Holly's face creased i̶n̶ ... d.
Are you saying ... ?'

'No, I'm afrai ... d
missing in Brigh ... g
by you last night ...

'The same?' S ... ne
same?' She shook ...

'We have reason to believe that your husband, Alexander Turner, was also married to another woman. I'm sorry, this must be very difficult . . .' DS Eames stopped and waited for Holly to catch up with what he'd just said.

'You're saying my husband was married to someone else?'

'Yes, that's what we believe.' Eames cleared his throat. 'I'm afraid there's something else, Holly.' He looked straight at her; it was better to be direct. 'Your husband's clothes and personal belongings were found on the beach at Brighton. Although no body has yet been found. I'm afraid the evidence is that he killed himself . . .'

Also by Maria Barrett

ELLE
DANGEROUS OBSESSION
DECEIVED
DISHONOURED

Intimate Lies

MARIA BARRETT

WARNER BOOKS

A *Warner* Book

First published in Great Britain in 1997 by
Little, Brown and Company
This edition published in 1997 by Warner Books

A CIP catalogue record for this book
is available from the British Library.

ISBN 0 7515 1510 8

Typeset by Palimpsest Book Production Limited,
Polmont, Stirlingshire
Printed and bound in Great Britain by
Clays Ltd, St Ives plc

Warner Books
A Division of
Little, Brown and Company (UK)
Brettenham House
Lancaster Place
London WC2E 7EN

For E.B.
Thank you for sleeping.

Acknowledgements

First and foremost, in writing this book, I should like to thank Lily, who, with only one exception, is the best baby in the entire universe. Secondly, my heart-felt thanks go to Emma Aylward who has coped with a pregnant, breast-feeding, then pregnant again boss with calm control, silent efficiency and a smile throughout. I am certain that the children have been easy in comparison to me. My parents have been as brilliant as they always are and the painstaking research and rewriting has only been possible because of one person, PC Stephen Davies of the Metropolitan Police, who has answerd endless questions, arranged visits, sent me information and treated my almost constant inane enquiries with the upmost courtesy. Thank you so much. Other important people have been Phillipa Vernon-Powell, Edward Glauser, John Lamming, Simon Batten, June Barrett and the press department of the Salvation Army. Credits are also due to my editor Barbara Boote, Helen Anderson and to Mic Cheetham. And finally, as I always do, I have to mention Jules. The year of this novel has been one of enormous joy and very great sadness, Julian has remained constant throughout, a true friend. Thank you.

17 DECEMBER 1993

Chapter One

Brighton, Winter 1993

The weather was bleak, the sort of icy, grey December day that chills right through to the soul, with a sleeting wind that whips the life out of everything. The sea was a dark, swelling mass, and the waves that crashed onto the stone beach brought with them a season's worth of debris. The seafront was deserted this dreary afternoon and it smelt damp. Damp, cold and miserable.

The girl walking down onto the seafront had not been a soldier long and she wore her uniform with great pride. She loved the dark navy skirt and jacket with the smart black buttons, the bonnet with its maroon ribbons and white writing, clear and sharp against the dark red background. It made her feel important, helping people, bringing Salvation.

Now she wished she had worn her cape. She shivered as an icy gust blew in from the sea and chaffed her face but she strode on, purposeful, strong. She wanted to feel the power of God and the place she felt it most was down on the beach, at the water's edge, open to the elements, to God's hand. She walked along the promenade for some time until she was out of sight of the big hotels, then she turned and looked across the stony stretch of beach at the magnificent sea. Putting her hand up to her eyes, she peered into the distance. She squinted, looked away for a moment then turned back to concentrate once more. Yes! Good Lord, she was right! It was a figure, a man, down there on the beach, huddled behind a wave break, in what seemed like a state of undress. She scrambled over the rail, jumped down onto the beach and shouted in the man's direction.

'Excuse me! Hey! Excuse me!' Her voice carried faintly on the wind. She waved her arms frantically and shouted again. The figure turned. 'You can't swim today!' she hollered, gesticulating that no swimming was allowed. 'No swimming!' she shouted again.

He must have been about a hundred yards away from her. Obviously he felt this was too far to shout: he merely held up his hand to show he understood, then looked to be getting dressed again. She peered at him for a few minutes more, then, satisfied that he had got the message, turned away and continued up the beach to her preferred spot.

She had been walking for a couple of hundred yards or so when it suddenly struck her that perhaps the man had not been intending to swim in the first place. She spun round and scanned the distance for sight of him, her hand up to her eyes. She could see nothing. Moving forward, she tried to keep her focus on the spot she remembered. Suddenly, she saw it. She broke into a run.

A short while later, reaching the pile of clothes, she dropped to her knees and began to rifle through it frantically. She found a wallet, keys, shoes, overcoat, underwear: everything a person would leave if they had thought about drowning themselves. She jumped up and raced to the water's edge, feelings of guilt engulfing her. She should have waited, she should have made sure he was all right. She hardly noticed the freezing water as it poured over her shoes, soaking her feet and ankles. Seconds later, unable to spot anything, she turned and fled. She had to get to a phone, ring the police.

The phone box was in a dark back street behind the Arun Guest House, a seedy, run-down building towards the Kemp Town end of the seafront, but she was too busy blaming herself to notice her surroundings. She yanked the door open and slipped inside. Picking up the receiver, her hands stiff with cold, shaking with panic, she dialled the emergency services. Moments later, she'd been put through to the police, and was about to speak, when the receiver was ripped from her hands. She spun round but never got a word out.

Her cry was extinguished before it left her lips.

The CAD room, Brighton Police Station, 2.30 pm

The radio operator took the call. She listened for about twenty seconds, heard nothing, then put out a trace on the line. The location came through, she made a request over the air and ten minutes later a squad car in the area found the phone box. It was empty. The PC lifted the receiver, which had been left dangling.

'This is PC Hardham, Brighton Police. There's no-one here, you can disconnect the line now.' He waited for the dial tone, then replaced the receiver again. He quickly looked round the phone box – no sign of anything suspicious – then went back to the car.

'Nothing, Sarge, some Christmas joker again.'

The Sergeant nodded and got on the air. 'Bravo Charlie, over, we're at Tyke Street public phone box, Kemp Town. We've searched the area with no trace, believe bogus call. The line is cleared.'

He switched off his radio. 'Get in, Bob, it's flipping perishing out there!'

The PC opened the door and climbed in beside him. 'You want me to do a quick recce of the area?'

The Sergeant shook his head. 'Don't bother. It's the third this week,' he said. 'Bloody piss artists!' He started the engine and glanced over his shoulder as he pulled out. 'Christmas! More trouble than it's worth!' he muttered. 'I'd cancel it if I were in government.'

Eastham, West Sussex, 3 pm

They were running late. Jill lifted Sophie's bag into the boot of the Range Rover and bent to pick up the basket containing the Christmas pudding, peach chutney and three bottles of wine for her mother-in-law. She tutted irritably as a small clump of mud from the grass transferred itself from the underneath of the hamper to the pale caramel-coloured cashmere of her coat. She brushed at it, scraping the tiny remaining mark with a manicured fingernail, then, satisfied it didn't show, slammed the boot shut and walked round to the driver's side of the car. She climbed inside and gave her face a quick check in the mirror. Her appearance, as usual, was immaculate. Jill Turner looked worth every penny she spent on herself.

At thirty-nine, Jill came across as at least seven or eight years younger. Her hair was cut and coloured every six weeks into an expensive sleek blonde bob, her clothes were Jaeger with a smattering of the cheaper designers, and her tall, slim body had been worked on and worked out every other day for years. Jill adored her husband and in the course of her marriage had made it her duty to be everything he could ever want in a wife. She took the role very seriously and her comfortable, insulated lifestyle meant she could enjoy it to the full. Jill was by no means stupid, but she had found as she got older that she had no desire to acquaint herself with things in the world that didn't directly relate to her own situation and as a result had become rather insular and cushioned. It was something that drove her stepdaughter Sophie almost insane with anger.

Sophie glanced out of the window at her stepmother waiting inside the car and said, 'No, don't go yet, Pol! Please! Stay and chat for a few more minutes!'

'Sophie, I can't! Mum says I have to get off the phone now. Sorry!'

'OK. Can't be helped. We're picking up the dwarf from school today anyway and staying the night at Granny's – our annual handing over of the Christmas goodies. We should have left ten minutes ago.' The dwarf was Sophie's half-brother, ten-year-old Harry. Checking the underside of her boots for mud, Sophie saw that they were clean and leant back against the glass, putting her feet up on the newly upholstered cushions of the window seat. She glanced down at the Range Rover, saw Jill looking up at her, and turned her face away to cover her smile. 'You going to Peter Kitcher's party?'

'Yes, if I'm allowed.'

'Right, I'll ring you the day before, to see what you're wearing.'

'OK. Oh, Sophie, I do miss you! School's pretty dull without you.'

'I bet!' Sophie laughed. She had played every trick in the book to get expelled, with all her friends and half the sixth form in on the scam. She wanted out, she wanted to be at home with her father and she didn't see why the hell Jill should get all the attention. She did it in the end – kicked out with only twenty-four hours' notice, for entertaining one of the boys from St Richards in her room. He hadn't been much cop but it had been worth it for the rumpus it had caused.

'See you next weekend then,' she said. 'Unless you can come . . .'

Polly cut her short. 'No chance!' she said flatly. Sophie's best friend had been banned from mixing with her: calls were allowed but visits were strictly off limits. 'See you at Peter's, Soph! That's if I can wangle it.'

'All right, see you then. Bye!' Sophie glanced out at Jill again and clicked the button to cut Polly off, but continued to hold the receiver for a few minutes more just to irritate her stepmother. Finally Jill climbed out of the car and Sophie hung up. Opening the window, she shouted that she was just coming and slammed it shut again, making the glass rattle. She saw Jill's look of fury as she turned and ran down the stairs and it filled her with a mixture of loathing and glee. She set the burglar alarm, sauntered out through the front door and slammed it shut.

'Sorry, Jill! It was a long call, I . . .'

'Get in the car!' Jill snapped.

Sophie opened the passenger door, made to climb in, then suddenly stopped short. 'Oh, no! I've forgotten my bag!'

Jill's jaw tightened as she walked round to her side of the car, removed the keys from the ignition and handed them to her stepdaughter. 'Do you do this on purpose?' she asked sarcastically.

'No! Of course not!' Sophie called as she ran back to the house. She opened the door, turned off the alarm and picked up her bag. 'Much!' she muttered under her breath, then she reset the panel and walked back out of the house. 'Ready!' She handed the keys to her stepmother and climbed into the car.

Jill took a deep breath, walked back round to her side and yanked open the door. She found that her hands were shaking and had to grip the steering wheel for a few moments before starting the engine. She had to talk to Alex. He had to do something about Sophie, he simply had to! It was all right while she was away at school, and Alex was around in the holidays, but now, with her at home all the time, mixing with those awful friends from the local college, and with her rudeness and her irritating manner, not to mention her dress sense . . . Jill revved the engine and slammed the car into reverse.

'I hope you've brought something decent to wear at Granny's tonight,' she said tightly. 'I hardly think that leggings, Doc Martens and that tatty old jumper is appropriate for dinner at the golf club.'

'No,' Sophie answered, taking out a bubble gum and stuffing it into her mouth. She chewed for a minute in silence, then blew out an enormous bubble. 'You wouldn't!' The bubble exploded over her chin.

Brighton, 4.30 pm

The daylight had completely gone by the time the Alco Office Systems party tumbled out of the Metropol Hotel after their Christmas lunch. Even though it was only four thirty, there was no question of their going back to the office – they were in no shape to work. The small drunken group staggered onto the pavement, their faces lit by the garish glare of the seafront neon signs and the orange street lamps, their laughter lost against the noise of the early evening traffic.

'Come on, lads! Onto the beach!' one of the young salesmen roared, running out into the road and darting through several gaps in the oncoming cars. 'Jeronimo!' He laughed as tyres screeched and horns tooted, smacking the bonnet of one car that missed him by inches with his fist. He made it to the other side and hollered across the road: 'Chicken shit! Come on, boys!'

Three of the others did the same, calling to the girls.

'You must be joking!' one of the secretaries screeched across the line of cars. 'No way!'

The four men broke into a stumbling run along the promenade, pulling each other as they went. The first one jumped over the railings down onto the beach. 'Coming swimming?' he shouted. The others jumped down after him and they lurched towards the water's edge, falling and yanking each other up, collapsing into laughter. By the wave break one of them stopped. He leant against the wet timber, dizzy and out of breath, and dropped his head down, closing his eyes for a moment. When he opened them, he saw a pile of clothes, just to his right. He bent, looked more closely at them and suddenly shouted to his mates. He didn't know what he'd found but looking at them gave him a sick feeling in the pit of his stomach. Some poor bastard had topped himself, he reckoned. What a thing to do, just before Christmas.

Twenty minutes later, he was standing with his three mates and a police officer on the promenade, going over the details one last time. He glanced out to sea at the lights on the horizon and the PC said, 'That'll be the coastguard. They'll be searching for the body.' The young man shivered and dug his hands in his pockets. He'd sobered up pretty damn quick.

'What if they don't find it?' he asked.

The PC shrugged. 'It's unlikely they will. Not in these conditions, not tonight.' He folded his notebook away and glanced out to sea. 'Poor bastard. I wish he'd given it more thought. It's a bloody nuisance, clearing up a suicide.' And with that, he walked back to the squad car and radioed in with his details.

Eastham, West Sussex, 9 pm

The patrol car sped along the country lane, then braked to a halt as it reached the white gate to South Ridge Farm. Sergeant Pierce parked on the grassy verge, swung open the gate and walked up the gravel drive in the glare of his headlights. As soon as the message had come in from the Brighton nick he'd set off to check the address and the next of kin. The house was dark, with only one light on in the front room – probably on timer switch, he thought. He rang the bell and banged the brass knocker for good measure, but there was no response.

'Excuse me? Hello?'

Sergeant Pierce turned, stepped out of the porch and saw a woman walking up the drive towards him.

'I was just passing, walking the dog. Is no-one in?'

'No, it doesn't look like it.'

'How odd! Alex Turner is due back this evening, he's been in

Geneva. Roddy! Here, boy!.' The woman stopped and whistled at a large black Labrador ferreting in the bushes. 'Wait a mo.' She hurried after the dog and grabbed its collar, hanging onto it and bringing it to heel. 'Sorry, yes, the Turners. Jill Turner is away for the night at her mother-in-law's and Alex is due back this evening. They leave a key with me and details of their comings and goings, just in case, you know.' The woman struggled with the dog for a few moments and brought him back under control. 'I keep my eye on the house for them. Mrs Birch, from South Ridge Cottage.' She clipped a lead onto the dog's collar and straightened. 'There's nothing wrong, is there?'

'No, madam, nothing to concern yourself with. It's Mr Alex Turner, is it?'

'Yes, that's right, Alex.' The woman's face was openly curious. 'And Jill.'

'Right. Thank you.' He'd have to leave it until the morning now. He walked down the drive and held the gate for Mrs Birch. 'At least the rain has stopped,' he commented. 'No fun walking the dog in this weather, I should imagine.'

'No, it isn't.' She hovered by the car as he got in, obviously hoping more information would be forthcoming. It wasn't.

'Thank you for your help.' He slammed the door shut.

'Oh yes, right.' Mrs Birch turned round and set off down the lane, waving as the police car drove past. It was a shame she was off early in the morning, she thought, pulling Roddy hard to heel, otherwise she'd have been able to call round to the farm for a coffee. She liked to be up on the gossip – it was the only thing that made village life bearable.

Chapter Two

London, 6 pm

Holly Grigson lifted her head from her work and looked out at the pavement as a couple stopped and peered in the lighted window of the gallery. She watched them for a moment, pretty sure they weren't going to buy, and saw them turn towards each other and exchange a swift kiss. It stung her, made her feel pitifully sad for a split second, then she went back to her task and ignored them. If they wanted something they'd come in, if not, then she could do without watching people in love – it only made her dwell on her own situation, and she didn't want to do that, not tonight, not the week before Christmas.

After a while, she finished her work on the catalogue of paintings and glanced at her watch. She stood and stretched, then walked across to the door, flipping the open sign over to closed.

'I reckon I could make a go of this place given half the chance,' she said aloud. She crossed to the two works she had sold that day, propped side by side against the wall. 'If he made a little less money then maybe I could make us a little more!' She stood and stared at the paintings for a few minutes, pleased with herself for selling them, for having chosen them in the first place, despite what Sandy advised – and then she remembered the row. The satisfaction instantly gave way to annoyance; annoyance that

Sandy wasn't here to see that she could do it, and ultimately that the gallery for which she had fought so long and hard brought her little more than frustration and regret. Her husband was the major earner – he made the big deals that kept the gallery funded – and as a result he called the shots.

'Let's face it, Holly,' she said, indulging in her habit of talking to herself as she gathered up her things, 'your father was right, you should never have given up the law.' She pulled a black cashmere poncho over her head and put a hand through her hair to calm the static. 'You should have stuck to what you knew, my girl.' She walked across to the light panel and flicked the first two switches; the lights in the back went off.

Just as they did so, the door opened and she spun round. 'Oh Lord!' She flicked the lights back on again and looked across at the young man who'd just walked in. 'Gosh, you made me jump!'

He was carrying a huge, scruffy portfolio – obviously not a customer. As he stepped forward, the portfolio slithered out of his grasp and fell noisily to the floor. He began a stuttering apology, tailed off and then stared silently down at his feet, embarrassed by his clumsy entrance. He shouldn't have come. He was taking the risk of seriously pissing off her husband, but he was fed up with not knowing what the hell was going on. He was selling to Sandy Turner and the Grigson Gallery and not getting any feedback. No reviews, no attention. He looked up and opened his mouth to explain.

'Look,' Holly said before he had the chance, 'I'm really sorry, but we're closed.' She didn't have the energy tonight to go through a young hopeful's portfolio, offering nice words of encouragement. It had been a busy day and Holly's brief, rosy glow of satisfaction had evaporated with thoughts of her husband. 'Apart from which, I don't usually take unsolicited works.'

The young man nodded, pushed a strand of hair off his face and stared down at the ground again. He should have given her a piece of his mind but he didn't have the nerve. Sandy Turner had warned him about her and he couldn't afford to upset her. The last thing he needed was to lose the steady income he already had from them. He smiled apologetically. 'Oh well, it was worth a try anyway.' He shrugged and turned towards the door.

Holly watched him for a moment. There was something so unaggressive about him, so gentle and appealing, that she found herself saying, 'But I could always spare you five minutes if you like, have a chat?' She regretted it the instant she'd said it. She'd bloody gone and done it again; she just could never say no.

The young man turned back. 'Really?' This was nothing like he'd been led to expect. She was really quite nice.

Holly stared at him. He looked so shocked that, despite her misgivings, she laughed. 'Yes, really,' she said. 'It is Christmas, after all! Plonk your stuff down there and I'll put the kettle on. Would you like some tea?'

'Yeah, great, I'd love a cup! Milk, and three sugars. Are you sure?'

'Of course!' Holly glanced away for an instant, then dismissed her fleeting moment of self-pity. 'I've got nothing else to do tonight, so why not?'

She put the kettle on in the small kitchen area and was walking back into the gallery, pulling her poncho over her head, when the door opened again.

Holly stopped short, the poncho half on and half off, and stared at the man who'd just walked in.

'Hello, Holly.'

She stood perfectly still, forgetting that she had a blanket on her head, forgetting everything for a split second, then the man said, 'What's that thing on your head?' and she blushed furiously.

'It's not on my head!' she snapped. 'It's my poncho, I was in the process of taking it off, actually!'

'I see.'

'No you don't! You don't see at all! You never did, that was your problem!' Holly's heart was thundering in her chest at the sight of him and she had to catch her breath. She yanked the poncho off her head and threw it at the desk. 'Anyway, what on earth are you doing here, Kit Thomas? You're supposed to be in New York! And how did you find the gallery?'

'Your father – he gave me the number – and I am mostly in New York, but I'm here for a week or so, on business.' Kit dragged his eyes away from her face and glanced down at the young man who was kneeling on the floor. He had to. He was so startlingly aroused at the sight of her, her cheeks blazing, her small, lithe body tense and coiled like a spring, that he thought if he stared at her for a moment longer he would be across the room and pinning her to the wall with his whole body. A mistake, a big mistake. 'Hi,' he said to the young artist. 'Kit Thomas.'

'Hello. Adrian White.' The two men shook hands, Kit feeling relief that this wasn't Holly's husband, but trying not to let it show. 'Listen,' Adrian said, 'I think I ought to be going. I can come back another time if you like?'

'No!' Holly said.

'Yes!' Kit said at exactly the same time. They glared at each other.

'You really don't have to,' Holly said quickly. 'I'm sure Mr Thomas is just about to . . .'

'No, I wasn't, but if that's what you want Holly, then . . .'

'Look, I'm out of here.' Adrian fastened his portfolio and stood up, digging around in his pocket. 'Here's a card with my number on. Maybe I can call in another time? Your husband . . .'

'My husband what?' Holly interrupted.

Adrian shrugged. He had been about to explain, but again lost his nerve. This was one hell of a situation – these two were oblivious to anything but each other. He held out the card.

Holly took it and absently dropped it into the battered carpet bag she used as a handbag. 'I'm sorry. Yes, do come back another time.'

The young artist picked up his portfolio and struggled to tuck it under his arm. 'I will. Thanks anyway, for, er . . .' He left the sentence unfinished as Kit opened the door for him.

'You all right with that?' Kit asked.

'Yeah, thanks.' Unwisely, he held up his free hand in a wave and nearly dropped his burden, but managed to steady himself before Kit could help. 'Bye then.' The door slammed after him and Holly picked up her poncho.

'Very gallant!' she said. 'Shame you drove him away in the first place.'

'I drove him away! I only came in to say hello. It was you who flew off the handle and . . .' Kit stopped. He sighed, glanced away for a minute, then looked back at Holly and said, 'Truce?'

Holly held his gaze for as long as she could, then turned towards the desk and fiddled with some paper. 'Truce,' she mumbled.

'So, how's the gallery going then?' Kit asked eventually, after an awkward pause. He wanted to cross the room, to be closer to her, but her body language told him to keep his distance.

'Fine!' Holly answered with false brightness. How could she explain about the gallery, about the thing she'd had to beg, steal and borrow for to set up, the thing she had wanted more than anything else, but was in reality nothing but a disappointment to her? 'Just fine!' she added.

'Good.'

Silence. Oh God, Holly thought, why did he have to come back now? The last time she had seen Kit Thomas had been eighteen months ago, when she had lain next to him, naked, warm, filled with a terrible mixture of elation and fear, knowing he was the only man she would ever love and cursing herself for finding that out. She had told him she wanted him but she needed some freedom, some time. She had tried to explain about the gallery, about her independence, her need to succeed with it, make it work. All she wanted was a little more space, to be able to go on as they were, but a week later he had gone. Three lines he wrote, just three lines: 'Holly, I love you, but I have a life too. I've waited two years, I can't wait forever. Take care of yourself, be everything you want to be. Kit.' Three measly, miserable lines and she never heard from him again. Bastard!

She looked up. 'You never wrote,' she said.

'You got married, Holly,' he reminded her. 'I didn't think it was appropriate.'

'No, perhaps not.' Of course she got married! Three months after he'd left she had found someone who wanted the gallery as much as she did, someone who understood, someone who . . . She sighed. Someone who she should never even have gone on holiday with, let alone married.

'What about you?'

'No,' he smiled. 'I didn't get married.' How could he have got married? It had taken him a year just to get through one day without thinking about her. 'I have a very nice girlfriend though,' he added quickly. 'I may get hitched at some time in the future, you never know.' At least, that's what he'd thought when he left New York. Only now, looking at her, he wondered hopelessly if he would ever be free of loving Holly Grigson.

'Where's your husband?' he asked quickly, to change the subject.

'Abroad – selling, I think, or buying, one of the two.' Holly shrugged and pulled a face. 'Italy.' She didn't mean to sound unhappy and resentful, it just always came out that way. She had tried to be involved, time and time again, but always to no avail. Sandy was aloof, secretive almost, and in the end she had simply lost heart. And this was her precious gallery.

'I see.'

'Yes, well.' Holly turned to the desk and picked up her bag. 'Look, Kit, it's really nice to see you but . . .'

'Don't lie, Holly,' he said wearily.

'OK!' Holly shook her head. 'Kit, this is one hell of a shock for me and I'm really too stunned to want to prolong the ordeal any longer. Please go and let me lock up. Enjoy your trip and give my regards to your girlfriend back in New York.' She pulled on the poncho and straightened it.

'Black suits you,' Kit said. 'You look good, Holly, exactly as I remember you.'

'No,' she answered coldly, 'not exactly. We all change, Kit.'

He sighed. 'Yes, you're right, we do all change.' It had been a mistake to come but oddly he didn't regret it. 'Look, Holly, here's my hotel, if you need, or want, for some crazy, whimsical reason, to contact me.' He smiled as he held out the card. 'Don't just drop it in your bag and lose it – put it in your purse. I'm there until the end of the week.'

Holly smiled back. She had forgotten just how captivating Kit's smile was. 'Please, Kit, have you ever known me to be whimsical?' she teased.

'Yes, often,' he answered and they were both silent for a moment, remembering the mad, exciting, extraordinary things they had done together, Kit always the cautious one, while Holly had been dangerously crazy. 'Shall I wait for you to lock up?' he asked eventually.

'No thanks. I do it on my own most nights, anyway.' She moved across to the light panel and began to flick the switches for the second time that evening.

'I'll leave you to it then,' Kit said. He had turned towards the door and opened it, feeling the need to put some distance between them.

'Yes.' Holly stopped and turned. In the half-light, in her red and black floral mini-skirt, her black poncho, crimson tights and flat black loafers, she looked like an adolescent, seventeen or eighteen, fresh-faced and lovely, and Kit wondered how someone with such intensity of experience and emotion could appear so young and uncomplicated.

'Goodbye, Holly,' he said. 'It was good to see you.'

'Goodbye, Kit.' He was the same wonderful Kit: charming, equable, solid. Holly turned back to the lights so that she didn't have to see him leave. She heard the door slam, his footsteps on the pavement, receding, then silence. Her only coherent thought was one of gratitude that she didn't have to see her husband. She wouldn't have been able to face that.

It was late that evening when Holly finally climbed the stairs to her second-floor flat, heaving three packed carrier bags up with her. She dumped them by the front door of the flat, rubbed her fingers where the blood had drained away and then ran down for the remaining four. She lugged those up, a huge bunch of flowers tucked precariously under her arm, bottles chinking and the free-range eggs wobbling dangerously in their carton. Just as she reached the top step, she stumbled and dropped the whole lot. Helplessly she stood watching a very ripe piece of Brie bounce down several steps before splitting open and oozing out onto the moth-eaten carpet.

'Damn, piss and damn!' she snapped. This wasn't enough to express her feeling. 'Bugger!' She kicked the rest of the shopping towards the flat door, picked up the overspill, then went to retrieve what was left of the cheese. Dropping it all in a pile, she opened the door and walked inside, letting it slam shut on the horrible mess behind her. She headed straight for the fridge, grabbed a bottle of white Burgundy and poured a liberal amount into a large wine glass. Slumping down onto the floor, she leant against the cupboard and swallowed half the amount in one go. 'Jeesus!' She let her head fall back and closed her eyes. Half a ton of trashed groceries was all she needed.

Holly had been shopping. It was her standard remedy for depression, to take herself to the supermarket and indulge in a frenzy of food buying. Three flavours of Häagen-Dazs ice cream, four expensive cheeses, fillet steak, bags of herb salad, extra virgin olive oil, out of season strawberries and tinned rice pudding for starters. She walked her trolley up and down the aisles, looking at each product, noting the special offers, squeezing the toilet paper to check for softness and sniffing the air fresheners – air fresheners she had no intention of buying. She heaped packs of tortilla chips on top of tins of tomatoes and three different types of spicy sausage. She bought two new face creams and stocked up with vitamins. She would take the capsules for a week then forget all about them the morning she had a hangover and then never bother with them again.

Only now, sitting in her small but compact kitchen – the estate agent's description, not hers – Holly realised she had to face the consequences of her mood: a hallway full of bags and a decided lack of space. She rubbed her hands over her face and sighed wearily. There was nothing else for it: she couldn't leave it rotting out in the hallway for days, and besides, part of the impetus for going to the supermarket in the first place was to prepare a gourmet meal for Sandy on his return. She stood up, kicked off her shoes and plodded heavily through the flat to fetch the groceries. She picked up the stray items, carried them into the kitchen, put them away, then systematically went back for each bag and unloaded it straight away until she had cleared the hallway and stocked the fridge, along with most of the cupboards. She poured another glass of wine and walked into the bedroom. Sitting on the edge of the bed, she looked around at the room she shared with her husband.

'Oh God,' she said, knowing that a gourmet meal wasn't going to make up for very much. They would eat it and talk about the gallery and about what she had sold in Sandy's absence – which would almost inevitably look very little compared to his deals. Then they would go to bed and maybe even make love, seeing as he'd been away for a few days – not love really but sex; they'd have sex – and Holly would moan reasonably convincingly and think about whatever stray subject came into her mind.

'Oh God,' she said again. Suddenly she stood up and walked across to the wardrobe. Opening it, she bent down and fumbled in the jumble of things at the back until she'd found a shoe box. She dropped to the floor, pulled her legs up under her and took the lid off the box. The papers literally spilled out: photographs, letters, receipts, postcards, menus, a huge, muddled mess of memories. She picked up a snapshot and smiled. Kit's bottom, the back of him, a deeply tanned, athletic body, running away, out of view, his hands up in the air in protest, his bottom, white, muscular, astonishingly sexy. It was France, the summer, and they were the greatest of friends – friends who became lovers, at the wrong time and in the wrong place . . . Holly dropped the picture and flicked through the rest of the things, picking out a postcard scene, a sweet wrapper – the oddest of mementoes – and wondered why she had kept half of it. Then she remembered: most of the time she had spent with Kit had been so magical that she had wanted to take a bit of it away with her and keep it, a small piece of happiness, tucked in a box forever.

But the instant that thought entered her head, Holly stood up, bent to scoop all the things back into the box and then stuffed it down inside the wardrobe again. She was married now, Kit was in the past, and she didn't have time for sentimentality. She would make a stunning meal for Sandy; she would clean the flat, change the bed, arrange the flowers. Her father had been wrong – she had proved him wrong. She had made a success of things, she knew she had. Maybe she *had* given up a good career in law, after years' worth of expensive Law School education, but in opening the gallery, she had become involved with something she loved desperately. And maybe she had rejected a man she'd been in love with for years and made a marriage Tobias Grigson had given three months at the most. But look at me now, Holly thought, stripping the bed, chucking the duvet on the floor and yanking the pillowcases off the pillows. Hell, I've got a gallery making a good profit, a nice lifestyle, I'm happy and I'm damn well still married, aren't I? She stopped, put the pillowcase up to her face and breathed in the faint, lingering aroma of her own perfume. There was no trace of her husband's scent – no photograph of him come to think of it, by her bed or in her purse; no razor or shaving foam, he took it with him; very little in fact, to show that he even lived there.

'Oh God!' Holly cried for the third time. Hurling the pillowcase onto the floor, she put her hands up to her face and burst into floods of tears.

Chapter Three

Holly woke with a start. The first thing she saw as she opened her eyes was the television – still on. She groaned and sat up, taking in the remains of her ready meal on a tray on the floor, an empty wine bottle, a half-eaten box of chocolates and, just by the door, the flowers, still in their paper and already wilting. Wincing at the hammering in her head, she stood up and walked across to open the curtains. According to her watch, it was seven twenty. It was only just light, and Sandy's flight had left Rome at seven

'Oh shit!' she muttered, hurrying through to the bedroom. The bed was still in disarray, unmade up, the dirty sheets on the floor. No cleaning had been done, no flowers arranged and no preparations made for dinner that evening. 'Shit,' she muttered again. 'Shit, shit, shit!' She rushed into the bathroom, turned on the shower full pelt and stripped off. She would dash round the flat with the vacuum cleaner, book a table for lunch at Sandy's favourite restaurant and serve a simple steak with salad for dinner. She would salvage what was left of the flowers, throw them into a vase and find something really special to wear.

Leaping out of the shower, Holly grabbed a towel, rubbed herself dry and wrapped it round her torso, then dashed into the bedroom and flung open the wardrobe doors. She began piling things onto the bed in one heap, then discarding them in another. Sandy had never really approved of the way she dressed and she was conscious of that now as she searched. She always bought things impulsively and she liked the unusual, putting things together that shouldn't really have gone but which somehow looked amazing. The effect was very offbeat, but in an expensive, designer way.

'Shit!' Holly said again, choosing that as the word of the day. She couldn't see anything to tempt her, or please Sandy. 'Ah, yes! That's it!' she said suddenly, spotting a long, close-fitting black wool skirt, with a split up the back. 'Perfect,' she muttered, gathering up a huge bundle of clothes and stuffing them back into the wardrobe. She rummaged through her drawer for a sweater, found a long silk and wool tunic in dark red, and then dug out a long, pleated velvet scarf overprinted with a baroque design and some black suede square-heeled shoes. She dumped it all on the bed, found a pair of tights, bra, knickers. These were both an expensive French make, and had once been white lace but were now grey chain mail, dyed, as all her underwear seemed to be, a grubby non-colour in the wash. Going to the dressing table, she bent to see her reflection in the mirror and deftly edged her eyes with mascara and dark grey eyeliner, then dusted some translucent powder over her cheeks. After swiftly getting dressed, she took a red lipstick from a basket full of them, put it in the pocket of her tunic and went through to the sitting room.

An hour later, Holly had vacuumed, dusted and rearranged the flat. The flowers had survived, just, and a liberal squirt of polish into the air of each room made it smell clean, even if it wasn't. She grabbed a banana and a yoghurt from the fridge, dropped them into her carpet bag and pulled on her coat. She would phone the restaurant from the gallery, book a table for one o'clock and do everything she could to make today special. She smiled as she left the flat, her mood hugely improved on the night before. How dare Kit Thomas come waltzing back into her life and think he could make the slightest bit of difference, she thought, bouncing down the stairs. But of course it had completely escaped her notice that this spurt of uncustomary effort for her husband might just be because of someone else. It was a cover-up, only Holly had no intention of admitting as much.

Later that day, at twenty minutes to two to be precise, Holly sat in the window of Luigi's restaurant and watched the activity on the pavement outside. She glanced at her watch for the second time in ten minutes and took a sip of wine. She had begun to worry.

For once in her life, Holly had been organised enough that morning to ring the airport and check that the flight from Rome had landed on time. This verified, she immediately rang Luigi, begged for a table and promised to be there at one exactly. So when Sandy didn't turn up at the gallery during the course of the morning, and after she had tried his mobile phone several times, she decided to leave him a note on the door and wait for him at the restaurant; she didn't want to miss the table. Only now, with him already several hours late arriving back, the place full to bursting point and Luigi watching her every move, she was beginning to think she'd made an embarrassing mistake. She decided to give it five more minutes, then apologise profusely to Luigi, let someone else have the table and slink out of the restaurant. She wouldn't forgive Sandy lightly for this one!

Ten minutes later, Holly was out on the pavement. She turned up the collar of her coat and hurried away from the restaurant, striding down the street. Apart from the nagging worry, she was absolutely furious. She had been humiliated and let down and she'd left the place with her cheeks burning, convinced that the whole restaurant was watching her.

Back at the gallery she decided to go after some answers. She rang the airport again and found there was another flight out of Rome that afternoon at two, only no-one could say if Sandy was on the passenger list or not. Her next call was to the travel agent.

They made all Sandy's bookings, they would know what the hell was going on.

'Hello, this is Holly Grigson from the Grigson Gallery. I believe my husband made some travel arrangements through you recently, to fly to Rome?'

'Ah, hello, Miss Grigson. No, I'm sorry, but the last time we made arrangements for Mr Turner was a month ago, a trip to Iran, I believe. Hang on a moment, would you, I'll just . . .'

'Are you sure? He said he'd booked with you!'

'Yes, pretty sure . . .'

There was a thirty-second silence, then the agent came back on the line. 'I've got your account details up on the screen now, Miss Grigson . . . er, yes, here it is. The last trip we booked was to Iran, flights and hotel in . . .'

'Oh.' Holly felt the smallest twinge of panic in the pit of her stomach. 'I must have made a mistake,' she said. 'I'm terribly sorry.'

'No problem.'

'Look,' she went on quickly, 'you couldn't do me a favour, could you? I've got the name of his hotel in my diary – could you possibly find the number for me and give me a ring back?'

'I can find it right now, if you hang on.'

'Brilliant, thanks!' Holly rummaged in her bag and pulled out her diary. 'It's . . . ah, here, it's the D'Inghilterra, on the Via Bocca di Leone, number fourteen.'

'Right, stay on the line and I'll look it up.'

Holly held the receiver away from her ear while the standard piped music came down the line. A minute or so later the agent came back on.

'Miss Grigson?'

'Yes, still here.'

'I've got the number for you.'

'Great! Fire away.' She scribbled down the number, then

repeated it back to him to be sure she had it down correctly. Thanking him profusely, she hung up, then immediately dialled Italy.

Ten minutes later, Holly sat at the desk in the gallery and wondered what the hell to do next. She felt suddenly desperate. It was now three o'clock in the afternoon and she could find no trace of Sandy's movements over the past few days. He had never made a booking with the hotel and certainly had never arrived there. He had made no travel arrangements with his agent, which in itself was highly unusual, and she had no way of knowing if he had even taken a flight to Rome. All she knew was that he had packed last Friday, then written his hotel name and his itinerary down in her diary. She also knew he'd taken his passport, because she'd seen him put it in his briefcase.

She stood and began to pace the floor. What if he'd left her, just walked out? He knew she wouldn't check his schedule – why should she? She trusted him and she'd never rung him in the past while he was abroad, never having felt the need to. Suddenly Holly stopped. What if he'd had an accident? The hotel manager didn't exactly speak perfect English and could easily have misunderstood. What if he had made a reservation but never made it to Rome? They would have cancelled the room perhaps, thought no more of it. What if he'd been mugged, or been in a car accident on the way to the airport, or worse, mugged in Rome, left murdered in a back alley? The panic rose in her chest.

'Calm down, Holly,' she muttered. 'Just calm down!' She took a deep breath and stood still. This was ridiculous. She was being paranoid, imagining things. The chances were that Sandy had simply changed his plans, used another agent. Perhaps he'd found the hotel was overbooked on his arrival and been forced to go elsewhere. Of course he wouldn't have bothered her with the details, he would have been too busy. That was it, that had to be it!

Perhaps she should ring a friend, for moral support. She could do with someone to talk it over with, to help her see things rationally, stop her worrying. She thought hard. Holly had lots of friends but no-one she was that close to. No, perhaps not. She really didn't know what to do; she just couldn't seem to think straight.

Suddenly it came to her: she should go home. She wasn't sure it was the best idea but it was the only one she could think of. She couldn't stay in the gallery for the rest of the afternoon, worrying and pacing the floor. At least if something had happened to Sandy it was more than likely she would be contacted at home. She bit her lip. What if someone had been trying to contact her all day?

'Home,' she muttered, gathering up her things in a rush. 'I must get home!' She hurried to the door, forgot the lights, then ran back to switch them all off.

Minutes later, she was on her way to the tube.

Jill indicated, swung the Range Rover into the entrance of South Ridge Farm and looked over her shoulder at her son behind her. 'Harry, gate please.' Alex usually left it open when he was home but she thought nothing of it.

Harry unclipped his seat belt, jumped down and ran across to the white five-bar gate. He released the catch, took a short run up, then leapt onto the bottom rung, taking a free ride as it swung open.

Jill smiled at him and drove on up to the house. She leant out of the window and called, 'Leave it open, Harry! I'll be out again later this afternoon.' He waved, hooked the gate up and ran up the drive towards them.

'Where's Dad's car?' he shouted, heading for the porch and holding his finger over the doorbell.

'I don't know, and don't do that, Harry, it'll ruin the chime!'

Jill glanced over her shoulder before she put the key in the lock. 'Sophie, could you bring some of the other bags in, please, not just your own!' She opened the door, went straight to the cupboard and turned off the alarm.

'I suppose you do know when Dad was due back?' Sophie said, dumping one of Harry's cases down in the hall and heading for the stairs with her own rucksack.

'Yes, I do. It was last night.' Jill refused to rise to the bait. If Sophie wanted to be in a strop the whole time, then it was her problem. 'I rang the airport from Granny's; his plane landed on time.'

'Oh really?' Sophie loaded the remark with as much sarcasm as she could muster and continued up the stairs.

'Yes really,' Jill murmured to herself. She felt a bit guilty, to be honest. Once she'd known Alex's plane had landed safely she had gone to bed without bothering to ring again, but perhaps she should have rung the house, found out what his movements were today. 'He's probably gone to the office,' she said. Sophie had stopped halfway up the stairs and stood watching her warily, making Jill feel edgy. 'I'll just give him a quick buzz and see where he's got to. Harry!'

Harry's blond head appeared round the door.

'Cases!' Jill ordered. 'Inside and upstairs. Now!' She went through to the kitchen, saw it exactly as she'd left it the day before and felt a small twinge of disappointment. Alex usually took the day off after a trip and she'd been looking forward to seeing him. She picked up the phone, dialled the office number and waited. Seconds later she got the line unobtainable tone. She tried a second time.

'How odd!'

'What is?' Sophie had come into the kitchen. She walked across to the fridge and took out a carton of skimmed milk.

'Alex's number, it's unobtainable.'

'Perhaps there's a fault on the line. Ring the operator.' She poured herself a glass of milk.

'Good idea,' Jill said. 'Put the kettle on, would you? And see if Harry wants a drink.'

Sophie sighed heavily and banged her cup down on the work surface.

'If it's not too much trouble, that is!' The operator answered the line. 'Yes, I wonder if you could check for a fault on this number? I keep getting line unobtainable.' Jill gave Alex's number. 'Oh, right, yes, it's Eastham 142. Thank you.' She hung up. 'They'll call the engineers and ring me back,' she said to Sophie, who wasn't in the slightest bit interested. 'I'll just try the mobile.' She checked the number in her diary, then dialled again. 'That's very strange,' she said. 'Sophie? The phone's switched off!'

Sophie looked round and shrugged. 'It's probably nothing. Don't panic, Jill!'

'I'm not panicking, Sophie, I'm just concerned, that's . . .' The phone rang. 'Hello. Speaking. Oh. I see. Are you sure?' Jill put her hand over the mouthpiece. 'The phone's been cut off,' she hissed. Sophie stopped drinking and looked across at her stepmother. 'I see,' Jill went on, 'OK. Thank you.' She replaced the receiver. 'What the hell's going on?'

'Search me!' The doorbell went. 'I'll go,' Sophie called, already on her way out of the kitchen.

Jill stood where she was, hearing a murmur of voices in the hallway, then started as Sophie called out, 'Jill! Can you come here?'

Jill hurried out to the door and blanched at the sight of the policeman. Swallowing down her fear, she tried to smile. 'Hello. Can I help?'

'Yes, I think so. My name's Sergeant Pierce, from the Eastham station. Are you Mrs Turner, Mrs Alex Turner?'

'Yes, that's right.'

'I came to ask you about your husband, Mrs Turner. Is he at home?'

'My husband?' Jill's hand went up to her throat. 'No, he isn't. What's happened? He should have been back from a business trip last night, but there's no sign of him here, and I can't get hold of him, the phone's been cut off . . .' She stopped, realising she was gabbling, sounding hysterical. 'I'm sorry. I'm a bit worried about him.'

'It's perfectly all right. Are you saying you think your husband might be missing, Mrs Turner?'

Jill cleared her throat. She could see Sophie's face, strained and white, out of the corner of her eye. 'I don't know, not missing exactly. I'm not sure. Sophie, can you run upstairs and see if Alex's case is in the bedroom?'

Sophie darted upstairs before the policeman could stop her, then reappeared and called down the stairs over the banister. 'No, it's not!'

Jill stared at Sergeant Pierce. 'There's a problem with his phone, I can't get through to him. I really don't know what's happened to him . . .'

Pierce waited a few moments. He hated this sort of thing, and it was particularly awful, just before Christmas. 'Mrs Turner, would you be able to accompany me down to the police station?'

'The police station!' she gasped. 'Why? What's happened? What's going on?'

'Some items of clothing were found last night on the beach at Brighton, Mrs Turner, items we believe might belong to your husband. I'm afraid it might be bad news. We'd like you to identify the belongings.'

'Items of clothing? Belongings?' Jill shook her head. 'No, that's impossible. My husband flew to Geneva yesterday morning, and then flew back last night. It couldn't be him.'

'Are you sure of that, Mrs Turner?'

'No, but . . .' Jill stopped. 'What belongings?'

'His driving licence, wallet, car keys, among other things.' Sergeant Pierce stepped forward. 'I'm sorry, this must be very difficult for you. May I come in and wait for you to get ready?'

'Oh God!' Jill put her hand up to her head. 'Yes, er, sorry.' She stepped back and turned towards the kitchen to fetch her coat, moving as if in a daze. 'Sophie, you stay here with Harry,' she said faintly, walking back into the hallway, half pulling her coat on, then going back for her handbag. 'I'll ring you from the station. I'm sure it's all some kind of dreadful mistake, I'm sure . . .'

But Sophie already had her rucksack over her shoulder. 'No! I'm coming with you. He's my father!'

Jill stopped. She looked at Sophie, then at Sergeant Pierce. 'I don't think you should, Sophie, I think . . .'

'I don't care what you think! I'm coming!'

Jill swallowed hard. She felt suddenly near to tears. She sat on the chair by the hall table and put her head in her hands.

'Are you all right, Mrs Turner?' Sergeant Pierce asked solicitously.

Jill looked up. 'Yes, sorry. I feel a bit faint, that's all. It's probably the shock.' She shook her head and took a deep breath. 'Sorry,' she said again.

'Miss Turner, it might be better if your mother comes on her own . . .'

'She's not my mother,' Sophie spat. 'She's my father's wife . . .' Her voice wavered and she turned away.

'Look, Sophie, Harry can't stay on his own. I'll ring you as soon as I know anything. Please . . .' Jill stood and went to touch her stepdaughter's arm but Sophie pulled away. 'Harry!' Jill called up the stairs. 'I'm just popping out for an hour or so.' Harry's head appeared over the banister. 'Sophie's staying here.' She blew him a kiss. 'I'll see you later.'

Walking out of the door, Jill looked back at Sophie. 'Try not to worry,' she said, but Sophie didn't turn round. Jill stared at her back for a few moments, then sighed and followed Sergeant Pierce out to the car, silently closing the door behind her.

The room was grey and cold, and all Jill could think of was how it could do with a lick of paint, something warmer like rose pink or saffron. She sat down and someone brought her a cup of tea, in a small plastic cup. She shuddered as she took a sip – it was horribly sweet, and she hadn't taken sugar for over twenty years. She drank it nonetheless, sitting huddled in her coat, her arms folded across her body defensively, her legs crossed, her knees pulled up.

'Mrs Turner?'

Jill looked round.

'DS Lewis. I have the things we recovered from the beach, Mrs Turner. Would you mind taking a look at them for me?'

Jill shook her head and stared blankly at the two plastic bags as the officer dropped them on the table. He removed the clothes first and laid them in a neat pile in front of her. She swallowed, then leant forward and picked up the shirt. Almost immediately, she let it go. It made her feel sick to touch it. They were all Alex's, she knew at a glance. She gazed at the smaller bag, containing the personal items: his watch, his wallet, his keys. Her vision blurred.

Putting her hand up to cover her face, she nodded. 'These are my husband's things,' she whispered. Terrified she might cry, she bit the inside of her mouth and turned away.

An hour later, Jill left the station. The situation had been explained to her but she'd hardly taken any of it in. She had filled out the missing persons form, been given Alex's personal belongings, drunk more tea with sugar in it and somehow survived. She sat in the back of the police car, her whole body numb, and watched the outskirts of Brighton pass by, row upon row of terraced houses, roadworks and finally the rolling Downs, carved up by the new London to Brighton road.

Why? she kept thinking. Why? This sort of thing doesn't happen to someone like me; it happens to other people, people who have no control over their lives, people in a mess. The landscape changed again: open countryside, fields, winter green and churned earth under a thunderous grey sky and the dark shadow of the hills. The car turned into the village of Eastham and Jill saw her neighbour walking the dog. Bloody woman, she thought, she'll know by tonight, they all will. She dropped her chin onto her chest and turned her face away, overwhelmed by a sudden surge of grief.

'Mrs Turner?'

She hadn't even felt the crunch of the tyres on the gravel drive.

'Would you like the WPC to stay with you for a while?'

Jill shook her head. She saw Sophie's face in the window on the second floor – a small, pinched, white face, watching, waiting. As Jill thought of both Alex's children, of their pain and their distress, she didn't know if she had the strength to face it.

'Thank you, but I'll be fine.' She reached for the door, and the WPC climbed out with her.

'Are you sure?' she asked.

Jill nodded, not trusting herself to speak. It was the sympathy and understanding that did it; the temptation to break down was almost overpowering. 'Thank you.' She glanced up at the window and saw that Sophie's face had gone. 'I have to tell the children,' she said. 'We need to be alone.'

'Of course.' The WPC waited for Jill to put the key in the lock. 'Is there someone you could call, to help out this evening if you need it, a neighbour or a friend?'

Jill nodded again but she was lying. There wasn't anyone. She was a private person; she had never been one to share her problems – but then she'd had very few. She turned before she went inside. 'You've been very kind.'

The WPC smiled sympathetically and Jill went inside. As she closed the door behind her she heard the patrol car reverse then move off slowly up the drive. She looked up and saw Sophie.

'What's happened?' Sophie demanded. She stood on the bottom stair and held the banister with her right hand. Jill noticed her knuckles were white with the force of her grip.

'I'll get Harry,' she answered. 'Go into the kitchen, I'll be down in a minute.'

'You're upset,' Sophie accused as Jill went past her. She grabbed at her sleeve. 'Why? Tell me why!'

Jill shook Sophie's hand away. 'Go into the kitchen, Sophie.' She walked up the stairs and across the landing into her son's bedroom, knowing that Sophie was watching her. She tried to keep her head up, her face composed, but in spite of herself, she looked stooped, diminished by grief. Downstairs, Sophie felt a moment of such intense panic that she thought she might suffocate on it.

Jill stood and both children sat. 'Something has happened to Daddy,' she began. 'Something awful, we think.'

She watched Harry's face. She wanted to look at both of them, to try and help Sophie as well, but she couldn't. Harry was her son, it was for him that her heart bled. Sophie turned her face away towards the wall.

'Some of Daddy's clothes were found on the beach at Brighton,' Jill went on, 'and I've had to report him missing.'

'He went swimming?'

'In a way, Harry, yes, sort of.' Sophie snorted derisively and Jill had to bite her tongue. 'We think that he might have drowned,' she said, as gently as she could. 'I'm afraid that Daddy might be . . .'

'Oh for God's sake, just say it!' Sophie suddenly cried out. 'Don't be so bloody pathetic! He's dead, isn't he? He's never coming back. Say it, for God's sake! He's dead. *Dead!*'

Harry shook his head. His face was so earnest, so confused. 'I don't understand, Mummy,' he said. 'What's Sophie . . . ?'

But as Jill went forward to her son, Sophie ran for the door, knocking her sideways. It was a sudden, violent movement and she stumbled momentarily, falling hard against the edge of the table, grazing her hip bone. Sophie ran up the stairs.

'Mummy!'

'I'm fine, Harry. It's all right, I'm fine.' Jill gripped the back of the chair as a searing pain shot through her pelvis. She tried to breathe evenly, to cover it. 'Come here.' She held out her arms and hugged her. Then she knelt, with her face at the same level as his. 'The police think that Daddy is dead, Harry,' she said softly. 'Sophie is right, I don't think that he is ever coming back.'

'Not coming back?'

'No, I don't think so.' Jill tried to hold him close but his body was tense and unyielding. He pulled back.

'Why?' he whispered.

Jill stared at the anguish and fear of a ten-year-old. 'I don't know,' she replied. She had no answers, no words to describe the desolation she felt. 'Sometimes people do things that we can't explain, sometimes . . .'

Harry shook his head. 'No . . .' He had tried to hold back the tears, but now, they spilt down onto his cheeks. 'Not Daddy,' he said. 'Daddy doesn't ever do those things . . .' He began to cry. 'Not Daddy . . .'

Chapter Four

Holly sat in the dark. She had the telephone in front of her, her business address book open, a stack of paper and a pen, unused, lying on top of it. For over four hours, she had done nothing except sit and wait. She stared at the wall, at the flash of the car headlamps as they came around the corner into Bishop's Road and shone in through the window of the flat, a beam of light illuminating one long, thin patch of the room, then disappearing forever. She knew she should do something, only she didn't know what.

The thought had occurred to her before, more than once, that she didn't really know Sandy. She knew nothing of his friends, or even if he'd had any before they married. As a couple they entertained her friends, never his. He had come into her life as a single package, with no emotional baggage, no domineering parents, nothing but him and his love of art, his ambitions for her and the gallery. It was a thought that Holly had instantly dismissed every time because it gave rise to questions that she didn't have any answers to. But it was a thought that went round and round in her head as she sat there now with an empty sheet of paper in front of her, waiting for the names and numbers of non-existent friends, people who might know where her husband was.

An awful feeling of desperation swept over her. Her husband was missing, and for the first time in her life, Holly did not know what to do. She didn't know who to call, where to look or what to think. She put her head in her hands and closed her eyes. If only the phone would ring, if only she could have some idea, some clue as to what had happened. He couldn't have been on the second flight from Rome – if he had been he would have materialised by now. For all she knew, he could have been missing since the moment he walked out of the flat on Friday, almost four days ago. He could have been mugged or murdered, had an accident, lost his memory. *Anything* could have happened to him, and there again, she had to face the grim truth that nothing at all might have happened, that he might simply have upped and left and she'd find a letter, a week from now, saying sorry and thanks but he had met someone else.

Holly wanted to weep but no tears would come. If only she knew, had some idea. If only he would call!

Suddenly the phone rang and she jumped.

She sat for several moments just staring at it, unable to move. Then, reaching out, her hands trembling, she picked up the receiver. Her heart was pounding.

'Hello?'

'Holly, this is Kit. I'm sorry to ring you late like this, but I was wondering . . . Holly? Are you all right? . . . Holly?'

Holly dropped the telephone. The sound of his voice was such a shock and such a relief that she couldn't speak. She put her hands up over her face and began to cry.

'Holly? Are you crying? What's happened? *Holly!*' Kit's voice rose frantically. 'Look, Holly, just stay there, all right?' He had already reached for his coat and pulled it on with one hand. 'Don't move, Holly!' he shouted, grabbing his wallet off the side. 'I'll be right over, OK?' Seconds later, the line went dead.

'I'm sorry . . .' Holly hiccuped. 'I just didn't know what to do and then when I heard your voice and . . . Oh God!' She covered her face with the already sopping handkerchief and Kit held her hand.

'I feel so stupid!' she choked out. 'I just don't know where he is. I've no idea who to call or if he's even missing!' She made to blow her nose, then stopped and said, 'Should I phone all the hospitals? I didn't know if that's what people do when someone goes missing but then I realised that I hardly know Sandy at all really and he could have gone off on some foreign trip and this could all be some kind of elaborate imagining . . .' She blew fiercely and Kit stood to get some loo roll. The hanky was finished; he hoped she wasn't going to give it back to him. 'What if he's had an accident?' Holly said, following him down the passage to the bathroom. 'Would they ring me? Would the police be round?' Silently she took the roll of toilet paper and handed Kit the handkerchief. He dropped it into her dirty laundry basket as she peeled off a length of tissue and blew her nose again. She was calming down now, and he wondered briefly why the thought of an accident didn't throw her into paroxysms of renewed wailing.

'Holly,' he said, walking across to the sink and filling it with cool water. 'Why don't you wash your face and bathe your eyes? You'll feel a lot better for it. Then we can sit down and go through all the possibilities. You must do something or you'll be insane with worry by the morning.'

She nodded, handed him the loo roll and the bit she'd blown her nose on, stripped off her tunic and bent over the sink in her grey lace bra. She splashed and Kit turned away. He remembered the underwear and Holly's ineptitude with the washing machine. He also remembered that she'd always said with him it didn't ever matter because her knickers were off so quick it was hardly worth wearing them, let alone worrying about what colour they went in the wash. She put her hand out for a towel and fumbled blindly in the air until he handed her one. She dried her face, a harsh rub, then glanced in the mirror. She looked a fright – blotchy, red and swollen – but she made no comment. She simply ran a comb through her hair and turned. 'I do feel better,' she said. 'Marginally.'

'Good.' Kit tried to keep his eyes on her face but he couldn't help glancing down at her body. He wished he hadn't; it was the same body, it did the same things to him. He turned and headed down the passage.

'Kit?'

'I'll be in the sitting room,' he called. He stopped off in the kitchen and went straight to the fridge. Taking a bottle of wine out, he poured two glasses and swallowed down half of his before refilling it and taking them both through to the small living room. He placed Holly's glass down on the mantelpiece and looked around him. The flat was exactly the same. Exactly. The same battered cream sofas, the stripped wood floor, the printed silk cushions, the Persian rug with the cigarette burn and the two huge abstract paintings on opposite walls, facing each other. Cream, white and beige everywhere, the splash of colour from the paintings standing out in violent contrast. Books lined one wall, and piles of them littered the floor: art books, photography books, interiors. A round bowl crowded with dark pink, purple and red anemones, their black centres scattering ash-like pollen over the table. A sculpture, Elizabeth Frink; an eighteenth-century writing case; a photograph of her father in an Indian carved sandalwood frame next to a half-full perfume bottle; two red lipsticks; three invitations; one postcard from Hanoi. It was just as he remembered it, the female chaos, Holly's own peculiar brand of charm. Kit felt uneasy. There was no wedding photograph, no smiling face of Sandy Turner, no masculine detail at all; the room was wholly feminine, completely Holly's.

'This for me?'

Kit turned. Lost in thought, he hadn't heard Holly come back into the room. She took her glass and swallowed down a large gulp of wine. He watched her for a moment, then said, 'Your husband's very tidy.'

Holly tensed. 'Yes,' she answered stiffly, 'he is.'

Kit nodded and continued to look round the room.

'Not everyone's like you, Kit!' she suddenly burst out. 'Not everyone comes for the evening and manages to make it look as if he lives here!' She was referring to Kit's old habit of leaving things all over the flat – shoes in the bathroom, jumper on the floor by the sofa, jacket in the kitchen. He always left his loose change on the mantelpiece, his keys by the door. 'Sandy just kept himself to himself, that's all!'

Kit looked at her. 'Kept?'

She stared back at him, the realisation of what she'd just said sinking in. Then suddenly she slumped down onto the sofa. 'Oh God!' She put her head in her hands. 'Did I really say kept?'

'Yes.'

She glanced up. 'What am I going to do, Kit?'

'Ring the police,' he answered. 'I don't think there's any other option.'

'The police?' Holly was instantly alarmed. 'No, I can't do that, not yet, he might turn up, he might . . .'

'Holly, it won't do any harm. All you do is go down to the police station and report him missing. If he does turn up then no-one thinks any the worse of you. It's not as if you're overreacting. You're worried, he's not here and he never turned up to where he said he was going. Come on.' He picked up the phone and handed it to her. 'D' you want me to look up the local station for you?'

She bit her lip, then finally nodded. Minutes later she dialled the Chelsea area control room and was put through to her local station.

'They want me to go down,' she said, hanging up after her call. 'I need to fill in a missing persons form.'

Kit picked up his jacket.

'What're you doing?' Holly stood and stared at him.

'Coming with you.'

She turned away, shocked. This wasn't Kit: Kit always waited to be asked, he always hesitated. 'I see,' she said tensely. She didn't know what to do, how to react.

'Good, I'm glad you see, because you often didn't.' She turned back and he smiled. 'In the past.'

Holly said nothing but walked across to pick up her bag. She pulled on her overcoat, fastened it and walked past him to the front door. 'Coming?' she snapped.

'Yes,' he answered coolly. He followed her out of the flat, down the stairs and outside to his rented car.

Jill eased her hand gently out of Harry's and quietly stood, moving away from him to switch off the lamp. She glanced down at him to make sure that he was asleep and touched his hair. Then she crossed the room to fold his clothes, laying them neatly on the chair, and to pick up a couple of books, replacing them on the shelf. She left, plugged the night light in on the landing and walked slowly downstairs. She wanted to sit and weep, relieving herself of the burden of grief and guilt, but she was too shocked and exhausted for tears. Instead, she made some tea and sat in the dark kitchen, warming her icy hands around the mug, numb, motionless, thinking that whatever she had done, she did not deserve this. Harry and Sophie did not deserve this.

She looked up at a figure in the doorway.

'D'you want some tea?'

Sophie shook her head. Her small, thin face was ashen, with dark shadows under her eyes, and her eyelids looked swollen and sore. Her gaze was hostile. She stood half in, half out of the room and said, 'What are you going to do?'

Jill put her mug down on the table and rubbed her hands over her eyes. She had no idea. What did people do in this situation? How did they cope? Should she assume Alex was dead, grieve, be a widow? Or should she keep hoping, waiting until a body was found before she got on with her life and tried in some way to get over the horror and misery? She looked up at Sophie. 'I don't know,' she said wearily. 'I just don't know.'

Sophie's jaw tensed. 'You think he's dead, don't you?'

Jill looked away. 'Yes, I do.'

'But how could you?' Sophie hissed. 'You know he'd never do that to us, you *know* he wouldn't!'

'Sophie, I don't know anything at the moment,' Jill countered. 'I'm so confused and upset and shocked I can hardly think straight.'

'He didn't kill himself,' Sophie said. She had moved closer to Jill and her face was lit from behind by the hall light. She looked both intimidating and like a small child, terrified and alone. 'I know he didn't kill himself, I know it in my heart.' She stared at Jill for a few moments, her eyes full of pain. 'And you'd know it too, if you'd loved him, like I did . . .' Tears choked her voice and she swallowed painfully. 'You never loved him and you never loved me and I know that whatever happened he would never have left me alone . . . not like this . . . not with you! He would never have . . .' A sob escaped her and she put her hands up to cover her face. She began to weep, noisy, broken sobs. Jill reached out to touch her but she stumbled back, repulsed by the action. Moments later she turned and fled up the stairs.

'Sophie!' Jill struggled to her feet. 'Sophie, come back here!' She ran into the hall and up the first few steps, then stopped as she heard Sophie's door slam at the top of the house. It was no good trying to comfort her, not now. Jill sank down on the stairs. Sophie would have to learn to cope, she thought angrily. She would have to face it as Jill was facing it – she wasn't a child, not like Harry. She had to show some strength, some character. No more histrionics, no more tantrums. Jill pulled her knees up under her, buried her head in her arms and wished to God, as she had done since the nightmare began, that she could cry.

It was almost midnight when she finally went upstairs to bed.

She was dreading it: switching on the bedside lamps, turning back the covers, drawing the curtains. They were the bedtime rituals, the motions gone through almost every night for the past fourteen years in the company of her husband. Sitting on the edge of the bed, Jill looked around the bedroom at the pale yellow chintz, the polished walnut tallboy, her dressing table, the matching silk-covered Regency chairs. She saw the photographs, perfectly arranged, the antique perfume bottles, the vase of white and yellow freesias, the order, the elegance and beauty of the room, and she thought, no, this sort of thing doesn't happen to people like us. It can't! We, I, don't deserve this. What have I ever done to deserve this?

She stood and walked across to the mirror. She had tucked a couple of the postcards Alex had sent her over the years into the frame, silly, romantic cards, and now she took one out and looked at the familiar, illegible scrawl on the back.

'You bastard!' she suddenly spat. 'How could you do this to me?' She tore the card in two and stuffed it into the drawer. Only she didn't really feel angry. Anger would have fuelled her spirit, her determination. No, she felt helpless, desperate. She had no idea how she was even going to get through the night, let alone face the awful loneliness and humiliation of the next few days. Me, I'm the one who will suffer, she thought, looking at her reflection, not you, Alex. Whatever pain you felt, you've left me with much worse. She closed her eyes on the image of a middle-aged woman, lonely and in despair, but when she opened them again the woman was still there. She turned away and switched off the lamp. Still fully clothed, she lay down on the bed, pulled the duvet over her and listened to the silence of her suddenly awful, empty life.

At one am Jill woke with a start. It didn't feel as if she'd slept, more as if she'd just lost consciousness for a few minutes. She heard the pitiful sound of weeping and immediately sat up, swinging her legs over the side of the bed. She hurried out of her bedroom and across the landing to Harry's room, but halfway there she stopped. It wasn't Harry crying, it was Sophie. Standing motionless, Jill felt a wrench in her stomach at the noise. She turned and walked towards the bathroom, her footsteps silent. Easing open the door, she saw her stepdaughter, huddled over the toilet, sick, weeping and desperate. A child, a lonely, frightened child of seventeen.

'Sophie, please . . . please don't cry . . .' She moved uneasily forward but Sophie jerked her head round.

'Go away!' she cried. 'I don't want you! I don't need your pity!' She covered her face with her hands while Jill stood there, helpless. The fact that it was Sophie rendered her inert, useless. Sophie was right – Jill was unable to feel anything but pity; she was paralysed by her own grief. She stepped back, suddenly anxious to get away. She should have stayed, hugged Sophie, done or said something, anything, but she couldn't. The gulf between them was too wide; there was too much that had gone before, both pain and misunderstanding. So Jill edged out of the bathroom and closed the door behind her. She walked back to her room and lay down on the bed in the dark, eyes wide open, feeling and seeing nothing. And she lay like that until the cold grey light of morning.

Holly stood by the window in her bedroom and stared out at the street. It was nearly two am and the tall, narrow houses in Bishop's Road were dark and silent, sleeping in peace. She bit the nail on her forefinger and wished for the hundredth time that day that she hadn't given up smoking; she longed for some small action to break the inertia. Turning away, she glanced back at the empty bed, its clean, fresh sheets unused, the pillows still plumped, their cases neatly ironed. She pulled her robe in a little tighter around her body and walked across to the door. She couldn't face going to bed – she knew she wouldn't sleep and she didn't want to lie in the dark, alone and thinking, brooding.

Padding down the corridor to the kitchen, she saw the light still on in the sitting room and looked round the door. He had irritated her by insisting he stay after they'd been to the police station, but now, in the cold night air, she was relieved of the company.

'Kit?'

He looked up from the book he was reading.

'D'you want some tea? I can't sleep, I'm making myself a cup.'

'Yes, OK.' He sat up on the sofa and threw off the rug, reaching for his sweater. The heating had gone off and the flat had a certain chill about it. Standing, he followed Holly into the kitchen and sat on the edge of the unit while she filled the kettle. She puzzled him, with her silent resignation. There was no passion in her worry, no wild panic or fury. She seemed to have accepted that Sandy was missing with a calmness that was very unlike Holly: no shouting, no weeping, no drama. It worried him.

'Are you all right, Holly?' he ventured some time later, having watched her every move. 'You seem . . .' He shrugged, not sure how to put it.

'I seem what, Kit?' she asked coolly, her back to him at the sink. There was something about his tone that annoyed her, something intimate that didn't belong there. God, he'd only been home five minutes and already he thought things were the same as they'd always been! Holly tensed as she turned to look at him.

'I don't know,' he answered. 'Sort of removed from it, worried, of course, but not your usual . . .'

'My usual terrible, uncontrollable self, is that it?' Holly's annoyance escalated. 'How would you know what my usual reaction is nowadays?'

'I wouldn't, but I just thought you might . . .'

She cut him off. 'Might what? Hmmm? Be weeping and wailing, flooding the kitchen floor?' Her nostrils flared and she bit her lip in an attempt to control the sudden temper that threatened to swamp her. It wasn't him, really; it was everything, the whole ruddy mess, and then again it *was* him, thinking that he could simply turn up and pretend that everything was all right, as it had been, with none of the pain and despair and mistakes in between. She looked at his face. 'Is that what you want me to do?' she asked. 'Sob uncontrollably, be utterly helpless?' She shook her head. 'Sorry to disappoint you, but I had enough of that two years ago.'

The hit was a direct one, and Kit flinched. 'Look, I didn't mean that!' he snapped. He was annoyed too, now; she made it sound as if it was all him. Christ, he'd done his own fair share of hurting, hadn't he? 'I just meant . . .'

'Oh for God's sake, Kit, I don't really care what you meant, or what you think or what the hell you're doing here!' Holly felt tired and confused 'Either just shut up or go away, all right?'

Kit glared angrily down at the floor. She's in a state, he told himself, be tolerant, don't spoil things. 'I'm sorry, I just didn't understand your reaction. I thought you might want to talk.'

'Talk!' Holly snorted derisively. Suddenly she lost control and banged her mug down, sending tea slopping onto the work surface. How could she talk, or even begin to explain her feelings to him? Christ, she could hardly make sense of them herself! And who did he think he was, coming into her life after a long and painful absence and expecting her to open up to him as if he'd been there all the time? 'You want me to talk, do you?' she demanded. 'Well here it is, OK? I am upset, but not in the way you think I should be. I hardly knew my husband; I don't even know if I loved him; in fact, I don't know anything at the moment, except confusion and anxiety. There, are you satisfied now?'

Kit stared at her. His first reaction was to fight back but she was under pressure, distraught, so he held his tongue. 'There's no question of being satisfied, Holly . . .'

'Isn't there?' she sneered.

'No!' This time Kit did snap, he couldn't stop himself. 'I just thought you might want help, that's all.'

'If I need help, I'll ask for it,' Holly said icily.

Kit jumped down off the side and stomped across the kitchen to chuck his unfinished tea down the sink. He'd had enough. This was getting them nowhere. 'Right then, I'll go. You obviously don't want me here.'

'You're damn right I don't!' Holly countered. She turned away.

'Fine!' he snarled. 'I'm off!'

'Fine!' Holly called after him as he marched into the sitting room and grabbed his things. 'Good!' She followed him out into the hall.

'Goodbye!' he shouted, storming out of the flat and down the stairs. He didn't turn or wave or glance back. At the bottom he stopped and turned up the collar on his overcoat before yanking open the main door and slamming it shut after him.

'Goodbye to you too!' Holly bellowed after him. She banged the door of the flat, making the letter box rattle. Then she slumped down onto the hall chair, dropped her head into her hands and suddenly felt very stupid and very miserable.

Chelsea Police Station, 3 am

The CAD room was quiet; it was that time of the morning. The PC on the message desk yawned and stretched. It was late, near the end of his shift, and he needed a coffee.

'Want a drink, Sarge?'

He stood and dug in his pockets for some loose change. As he laid a few coins out on the desk the phone rang. He answered it, listened for a few minutes, then said, 'Can you hang on for a short while?' He pressed the hold button.

'It's Missing Persons Index, Sarge, about an enquiry form 584, logged on tonight. Apparently an identical form has been recorded from Brighton Police.'

'OK, tell them we'll get back to them.'

The PC spoke quickly then hung up.

'Sounds like someone's mucked up, doesn't it, Sarge?'

'Could well be. Let's get the form out and have a look. Who filed it?'

'Mannings.'

'Get him in here then, with the form.'

'He's out on patrol, Sarge.'

'Just the form then, Constable!' The Sergeant's irritation flared. He'd been hoping for a reasonably quiet end to the night.

'Right, Sarge.'

The Constable walked off down the corridor and the Sergeant rubbed his hands wearily over his face.

'Here it is, Sarge, form 584. Looks to be filled in correctly.'

'Let's have a look.' The Sergeant checked all the details, then picked up the phone. 'It's all right, Dave, I'll deal with it.' He waited for the line to connect.

'Hello, Missing Persons Index? This is Sergeant Pete Davis from Chelsea Police Station. Regarding the form 584, reference number CD2331. As far as we're concerned, we've got a bona fide enquiry here. Can you tell me what the problem is?' He was silent for a few moments. 'Yes, sure, it's here in front of me, go ahead.' He glanced down the form as the voice at the other end read out the information, checking it all off. 'Yes, I see,' he said a few minutes later. 'We'll get on to Brighton now then. Thanks.' He hung up. 'Get Brighton nick on the phone, will you, Dave?' he said. 'This is a right oddball, this one.'

'Right, Sarge.' the PC walked across for the station directory and the Sergeant stood, stretched and massaged the base of his spine. 'Terrific bloody timing, Missing Persons!' he said. And taking the phone, he spoke to the duty officer in Brighton.

Chapter Five

'What is it, Pete?' Chief Superintendent Hart had just got his coat off when Sergeant Davis knocked. 'First of the day's problems, I expect! Come on in.'

Davis walked into the open office and put a sheaf of stapled papers down on the desk. ''Fraid so, sir,' he said. 'Bit of an odd one this, too; glad to be handing it over!'

'What is it?' Hart picked up the top sheet, glanced down it and turned the page. 'Form 584, what's the problem with it?'

'Brighton nick,' Davis answered. 'It's all down there, along with their copy of the form.'

'Ah . . .' Hart continued to read. 'I see.' He looked up. 'One for CID I think, don't you?'

The Sergeant smiled.

'Robert?' The Chief Superintendent called through the door in the partition wall. 'In here!'

DS Robert Eames appeared almost immediately. 'Sir?'

'A problem for CID, Robert, I'll let Sergeant Davis explain. A missing persons investigation.' He stood and came round the desk. 'Coffee?'

Both officers nodded. 'Right.' He headed for the door. 'You could put one of our new trainee investigators on it if you like, Robert. Let someone else do all the leg work!'

Eames smiled. 'Good idea, sir, get the lazy buggers working!'

Holly hadn't slept. She sat up in bed at eight am with a mug of tea and wondered whether or not to open up the gallery that morning. In fact she had been worrying about it for over an hour, but had found herself completely unable to reach a decision. She sipped her tea as she went over the question one more time and huddled down under the covers. All she really wanted was to close her eyes and go to sleep, to blank it all out – the row with Kit, Sandy's disappearance, the doubt and the confusion, the anxiety. She wanted to wake up to find that none of the past twenty-four hours had even happened. As she put her mug down on the bedside table, the telephone rang, shaking her out of her inertia.

'Hello?' She reached for the pen and paper she had put by the bed the night before but her hand stopped in mid-air.

'Oh, I see.' She took a sharp intake of breath. 'Yes, of course, I can get down there right away. A problem, you say?' She let the breath out slowly, tensely. 'No, of course you can't, I understand. I'll be there as soon as I can.'

She hung up and threw back the duvet. Rushing across to her bag, she rummaged for several minutes, peering into the muddle, then pulled out her purse and found Kit's hotel number. 'Oh thank God for that,' she murmured, running back to the phone. Without questioning what she was doing, she dialled.

'Room 114 please.' She waited. 'Kit! Thank goodness!' She rushed on without pausing to take breath. 'The police just rang, they've asked me to go down to the station. There's been some kind of development but they wouldn't say wh . . .' She stopped as Kit interrupted her. 'Oh . . .' she said in a small voice, then, 'I see.' She bit her fingernail. 'No, of course not! Sorry, I didn't think. A meeting? Yes, obviously. Sorry, I . . .' Her voice trailed off. Acute tension was suddenly replaced by disappointment. She put her hand over the mouthpiece and took a deep breath, tears dangerously close, then stood winding the telephone wire tightly round her finger as she listened to him speak.

'No, of course I understand,' she murmured. She'd been foolish to expect anything else after the row last night. 'Yes, you must, of course . . .' She dropped onto the edge of the bed, tired and miserable. 'I'll let you know, yes, later on.' The thought of going down to the station on her own, of what she might have to face there, brought the threat of fresh tears. She should never have called, of course he wouldn't help. It had just seemed the obvious thing to do to pick up the phone.

She swallowed hard, caught her breath to stop a sob, and said quickly, 'I really must go or I'll be late. Thanks anyway. Bye!' She hung up. 'You stupid, stupid woman!' she cried out loud, covering her face with her hands. But the room was empty and unresponsive, and her voice was swallowed up by the silence.

In his hotel room across London, Kit slammed down the phone and paced the floor for a few minutes before picking up the receiver again and dialling his London office.

'Hello, Lucy Yates please.' He waited to be put through. 'Hi, Lucy, it's Kit Thomas.' Lucy Yates was the solicitor working on the British side of the deal he had come over for. 'Have you got everything ready for the meeting this morning?' He drummed his fingers on the bedside table. 'Good, well done. Look, something's come up, Lucy.' He knew he was being foolish, even as he spoke. He had told himself last night to stay well clear, that she hadn't changed, it was all take and no give, but he couldn't stop himself. 'I might have to leave the meeting an hour or so early,' he went on. 'D'you think you can manage to wrap things up on your own?' He stood as he listened to her answer.

However unreasonable Holly's behaviour had been last night, her husband had disappeared, she needed him and he couldn't leave her to face all this on her own. 'Great!' he said. 'That's a lot of help, thanks. I'm on my way in now so I'll see you in about twenty, twenty-five minutes, tube permitting.' He reached for his coat off the back of the chair. 'Yup! See you in a while.' Hanging up, he clicked his briefcase shut and pulled on his overcoat.

He had gone to bed angry, had woken up determined to forget the whole bloody thing with Holly, and an hour later he was rearranging his meeting to be with her. He grabbed his case and headed for the door. So nothing's changed, he thought, walking out towards the lifts, but instead of infuriating him, he found the idea strangely exhilarating. He smiled and went on down to the hotel lobby.

Holly sat huddled inside her coat and sipped the coffee the WPC had brought her. It wasn't cold in the station, but she couldn't seem to stop shaking. Her hands trembled, and she had to grip the cup tightly so that it didn't show.

She looked up as Detective Sergeant Robert Eames came back into the room and thought what an unlikely police officer he made. A short, neat young man with an officious air and small round glasses, he would have looked better in a bank.

'Sorry to have kept you, Miss Grigson.' He sat down opposite Holly and took out his cigarettes. 'D'you mind?' He tapped the packet, then proffered it to her.

'No, thanks.' Holly attempted to smile. 'I gave up a year ago. I wish now I hadn't.'

Eames nodded, lighting up. He inhaled, then said, 'Miss Grigson, Holly, I'm sorry to have to do this again, but could we just clarify a few points one more time on the form?'

Holly hesitated. She didn't really know what was going on, as she had been given only a brief explanation for all the questions, the checking and the waiting. 'Look,' she began, 'I don't know what this is all about but I've answered your questions once already and

I really don't see why I have to go through it all again without some kind of reasonable explanation.'

Eames flicked his ash and Holly noticed his hands, pale-skinned and plump. 'I do understand, Holly, but at this moment all I can say is that we are not investigating you in any way, we are simply trying to verify the facts in this case. There's a problem with the missing persons form and I need to be quite sure of the information this end before we investigate the matter further.'

'Investigate?' Holly tensed at the word.

'Look into.' Eames took out the form 584 Holly had filled in the previous night. 'Can I just go over the details you gave us?'

Holly sighed. 'Yes, all right.' She couldn't see that there was anything she could usefully add to what she'd already told them.

'Your husband's full name was Alexander Richard Turner?'

Holly nodded.

'Date of birth, twenty-first of April 1948; age forty-five; born London, UK. He is British, white, height six feet two inches?'

'Yes.'

'Now – marks, scars, tattoos, physical peculiarities. You've written here that apart from the skin markings, freckles, etcetera, the only definitive mark is a small one-inch scar on his neck, the left side, just above his collar line, from the removal of a mole. Is that all?'

Holly nodded.

'You're quite sure that's all there is? No false teeth, birth marks, other scars?'

'No!' Holly shook her head in disbelief. 'I've already told you. Why d'you want to know anyway?'

'I'm sorry, I don't want to distress you any more than you already are. I have to ask.'

Holly dropped her head down and pulled her coat tight around her. 'Go on,' she said quietly.

'Build, medium; hair, light brown, short, slightly wavy, greying at the sideburns; eyes, green; no glasses or contact lenses. Complexion, fair; no moustache or beard. Now, clothing. Your husband was wearing a suit, navy pinstripe, off the peg, Austin Reed; shirt, M & S, striped, can't remember particular detail; tie, red, again can't remember particular detail. Shoes, black leather brogues, Churches, size, don't know, about eleven. A navy wool top coat; a watch, Tag Heuer, stainless steel, gentleman's diving watch. Yes? All correct?'

Again Holly nodded.

Eames placed the form back in the file and glanced at another form below it. Apart from the address, the occupation, and the date and time last seen, the details on both forms in his file – the original and the faxed copy from Brighton – were identical. He reached for the driving licence and looked at it again. The driver number, date of test pass and date of birth were all exactly the same as the faxed copy from Brighton. The marriage certificate was bona fide, Holly Grigson was who she said she was, and there was no recent photograph – not unusual for someone with something to hide. He closed the file and took a breath.

'Holly, one last question, I'm afraid. Do you know anyone at all in the West Sussex, Brighton area?'

'Brighton?' Holly echoed.

'Or West Sussex?'

She thought for a moment. 'No, no-one, not as far as I can remember anyway.'

'I see.' DS Eames reached for his cigarettes again, then stopped, thinking better of it. 'Holly, will you excuse me for a few moments? I just want to check something with my superior.'

Holly nodded. 'Then can I go?'

Eames stopped and looked back at her. Poor woman, she didn't deserve this; no-one did for that matter. 'Yes,' he said, 'then you can go.'

He walked out into the corridor and across to the Chief Superintendent's office.

'Sir?' He knocked lightly on the half-open door.

The Chief Superintendent had been deep in conversation with one of Eames' superior officers, DCI Heeley, and both men looked up as he appeared.

'Yes, Robert?'

'Sir, I've got Holly Grigson next door.'

Hart looked momentarily blank.

'The duplicate form 584?' Eames prompted. 'She's the person who filed the second form.'

'Oh yes, that's right. Go on.'

'Well, sir, I've been through it all twice, checked the details again with Brighton, and it's as we thought. I just wanted to check it with you before I went ahead and told her.'

'Right. Looks pretty straightforward, does it?'

'Well, to be frank, sir, I'm not really sure. It seems a bit odd, the fact that Miss Grigson had no suspicion whatsoever. She seems a very intelligent woman and yet from what I can tell, she hardly knew her husband at all. She married him within a short space of meeting him, and knows virtually nothing about his background. I don't know, there's nothing ringing alarm bells but I just feel something doesn't add up.'

Chief Superintendent Hart held out his hand for the file. He opened it, glanced briefly at the details, then handed it across to DCI Heeley. 'Have a look at this, will you, Pete?' He reached behind him for his cap. 'I haven't got time myself, I'm afraid. I've got a meeting that I should have been at . . .' he glanced at his watch, 'five minutes ago.' He stood up. 'I'll put DCI Heeley in charge, all right? Talk your worries through with him.'

DS Eames nodded and attempted a smile as the Chief Superintendent moved past him into the corridor. Heeley was famous for his dislike of graduate entry. Gentlemen policemen, he called them, the boys who don't like to get their hands dirty.

'Let me know how it goes,' Hart said. He fitted his cap onto his head and hurried away.

DCI Heeley looked down at the file and read for a few minutes, leaving DS Eames to stand uncomfortably in the doorway. Finally Heeley looked up. 'There's one born every minute,' he said. 'Why do they do it, Detective Sergeant? Never fails to amaze me how stupid some women can be.'

Eames bit back instant irritation. He prided himself on being politically correct. 'Just women, sir?'

Heeley ignored the comment. 'A wife knowing sweet FA about her husband's double life is nothing new, DS Eames. In my experience, these women only see what they want to see; they turn a blind eye to the rest.' He glanced at the file again. 'Did she say anything to make you suspect that this could be some kind of faked death for an insurance fraud?'

'No, sir.'

'Is there any other crime you might read into this, apart from the obvious one?'

'No, sir.'

'Well then.' DCI Heeley looked directly at DS Eames. He was exactly the sort of officer he didn't like: a smart aleck with a degree stuffed up his arse who was looking to score points. Heeley held out the file. 'Wrap it up, Detective Sergeant, and don't waste any more time on it.'

Eames took the file without answering, to Heeley's irritation. 'You might ask Miss Grigson to identify the personal belongings, if you've nothing outstanding.' The sarcasm was heavy; it was obvious there was nothing outstanding. 'Ultimately we've got a crime and it'll need to be dealt with correctly. We need as much evidence as possible.'

'Yes, sir.' DS Eames kept his face blank but the dislike was mutual. 'I'll organise a car to drive Miss Grigson down to Brighton.'

'Do that.' Heeley smiled, but there was no warmth in it. 'Once the personal effects have been identified by her as well, I think we can safely go ahead and charge the crime.'

'Right, sir.' He tucked the file under his arm. 'And who should I charge the crime to, sir?' Heeley scowled by way of response, and Eames left the office.

Holly refused the offer of another coffee and nodded blankly in reply to the WPC's comment on the weather. She turned as DS Eames came back into the room and looked hopefully at him. The hope faded the instant he sat down.

'Something's wrong, isn't it?' Holly said.

DS Eames kept his face impassive. 'Holly, I'm afraid I have some bad news for you.' He took a short breath and went on. 'There has been another missing persons report filed on the central computer, logged on at Brighton Police Station, and that's what we've been checking, last night and most of this morning. We've been in contact with Brighton and it would appear that the details on the form are identical to your own. Mr Alexander Richard Turner was reported missing by a woman claiming to be his wife, a Mrs Jill Turner.'

Holly's face creased in a frown. 'I don't understand. Are you saying that there are two Alexander Turners?'

'No, I'm afraid not. It looks as if the person reported missing in Brighton is the same one reported missing by you last night.'

'The same?' Surely he wasn't saying . . . 'The *same?*' She shook her head.

'We have reason to believe that your husband, Alexander

Turner, Sandy Turner, was also married to another woman. I'm sorry, this must be very difficult . . .' DS Eames stopped and waited for Holly to catch up with what he'd just said.

'You're saying my husband was married to someone else?'

'Yes, that's what we believe.' Eames cleared his throat. 'I'm afraid there's something else, Holly.' He looked straight at her; it was better to be direct. 'Your husband's clothes and personal belongings were found on the beach at Brighton. Although no body has yet been found, I'm afraid the evidence is that he killed himself.'

'Killed himself?' Holly shook her head. She simply didn't believe it. 'That's ludicrous! Why on earth would he want to . . . ?' She stopped. Sandy was always away, abroad she'd thought, but he could have been anywhere, with anyone.

'He may have found the strain of leading a double life too much,' Eames said gently.

'But how? How can someone get married twice in this country? Surely he would have been found out? Surely he couldn't just get away with it?'

'It's not that difficult to commit bigamy in the UK, I'm afraid.' DS Eames shrugged. 'Just as it's not that difficult to obtain false documents, a driving licence, credit cards, a passport.' He shook his head. 'This would probably never have come to light if it hadn't been for your husband's, er . . . Mr Turner's, suicide.'

'Mr Turner . . .' Holly's voice trailed away. She tried to swallow but her throat was painfully dry. 'You're saying he's not my husband, aren't you?'

DS Eames hesitated, then nodded. 'The other woman in Brighton . . .'

'Mrs Turner?' Holly said.

'Yes. That marriage appears to be the first and therefore legitimate. I'm sorry, we checked with records at St Catherine's House.'

'I see.' But Holly didn't really see. She felt utterly confused. It was all so impossible, so far-fetched, like being part of some incredible drama. 'Suicide?' she croaked.

'Would you like some water, Miss Grigson?'

'Er . . .' Holly dropped her head into her hands. 'Yes, please,' she mumbled.

Eames nodded at the WPC, who silently left the room. She returned almost immediately with a glass of water and Holly took it, her hands shaking. She sipped but felt suddenly sick. Dropping her head down again she covered her face with her hands. 'I'm sorry,' she whispered. 'It's the shock. I . . .' Moments later she looked up. 'You're sure? There's no mistake, is there?'

DS Eames shook his head. 'If you feel up to it, we'd like you to identify Mr Turner's clothes, his personal belongings. That way there would be no doubt.'

'Yes, of course.' Holly stood up shakily.

'There's no hurry, Miss Grigson, please, take your time.'

'I'm fine,' Holly said. She held onto the back of the chair and her hands were white with the force of her grip. 'Really.'

DS Eames and the WPC exchanged glances. It sometimes happened like this. Some people dismissed the shock immediately, in an attempt to be normal, but it was a bad sign. It would hit them later, twice as hard.

Eames stood up. 'Are you sure you can cope with this now? We can take you home and arrange it for later today, or tomorrow, if you prefer.'

'No, I'd rather do it now. Get it over with.' She rummaged frantically in her bag. 'Can I make a phone call, before we go?' She found her purse.

'Of course, WPC Pierson will show you where you can ring.' DS Eames walked towards the door. 'I'll get a car organised,' he said. 'Let WPC Pierson know if there's anything else you want.'

Holly nodded. She opened her purse and took out Kit's card. She looked at it for a few moments before dropping it back. There was no point, Kit would never come. Besides, what could he do anyway?

Silently, she followed the WPC out of the room and along the corridor to the front desk.

Jill let herself into the house and stood just inside the hallway, slumped against the door. She stared at the familiar surroundings – her home, her family's home – and the sight of it made her feel sick. Putting her hands up to her face, she slid down to the floor and closed her eyes. She had never felt so helpless, so desolate and alone in her entire life.

'Jill?'

She looked up slowly and saw Sophie, standing motionless halfway down the stairs, her gaze resentful and accusing. 'Where've you been?' she demanded.

Jill took a breath. When she spoke her voice was weak and she knew she sounded pathetic; she hated herself for it. 'The police station in Brighton called early this morning and I had to go down to answer a few questions about Dad . . .' She stopped. The word stuck in her throat. 'About Alex,' she said. 'I didn't want to wake you.'

'You should have told me!' Sophie protested. 'I have a right to know! I could have come with you, I . . .'

'No you couldn't!' Jill suddenly snapped. She struggled to her feet, the effort of it exhausting her. 'It was personal, it didn't involve you!' She walked into the kitchen. She had decided on the drive back from Brighton not to say anything about Alex, not now, not yet, not to anyone. She had to attempt to come to terms with it herself first, to try and work it out in her own mind before she could explain it to anyone else. She felt overwhelmed by his betrayal, his deceit; it made her feel physically sick. Like an automaton, she began to lay things out for tea: a mug, the sugar bowl, a jug of milk. Turning the tap on, she picked up the kettle and held it under the jet of running water. All the lies – the so-called business trips away, the late meetings, the overnight stays in London; it had gone on for almost two years and she had known nothing. What a fool she must have been! How could he have done it? How could he have married again, living half a life in London and half a life here with her, half a life filled with lies and deceit? She just couldn't believe it.

'Jill! For Christ's sake!' Sophie grabbed the kettle out of her hands and turned off the tap. 'What's the matter with you? God, you nearly flooded the place!'

Jill stood helpless while Sophie yanked the plug out of the sink and threw a tea towel onto the floor to mop up the water. 'You're soaked.'

'Yes, I . . .' Jill broke off and looked down at her drenched jumper, stunned at her incompetence. No wonder Alex had found someone else, no wonder he had . . . 'Oh Christ!' she cried. 'Look at the state of me!' Reaching for another tea towel, she began to rub frantically at the wet stain on her jumper. 'God, I'll have to change now. I can't go back to the station looking like this, I can't let people see me like this . . .'

Sophie moved away, horrified. It was as if nothing else mattered: all Jill could think about was herself, what she looked like, what people thought. Jill stopped and glanced up. She had felt Sophie's hateful gaze.

'Why d'you have to go back to the station?' Sophie asked, her voice edged with panic.

Jill dropped the tea towel onto the work surface. She had to go back with Alex's personal belongings, for the other woman to identify. How could she explain all that?

'It's nothing much,' she lied. 'Just a few details . . .'

Sophie continued to stare at her stepmother. 'That's not true. You're hiding something!'

Suddenly Jill turned away. She wasn't sure she had the strength to face this, not now. She took a deep breath and closed her eyes. All she wanted to do was pretend everything was all right. Pretend it hadn't happened. After this latest shock, she couldn't think straight, let alone lie convincingly. She longed for two days ago, for blissful, contented ignorance. Finally she looked round.

'Sophie, go up to your room please. I haven't the time to talk about this now.'

But Sophie stood where she was. 'You're lying,' she accused. 'You're hiding something about Daddy!'

Jill put her hands up and wearily massaged her temples. She was hanging onto her sanity by a thread. 'Sophie, please,' she murmured tightly. 'Just leave it for now, all right?'

'No it's not all right!' Sophie cried, moving closer. 'You're lying and I know it!' Her voice rose hysterically. 'Don't think you can get away with it, don't think you can . . .'

Jill's hand came up out of nowhere. She hit her stepdaughter with her open palm and the force of the blow knocked Sophie off balance. She stood stunned, her hand against her burning cheek, and stared at Jill.

'I hate you,' she whispered. 'I hate you, I hate you, I hate you!' And suddenly she spat on the ground between them. 'Pig!' Turning away, she stuffed her fist in her mouth to stop herself from crying and fled up the stairs.

Jill stood motionless. She raised her right hand and looked at it. The fingers shook; the palm was flame red from the blow.

'Oh Christ!' She put it up to her mouth and pressed her lips against the stinging flesh. Then she dropped her head down and closed her eyes. 'You bastard, Alex,' she muttered. She had never in her life before lost control, never. 'This is what you've done to me . . .' she whispered hoarsely. 'This!' She dropped her hand down and clenched her fist. 'This!' Suddenly she smacked the sideboard with all her force and swept the mug, sugar bowl and milk off it onto the floor. There was an almighty smash, then her legs and feet were drenched with milk, and the floor was littered with sugar and hundreds of splinters of shattered glass and china.

'Damn you!' she screamed. 'Damn you!' She sank to her knees, oblivious to the chaos around her, her body racked with hard, dry sobs.

Later that afternoon, Jill stood and reached for her coat. She had seen enough of the interview room at Brighton Police Station in the past twenty-four hours to last her a lifetime, and she was anxious to leave. She glanced momentarily at the plastic bag on the table containing Alex's things, then turned away.

'Thank you very much for your time, Mrs Turner,' the Detective Sergeant said. 'I appreciate you bringing your husband's things down here.'

She nodded and pulled on her coat, waiting for him to open the door.

'Are you all right to get back to Eastham?'

'Yes, thanks.' Walking out into the corridor, she fastened the buttons on her coat and turned the collar up, flicking her hair over it. Her immaculate appearance gave no hint of what had happened earlier that day. She dug her hands in her pockets and followed the police officer the length of seemingly unending grey passage to the locked glass-panelled doors that led out to the front desk. She glanced through them, waiting for him to key in the number, and saw a slim young woman booking in. She tensed.

'Mrs Turner?' The officer held the door for her. She walked out, then stopped as the woman turned.

For a moment Jill stood perfectly still and held her breath. She knew instinctively who the woman was and a feeling of panic washed over her. She stared at Holly and Holly stared back. It was a matter of seconds but it felt like an eternity.

'This way please, Mrs Turner.' The officer motioned for her to go forward and Jill started. Averting her gaze, she walked past the woman, noticing her scent, rich and woody, expensive, exotic. It made her feel sick. At the main doors to the station she turned; she couldn't help it. Holly was still there, staring after her, a terrible mixture of pain and understanding on her face, and Jill saw then how beautiful she was, how strange and young and startling. She turned away, shook the Detective Sergeant's hand and walked down the steps to the car. If she had been able to cry, she would have done so then. She would have wept for fourteen years of innocent happiness that had been shattered in twenty-four hours and the fleeting glance of another woman.

Chapter Six

Holly took a taxi home from Chelsea Police Station. Exhausted, she stared blankly out of the cab window at the lighted shop fronts along the King's Road and the steady flow of late-night shoppers.

At Bishop's Road, she alighted and paid the driver, hardly aware of the fare, telling him to keep the change even though she'd given him a twenty-pound note. She stood for a moment on the steps of her building, shivering in the chill wind, and looked up at the dark, empty rooms of her flat on the second floor.

Kit stood up when he heard the door. He had been sitting on the stairs outside Holly's apartment for over two hours and had even read the flat share column in the *Evening Standard*. He was bored, tired, cold and anxious. He had been to the police station at lunchtime and been told that Miss Grigson was out with an officer. That was nearly six hours ago. The ensuing time had been spent loitering in Bishop's Road until he spotted a neighbour he recognised and persuaded her to let him in to the house. This achieved, he waited in the hallway, huddled by the ancient radiator, which gave off an hour of feeble warmth, then died. As a last resort, he read the fire regulations until a kind-hearted tenant coming in from work had given him his copy of the *Standard*, which he'd devoured, from cover to cover. Of course he should have gone home and waited for Holly to call, or even gone back to the office. But she might not have rung him and he couldn't take that chance.

Hearing footsteps, he looked over the banister at the ground floor and saw Holly's figure as she slowly climbed the stairs. He could see from the way she moved that she was tired, that something had happened, and he felt suddenly awkward, doubting if he should be there. He dug his hands in his pockets and waited for her.

As she came round the corner, she looked up and started. 'Jesus! Kit!' She put her hand up to her chest. 'God, you scared me.'

'Sorry, Holly, I should have thought . . .' He came down the top three steps towards her. 'I should have called out or something.'

'Yes, you bloody well should have!' The shock at seeing him standing there caused a spurt of irrational anger. He really had given her a fright and her pulse was hammering in her throat. 'What on earth are you doing here anyway?'

Kit hesitated. His automatic reaction would have been to snap back but he could see she was in a state. He took a breath, then said, 'I came to see if you needed help.'

'Help?' Holly snorted, pushing past him to her front door. 'Ha bloody ha!' She'd needed help twelve hours ago and he'd been too damn busy to give it! She turned, feeling all the anger, shock and humiliation of the day well up inside her. 'I don't need your help. I don't need anything from you, in fact. So, if there isn't anything else?' She glared at him.

Kit's patience snapped. 'Yes, there bloody well is!' he snarled, scowling back at her. 'I cancelled my meetings as soon as you rang me, I've waited here all afternoon in the freezing cold to make sure you're all right, and the least you can do is tell me what the hell has happened!' His voice rose indignantly. 'You needed my help this morning, remember?'

'That was this morning!' she shouted. 'A lot can happen in twelve hours!'

'Oh yeah? Like what? Tell me what's happened!' he shouted back.

'No!' Holly cried. 'And don't yell at me! How dare you come here and hang around my flat for hours thinking you have some kind of right to my life! How dare you demand to know what's happened! It doesn't involve you, it's none of your bloody business!'

'No? OK, fine!' Kit turned to go. 'I'll leave you to it then, to your lonely, miserable independence. Just don't call me next time you think you might need something. Save me the wasted time and energy, all right?'

'All right!' Holly yelled back. She fumbled with the key in the lock and swore as the door jammed. She shoved, unable to budge it, and cursed again, her voice cracking. She hung her head, suddenly incapable of doing anything, blinded by tears. Kit looked back at her and his stomach lurched. Why the hell did she have such a capacity for churning him up?

'Christ, you're a bloody difficult woman!' he snapped. He walked up the few stairs between them and took the keys out of her hand. Dealing swiftly with the locks, he swung open the front door and Holly stumbled inside.

He hovered on the landing. 'Holly?'

She had her back to him, rifling frantically in the hall table drawer for some tissues.

'Holly, look . . .'

'Go away,' she croaked. Unable to find any tissues, she wiped her face on her sleeve. She couldn't stop weeping now she'd started.

'Holly, please.' Kit moved towards her but she edged away. 'Holly, tell me!' He put his hand on her shoulder and left it there. 'Please,' he whispered.

She turned round. 'What a mess,' she mumbled. She looked at him, her face red and blotchy, her nose swollen, her eyes streaming, and he felt such desire, such love, that it took his breath away. 'What a bloody awful mess,' she whispered. 'I'm sorry, I shouldn't have shouted at you, you were only trying to help. I really am sorry . . .'

He moved forward and put his arms around her, and she burst into noisy sobs soaking the shoulder of his cashmere overcoat and making him hard at the feel of her body, even through their six or seven layers of clothing.

Twenty minutes later, nursing a brandy, Holly sat on the floor of her sitting room, leaning against the sofa with a blanket tucked round her and her knees pulled up to her chin. She watched Kit as he struggled with the gas fire, as inept as he'd always been with anything remotely practical. He lit three matches, burnt his fingers twice and finally, after five fraught minutes, managed it. He sat back and said, 'These bloody gas fires are impossible!'

Holly smiled. He always blamed the appliance.

'Are you sure it's safe? It looks a bit dodgy to me.'

'It's quite safe, Kit,' she said.

He nodded and sat back opposite her, eyeing the fire warily. Holly felt relieved that he was here; it made her feel normal. She looked across at him as he turned away from the fire and they stared at each other for a few moments, both aware of the familiarity of the situation. Kit said, 'D'you want to tell me about it, Holly?'

'About the bloody awful mess?'

'Yes.'

She looked away, at the fire, at his shoes across the room, his jacket on the sofa, at her hands around the glass. 'Sandy was already married,' she said. 'He was a bigamist.'

Kit drew in his breath. He said nothing.

'He was married to another woman, before he met me. He had an investment business in the City, a house in West Sussex, in a village called Eastham . . .' She stopped, on the brink of tears again, and cleared her throat. 'I looked it up, when the policeman was out of the room, it was on the form faxed from Brighton.' Still watching her hands, she continued, 'His clothes were found on the beach there, two days ago. He apparently committed suicide.' Her hand jerked uncontrollably and the dark amber liquid slopped over the side of the tumbler. 'Oh damn!' She put her fingers up to her mouth and sucked the spilt brandy off them, then took a large gulp from the glass. She was silent for a while and Kit dared not look at her. He could feel her tension, hear the shock and confusion in her voice.

'None of this would have come out,' she went on, 'if it hadn't been for the suicide. He could have gone on living with me, and her, for as long as he liked, and no-one would ever have known, except him.' She took another gulp of brandy and waited for the warmth to hit her stomach. 'Legally I'm not married.' She smiled ironically at Kit. 'Lucky I didn't change my name, isn't it?'

Suddenly she put her head down on her knees and squeezed her eyes shut. The tears slid out from under the lids and trickled down her cheek. Kit moved forward and gently wiped them away with the tip of his finger. Holly looked at him. 'I'm not crying for me,' she said. 'Or for him. I'm crying because . . .' Her voice broke as she tried to hold in a sob. 'I'm crying because I'm so relieved and because that poor woman in Brighton who probably really loved her husband, who has a child, a whole life with him, not just eighteen months, had to find out all this and . . .' Kit handed Holly his freshly laundered handkerchief. 'And because it's all been such an awful waste of time.' She blew her nose and took a deep breath. She was silent for a while, twisting the hanky round and round her fingertips. Finally she lifted her head and looked away from Kit to the fire. 'You're shocked, aren't you?'

'Shocked?'

'That my husband . . .' She stopped to correct herself. 'That my so-called "husband" has committed suicide and that I feel relieved.'

Kit shrugged. He was stunned by the whole thing but he couldn't say so. He didn't want to risk Holly shutting him out.

'I never loved him, you see,' she murmured. 'I hardly knew him.

70

It wasn't a marriage, it was a business partnership.' She shook her head. 'I thought the success of the gallery was so important, I thought it was everything, and I kept fooling myself that I was happy . . .' She broke off and looked at Kit. 'I knew in my heart there was something wrong, though. It was as if he didn't really belong here, you know? In the flat or in my life. He was so often away . . .' She swallowed down more brandy, but she didn't say what she was thinking – what they were both thinking – that he would surely have been with his wife. 'I told myself I was happy,' she said, 'even thought I was up to a point, but then this afternoon, after the shock and humiliation had passed, all I felt was relief – that I didn't have to go on with it any more, that it was all over.' She drained her glass. 'God, how awful! I feel ashamed of myself.'

Kit picked her tumbler off the floor and walked across to the table to refill it, feeling the need to do something, to ease the impact of what she'd just said. He poured a measure into the glass, drank it himself, then poured another and took it back to Holly.

'Do you think there's something wrong with me?' she asked, taking the glass. 'Should I really feel this numb?'

He nodded. He was relieved she felt numb; it would insulate her for a while against the awfulness of what had happened.

'I suddenly feel very tired,' she murmured, 'and more than a little drunk.' She held the glass out to him. 'You have this, you look as if you need it more than I do.'

Kit couldn't help smiling. She had always been able to pick up on every nuance of his emotions. He took the tumbler and drank the brandy down in one.

'What a mess,' Holly said.

'Yes.' He placed the glass carefully down on the floor. 'What a mess.'

She leant her head back against the sofa and closed her eyes. The movement was slow and erotic and Kit saw an image of the same movement flash into his mind – a memory of Holly naked beneath him – and he jolted at the force of it. He uncrossed his legs and stood. Holly opened her eyes.

'I should go,' he said. 'Let you get to bed, get some rest.' She moved her head to the right and stared at him. Then she held out her hand. He took it, meaning to hold it for a moment, to squeeze it, show her he cared, but it didn't go at all like that.

'Don't go,' Holly whispered. 'Please.'

He squatted down in front of her and brushed her hair off her face with his other hand. 'I think I should.' But she caught his wrist and held both of his hands. 'No, don't.'

He looked at her face. 'Holly, I . . .'

She reached up and kissed him. Her eyes were closed and he watched her expression of complete abandonment. He wanted to leave, to do the right thing, but he couldn't move. He remembered the expression. She released his hands and he moved them to her hair. He tangled his fingers in it and held her face close to his own, gently kissing her open mouth, tracing the curve of it with his tongue. She moaned and slipped her fingers inside his shirt, her nails trailing the skin on his neck, making him shiver. He dropped onto his knees, let go of her hair and pulled her body up to him, kissing her deeply now, pressing her hips into his groin so she could feel his erection. She moaned again, and he fumbled with her shirt, eager to touch her skin, to run his hands along her spine and around to her breasts. He was so desperate for her his mind spun. She threw her head back and he bit the hollow of her neck, moving his mouth down, roughly pulling her shirt up over her chest, sucking her nipple, hearing her cry out.

The telephone rang.

For a moment they froze. They were so still that Kit could feel the pulse in Holly's neck, hear his own heart pounding. They listened in silence, sure it was about to stop, but it rang on. Seconds later, Kit moved.

'Leave it,' Holly whispered but she had opened her eyes and the room seemed to be filled with the piercing bleep. Kit sat back. Suddenly unable to look at her, he dropped his gaze as she stood and straightened her shirt. She waited half a minute longer, then walked out of the sitting room. In the hallway he heard her pick up the receiver and answer the call. He stood, slipped on his shoes and reached for his jacket, then dug his hands in his pockets and waited. A short time later, Holly came back into the room.

'That was very odd,' she said. She took in the fact that Kit had prepared to leave but made no comment.

'What was?'

'That call. It was a friend of Sandy's. The first to ever call here.'

'Really? What did they want?'

'To have dinner, a drink.' She shrugged and bent to pick up the brandy glass. Taking it to the table, she poured another measure and drank some. 'I've never heard of him before, Sandy never mentioned him. He lives in New York, but he's in London for a while on business. I told him it was impossible.'

'So?' Kit could see the call had upset her. He sat on the arm of the sofa. 'What was odd about it?'

'He asked me if everything was all right. It was weird, as if he knew something.' She hugged her arms round her self and took another sip of brandy. She was suddenly cold and very tired.

Kit shrugged. 'It's probably nothing, Holly. He may have just picked up on your voice.'

'Yes, I suppose so. But he also asked if the gallery was going well, so he must know all about me, even if I didn't know anything about him. Don't you think that's odd?'

Kit put his hands on her shoulders. 'No, I don't. Sandy probably, talked to him about you.' She flinched at the name. 'Look,' he said, bending to kiss her cheek. 'Stop worrying and try to get some sleep, all right?'

She nodded.

'Don't see me out. Go to bed.' He smiled and moved away

towards the door. Neither of them acknowledged what had just happened between them. The phone call was probably a blessing in disguise, Kit thought, as he went out of the flat, closing the door behind him. I should have been more careful.

I should never have let it happen, Holly told herself, as she watched him leave from the window, a tall, solitary figure disappearing down Bishop's Road in the shadow of the street lamps. It won't happen again, they each thought, separately, but at the same time. Kit dug his hands in his pockets and crossed the road towards the tube; Holly turned away and switched off the lamp.

She lay down on her bed, fully dressed. It wouldn't happen again. She wouldn't let it. There was no future in it, none at all.

Chapter Seven

Jill retrieved Harry's dirty pyjamas from the floor of his bedroom, dumped them in the laundry basket and took a clean pair out of the drawer. She laid these in his case on top of his other clothes and rifled through the neat piles to check she had packed everything he might need. That done, she closed the case, fastened it and went to the top of the stairs.

'Harry! Will you come and sort out what toys you want to take with you to Granny's!' She waited for him to appear in the doorway of the kitchen and her heart ached at the sight of him. He looked so small and forlorn that she hated Alex for a moment, hated him with a force that took her breath away.

'I don't want to take anything,' Harry said. He stared down at the ground and waited for her to argue with him, but Jill didn't have the strength.

'I'm sure you'll find things to do there,' she mumbled, turning away. She went back to his room and picked up his case from the bed. 'Have you finished breakfast?' she asked as she carried it down the stairs. Harry nodded and Jill dropped the case down the last few steps. 'Good!' she said with false brightness. She stood for a few moments to get her breath back. She had never had to lug cases around before; she had never had to do anything on her own.

Harry went back into the kitchen and took his cup and plate over to the sink. He ran the hot tap and rinsed them, something he had previously always left for his mother, then he picked his coat up off the chair, and said, 'You look nice this morning, Mummy.'

Jill turned from the front door and smiled. 'Thank you!' Her voice cracked with tears and she coughed to cover it up. In twenty-four hours her son had taken on the responsibilities of his father without even knowing it. She looked away and wiped her eyes with her handkerchief, careful not to smudge her mascara. She had taken great trouble over her make-up this morning, slowly and painstakingly creating a mask, without which she would never have been able to brave the day.

Taking a deep breath, she went outside to open the car boot and Harry emerged a few minutes after her with his case. He struggled to where she was standing and dropped it, narrowly missing her toe.

'Crikey, Mum! What on earth have you got in here? It weighs a ton!'

Suddenly Jill smiled and bent to hug him.

'What's that for?' he demanded.

She stood back and shrugged. 'You're not too old for a hug, are you?'

Harry kicked a stone by his foot. 'As long as it's not at school,' he mumbled.

Jill lifted his case into the boot. 'Get in,' she said. 'Let's get going.'

By taking Harry to her mother-in-law's, Jill hoped to protect him from finding out the truth about his father. She didn't want him to know, not yet, maybe not ever.

Harry climbed in the front next to his mother and reached for his seat belt.

'Have you said goodbye to Sophie?' Jill asked.

'Sort of. She's in a rotten mood. She hardly said anything when I went into her room, she just stared out of the window.' He picked up his rucksack and unzipped it, looking for his Game Boy. 'Why isn't she coming to Granny's?'

'I expect she has some school work to do,' Jill said.

But Sophie had no school work to do; Jill knew that. She had simply refused point-blank to go to her grandmother's, declaring that she wouldn't leave the house in case news came in of Alex. Jill glanced up at the window seat on the second floor. Sophie was there, staring out at them, her pinched, white face set in a grim expression of pain. Jill thought about waving, then changed her mind. It was the expression that incensed her – as if no-one else had a right to any pain or grief except Sophie, as if she had the monopoly on suffering!

Jill revved the engine and reversed, the tyres spinning on the gravel drive, then roared off without a backward glance at her stepdaughter.

Sophie watched the Range Rover from the second-floor window until it had disappeared down Little Hill and round the corner. She had wanted them to see her, wanted Jill to wave so that she could ignore the gesture, but Jill hadn't. Irritated, she slumped down onto the cushions and closed her eyes. She felt desolate and alone. She had longed to go to her grandmother's, to escape to a loving and warm environment, but she had stayed to spite Jill. She was driven by cussedness and a desire to hurt her stepmother, to make her register some of the pain she was feeling herself. She knew her father wasn't coming back but she couldn't admit it: admitting it was giving in to Jill, and for as long as she could remember she had been completely unable to do that.

Opening her eyes, Sophie stood and ran a hand through her hair. It was dirty but she couldn't be bothered to wash it. In fact it was a statement: she was taking a stand against Jill and the way she perpetually fussed over how she looked. Even now, in the midst of her so-called grief, Jill still managed to make up her face and dress to impress. Sophie simply couldn't understand it. She looked as she felt, seeing no reason to pretend. She went downstairs to the kitchen, passing the mirror in the hall and glancing at herself as she did so. In her ankle-length Indian print skirt, clumpy boots and long, ripped sweater she looked a mess, but she didn't care; at that moment she didn't care much about anything at all. She stood for a few minutes and stared at her reflection. Her face was so like her father's that it hurt. Suddenly she whirled round, grabbed her coat off the banister, took the front door keys from the drawer and slammed out of the house, the small panes of glass in the side window rattling as she went.

Holly drove through the small village of Eastham as slowly as she dared. She was lost and needed to get some directions, but was anxious not to attract attention. Spotting the post office, she stopped and hurried in to ask her way. An officious woman with a dog seemed keen to help, and came out with her to point out the route. Holly thanked her and climbed back into the car.

It was still early – only nine thirty – but she was running late. She had wanted to be there just after breakfast, in order to make sure that someone was in. She switched the engine back on and set off. Her hands were shaking as she tried to yank the wheel of her old VW round, and she had to stop and take a deep breath to calm herself. She was almost there now but was still undecided about what to say or how to handle it. All she knew was that she had to make contact.

Completing her three-point turn, she waved at the woman with the dog and drove on.

She hoped to God she wasn't making a grave mistake. She had acted on impulse in deciding to come. That morning she had woken after a troubled, disturbed night, and it had simply seemed the obvious thing to do. It wasn't macabre curiosity; it was a basic need to know more about the man she had lived with, who had deceived her so terribly. No-one knew she had come, no-one had asked her to justify her decision or think it through and, as she saw the gates to South Ridge Farm up ahead, her stomach churned. Perhaps she should have given it more thought.

She swung the car through the open gates and drove slowly up towards the house. It was beautiful, a family home, ageing and mellowed but cared for and well maintained. She stopped the car and sat staring up at it, her hands in her lap.

'Oh God,' she murmured. A feeling of utter misery washed over her and she realised that she should never have come. She should have left Sandy's other life where it was, where it belonged, a million miles from her own. Reaching forward, she quickly switched on the engine again and shifted the car into reverse. She began to turn the wheel but stopped suddenly at the sight of a young girl walking towards her. The girl gestured at her to wind down her window and, cutting the engine, Holly warily complied.

'Can I help you?' The girl was edgy, shifting from one foot to the other and staring at a point somewhere just above Holly's head. She was no more than sixteen or seventeen, but the resemblance to Sandy was staggering – the same tall, willowy shape, the same green eyes and wavy, light brown hair. Holly could do nothing but stare. The fact that Sandy had a daughter had thrown her completely off balance.

'Are you looking for someone?' the girl persisted.

Holly started. 'Yes, I . . .' She stopped, confused about what to say. 'I'm sorry, I was looking for Mrs Turner,' she finished truthfully.

'She's out,' the girl said aggressively. 'Sorry.'

Holly shrugged. 'It doesn't matter, I shouldn't have come any . . .' She broke off and looked down at her hands. She felt stupid; this had been a big mistake. Tears of self-pity stung her eyes. Reaching forward, she restarted the car, and began to move off slowly. 'Thanks anyway,' she croaked. 'Goodbye.'

'Wait!' The girl waved her arm in the air. 'Hang on a minute!'

She hurried after the car and Holly stopped again, yanking on the handbrake.

'Why shouldn't you have come?' the girl asked.

Holly sniffed and wiped her face on the back of her hand. 'I just shouldn't have,' she said. 'It doesn't matter.'

The girl watched her silently for a short while, hands on her hips, dark green eyes suspicious, then she glanced back at the house and said, 'D'you want to come in and wait? Jill won't be that long. She's gone to my grandmother's in Henfield, to drop my brother off.' She didn't issue the invitation out of kindness; her curiosity had got the better of her. The woman in the car had to be crying for a reason.

Holly shook her head. 'No, thanks, I've got to get going.'

The girl continued to watch her. Then, without warning, she said, 'Why are you crying? And what are you doing here? Is it connected to my father?'

Holly couldn't look up. She stared down at her fingers, knotted together in her lap, and felt the intense scrutiny of Sandy's daughter. Finally she glanced up. 'I'm crying for all sorts of reasons,' she said quietly. 'I'm sorry, but I can't even begin to explain them and . . .' she broke off, took a breath and finished, '. . . and no, it's not connected to your father.' Biting the inside of her lip, she said, 'Why should it be?'

'No reason,' the girl answered sulkily. She felt guilty; she shouldn't have interfered. 'Sorry,' she added half-heartedly.

Holly shrugged and glanced away.

'Look, I really shouldn't have pried,' the girl said. 'It was rude. Are you sure you won't come in for a cup of tea? You look as if you could do with one.'

Holly hesitated for a moment before replying and the girl added, 'To be honest, I could do with the company.'

There was no refusing now. So Holly nodded, switched off the engine and climbed out of the car. She smiled nervously and the girl smiled back. They walked together towards the house.

'D'you want tea or coffee?' The girl had taken her jacket off and hung it over the banister but she left her boots on, thick with mud.

'Er, tea, please.' Holly stood and stared at the trail of grubby footprints on the thick cream carpets as the girl walked on into the kitchen. The girl turned and caught Holly's eye. There was no remorse in her expression, more a grim satisfaction at the mess. Holly followed her into the kitchen.

'I'm Sophie by the way,' the girl said, filling the kettle.

'I'm Holly, Holly Grigson.'

'D'you live round here, Holly?'

Holly stood awkwardly by the door, unsure of what to do with herself, and how much information to give away. 'I live in London,' she said. 'I run an art gallery.'

'Really?' Sophie turned. 'I want be a painter, I've applied to Brighton Art School.'

Her face was suddenly animated and Holly could see for the first time how pretty she was. For some reason it made her immeasurably sad. She looked down at the floor. What sort of man had Sandy been, that he could risk losing all of this? Glancing up again, she said, 'Well, good luck. Is that for your degree?'

'No, my foundation course. I'm doing my A levels at the moment.'

'I see.' Holly wanted to ask her age, to get things perfectly straight in her head – all the details, all the facts.

'I'm a year younger than everyone else in my form and Dad said . . .' Sophie stopped abruptly and turned to take two mugs out of the cupboard, then hunted for the tea and sugar bowl. Placing everything on a tray, she walked across to the fridge for the milk and Holly caught sight of her face. It was ashen and she was biting her lip so hard that the colour had drained from it. She took the milk back to the sideboard, poured it into a jug and made a pot of tea. All this time she said nothing, and Holly felt for her.

Carrying the tea to the table, Sophie pulled a chair out for her guest and said, 'My father wanted me to take a year off before my foundation course but I think I should go in September, if they accept me.' Her voice was unsteady and, without thinking, Holly gently touched her arm. Sophie looked down at the hand and stood completely still for a moment. Then she smiled. It was the first gesture of sympathy and comfort that she had been offered, and she never thought to question how Holly might have known. 'Dad said there was no hurry,' she went on quietly. 'To be honest, he didn't really want me to go, he didn't understand much about art, but I love it and I don't see any point in waiting around.' She poured the tea. 'Do you?'

'No, not really.' Holly helped herself to her three sugars, stirred her tea and caught Sophie staring at her. Jill didn't take sugar and she had nagged Alex, Harry and Sophie about their one lump each for as long as Sophie could remember.

'D'you want a chocolate biscuit?' Sophie suddenly asked. She liked this woman, felt comfortable with her.

'I'd love one!' Holly said. 'Tell me where they are and I'll get them.' A brief look of surprise registered on Sophie's face, then she grinned. Jill disapproved of chocolate almost as much as she did sugar, so the seal on the friendship had been set. Sophie liked Holly Grigson. She was an unexpected bright light in what had been a very dark and miserable forty-eight hours.

Jill swung the Range Rover into the drive of South Ridge Farm and braked urgently, narrowly missing the car parked halfway down. It looked as if someone had simply abandoned it, and she sat feeling shocked at the near collision and fuming at the irresponsibility of the car's owner for several moments before reversing and parking on the main road. She climbed out, grabbed her bag off the front seat and stormed up to the house. It was one of Sophie's awful friends from college, it had to be. The bloody fool had damn near caused an accident. Opening the front door, Jill left the keys in the lock and slammed it shut behind her. 'Sophie? Where the hell are you?' She stomped into the kitchen.

'Oh!' For a moment Jill froze and stared at her stepdaughter and the woman with her. She recognised Holly instantly. Feeling for the wall, she gripped it, her head suddenly dizzy, and took a deep breath. She was silent and Holly felt herself suffocating in the deathly hush. Then Jill looked up.

'I think you had better leave,' she said icily.

Holly nodded wordlessly and stood up.

'What do you mean, she has to leave?' Sophie looked nervously from her stepmother to Holly. She felt suddenly caught in the middle of something terrible and began to panic. 'What d'you mean, Jill?' Her voice rose. 'What's going on?'

'I'm sorry,' Holly mumbled. 'I'm really sorry, I . . .' She moved towards the door, unable to look at Sophie.

'Holly?' Sophie caught her arm. 'Holly, why're you going? What's happened?'

Holly looked over her shoulder. 'Sophie, don't, please.'

'Sophie, go to your room!' Jill suddenly shouted. 'Go on! Go!'

Sophie dropped her hand and her face flushed dark red. Her pain and humiliation at being shouted at in front of her new friend was so great that Holly could feel it herself. She walked past Jill to the door, grabbing her coat.

Sophie hurried after her. 'Holly, I don't understand!' she pleaded, standing in the hallway.

But Holly was unable to speak as she struggled to get the front door open, her heart pounding in her chest.

'Holly? Please, tell me what's . . .'

Finally Holly yanked the lock back and fled out of the house.

'Holly!' Sophie ran out and watched as Holly fumbled her car door open with shaking hands, then clambered inside. The door of the Beetle slammed and Sophie watched the car spurt forward, heard the engine stall and saw Holly put her hands up to her face for a few moments. Then Holly seemed to compose herself, the car started again and the little VW sped out of the drive, disappearing from view. Bitterly confused and ashamed, Sophie turned back inside the house. She walked into the kitchen and went for her stepmother.

'Look what you've done!' she shouted. 'Just look! I'm not allowed any friends now, am I? Christ, if Dad had been here, if he'd seen . . .' Sophie broke off; Jill had her back to her. 'Christ, Jill!' she cried. 'You are such a fucking bitch!'

Jill spun round as the words slapped the air. 'And you, you are a stupid little cow!' she spat back. The sight of that woman in her home, the sight of her with Alex's daughter, had incensed her. She was so angry that she shook. 'You know who she is, do you?' Jill shouted, suddenly unable to stop herself. 'You know who your friend is?'

Sophie's expression changed. She looked momentarily confused and shook her head.

'Well, I'll tell you then!' Jill yelled. 'She's another of your father's wives! His third wife, to be precise. Only this time he didn't bother to get divorced. He just went ahead and made a life in London with her, married her, committed a crime, a crime he would have gone to prison for if he hadn't been such a bloody coward and killed himself!' She moved closer to Sophie. 'You didn't know, did you?' she hissed. 'Miss clever dick didn't know! No, he deceived you, and me, and Harry. All of us! He laughed at us behind our backs, enjoyed the risk, the lies, the . . .' She broke off, her chest heaving. Her face was so close to Sophie's that Sophie could hardly breathe. She backed away, smacking her spine against the edge of the kitchen table.

'Shocked, are you?' Jill sneered. 'Upset?'

Sophie shook her head in disbelief. She edged round the table, away from Jill. She was terrified. 'I don't believe you,' she murmured. 'I don't . . .'

'What the hell do you think I feel, then?' Jill cried. 'How the hell do you think . . .' She suddenly stopped and put her hands up to her face. She stood there for what seemed like ages, struggling to control herself as Sophie stood paralysed with shock and fear. Then, spinning round, Jill ran up the stairs and slammed into her room.

Sophie's legs gave way. She sank to her knees and buried her face. She wasn't crying, she was too stunned and frightened to cry. She had never seen Jill like this before. Suddenly, she heard thumping overhead.

'Jesus!' She jumped up, steadying herself on the kitchen table, and ran to the door. Jill was stumbling down the stairs, her arms full of Alex's clothes – suits, shirts, ties, shoes. Her face was drenched with tears, although she seemed to have no idea she was crying.

'Jill?'

Jill glanced up and lost balance. She slipped on the step and her ankle gave way.

'Jill! For God's sake!' Sophie started up the stairs, but stopped as Jill managed to right herself, grabbing the banister. She let the massive pile of clothes drop and they tumbled to the bottom. Then she turned and ran back up to her room.

Sophie stood helplessly and stared down at her father's things. As she bent to pick up a tie, Jill appeared on the top step with what looked like the rest of his wardrobe.

'Jill, what are you doing?' Sophie cried.

But Jill didn't seem to hear her. She struggled down with her burden and shoved past Sophie into the kitchen. Sophie heard the back door open and ran to the window. Jill was out in the garden, half running, half stumbling down towards the bonfire site at the bottom. Sophie ran out after her.

'Jill, what are you doing?' she yelled, grabbing Jill's arm in an attempt to hold her back, but Jill violently pulled herself free.

'Get away from me!' she screamed. 'Let me go!'

Sophie fell back. 'Jill, please stop it!' she shouted.

She watched Jill dump the clothes in the burner and turn. Her face had collapsed and she was crying openly, the mascara running in a thick black channel down her cheeks. There was absolutely nothing Sophie could do. She wrapped her arms around her body and stood motionless in the freezing December wind as Jill ran back to the house and brought the rest of Alex's things out. Three times she did it, labouring with the mound of clothes from the floor in the hall, the albums of family photographs, her wedding album, Alex's letters to her, his postcards. And all the time she did it she wept, not even conscious of that fact.

Finally she dropped everything in the burner, a massive pile representing their life together, and ran to the garage for the petrol. Sophie watched her soak the pile in fuel, then she turned away, unable to witness any more. Slowly she walked back to the house. The last thing she heard before she closed the kitchen door was the whoosh of fire as the whole mound caught light, and the last thing she smelt was the terrible stench of burning.

Much later, as the daylight disappeared and the darkening sky was lit by the glow of the still smouldering fire, Sophie moved stiffly away from the window where she had sat all afternoon and went to fetch a blanket from the bedroom. She made a mug of tea, poured a good measure of whisky into it, then put her coat on and took it outside.

Crossing the cold damp grass, she saw Jill, huddled in the far corner of the garden, her body hunched up like an old woman's. She crossed to her stepmother and squatted down beside her.

'Here,' she said, 'drink this.'

Jill looked up. She stared at Sophie for a moment as if she'd never seen her before, then she took the mug. As she wrapped her hands around it, Sophie placed the blanket over her shoulders.

'I'm sorry,' Jill whispered.

Sophie shrugged in the darkness and they both sat in silence, staring at the fire for some time.

Finally Sophie stood. She held her hand out for Jill and was relieved when Jill took it. They stood together.

'He didn't do it,' Sophie said quietly.

Jill didn't even look at her.

'I know he didn't marry Holly and I don't think it was him on the beach.' Sophie took a deep breath, encouraged by Jill's silence. 'I am sure that Holly's husband wasn't Dad,' she said. Jill turned to her and for the first time Sophie saw how ravaged she was by shock and grief. 'He loved us too much,' she murmured, 'all of us.' And squeezing the hand that she still held, Sophie led her stepmother back inside the house.

Chapter Eight

Holly stood on the seafront at Brighton and shivered in the chill wind. She had been there for a couple of hours. Pulling her coat in tight and lifting her shawl up over her head, she tied it under her chin and finally climbed down the steps onto the shingle beach. She wanted to be where Sandy had stood, where he had made that last decision to leave behind him a chaos of pain and deceit.

The sea was grey and forbidding, and the sky was leaden with dark clouds. Looking out, Holly felt a cold finger run the length of her spine and huddled further into her coat in an effort to get warm. She walked down to the water's edge, smelt the cold sea, the damp wind, and felt the spray of freezing water on her face. Then she turned away and trudged back to the steps. Climbing up to street level, she sat down once again on the cold iron bench she had been sitting on all afternoon and closed her eyes.

Holly felt something wasn't right. As she sat between the roar of traffic from the main road and the crashing of the sea, she just felt in her heart that something wasn't right. Things didn't fit. Ignoring the cold and the noise as best she could, she tried to think back over the events of the morning. Snippets of dialogue floated in and out of her head; an image of Sophie formed momentarily in her mind, to be replaced by the memory of Jill, angry and distraught in the doorway.

She let out a deep breath. 'I shouldn't have gone,' she muttered to herself. 'It was bloody foolish!' It had stirred up all sorts of emotions, made her feel miserably ashamed and given rise to this peculiar sense of unease. For reasons that she hadn't quite worked out yet, Holly had an eerie instinct that the whole situation was very wrong. She opened her eyes and stood up. Turning away from the sea, she dug her hands in her pockets and walked off.

It could all, of course, be her imagination, she considered, heading back towards her car. She wasn't thinking straight at the moment. She'd made too many mistakes in the past twenty-four hours – she shouldn't have come to Sussex and she shouldn't have let Kit . . . Suddenly she stopped dead in the middle of the pavement. Kit: just the thought of him threw her. 'Damn him!' Holly snapped out loud. She began to walk again, increasing her pace, her heels clicking smartly on the stone as she went.

It was her imagination, she decided, in an attempt to put Kit firmly from her mind. She was seeing things that weren't there, dreaming them up; maybe because she wanted to. The situation with Kit last night was a classic example – falling for the same old routine, almost making one hell of a fool of herself. She would have to tell him it didn't mean anything, she decided on reaching the car. She would ring him that evening and explain that she'd behaved as she had because she was confused, in a mess.

Unlocking the VW, Holly waited for a gap in the traffic before opening the door and climbing inside. It was freezing in the car so she started the engine, turned the heater on full blast and sat for several minutes with her coat, gloves and shawl on, waiting for it to warm up. That was it, she resolved. She would put this whole thing out of her mind, forget it, forget Kit. She took off her outer layers, ready for the drive back to London. It wouldn't do any good, this intuition that something didn't add up. Where would it get her, except in more of a mess than she already was? She clicked in her seat belt and shifted into gear. She must try and put it all behind her, she thought miserably.

Glancing over her shoulder, she pulled out into the stream of cars and started the long journey back home.

Sophie sat back on her heels, blew the taper out and watched the small glow of red in the bottom of the grate. It caught quickly, the kindling smoking for a few seconds before breaking into flame. She held a piece of newspaper up over the fireplace and waited. A couple of minutes later, she removed it. The fire had taken.

'Well done,' Jill said. She sat across the room on the floor, her knees tucked up under her, the blanket wrapped around her body. She had stopped shivering but couldn't seem to get warm; her hands were like ice. 'I didn't know you could make a fire.'

Sophie kept her eyes on the grate. 'Dad taught me,' she answered. 'He said I should learn because you had no idea and were always worried about chipping your nail . . .' She stopped and swallowed. She hadn't meant to sound rude; it was just the truth and her father had meant it without malice or criticism. There was a tense silence and Sophie waited for Jill's irritation. Warily she glanced over her shoulder.

Jill looked up and smiled sadly. 'He was right,' she said. 'I hate making fires, I'm useless at it.'

Sophie smiled back. 'Come and sit here, it'll really get going in a few minutes.' She stood and wiped her hands on her skirt. Her jumper was covered in coal dust and she brushed at it without any success. 'I think I'll go and ring Harry,' she said. 'Check he's all right.'

Jill attempted to stand up but her legs were too weak. 'I should ring,' she said quickly. 'He'll wonder what's happened to me . . .' Her voice broke. She really didn't have the strength to keep up the façade any longer and she put her hand up to her face to cover her tears. Sophie stood awkwardly across the room.

'I'll tell him you're down at Circle C because we ran out of milk,' she offered.

Jill nodded, fumbling in her pocket for her tissues. 'He'll think . . .'

'He won't think anything,' Sophie interrupted. 'D'you want a drink?'

Jill shook her head. 'No thanks.'

Sophie shrugged and started for the door.

'Sophie!' Jill suddenly called after her.

Sophie stopped and turned round.

'Why?' Jill asked quietly.

Sophie looked down at the ground. There was a silence, which seemed to last forever, then she glanced up again. 'You never needed me before. I was surplus to requirements.' And with that she walked on across the hall and into the study to telephone her half-brother.

Jill moved across the room and sat down in front of the fire. The effort of that alone exhausted her. For the past forty-eight hours she had kept going in a state of shock, eating nothing, lying awake at night, steeling herself against the pain and humiliation of it all. Now, in the aftermath of her collapse, she was drained of all energy and strength. She had burnt herself out.

Resting her head back against the armchair, Jill thought about what Sophie had said. She was right, of course. Jill had never needed her, had never even wanted her really. Jill's life had revolved around Alex and Harry, with herself as the central pivotal point. Sophie had been tacked on the end, her father's afterthought, the result of unfortunate circumstances.

'Harry's fine,' Sophie said, coming back into the room. 'He sends his love.'

Jill lifted her head and smiled. 'Thank you,' she murmured. Sophie shrugged in the odd, slightly aggressive way she had and Jill suddenly realised that she had been misinterpreting the action all these years. She sat up as Sophie perched on the edge of the sofa opposite her and wondered sadly if either of them would ever be able to cross the barrier of misunderstanding that had existed for so long. She looked at her stepdaughter and saw the tense, closed face, an expression that looked like contempt but which she now knew covered insecurity. She waited for Sophie to speak. There was something Sophie wanted to say, this much Jill understood; this far she felt they had come in the past few hours.

Sophie fiddled with the fabric of her skirt, pleating it between her fingers, wondering how or where to begin. She dropped the patch she had neatly folded and began on another. At last she spoke. 'I meant what I said in the garden, about Holly and Dad.' She swallowed, waiting for Jill to interrupt. When no retort came after a minute or so, she went on. 'It's only a feeling I've got, but I just think that maybe you should meet Holly, talk to her . . .' Her voice trailed away as she lost confidence. Jill was still silent. Sophie struggled on. 'She didn't fit, Jill; she just didn't make any sense! I loved my father, I knew him and watched him and I tried to be like him. I just can't see it, not with someone like Holly; she's all wrong, she's . . .' Sophie broke off and swallowed hard. She saw the pain register on Jill's face and stared down at her hands. 'If you rang her maybe, spoke to her,' she murmured, 'then you might understand . . .'

Jill sat huddled in the blanket and watched her stepdaughter. She was at once both touched and incensed by what Sophie had just suggested, but she tried to keep calm. 'Why is she all wrong?' she asked. 'What doesn't fit?'

Sophie took a breath. 'Well, she was really sparky and kind of assertive, in a way that Dad would never have really got on with. Her clothes were beautiful, all dark and rich, and she smelt exotic, woody and eastern, and her nails, she bit her nails because she had given up smoking a year ago and needed something to do with her hands, she said.' Sophie's face was flushed and when she stopped speaking she was slightly out of breath.

Jill waited for more but Sophie seemed to have lost her nerve.

There was another strained silence then Jill said, 'What about the police, the form, Holly Grigson's statement? It all fits so neatly now it's out. Your father was away so much, Sophie – weekends, weeks at a time, in Jersey or Gibraltar or God knows where. He told us, it was for business, but it seems more than likely now that he was with this Holly woman. And what about all the evidence that she was married to Alexander Turner? To the same Alexander Turner that I was married to – your father?'

Sophie shrugged. She couldn't explain all that, she only knew what she felt. Defeated, she began to stand up.

'No, wait,' Jill said, 'I'm not dismissing what you said.'

'You're not?'

'No.' She desperately wanted to give Sophie a chance, but she wasn't at all sure of the logic of what her stepdaughter had suggested. If Alex had wanted someone else, wouldn't he have chosen someone completely different to her? Wouldn't that have been the real thrill of living two lives, that they were both totally different, alien to one another?

'Why are you so convinced that Daddy wouldn't have wanted someone very different to me?' she asked. Sophie looked so aghast at the question that Jill almost smiled.

'Because it just wasn't like him!' she exploded. 'He was so set in his ways, so positive about what he liked and didn't like. He hated smoking; he hated the smell of musk and sandalwood – don't you remember? He always said they were so strong, so overpowering.' Sophie stood up and walked across to the window, unable to sit still any longer. She looked out at the smouldering bonfire for a few moments, the pile of her father's things, then she went on. 'Dad loved pale colours, blond colours, your colours, he hated my "arty ethnic phase", as he called it, and he knew nothing about art.'

'Art?'

'Yes! Holly runs an art gallery, in London. She wouldn't have married anyone who didn't understand her business. Well, that was the feeling I got from her, anyway.'

Jill sighed heavily and shook her head. 'You seem to be going on an awful lot of feelings, Sophie.'

'You think I'm being stupid, don't you?'

'No!' Jill protested. 'I just . . .' In truth she didn't know what she thought. Sophie's faith was so frighteningly strong that Jill felt herself bending under the force of it, even against her better reason. She had seen the forms, spoken to the police, she had witnessed the evidence, and yet she could hear what Sophie was saying and some of it made sense, she had to admit. She rubbed her hands wearily over her face. 'What do you think I should do, then?'

Sophie clenched her fists by her side in triumph. 'You could ring,' she suggested quickly. 'Tonight, before you lose your nerve. I wrote the name of her street down; you could ring directory enquiries.'

Jill shook her head. 'You had it all planned, huh?'

'No! I . . .' Sophie broke off when she saw Jill's smile. Blushing, she smiled back. 'I want to help,' she mumbled.

Jill nodded. Getting to her feet, she winced at the painful stiffness in her legs and held onto the edge of the armchair to support herself. 'I think I'll have a bath,' she said, 'then a large drink before I take your advice.' She walked across the room and touched Sophie on the arm before turning towards the door. 'Thank you,' she said quietly. Sophie shrugged in her customary way and for the first time ever Jill really understood the gesture. She went on her way upstairs. Nothing else was said; nothing else needed to be.

Holly eventually found a parking space three roads down from her own and swore at the time and effort spent doing so. She climbed out of the VW, locked it and headed off towards Bishop's Road. It was the one thing she hated about living in London, the nightly scramble for a space even remotely near her flat.

The walk to her building was brisk and she was out of breath by the time she had climbed the three flights of stairs up to her flat. She put the key in the door and leant against the wall for a few moments to get her breath back. She was so tired that she felt she could have just closed her eyes and gone to sleep standing up right there. But she was cold, too, and hungry, so she heaved herself forward, opened the door and went on into the flat. The first thing she did was stop in the hall and play back the messages on her answerphone.

'Good morning, Holly, this is Guy Ferreira – we spoke last night. It's nine thirty am and I'm ringing to see if you might be free for lunch. Could you call me at my hotel when you wake, or get back in, if it's within the next hour and a half? Thank you.'

The tape bleeped and Holly stopped it. She rewound that message and listened to it again. It was Sandy's friend, and for some reason hearing from him once again unnerved her. The message was innocuous enough, but it just didn't feel right. She shivered and decided to ignore it. This intuition business was turning into paranoia. The tape moved on, and the next message was from Kit.

'Hi, Holly, it's me.' There was an uncomfortable pause, then he went on, 'Holly, er, are you all right, I mean, after last night?' Holly flushed. There was another pause and finally: 'Ring me if you need to, or want to. I'm in the office all day and back at the hotel around seven.' The phone clicked off and she felt an overwhelming disappointment that there was nothing more from him. 'Oh, Kit,' she murmured, leaning back against the wall. She really thought she'd made a decision on the way back from Sussex. She rewound his message and closed her eyes to listen to his voice. Perhaps she'd been hasty, perhaps she should reconsider? She sighed heavily, her eyes still closed, then the answerphone beeped and the final message came on. Holly jerked back to reality.

'Good morning, Holly, it's Guy Ferreira again, the time is ten am. You're obviously not there, no message.' Holly frowned at the peculiarity of this second message, pressed the home button and let the machine rewind as she walked on into the sitting room. She was still thinking how odd it was when she stopped dead, halfway into the room.

'Oh my God!'

She stared across at the bureau. The drawers had been pulled out, the contents scattered all over the floor, the shelves had been ransacked and the cupboard was open, the door broken off its hinges. She turned and ran into the bedroom. In there her wardrobe was open but only some of the clothes had been heaped on the floor. Her shoe box had been tipped out, all her letters, photographs and mementoes rifled through. The top two drawers of her pine chest had been emptied along with the drawers in the bedside table, but immediately taking stock, Holly saw that her jewellery box, two ropes of pearls hanging over the mirror, her camera and Walkman CD player were all intact. She wandered round for a few minutes, her heart pounding, a cold sweat on the back of her neck. Then she turned and hurried back to the sitting room to take a good look round.

The room had an awful feeling about it and Holly shuddered at the thought of who had been there, touching her things, looking at her personal letters, her photos. She moved around her possessions and realised that, just like the bedroom, everything had been moved and touched but nothing had been taken. The TV was still there, the mini hi-fi system, her silver photo frames, the antique porcelain. A spasm of fear clutched her stomach.

'Oh Jesus!' she muttered, stopping at the bureau and staring down at the floor. Everything had been thoroughly rifled through. Letters had been taken out of envelopes, bills removed from files, photographs turned over, postcards read, but nothing, as far as she could see, without touching anything, had been taken. She dropped to her knees and carefully picked over some of the papers. This was really beginning to terrify her. Turning over an envelope, she saw her emergency cash still folded and clipped together inside it, untouched. There were three hundred and fifty pounds, all in used notes.

Standing, Holly ran out into the hall to the front door. She stared at it, then ran into the bedroom at the back of the flat. She spotted the glass on the carpet at once, amazed she hadn't seen it the first time, then she yanked the curtains back and saw the wrenched catch, the smashed window. She slumped back against the wall, her whole body drenched in sweat. For one small, insane moment just then she had actually thought that Sandy had been there, that he was alive and had let himself into the flat to search for something. But it was definitely a burglary; the smashed window confirmed that. 'Oh God,' she murmured, feeling suddenly faint. If it wasn't Sandy, then who the hell would do this? And why hadn't they taken anything? Without thinking, she went and retrieved Kit's number from her bag, then picked up the phone.

'Kit? Hi, it's Holly. I'm sorry to bother you but . . .' Her voice failed her. 'Yes . . .' she managed to say, hearing his immediate reply, 'please . . .' Hanging up, she sat down on the floor, put her head in her hands and didn't move until twenty minutes later the main door buzzer sounded and she stood to let him in.

'I don't understand it,' Kit said, half an hour later. He had looked round the flat and double-checked with Holly that nothing had been taken. 'This is really odd!' He sat down on the edge of the bed and made a conscious effort not to look at the overturned shoe box. He had recognised his handwriting and photographs the moment he saw them and the temptation to know why she had kept it all was almost overpowering.

'It looks to me as if someone knew exactly what they were looking for, Holly,' he went on. 'I'd say this is a pretty professional job.'

Holly stood with her arms embracing her body. She nodded, chewing her lip.

'Have you any idea what it might have been?'

'No, I . . .' She broke off, catching Kit's gaze as it wandered down to the shoe box. Kneeling, she scooped all the letters, photos and mementoes up and stuffed them messily back into the box, then thrust it down inside the wardrobe. 'I have no idea, Kit. This is positively the last straw for me, it really is!' Her voice wavered. 'What with this morning, then the calls from this friend of Sandy's – I'm beginning to wonder if my intuition wasn't right. I just don't know what the hell's going on any more!'

Kit stared at her. 'Holly?'

She avoided his eye.

'What d'you mean, intuition? And what happened this morning?' Still she kept her head down. 'And what's this about calls from this friend of Sandy's? I think you'd better fill me in on what's been going on. You haven't given me the full story, have you?'

Finally she glanced up and shook her head.

'Right.' Kit moved past her to the door. 'Come on, into the kitchen where there's no debris and tell me what the hell's been happening.'

Holly took a deep breath, then followed Kit out. In the kitchen he sat at the breakfast bar and pulled a stool out for her. She perched, unsure of how much to tell him.

'Everything,' Kit said, looking at her face. 'Don't leave anything out.'

'I went down to Eastham this morning,' she began, 'to see Sandy's wife.'

'You did *what*?' Kit was astounded. He couldn't believe she'd done something so stupid. 'Go on,' he said, repressing the urge to tell her so.

'Well, I met Sandy's daughter, Sophie, but when his wife came home she threw me out.'

Kit said nothing but by the look on his face Holly could tell that he thought she had gone completely insane.

'I had to!' she implored. 'I had to see for myself what kind of life he had.'

'Wasn't that a bit selfish of you?' Kit's voice was incredulous. 'Another of your impulsive decisions, I expect,' he said sarcastically, 'with no thought for anyone but yourself!'

Holly stared down at her hands.

'So, you did that and got just deserts by the sound of it. Tell me, why did that confuse you?'

'God, you must be a bastard lawyer!' she suddenly cried. 'I'm not in court now, you know!'

Kit stared for several moments at the wall until he was calm enough to reply. 'No, you're not. I'm sorry, but I think it was a bloody foolish thing to do.' He paused. 'So, what happened? Why did it upset you so much? Surely you must have been expecting to be asked to leave?'

'Yes, but it wasn't that at all. It was Sophie, Sandy's daughter, and the house and his wife, Jill – it was all wrong. It didn't make any sense to me.'

'Did you seriously expect it to?'

'Yes! No! I mean, I did expect it to make some sort of sense. I thought it would help me get it straight in my head. I thought . . .' Holly caught a sob in the back of her throat. 'Oh bloody hell!' she burst out. 'You don't understand at all, do you?'

Kit sighed; he hated to see her upset. Reaching out, he touched her hand and said, 'Try me.'

Holly took several deep breaths, composing herself, then made a second attempt to explain herself.

'Sophie, Sandy's daughter,' she began. 'Well, she was so unlike him that it just didn't make sense. She looked like him – very like him, actually – but her personality, her mannerisms, the way she spoke, oh, I don't know, just everything about her, was completely different to Sandy. I couldn't see anything of him in her at all.' She stopped and saw that she had caught Kit's attention. 'And another thing, when she talked about going to art school, she said her dad didn't approve, didn't understand art. How could Sandy have pretended that? He lived, ate and breathed art; it was his life. It was the only thing we ever had in common, if I'm honest.'

'OK,' Kit said, 'let's try and work those two points through, shall we?' He paused for a moment to sift his thoughts. 'Firstly, I grant you that the comment about art school is odd, but lots of actors would hate their children to go on the stage. You see what I'm getting at? Sandy was in the business; he knew the pitfalls. Maybe he didn't want his daughter to struggle all her life and never make a living.'

'Yes, but what about her father not *understanding* art? Sophie said . . .'

'It was a comment,' Kit interrupted. 'She probably said it off the top of her head. She might never have meant it the way you took it.'

Holly sighed. 'And her personality?'

'Well, that's a bit easier,' Kit said. 'As far as I can see, there's no reason at all why Sophie should be like her father; hundreds of parents despair of the fact that their children are nothing like themselves. She could take after her mother, or not after either of them; genetics can play funny tricks, you know.'

'Yes, but she quoted him and seemed to adore him and almost, well . . .' Holly stopped. She was moving out of the boundaries of fact and into the realms of intuition again. She had no concrete evidence; Kit wouldn't understand.

'Almost what?'

'I got the feeling that she modelled herself on him, that she tried to be like him. Yet the whole time it seemed as if the man she was talking about was completely different from the man I knew.'

Kit was silent. He thought about what Holly was saying and could see why she was confused. She had suffered an enormous shock. What had happened was virtually impossible for her to comprehend. He thought she was making excuses, thinking up extraordinary ways out. He said gently, 'Holly, often no two people will see the same things in the same person.'

'Yes, but . . .' She stopped, thinking it pointless to continue.

'But what?'

'But it was more than that, Kit. I know you'll dismiss this, but I felt it so strongly, this sense of disconnection.'

'It was a feeling, Holly.'

'And feelings can be right!' she answered sharply.

Kit sighed. 'What about the calls from this friend of Sandy's? What's the problem there?'

'He rang twice this morning, to see if I was in. Don't you think that's weird? I've never heard of him before, then Sandy disappears, commits suicide, whatever, and he turns up out of the blue asking after my husband. Then this morning he rings the flat, checks I'm not in and the next thing I get burgled.'

'No, it's not necessarily weird; it could just be coincidence.' But Kit was beginning to worry. He usually only ever worked on logic and hard evidence, but he was beginning to think that Holly could be right. Things did feel odd; the situation didn't add up at all. However, he didn't want to alarm her. He placed his hand gently on her arm and said, 'Look, why don't we ring and get the glass fixed, report this to the police, then go back to my hotel and I'll book you a room?'

Holly hesitated, then nodded. 'Will you come with me?' she asked. 'I don't think I can face another session at my local nick on my own.' She attempted a smile, but her mouth trembled.

Kit picked up her hand and squeezed it. 'I'll come with you as long as you take up my offer of a room at the hotel. I don't like the idea of you coming back here on your own.'

'Done,' she said, and slipped off the stool. As she did so, she realised for the first time since she'd got in that she still had her coat and hat on. Embarrassed, she dug her hands in her pockets and said, 'Thanks, for all this I mean.'

Kit shrugged and got to his feet. 'D'you want to tidy up a bit first?'

'No, let's just go.' Holly turned towards the hall. She thought briefly about collecting up some things but dismissed the idea; she could buy a toothbrush at the hotel. Walking towards the front door, she waited for Kit to get his coat and took her keys off the table. As she did so the telephone rang.

For a moment Holly just stood and stared at it, then Kit appeared in the hall and, feeling stupid, she nervously picked up the receiver. She saw Kit move into the sitting room to give her some privacy.

'Yes, this is Holly Grigson.' She paused, stunned by the other voice, then said, 'Yes, of course, if you want to. Tomorrow? Yes, I'll just get a pen and write it down.'

Kit stood in the centre of the sitting room, waiting for Holly to finish her call. He looked at the bureau again and spotted the tiny silver desk clock that he had once given her, on the floor under some papers. Out of curiosity, he crossed and bent to look at it. Holding it in the palm of his hand, he saw that the face had been smashed, and guessed it had fallen in the trespasser's scramble over the desk. Reading the inscription on the back, he then looked at the time: it had stopped, at ten am.

Just then, Holly came into the room.

'That was Jill Turner,' she said. Her face was deathly pale except for two spots of intense colour on her cheeks. It gave her an odd, slightly mad appearance. 'She asked me to meet her and her stepdaughter tomorrow. Apparently they want to talk about Alex, I mean Sandy. They feel that things aren't quite right.'

Kit stood, still holding the clock.

'And that verifies what you said?'

'No, but it gives it a bit more credibility, doesn't it?'

'Yes, I guess it does.' He didn't like it, he didn't like any of it one little bit. Walking towards Holly, he slipped the clock absentmindedly into his pocket and said, 'D'you remember that clock I once gave you, Holly?'

'Yes, I've still got it somewhere.'

'Good.' He followed her out into the hall. 'Does it still work?'

'I don't know, to be honest. It's been tucked away in a drawer for ages.' She opened the door for them both, then slammed it behind them and dropped the keys into her bag. 'I think I put a new battery in a couple of months back, or maybe that was my camera flash?' She shrugged, then smiled at him. 'Why?'

Kit took her arm. 'No reason, just curiosity,' he lied. And together they went down the stairs and out into the cold night air.

It was eleven thirty pm and Detective Sergeant Robert Eames sat with the report he had just completed on his desk, staring at it. He had been doing exactly that for the past twenty minutes and was very unsure of what to do next.

His better judgement, in the guise of DCI Heeley, told him to ignore it, but his intuition told him to follow it up, or at least mention it to his superior. Had it been any boss other than DCI Heeley he would have been in there like a shot, but Heeley was a different matter. With him it was a simple case of intimidation – if that was ever simple, of course. Who would take his claim seriously? Heeley was revered in the force, with twenty years of unblemished service, while he was graduate intake, not very popular, with just three years under his belt.

Lighting a cigarette, Robert read through the form one more time but was still no clearer on the right course of action. He didn't want to be humiliated and he didn't want to be marked down as nit-picking, looking for crime. But there was something that kept niggling at him – something odd about the break-in, something odd about Holly Grigson. It was as if all the right pieces were there but they just didn't quite fit together. He smoked on for a few minutes, then reluctantly acknowledged that he needed to talk this through with someone. He walked along to DCI Heeley's office, knocked on the slightly ajar door, and went in.

'Sir?'

DCI Heeley was on the phone. He motioned for Robert to sit down, then carried on talking without making any effort to hurry the conversation to an end. Robert bristled at the slight.

'I didn't know you were on nights, DS Eames,' Heeley said sarcastically as he put the phone down.

'I'm not, sir, it's just that something came up and I stayed on.'

Heeley didn't even acknowledge the answer. 'Can I do something for you?'

'It's this, sir.' Robert passed the form across the desk. 'It's connected to the missing persons case two nights back. The same woman has had a break-in to her flat. There's nothing missing, but it's a bit odd. I thought I'd mention it.'

DCI Heeley read through the report. It took no more than a minute, then he dropped it down on the desk. 'Detective Sergeant,' he said, 'I have enough crimes to solve – serious crimes, ugly, violent crimes – without wasting my precious, overburdened time on petty, stupid incidents that most reasonable officers would know to ignore.' He picked up the phone again. 'Is that all?'

Robert retrieved the report, nodded and stood. Without another word, he walked out of the office and heard Heeley begin talking on the phone as he left. If Heeley had been even the slightest bit pleasant he would probably have done as he was told and let the matter drop. But now he had no intention of doing so. He was going to shake this bugger until something dropped into place. And when something did, he thought, switching off his desk lamp and pulling on his raincoat, then he was going to make damn sure Heeley knew about it. He was going to ram it down that bastard's throat, and with any luck, he just might choke on it.

Chapter Nine

Holly ordered coffee in the hotel restaurant and some toast. She wasn't in the slightest bit hungry but she had slept badly and had a stressful day ahead of her; she needed the nutrition. It arrived within minutes and she poured herself a cup of half hot milk, half coffee, then added three cubes of sugar. She took a sip, felt immediately better and started on the toast.

'Morning!' Kit stood at the table looking down at her, his dark suit on, *The Times* tucked under his arm.

Holly looked up. 'Are you breakfasting with me?'

'No, I had mine in my room earlier; I had some calls to make.'

She bit into her toast, heavily coated with butter and honey, and Kit shuddered. For a woman so slim, she had a remarkable lack of respect for diet.

'Wassitbisssness?'

'Sorry?'

Holly swallowed down her mouthful of toast. 'Sorry, I forgot I had my mouth full! Was it business?'

Kit hesitated, then pulled out a chair and sat down. 'Sort of. I cancelled my flight at the weekend and called my boss in New York to put in for a couple of weeks' leave.' He said it quickly, unsure of her reaction.

Holly dropped the piece of toast and stared at him. The very idea of Kit being around unnerved her. The last thing she needed, or wanted even, was any involvement. The other night had been a mistake, she kept telling herself that. She'd been lonely, upset; it should never have happened. 'You did what?' she gasped.

He met her gaze. 'You heard me.'

Holly's chin jutted out. 'Don't you think that was a bit presumptuous?' This was emotional blackmail, putting her under pressure! How could he think that one, stupid, insane moment of passion meant they were back to where they'd started? 'Perhaps it didn't occur to you that I might not want you to stay,' she said icily.

'Yes, it did occur to me,' Kit answered. 'But I decided that I would do it anyway.'

'Oh really?'

'Yes, really.' He held back a rising irritation, resisting the temptation to tell her she was being childish, and looked away.

'My God, Kit Thomas, you infuriate me, you really do!' Holly suddenly burst out. She didn't want him around – he would only confuse things! She felt herself begin to panic at the very idea of it. 'Why the hell do you think that you have some kind of divine right to interfere in my life?' She stared at the back of his head while he ignored her, and second by second her temper escalated. 'Kit? I'm talking to you, for God's sake!'

He faced her and raised an eyebrow. '*Talking* to me?'

'All right!' she snapped. 'I'm bloody shouting at you, then. Why should I care? You go around bossing and taking control as if I'm some kind of idiot, unable to survive without you!' She glared up at him, her face flushed, oblivious to the stares from the other diners. 'Well, I've done it for two years, haven't I? I can bloody well do it now!'

Kit's face was like thunder but he held his temper. As calmly as he could, he said, 'I am not on a piece of elastic, Holly; I am not here to come and go at your request. One minute you call asking for help, the next you're telling me to exit. You needed help and I made the decision to stay. I do not require your permission to do that, and if you think it has anything to do with the other night then you are sadly mistaken, because it damn well doesn't! That was a stupid error and we both know it. So, stop being so bloody childish and accept my offer when it's given.'

'Childish?' Holly scraped her chair back and stood. Kit had hit a raw nerve. 'Childish? Ha!' She threw her napkin onto the table. 'What's childish about wanting, no, needing to be independent?'

'But it's not independence, is it, Holly? It's wanting the upper hand all the time, wanting to make all the decisions.' Kit's own voice had risen but he was so angry that he was unconscious of the fact. 'Help me, Kit, go away, Kit – as long as it's you who dictates the terms then that's all right!' He stood up and they glared at each other across the table, indifferent to the commotion they were causing, the stares, the embarrassment, the hovering waiter.

Then all of sudden Holly's anger died, as instantly as it had erupted. 'When did you become so aggressive?' she asked sadly. 'All we've done is row since you came back.'

'I learnt through my mistakes, Holly,' Kit said. 'I either shout back at you or get trampled on. You always told me what to do. Even at the very end it was what you wanted – give me space, Kit, I love you on my own terms, Kit . . .'

'It wasn't like that! You know it wasn't. You're the one who . . .' Holly broke off and bit her knuckles, close to tears.

'Who what, Holly? Who did what you wanted, left you to get on with it!'

'Left me to get on with it? You walked out! You didn't listen to me, didn't understand, didn't . . .'

'Oh, I listened all right!' Kit said. 'And I understood. You wanted me out of your life so that you could get on with the gallery, get on with what you wanted!'

'No, that's not it! I . . .' She stopped again and the tears that had welled up in her eyes spilt over and rolled down her face.

Noisily, she sniffed, and wiped her nose and cheeks on the back of her hand.

He watched her for a moment, not knowing what to do. She had the power to anger him beyond belief and then suddenly to move him like no-one else on earth. Seeing her regain her composure, he swallowed hard and turned away. He wasn't going to back down, not this time. Before he walked off he glanced back over his shoulder. 'You have my number,' he said. 'I'm not going anywhere.' And without another word, he left the table and walked across the restaurant, nodding to the waiter as he went.

Holly slumped down in her chair and reached for her bag, searching in it for a tissue. She found one, blew her nose loudly and felt a little better. She watched Kit's back as he disappeared out of the restaurant. There was something so infuriating about this new Kit – something that really got under her skin and yet at the same time was intensely sexy.

So the other night meant nothing to him, did it? She thought miserably, plucking her napkin angrily off the table and going on with her breakfast. Well, it sure as hell meant nothing to me either! The bastard! How dare he even imagine that it did? She munched the rest of her toast, hardly tasting it, too upset to think about food.

'Bloody Kit!' she muttered. 'I'll be damned if I'm going to phone him.' And leaving the table of Japanese diners next to her speechless, she got up and stalked out of the restaurant.

By twenty past two that afternoon, Holly's resolve had weakened. She was feeling miserable and confused, and as she stood on the pavement outside the restaurant, waiting for Jill and Sophie, she wished she and Kit hadn't parted on such bad terms. She thought longingly of getting back to the gallery and calling him – but of course she wouldn't do it.

Sophie came up the stairs and Holly forced a smile, but her

morale was so low it came out more as a grimace. 'Hi,' she said, trying the smile again. 'Is your mum ready?'

Sophie nodded. 'She's just paying the bill.' She stood next to Holly and stamped her feet on the ground to warm herself up, digging her hands deep into the pockets of her donkey jacket.

Holly watched her, seeing so much of Sandy in her and yet nothing at all. She sighed and turned away.

Lunch with Jill and Sophie had been a dismal experience. She had listened politely for over an hour and a half to stories of a man she had no knowledge of, a man loved by his family, happy, inspired in his life. She had seen glimpses of her husband in the hobbies, the likes and dislikes, but she had recognised nothing in the humour, compassion and kindness that Alex Turner had apparently possessed. If Jill hadn't identified Holly's photograph, indeed if Sophie hadn't confirmed that she had the same photograph of Sandy at home herself, and if they hadn't matched up certain things – the mole on his neck that had been removed, his passion for sailing – then Holly would have been convinced she had married a different man. Now all she knew was that she had married the same man but brought out the very worst of his nature. She had been there for sex, perhaps, and a bed in London, but certainly not love, or even companionship, not in the sense that Jill had been.

She turned back as Jill came up the stairs and out onto the street. 'Thank you again for lunch,' Holly said. 'It was useful.'

Jill nodded and clipped her Vuitton bag together. It might have been useful to Holly, but it had been a terrible ordeal for her. She had watched this woman for the last hour and a half and seen nothing whatsoever that she could identify with. She was nice enough, obviously very clever, and attractive, in an earthy, exotic way, but she was so different to Alex that Jill couldn't see how it could have worked. Perhaps it hadn't – certainly there had been no spark, no glimpse of love in any of her conversation about Sandy.

'Is this a good place to get a taxi, d'you think?' she asked.

Holly glanced up the road. 'As good as any, I guess.' She kept her eye on the traffic, unsure of how to cover her dismay. It wasn't just Jill's description of Alex's character that had thrown her, she realised; it was the woman he had been married to. She glanced back and took in Jill's pale blond hair, the cream wool trouser suit and her soft cashmere overcoat. Jill was so vastly different to Holly that it made her wince. She glanced down at her own clothes – her black opaque stockings, with a hole in the thigh which thank God no-one could see, the Royal Stewart tartan mini skirt and crimson wool jacket, her shiny black patent lace-ups with a crepe wedge, and her poncho. There was nothing classic or chic about it – an image that she neither thought much nor cared much about, thrown together with haste and her own peculiar sense of style. Her hair was a mass of short, dark waves, forever unbrushed, tucked behind her ears to show large silver hoop earrings. Jill's chic bob moved with her, not a hair out of place.

Holly looked back at the traffic, feeling thoroughly depressed. Sandy had so obviously been happily married – why in God's name had he risked losing it all? And why had he chosen Holly, a choice she had always known was wrong, even if she'd never admitted it?

At last she spotted a taxi. Relieved, she ran out into the road to flag it down. She didn't want to think about this any more; she'd had enough. It was time to forget the whole thing. Sandy had gone; it was over. She needed to get away – from the gallery, from this awful mess and from the complication of Kit – before she made another terrible mistake with her life.

The cab slowed down and Holly ran over to speak to the driver. 'Victoria Station, please.' She beckoned to Jill and Sophie. 'Should get you there in plenty of time for your train,' she said.

Jill smiled tightly. She had no intention of going straight back to Sussex. She wanted to go to Alex's office and have a nose around.

Sophie had been right. Lunch might have been horrific, but it had brought it home to her that things didn't quite add up. In fact, they didn't add up at all. Opening the door, she held it for Sophie then climbed into the cab after her.

'Bye,' Holly said, then added, without conviction, 'it was great meeting you.'

Sophie smiled. 'And you.' Jill merely nodded.

Holly stood back as the driver switched on his meter and indicated, pulling out sharply into the traffic.

'Bye!' she mouthed. She held up her hand to wave, then turned away. Folding her hands inside her poncho and feeling it all had been a monumental waste of time, she started miserably for the tube.

The day was beginning to fade by the time Holly made it across London to the gallery, and the shops in the street had already started to light up. She waved at one or two of the owners as she approached the Grigson Gallery, then popped her head round the door of Patel's Grocery, three doors down, and called out hello to Mrs Patel.

'Oh, Holly! Thank goodness you are back!' Mrs Patel came hurrying out from behind the counter, her sari covered with a floral housecoat. 'You have had a problem with the shop, Holly dear. There was not a burglary, thank God, but the police were here last night and they were not able to get hold of you!'

Holly froze for a moment, then she turned and started for the door.

'Musti! Come here!' Mrs Patel called out to her husband. 'I am having to go with Holly to her shop.'

Mr Patel appeared from behind a beaded curtain. 'Let us know if there is anything we can be doing for you, Holly!' he called, taking up his place on the stool behind the counter.

But Holly didn't hear him; she was out on the pavement before he had finished his sentence and running towards the gallery. Fifty yards down she stopped dead and stared at the boarded-up door.

'Oh my God!' She was lucky: the plate-glass windows were intact; only the door had been smashed. 'Did the police do this, Mrs Patel?' She pointed to the tape and boarding.

'Yes. Holly dear, do you want to come in with us and sit down? You can ring the police from our telephone, if you like.'

Holly moved closer and pressed her nose against the plate glass, staring into the dark interior of the gallery. It all looked in place, she thought, mentally counting the paintings on the walls. 'What happened? Have you any idea?'

'Oh yes! We were in bed; it was about eleven o'clock. The alarm started and Musti got up and came down in his dressing gown. The police were here very quickly, Holly dear. It was only a matter of minutes, I think.'

Holly stood back. 'I wasn't in,' she murmured.

Mrs Patel shrugged. 'I think that whoever it was ran out of the back when they saw the police car. There was no-one there and the police constable said that he could not see that anything had been disturbed. It was probably kids, Holly dear, causing trouble.'

Holly nodded. The colour had drained from her face and she felt dizzy.

Mrs Patel took her arm. 'Come and have a cup of tea with us,' she said kindly. 'You will feel much better after something warm to drink.'

Holly nodded and let herself be led away. 'I should get over to the police station,' she said lamely.

Mrs Patel clucked her disapproval. 'Musti will drive you when you are feeling better, Holly dear.'

They reached the Patels' grocery shop and Mr Patel came out to help Holly inside, carefully and gently, as if she'd been injured in some way. She smiled as they fussed, and sat quietly drinking her tea, all the time a sick feeling of unease churning her stomach.

Seeing her face, Mr Patel said, 'I think Holly must be wanting to see the police now. Leave the tea, Holly dear. I will drive you right away. I'll just get my keys.'

Holly stood with relief. 'Thank you, you've been so kind.' She put her teacup down on the counter, eager to depart. She was anxious to speak to the police and get the facts so she could have things clear in her mind. She followed Mr Patel out to the car. 'I'll let you know what the police say,' she told Mrs Patel as she climbed in. 'Thank you again.'

'It is a bad business, Holly dear,' Mr Patel said, pulling out from the kerb. 'But it is nothing to worry about, I am sure.' Not quite convinced, Holly nodded, tried to smile and they drove on in silence.

An hour later Holly was back at the gallery. She had called a twenty-four-hour glazier and organised the refitting of the door. She had also made up her mind that she needed a break; she would close the gallery until the new year.

The police had dismissed the break-in as criminal damage only. They'd found nothing to indicate that anyone had moved or stolen anything, and Holly could see for herself that nothing was missing. This sort of thing happened all the time, she'd been told. It was nothing to worry about. She was lucky it had only happened once.

But Holly couldn't ease her feeling of alarm. It was a small, tight knot in the pit of her stomach and it kept nagging at her, making her tense, giving her the feeling that something sinister was going on. This whole thing was getting out of hand; she simply had to have a break.

Sitting at the desk with the business diary in front of her, Holly opened it at that week and reached for the address file. She had several things to do, the first being to ring Sandy's two appointments in the book and cancel them. She looked up the first address in the file, and dialled the number. The line was unobtainable.

'That's odd,' she muttered, immediately ringing directory enquiries. She gave the name of the client, the address Sandy had written down, and waited.

'Yes? Nothing at all listed under that name for that address? Are you sure? Can you try the same name in Grosvenor Street, not Road, or Grosvenor Avenue? Yes, I'll hold.'

She flicked through the address file again while she waited, to double-check Sandy hadn't written another entry for this client. The girl came back on the line. 'Oh, nothing at all? OK. Thank you.' She hung up. There was bound to be a reasonable explanation for it. Perhaps it had been noted down wrongly. She moved on to the second appointment, found the client's address and number and dialled.

'Yes, hello, could I speak to Mr George White please.' Holly tensed. 'You haven't? Are you sure? Oh, yes, I see. Thank you. Sorry to bother you.' She dropped the receiver back in its cradle and sat staring at the diary. No George White at that number, no Perry Lucas at the other. She fingered the cards in the address file, wondering whether to try them all, then dismissed the idea. It had to be a mistake. She must have got it wrong, misdialled. She rang the number once more, heard the same switchboard and immediately hung up. It had to be written down wrongly then – these things happened; people made mistakes all the time with phone numbers. Glancing at her watch, she decided to get on with her call to Sotheby's before they closed. Sandy had made an appointment to pick up some paintings he was having valued, and she needed to cancel it.

She got through to the contemporary art department, gave the name Sandy had written in the diary and was put through.

'Martin Hotten.'

'Hello, Mr Hotten, my name is Holly Grigson from the Grigson

Gallery. I believe you have an appointment with my husband, Sandy Turner.'

'I do?'

Holly was caught off balance. She hesitated, then said, 'I, er, I have an appointment written in my book. My husband was supposed to be collecting some paintings from you that you had valued for him. Paintings by Marcus?'

'I'm sorry, Miss Grigson, but I don't know anything about this. Are you sure it was me and not another valuer?'

Holly was stunned. This was crazy – she must be going mad!

'Miss Grigson?'

'Oh, er, yes, I thought it was you, but I must have made a mistake.'

'Can you hold on a minute? I can check with my colleagues, to see if anyone else knows something about this. What was the name of the artist?'

Holly's mind was spinning. She forced herself to respond. 'Thanks, but don't bother, really. Did you know my husband, Mr Hotten?'

'I'm not sure, I don't think so. A Mr Turner, you said?'

'Yes.' It came out as a whisper. She coughed to clear her throat. 'What about Marcus? Have you valued his work before?'

'No, I'm sorry, but I don't believe I have. Where is he from?'

'Oh, it doesn't matter.' Suddenly Holly felt flushed; she had to get off the phone. 'I'm sorry to have wasted your time, Mr Hotten,' she murmured. 'Thank you for your help.' Without waiting for an answer, she hung up and dropped her head into her hands.

'Oh my God!' she moaned. 'What the hell is going on?' She felt close to tears and had to bite her lip to stop them. Her hand hovered by the phone, on the point of dialling Kit's number, but she curbed herself and stood up. The last thing she needed was involvement with Kit; she was confused enough as it was. She paced the floor for a few minutes, the monotony of it calming her slightly, then she went back to the desk. She would do this on her own: ring the other numbers in the file, find out who and what were bogus, if any at all. Chances were there was a logical explanation for all of this; she just had to find it.

Sitting down, she turned to 'A', held her finger under the first number and reached out for the phone. She was being ridiculous, she told herself firmly; she had to get a grip! Suddenly, just as her hand touched the phone, it rang.

'Shit!' Holly jumped with fright. It took her several moments to compose herself before she felt strong enough to pick it up. 'Hello?' Her voice came out as no more than a faint whisper.

'Sophie!' she exclaimed. 'Yes, I'm fine . . . No, I haven't been here. Something happened to the gallery and I had to go the police . . . Have you? What, for the last three hours? Oh God, I'm sorry, I've been on the phone ever since I got in.' She broke off and listened. Sophie had been trying to contact her all afternoon. She was in a terrible state, practically incoherent. 'Look, Sophie, calm down, please, and tell me what's happened.'

Holly's hand crept up to her chest as she listened to the answer and the pulse throbbed in her neck. 'His office? Completely trashed? What, files, computers, everything?' She nodded, listening intently. 'How awful!' She felt a cold shiver run along the length of her spine. 'Yes, of course I can. Where's the office? Yes, I know it.' She wrote the address down on the pad in front of her.

'Have you rung the police?' She stood and reached for her poncho, still listening to Sophie's near hysterical voice on the other end of the line. What the hell were they doing in the City, anyway? Jill had said they were going straight back to Sussex. 'Good, well, stay put,' she said, 'and I'll get there as soon as I can.' Seconds later she hung up. Without another thought, she dialled the number she had by now learnt off by heart.

'Room 114 please,' she said to the switchboard. She waited nervously. 'Hi, Kit, it's me.' She stopped, suddenly unsure of how to go on. There was a silence, then she said, 'I'm sorry, you were right.' She had rarely apologised for anything in her life before. 'I found out some really odd things at the gallery this afternoon and now I've had a call from Sophie, Sandy's daughter.' She bit her lip and said quietly, 'I need your help, Kit, please.'

There was another silence and she held her breath, waiting for his reply. Moments later, she blinked back tears of relief, let the breath out and gave him the address of the investment business Alexander Turner had run from the City.

Chapter Ten

Holly jumped out of the cab on the corner of Broad Street and saw Kit up ahead. She called out, waving as he turned, then hurriedly paid the driver, not waiting for her change. She ran to where he was standing and stopped just in front of him, pale and breathless.

'Oh God, Kit! This is all really weird!' She broke off to catch her breath. 'I don't know what the hell's happening any more.'

'Let's wait and see,' he said. 'Come on. Number fifty-four, you said?'

'Yes.' Holly fell into step with him but struggled to keep up. He was six foot one and his stride was twice hers.

'It's here.' Kit glanced at the squad car. 'The police have arrived then.' He rang the entry panel and they waited.

'Hello?'

'Hello, Sophie? It's Holly.'

'Second floor,' Sophie said.

The buzzer went and Kit pushed the door open, leading the way inside. The building was Victorian but the interior had been gutted and redesigned in the nineties office vogue, with low leather sofas and glass tables. They crossed the reception area to the lifts and went on up to the second floor.

Sophie was waiting for them as they alighted. 'Hi. It's through here.' The lights were on at the end of the corridor and Holly could see the outline of two uniformed officers through the frosted glass panelling. The whole scene made her uneasy.

Minutes later, Holly stood with Sophie in the entrance to the suite of offices, Kit a pace behind them.

'Jill?'

Jill turned and gave a wan smile. She held out her hands to indicate the mess and Holly stared around her. The front office was a reception area, from which glass doors led through to the main room, a large open-plan space, with screen dividers for two partners and a secretary. Everything in it was in chaos. Computer terminals lay smashed on the floor, their screens shattered and keyboards ripped apart. Files had been shredded, papers ripped; a typewriter had been thrown through the glass doors. The plants were uprooted; chairs looked as if they'd been hurled around the room; and the contents of the coffee machine had been smeared over the desks.

Holly was stunned.

'When did all this . . .'

Sophie cut her short. 'We don't know. When Dad didn't show up two days ago, Jill tried to call the office but the lines were down. It could have happened then, or even earlier.'

'Weren't there any other employees? Someone who might have come in, seen this and called you?'

'No, there was just Alex,' Jill said, coming across to them. 'He did have a partner a few years ago but they split and from then on he worked on his own, only employing secretarial staff on a temporary basis.'

'How did you find out then, about all this?'

Jill looked momentarily embarrassed. 'I have a key to the office. I decided after lunch that, instead of going straight back to the station, I'd call in here. I thought it might help, to sort things out a bit.'

'Excuse me, are these two people involved, Mrs Turner?' The

police officer was pissed off at the interruption; they were wasting time.

'I'm sorry, er . . .' Jill broke off, not knowing how to continue.

Sophie filled in for her. 'This is a close family friend, Holly Grigson,' she said. 'And . . .'

'Kit Thomas,' Holly said quickly. 'He's . . .'

'A close family friend,' Kit said, and the women smiled.

The policeman ignored the wisecrack. 'Well, there's very little we can do here for the moment, Mrs Turner,' he said. 'We'll send the scene of crime officer in tomorrow, for prints and such like, but there's no urgency, if you're sure nothing's missing.'

'No . . . er . . .' Jill hesitated. She honestly didn't know if anything was missing. 'I don't think there is.'

'Good.' He turned and glanced at his colleague. 'One last thing – this partner you mentioned a moment ago. Is he still involved in the business in any capacity?'

'No, I don't think so.'

'OK, fine. If there's nothing else then, Mrs Turner?'

'Oh, no, of course not, er, thank you.' Jill stood aside to let the policemen past. She seemed to have become even paler than Holly remembered. It was as if the colour had drained out of her over the course of the past few hours.

'We'll leave you to lock up then,' the officer said, 'if you're happy to do so.' She nodded and smiled politely at the policemen. 'The duty officer will be in touch in the morning to let you know what time forensic will be over.'

'Thank you,' she said.

Holly and Kit moved to let the men past and then stood in the demolished office with Jill. They waited until the lift doors closed and they were alone, then Sophie said, 'D'you think they'll follow it up with Brighton, find out about . . .' She stopped and looked from Jill to Holly. 'We didn't mention anything about the, er, situation. Jill just said that Dad had recently committed suicide.'

There was a painful silence, and Holly stared hard at the ground, then Kit asked Jill, 'Are you all right?'

She nodded, then said, 'Actually, I'm not sure if I am.' She dropped her head down and took a couple of deep breaths while Kit reached for a chair and helped her into it. He patted her shoulder gently, feeling immensely sorry for her. She was shattered by all this, anyone could see that. Holly glanced up, caught the action and Kit's expression, then stared angrily back down at the floor. She wasn't jealous, but she couldn't see why the hell Jill needed sympathy. She had at least been happy, hadn't she?

Jill pinched the bridge of her nose hard between her forefinger and thumb, to try and stop the throbbing in her head. 'This is all so peculiar,' she murmured. 'I feel as if it's not happening to me.' She looked up. 'It can't be. Three days ago I was happily married to a man I loved and trusted. My life was happy, routine; I knew exactly what was happening. Now I don't even know what day it is.' She looked around the room. 'Why this? Why now?'

Kit didn't know what to say, or how to comfort her. He looked to Holly for support but she ignored him. She was thinking about herself, not Jill, but her thoughts were the same: why me, why now?

There was a tense, uncomfortable silence in the room, and Kit wasn't at all sure how to break it. He was a corporate lawyer; he wasn't used to sorting out emotional mess. Suddenly Holly looked up.

'The gallery was broken into last night,' she said. 'I found out this afternoon.' She hadn't planned to say it, but now she had she felt enormous relief.

There was a sharp intake of breath in the room, and Kit said, 'Jesus, Holly! Why the hell didn't you call me?'

She shrugged. She wanted to say, I held off for as long as I could, don't you understand that? I don't want to get involved with you; I want to deal with this on my own, only I can't! But instead she took a breath and said, 'There's more.' She stared down at her hands and fiddled with her wedding ring. 'Odd things have been happening there and I don't know what to think. Things that involve Sandy.'

'What things?' Kit moved towards her but she picked up a fallen chair and righted it, then sat with her body facing away from him and her arms folded defensively.

'I decided after lunch to forget all this and go away for a while,' she said.

Kit felt his stomach tighten. He stared at a spot above Holly's head and kept his face impassive as she continued.

'But I had to tie up some loose ends at the gallery before I could close it. That's when I found out what's been going on . . .' And without thinking whether or not it was right to do so, she told them all about Sandy's bogus clients.

When she had finished, she waited for someone to speak. Again there was a silence, only this time it was heavy with shock. The man that Jill thought she had known no longer existed. What shred of understanding she had left had been shattered by Holly's revelation. Holly glanced across at her. She was ashen, the immaculate hair and make-up doing nothing to hide the haggard despair on her face. Jill caught Holly's gaze, and at last found her voice. 'You are implying, Holly, that my husband was involved in something fraudulent, aren't you?'

Holly chewed her lip.

'*Aren't* you?' Jill demanded.

'I don't know, there's nothing concrete, I can't be . . .'

'But that's what you think, isn't it?'

Holly said nothing for several moments, then, reluctantly, she nodded.

Jill dropped her head down. 'Then we have to go to the police,' she said quietly. 'We have to tell them everything.'

'No,' Holly said quickly. 'I'm sorry but we can't do that.'

Jill jerked her head up. 'Why not?'

'Because this isn't just about your or my husband, it's about us as well, and that means that we could both be in a great deal of trouble.' Holly stared at her, her gaze unswerving. 'You do understand that, don't you?'

Jill flushed. 'Yes, I do.'

'I'm sorry,' Holly said. 'I just wish it were different.'

Sophie spoke up hesitantly. 'Jill, I . . . I don't know if I should say this, but . . .' She stopped, unsure of herself.

Jill nodded. 'Go on.'

'Well, the thing is, I mean . . .' She glanced sidelong at Holly, then braced herself. 'The thing is that I don't believe this. I don't believe any of it – that Dad could do anything illegal, or . . .'

Holly interrupted her. 'Are you calling me a liar?' Her voice was icy cold.

'No! I . . .'

The threat of confrontation spurred Jill into action. 'Go on, Sophie. Say what you want to.'

Sophie gave a small nod. 'You know, I've had this odd feeling ever since, well, since the police came round,' she said. 'You see, I really can't believe it. I know that you hear people say that when something awful happens – it's a natural reaction – but that's not what I mean. It's not that I can't believe it's happening – I *can*; it's all so real it makes me feel sick. But it's more than that. It's like, I could never, ever see Dad doing that, taking his own life.' She stopped and swallowed hard, struggling not to cry. Then, composing herself, she went on. 'I don't think what's happened – I mean this and Holly's flat and gallery – are coincidences, but I don't think it would be Dad. I just can't believe it would be him! You see, I can't ever remember him telling me a lie, not ever. Even when he and Mum split up and he met Jill, and then Mum died, he always told me the truth, no matter how hard it was . . .' Her voice petered out and this time her eyes did fill. Kit, not looking at her, dug in his pocket for his handkerchief. He was beginning to run out of clean ones; he'd have to do a job lot at the hotel laundry.

'So you think I made all of this up, do you?' Holly felt a pang of sympathy at the tears but she was too wrought-up herself to act on it.

'No, I don't think you've made it up, I just think . . .'

'You just think *what*? If I haven't made it up, what's the alternative?' Holly spoke much more harshly than she'd meant to.

'Stop it, Holly!' Kit said.

'Stop what?' His chastisement infuriated her. She knew when she was wrong; she didn't need him to tell her.

But Kit ignored her question and turned away towards Sophie. 'You all right?' he asked gently. She nodded and offered him back his hanky. 'Keep it,' he said, 'please.'

Jill decided to speak out. She didn't agree with Sophie but she did understand what she was trying to say. 'You know, last night, Sophie, when you first said this to me, I was too shellshocked to take it in. Half of me wanted to believe you and the other half had just been through hell at the police station. I still don't know what to think, but you are right about one thing. I can't ever remember Alex lying to me . . .' She broke off as her face flushed deep red. 'I mean, apart from this,' she stammered, 'if it's true . . .'

'If it's true!' Holly burst out. 'Are you doubting now that I was married to Sandy?'

'No! I . . .' Jill took a breath. 'I don't know what to think,' she said honestly. 'I'm very confused.'

'But you see what I was talking about, don't you?' Sophie said. She stared at Jill, defying her to answer.

Jill glanced at Holly, then nodded.

'And what was that?' Holly said icily.

'That you . . .'

'It's all right, Sophie,' Jill interrupted, 'I'll explain.' She could feel Holly's aggression and she didn't want Sophie to be hurt. 'Neither

Sophie nor I are at all sure that Alex would have been . . .' She stopped, braced herself, then said, '. . . would have been attracted to you, to your, er . . .' The moment she began it, Jill regretted it. She had no idea how to phrase what she wanted to say and she knew she'd done it appallingly.

'To my what?'

'I think Jill is trying to say . . .'

'Shut up, Kit! Let her say it!'

'To your type, Holly,' Jill finished. 'I don't mean to offend you in any way at all, but . . .'

'But I wasn't good enough for your husband, eh?' Holly snorted derisively. 'Well, I was good enough all the nights he spent in my bed and not yours!' she cried. 'I was good enough to . . .'

Kit was across the room and in front of her before she knew what had happened. He blocked her off from the other two and placed his hands on her shoulders. 'Calm down!' he hissed. 'Stop it!' He saw her face collapse and squatted down, hugging her in close to him. 'It wasn't meant like that,' he said gently. 'Jill has just said what you yourself have been thinking.'

Holly pulled back from him. 'And what's that?'

'That you two are so different, and that Sandy was a different man with both of you – am I right?'

There was a silence, then Holly nodded and broke her arm free to wipe her nose on the back of her hand. 'That he loved them but he didn't love me,' she said tearfully. 'That no-one can for the life of them see why he married me!'

Behind them Jill winced.

'So where does this leave us?' Holly asked miserably.

'It leaves us with one answer that we agree on,' Kit said. 'That there is something very odd going on here. This isn't just a suicide, or a simple case of bigamy.'

'Is bigamy ever simple?' Holly asked. Kit flushed.

125

'I'm sorry,' he said. He glanced over at Jill. 'I didn't mean any offence.'

Jill shrugged. She hadn't taken any offence. She had been preoccupied, only half listening. 'You know, something odd has just occurred to me,' she said. 'Something I perhaps should have thought of earlier but . . .' She stopped and wondered again if it could have been connected.

'Go on,' Kit said.

'Well, it was about three months ago. Alex was behaving in a most peculiar way. He was worried about something, only he wouldn't say what. He was sharp with me, bad-tempered. It was very out of character and I knew something was stressing him. I wonder if it has anything to do with all this?'

'I thought it was me,' Sophie said in a small voice. Both Kit and Jill turned to look at her.

'You noticed it too?'

Sophie nodded and Jill felt again the gulf of misunderstanding that had existed between them. 'He was always on the phone in the study,' Sophie went on. 'Every time I came in, he hung up or cut his conversation short. He was very distant for a while, tense. I thought you'd asked him to arrange another school for me, to get rid of me.'

Jill flushed. She looked down at her hands in her lap, embarrassed and ashamed. Sophie was right: that was what she'd wanted; not then, but a bit later. Alex had refused point-blank.

'Does all this really matter?' Holly broke in. She didn't want to say that Sandy was always sharp, often bad-tempered, and she didn't want to hear any more about him from Jill and Sophie.

Kit shrugged and stood up. 'Perhaps it doesn't. It's speculation until we have more facts. What we really need to know is what was happening at the gallery. If you have the keys, then maybe I should go over there and pick up the books and files, and anything else you think might be relevant.' He turned to face

Jill. 'You look tired. Perhaps you should take Sophie back to Sussex?'

Jill nodded.

'I can call you if anything important comes up.'

'Hang on a minute!' Holly interjected, suddenly furious that Kit had taken control. And she resented the tone he'd taken with Jill. Why didn't she get the same level of understanding? She was tired as well; she was bloody exhausted. '*I'll* go to the gallery, thanks, Kit, and, Jill, *I* can call you if anything comes up there.'

Jill looked from Holly to Kit. She was half out of the chair and felt she'd been caught in crossfire. She sat again.

'Holly, don't be childish,' Kit said. 'It's late, and it's far better if I go, all right?'

There was a silence while Holly and Kit glared at each other. Jill made to stand up again.

'No, it's not all right!' Holly answered icily. Jill sat down for the second time. 'It is my gallery and my responsibility. I will go.'

Kit shook his head and sighed. He didn't want her to go – he was concerned that whoever had been there last night might return – but he knew it was pointless to argue. Holly was upset and she was damned stubborn at the best of times. He left it.

Jill finally stood up. She was no expert on emotional matters, but she could see that these two had got it all wrong. They'd turned love into a battleground.

She pulled her coat in tight and glanced at Sophie. 'Let's go then,' she said, and Sophie stood. 'Everyone out, I have to lock up.'

Kit picked Holly's poncho up off the desk and walked over to her. 'Here,' he handed it across. 'Come on, we can share a cab.'

Holly nodded and pulled the poncho over her head. She had no intention of sharing a cab with him but she could tell him that outside.

'Thank you for your help, Kit,' Jill said. 'Oh! You'll need our number, in Sussex.' She extracted a card from her purse and handed it to Kit. 'We should be in late, around ten-ish.'

Kit tucked the card in his pocket and thought of the disorder and grubby chaos of Holly's carpet bag in comparison to Jill's neat, expensive purse. Holly was in the habit of writing her number on people's hands; she never had any spare paper in amongst the jumble and mess and she'd certainly never had any cards, as far as he could remember. 'Holly or I will ring later tonight, or first thing in the morning,' he said.

Jill nodded.

Holly had meanwhile moved to the door. She'd had enough. Jill's unending politeness got her down and she was anxious to get away.

Jill looked across at her. 'Goodbye, Holly.' She knew Holly had been offended tonight and didn't know what to say; she wished she'd handled it better.

Holly managed a polite half-smile. 'Goodnight. Have a safe journey back to Sussex,' she answered, in a poor imitation of Jill. 'Goodnight, Sophie.'

'Bye!' Sophie held up her hand to wave but Holly had already walked out.

Kit glanced at her and shrugged apologetically, then followed Holly out to the lift. She was a bloody difficult woman, Holly, impossible at times, but he forgave her for it. She was also easily the kindest, funniest and most exciting one he had ever met. He hopped into the lift beside her, knowing that she wouldn't have waited, and seconds later, they had left the building and were walking together down towards the main road.

'Well,' Holly said, 'if it's all right with you, then I'll give you my keys and get the next cab to Notting Hill. You go back to the flat and I'll meet you there.'

Kit sighed. He had no idea what he had done to upset her and he sure as hell wasn't going to ask. That had been his mistake in the past. 'Fine,' he replied. He spotted the free sign on a taxi and whistled, two fingers between his teeth. The cabbie saw him, indicated and pulled over.

Holly dug in her bag, while Kit gave the cab driver the address of the gallery, and finally pulled out her flat keys along with a moth-eaten packet of Polos. She gave Kit the keys and peeled the paper off the mints, offering him one.

'No thanks,' he said, to a rather dirty-looking sweet. Holly shrugged and popped two into her mouth. She climbed into the cab without another word, and the driver pulled out into the traffic. She saw Kit call out something but she didn't catch it, and she didn't care. It wasn't that she was angry with him as such; it was just that she was angry full stop – with Sandy, with events and with her whole damn life in general.

DS Eames had Sandy Turner's form 584 on his desk, an incident report for the break-in at Holly Grigson's flat and a copy of the Yellow Pages open in front of him. He had just circled the small advertisement for the Grigson Gallery in black ink when DCI Heeley walked into the office.

'Ah, DS Eames.' His tone was far from convivial. 'Single-handedly solving the crime of South London, I see.' He smiled at his joke, stopping at Eames' desk on the way through to speak to another officer. 'You're not on duty this evening, are you?'

Eames looked up. 'Just doing a bit of research, sir.'

DCI Heeley caught sight of the form 584 and all trace of humour left his face. 'Well, I bloody well hope that this research is on your own time, Detective Sergeant, because I'm not signing any friggin' overtime for you!' He picked up the incident report. 'Is that quite clear?'

DS Eames didn't look at him. 'Quite clear, sir.'

Heeley dropped the report down onto the desk. 'Good, because when I ask my officers to leave well alone I expect them to do exactly that. Understood?'

Eames kept his gaze averted. 'Yes, sir.'

DCI Heeley stared at the top of his head for a few moments, not at all sure if he'd got the upper hand, then, his voice heavy with sarcasm, he said, 'Go and have a drink with someone, Detective Sergeant, find yourself a friend.' He flicked the papers on his desk. 'Get a life, will you?' And with that he walked off.

Eames rubbed his hands wearily over his face. Maybe Heeley was right. What the fuck was he trying to prove? He'd been going over the Grigson case with a fine toothcomb and he'd come up with bugger all. There was nothing in any of the records anywhere that he could find to connect. Maybe he'd got it all wrong. He shuffled the form back inside the file and closed it; time to give in, he reckoned. He stood up just as the phone rang.

'DS Eames.' He glanced at his watch.

'Rob, it's Tony. I have to cancel tonight, I'm afraid. I've gotta work.'

Eames sat back down. 'No problem, mate.' Bugger it, he'd been looking forward to a drink. 'I'm pretty knackered and I've not eaten or anything yet.' He lit up a cigarette. 'Yeah, 'course I understand. How about Thursday next week?' He took his diary out of the inside pocket of his jacket and made a note of the time. 'Really? What, in the City? That's unusual, isn't it? You boys hardly ever have any real crime up there.'

'What, like Chelsea, you mean? Come off it, Eames!' Tony laughed. 'It was a bit odd, though. A company called Alex Turner Investments – the place was trashed but nothing taken. Some sort of vendetta job, in my opinion. Maybe they were into something dodgy. We'll find out soon enough.'

Eames' hand stopped, his cigarette halfway to his mouth. 'Alex Turner Investments?'

'Yeah, don't tell me you've heard of it? What, in the *FT* or something, Eamsie?'

'No, hang on a minute, Tony. Who reported it?'

There was a pause while Tony looked at the report. 'Mrs Turner. Why? What've you got up your sleeve this time, Rob?'

DS Eames sat silent for a few moments. He could hardly believe it. All that time he'd spent going over files, and one chance call had cracked it. Jesus! This was weird. He didn't exactly believe in fate, but what had just happened gave him the heebie-jeebies. 'Listen, Tony, you couldn't fax me a copy of that incident report over, could you?'

'What, now?'

Eames smiled, all thoughts of home and supper dispersed. 'Yes, now, if that's all right.'

'No problem, mate. Any clues as to why?'

'Not yet, Tony, but when there are you'll be the first to know,' Eames said. 'Thanks, mate, I appreciate it. See you Thursday.'

Still smiling, he hung up, and quickly made a note of the address on the advert he had ringed. He stubbed out his cigarette, immediately lit another, then made his way along to the CAD room. It was a hunch, but what the heck; some things were beyond explanation.

He was in luck: one of the civilian operators was on, a woman who had taken a bit of a fancy to him.

'Ali, could you check an address for me in Notting Hill? I want to know the station for that area.' He handed the piece of paper over and stood just behind the woman as the information was tapped in, staring at the bank of screens. The area station came up within seconds, and Eames noted it down then patted the woman on the shoulder. 'Thanks, Ali, I appreciate it.'

Back at his desk he dialled the Notting Hill station, spoke to the duty officer and was told they would call him back in half an hour or so with an answer. He went down into the canteen, had a cup of coffee and a stale doughnut, and whiled away twenty minutes over the the *Evening Standard* before making his way back to the office. Another half an hour and the call came through. The duty officer read the crime sheet out over the phone and Eames asked him to fax him a copy. He had been right; he was on to something – another break-in connected to the Turner case. Hurrying down to the fax machine, he picked up the fax from Tony and waited for the second document to transmit. When it came through, he added the copy of the crime sheet on the attempted burglary at the Grigson Gallery in Notting Hill to his file.

DCI Heeley can swing for it, he thought, tucking the file into his briefcase. Supercilious bastard! This is more than just coincidence – three break-ins, all in different areas and all connected to the same person or persons. There's something going on here and I damn well spotted it first.

He made his way along to Heeley's office, anticipating a thoroughly satisfying encounter, but Heeley was out. Disappointed, Eames left a note on the desk, with the time clearly marked at the top. It was eight thirty, and he damn well wanted Heeley to know that he was way over the end of his shift.

Holly arrived at the gallery in Ledbury Road at nine. First, she called in to the Patels, three doors down, to let them know she was there, then she went back and switched on all the lights, front and back. She locked the front door, checked the back was secure and opened up the safe. She wanted a couple of hours of peace to go through all the books, receipts, orders and files before reporting back to Kit.

Lighting the desk lamp, she dumped the stack of information down in front of her and shunted her chair forward to the desk. Opening the first set of accounts, she scrabbled around for some paper, then thought better of it, took her jacket off and pushed the sleeve of her jumper above her elbow. Most things she could remember, but she would write any essential figures and notes on her arm, then copy them down later at the flat. Carrying around bits of paper with important evidence on them made her nervous – in fact, this whole damn thing made her nervous, and she wasn't about to take more of a risk than she had to.

Kit helped himself to a large whisky and slumped down on Holly's sofa, putting his feet up on the coffee table. He was tired but the adrenaline of the past few hours was buzzing in his veins and he couldn't relax. Sipping his drink, he stared at the massive abstract painting on the wall opposite and let his mind wander back over the events of the past forty-eight hours. It was the best way to problem-solve, he'd always found: a malt whisky, peace and quiet and something to stare at.

An hour and a half later, the phone rang. His thoughts flew to Holly, and he was instantly worried. He had lost track of time, he realised, glancing at his watch. It was near eleven, and there was no sign of her. Jumping up, he hurried out to the hall and picked up the phone.

'Hello? Holly?'

It was Jill, sounding upset. 'Kit? Is Holly with you?'

'No, she's still at the gallery.' As he said it he felt a surge of panic in his chest. 'Why?'

'We've just got back and the house has been broken into. D'you think Holly's all right?'

'I don't know. Look, I'll ring her now and then call you back.'

'No, don't bother. D'you think you should get over there?'

'Yes, maybe.' Kit glanced a second time at his watch; Jill really didn't sound at all good. 'Jill, are you OK?'

She hesitated then said, 'Yes, a bit shaken, but OK.'

He made a snap decision. 'Good. Look, ring the police now and I'll collect Holly and bring her straight down to Sussex.'

'You don't mind?' She tried not to sound too relieved, but Kit wasn't fooled.

'Of course not. Just get on to the police now, all right? I'll ring Holly, and tell her to be ready. See you later.' He clicked the button and immediately dialled the gallery.

Holly gathered all the material she had been looking at together into one pile and switched off the desk lamp. She had got everything she needed. Pulling down the sleeve of her jumper, she stood up and made her way over to the safe. She was halfway across the gallery when she heard a noise at the door. She stopped and glanced behind her nervously, then peered out through the window, but but could see no sign of life on the street.

'You're being paranoid, Holly my love,' she said aloud to reassure herself. She had found out far more than she'd expected and was beginning to realise just how vulnerable she was. 'I think I'll double-check to make sure,' she muttered, crossing to the door. She stood and looked out at the quiet street for a few moments, staring hard. There was definitely no-one there. But as she turned, something caught the corner of her eye: a shadow across the pavement, or maybe it was a figure; it was so quick she wasn't sure. She peered out again, scanning the road, then she did something that she later decided was incredibly stupid: she unlocked the door and opened it, then stepped out and glanced up and down the street. She couldn't have been thinking straight, she told Kit afterwards. All she knew was that she felt spooked and that she had to get out of there. She could see nothing suspicious, so, satisfied it was her imagination, she turned without re-locking the door and hurried back to the safe. Squatting down, she leant forward and quickly shoved the files inside.

Seconds later the lights went out. She screamed as fear ripped through her, then she felt an almighty thud on the back of her neck. She fell forward, cracking her head on the side of the safe, and a searing pain shot through her skull. Then all was darkness.

*   *   *

Kit stood in the hall of Holly's flat with the phone in his hand, listening to the constant ringing signal and wondering what the hell to do. He had been trying to get through to the gallery since Jill's call, with no success. Holly had more than likely left, he told himself but he couldn't relax. If she wasn't on her way home then she could be still at the gallery but in some kind of trouble, unable to get to the phone, maybe even badly injured. Kit pulled himself up sharply and took a deep breath. He was panicking, something he rarely did. He pulled open the drawer in the hall table and rummaged under the papers and general junk for Holly's car keys. He found them, hung on for a moment longer, then dropped the receiver back in its cradle, grabbed his coat and slammed out of the flat.

He was convinced Holly was in trouble. He wasn't a believer in this intuition thing, but by God he could feel that something was very wrong – feel it in every sinew and nerve in his body.

Kit swung the VW up onto the pavement in front of the Grigson Gallery and jumped out. Running to the door and finding it locked, he peered in through the windows at the darkened interior, knocking on the glass and calling out. The closed sign was up; the gallery seemed to be in order, tidy and empty. It was more than likely that Holly had gone. Nevertheless, he put his hands up on either side of his face, to cut out the glare from the street lamps and get a better look. Everything seemed to be in place. Holly must have finished and left in the last half hour; she was probably already at home. He was about to turn back to the car, but something stopped him. He took another look, pressing his face against the glass, and spotted her coat still hanging behind the desk. Wasting no more time, he ran down the street and into the first open shop.

'Do you have a phone?' he shouted into the back. 'This is an emergency!'

Mr Patel appeared immediately and caught Kit's panic. He brought the payphone quickly up from under the counter. 'Is there anything I can be doing?'

Kit picked up the receiver. 'It's the gallery, three doors down,' he said hurriedly. 'I think something's happened to the owner.'

'Holly! My God!' Mr Patel turned and shouted several rapid words in Bengali to his wife in the back. She came running through to the shop front with a bunch of keys in her hand. 'Musti! Here!'

'These are her keys,' Mr Patel said. 'Quickly, we'll go! Come!'

Kit hadn't yet dialled; he held the receiver in his hand, unsure of what to do.

'Come!' Mr Patel shouted. 'Quickly! My wife will call the police.' Kit dropped the phone back and ran out after him.

At the gallery, Mr Patel peered briefly through the glass, then found the right key on his bunch and unlocked the door. He shoved it open and they both ran inside.

'The lights!' Kit called, moving across the gallery, towards the back. 'D'you know where they are?' The place was only semi-dark, the street lamps outside providing enough light to see. Both men searched the back for the lights. 'I think they're on some panel on the wall behind the desk,' Kit called again. 'I remember Holly . . .' His voice broke off. 'Jesus!' he suddenly shouted. 'Over here! Quick!' Just then Mr Patel found the panel and the gallery was flooded with light.

'Oh my God! Holly!' Kit dragged her by the feet from under the counter in the back and started to claw at the sack that had been tied over her head. She struggled, making indistinct noises. Obviously her mouth had been gagged. Kit talked to her, trying to reassure her, the whole time his hands shaking and his heart pounding with panic.

Once he'd untied the sack, he yanked it off her head. Mr Patel crouched the other side of her, holding her head and shoulders, while Kit tried gently to peel off the tape that had been plastered over her mouth. She flinched with every movement.

'Hold still, Holly, please. Hold still for a bit longer, while I . . .' He felt her jerk in pain as the tape ripped across her skin. 'Last bit, just try to hold still . . .'

'Hold still?' Holly suddenly cried as her mouth was freed. 'Hold still?' Her voice broke. 'Thank God you're not a doctor, Kit Thomas!' She sat up, put her hands over her face and burst into tears.

A short while later, sitting in the Patels' shop, a cup of hot, sweet tea in her hands, Holly went over the events of the past few hours with Kit. The Patels left them alone together at her request, shuffling about in the back, and popping in every few minutes to check she was all right as she attempted to convince Kit that despite what had just happened, she had been right to ask Mrs Patel to cancel the call to the police. She had no intention of reporting it. She also had no intention of going to the nearest hospital to be checked out, and told Kit so forcefully when he suggested it.

He stood opposite her, too agitated to sit, and tried very hard to understand her reasoning. He couldn't get past the feeling of desperation he'd had when he discovered her, the sense of complete panic that he might have lost her, and now, regardless of what she said or how she said it, that thought kept going round and round in his head.

'So, if you don't go to the police, Holly, then what *do* you intend to do?' he finally asked.

She shrugged.

'That's it? You just shrug and forget it?' He shook his head. 'Someone breaks into the gallery, takes the cash from the safe, duffs you up in the process and you don't want to go to the police!' He gritted his teeth. 'I just don't get it, really I don't! What if it's connected to this whole thing, what if . . .'

'What if, what if . . .' Holly interrupted. She put her tea down and slid off the stool, looking to Kit at that moment as if nothing at all had happened to her. But that was exactly what she wanted to look like. In fact she had been terrified, and she was still reeling with the shock, but she knew for sure that she didn't want to go to the police. Now she had to convince him. She hadn't told him about what she had found in the files, or the fact that they were now missing. She needed a bit of time and space to try and think it through without Kit going off like a loose cannon. She was in this thing up to her neck, implicated in whatever had been going on, and she wasn't going to hand herself over to the fraud squad until she had some idea of what she was up for. She crossed to him and put her hand on his arm. 'Look, Kit, I know what I'm doing, all right? I'm a big girl and I can look after myself.'

'Clearly!' Kit snapped. 'As you've just demonstrated!'

Holly pulled her hand away and moved back. 'OK,' she said, trying to keep her patience. 'If I have to spell it out then it's like this.' She jerked her head up and stared at him defiantly. 'I have no intention of reporting this to the police and you can kick up as much fuss as you like, but that is my last word. Now, you can either carry on with this thing my way, or you can go back to the States. I said I needed your help; I didn't say I needed you to tell me what to do, how and when!' She held his gaze for a few moments, then turned away and bent to pick up her bag.

Kit stared down at the ground. Bloody Holly, bloody, bloody Holly! How the hell could he go back to New York now, with all this going on? She knew he wouldn't, and she was using it just to get her own way again. 'OK,' he told her. 'We'll do it your way, for the moment.' He clenched his jaw. 'But I'm telling you this for nothing, Holly! If it goes wrong, if things get any more dangerous than they already are, then I am going to the police, with or without your consent. Is that clear?'

Holly looked at him. He was scowling, a hard glint in his eye. She nodded.

'Right, then let's go!' Kit said. 'It's a long drive.'

Holly tensed. 'I'm sorry? A long drive? What d'you . . .'

'Jill, the house in Sussex?' Kit prompted. 'I told you, earlier on, you . . .' He stopped; she obviously hadn't taken it in. 'Jill's house was broken into,' he said. 'Nothing was taken, as far as she could tell, but she's as nervous as hell and I said we'd drive straight down there.'

'When was it broken into?' Holly asked.

'Earlier today, I suppose. I don't know, she didn't say.'

'And nothing was taken?'

'Apparently not.'

Holly reached for her coat, turning away from Kit, not wanting him to see her face. This wasn't a shock – it was more than likely that Jill's house would be searched – but it was one more frightening event and she prayed to God that she could just keep her nerve.

Christ, I hope I know what I'm doing, she thought, as Kit called out to the Patels that they were leaving. Because if I don't, it seems from here on in that there's more than just my life to mess up.

Chapter Eleven

Kit indicated and pulled off the A3 onto the main road to Petworth. The rest of the journey would be cross-country and he glanced down to check the petrol gauge before leaving the outskirts of Guildford; it was the last chance to stop for fuel. The tank was quarter full – enough to get them to Eastham, and he'd rather keep going if they could help it. He sneaked a sidelong glance at Holly, huddled down in her seat, silent and brooding, and wondered if he should offer to stop. She had said nothing since they left London and he guessed that the reality of what had just happened might suddenly have hit her. He was tempted to reach over and touch her hand, but quickly thought better of it.

'Are you all right?' he asked instead.

'Yes,' she murmured.

'You sure you don't want to stop for a drink or something? Now's your last chance.'

'No, thanks.' Holly reached forward for her bag. Kit had guessed right – she felt sick and her hands were shaking no matter how hard she clutched them in her lap. At this point a year ago she would have lit up a cigarette; now she scrabbled around unsuccessfully amongst the debris in her huge carpet bag for the packet of Polos and pulled out a couple of loose sweets from the bottom. She wiped them on her scarf and offered one to Kit. He declined and she popped them both into her mouth.

'Howmuchfurtherisssit?'

'Sorry?'

She shook her head and sucked, then she removed one of the sweets and said, 'How much further is it?'

Kit smiled. It was one of the things that he found so sexy about her, the individuality, the disregard for manners, for doing what was right. Only Holly could pull out a half-sucked sweet and manage not to make it look revolting.

'You should be telling me,' he said. 'You're the one who's been here before.'

Holly shook her head. 'It was all such a blur two days ago that I can hardly remember driving down here.' She held the sweet up and looked at it. 'Besides which, I have the most monumental headache.'

Kit glanced at her again. 'And a pretty big bruise to match, by the looks of it.'

Holly groaned and rubbed the side of her head where she'd hit it, just above her right eye, then she put the sweet back in her mouth and sucked.

'You've no idea where we're headed then?' he asked.

She shrugged. 'Nah.'

'I see.' He tried to cover his dismay and said nothing. By his calculations it was about thirty miles, only he'd been relying on Holly to direct him once they were off the main road. What an idiot! It should have occurred to him that she'd driven down in a state and that she'd never find her way back. He should have rung Jill for directions.

'Shit!' he swore silently under his breath, then checked the petrol gauge again and put his lights onto full beam. They were well and truly out of town now. The road was pitch-black and the smell of wood smoke drifted up above the trees into the freezing night air. It made him nervous, not having a clear idea of the route.

'Holly, you don't have a map in the glove compartment, do you?'

'No, I usually rely on road signs, the generosity of passing pedestrians and prayer.' She looked across at him and he smiled through gritted teeth. 'Why?' she asked.

'Just wanted to double-check the route,' he answered, a little too quickly.

Holly narrowed her eyes. She was silent for a few moments, watching his face, then she said, 'You don't know where you're going, do you?'

Kit laughed. 'Of course I . . .' The car slowed and he pressed his foot down harder on the accelerator. 'Of course I . . .' It happened again. 'Don't be daft, Holly, I know exactly what I'm doing!' he insisted as the VW picked up a little speed down the hill. He turned to her briefly and smiled. Twenty seconds later, his foot pressed hard on the pedal, they began to slow down and the smile died on his face. 'Shit!' he muttered. 'Something's wrong with the . . .'

Holly leant across and peered at the dashboard. 'We've run out of petrol,' she announced.

'Petrol!' Kit snapped. 'We can't possibly have run out of petrol! The bloody tank's quarter full, it's nowhere near reserve, it's . . .' He broke off and looked at her. 'The gauge doesn't work,' he said. She nodded. He indicated, pulled the car onto the grass verge and cut the engine. Switching off the lights, he dropped his head in his hands and stayed like that for several moments.

'Why the bloody hell didn't you tell me?' he said finally.

'I didn't think! How was I supposed to know that we'd run out of petrol?'

Kit sat in silence and stared out at the darkness. 'You weren't,' he answered grudgingly, after a long pause.

'No, I wasn't!' Holly said firmly. 'So, what next?'

'I get out and walk, I suppose. Unless you brought your mobile phone with you. Did you?'

'No, I'm afraid not.'

Kit sighed irritably and glanced behind him. It was past

midnight and the hope of another car passing was minimal. If one did come along then the chances of it stopping were a thousand to one, he thought, unclipping his seat belt.

'Where're you going?' Holly demanded.

'To find a phone box or a petrol station, whatever comes first.'

She unclipped her own seat belt and reached for the door handle.

'Alone,' Kit said, placing a restrictive hand on her arm. 'You are staying here, locked in the car.'

'No way!' Holly interjected.

'Holly! It's perfectly safe. The car will be locked, you'd be a lot better off . . .'

'No way José! You are not leaving me here and that is final!' She opened the car door and climbed out, and he followed suit. She stood straight and stared across at him. 'Sorry, Kit, but I am not staying on my own in this car in the middle of nowhere!'

Kit glared at her across the bonnet. After what had just happened it was perfectly understandable that she felt anxious, but she wasn't thinking properly. It really was safer for her in the car. 'Look, Holly,' he said, trying to be patient. It was late, he was exhausted – they both were – he didn't need any antagonism. 'I'd really rather you didn't come with me. Think what you like, but it's a hell of a lot safer and more comfortable here in the car than walking along a road, unlit, in the freezing cold without a frigging clue as to where you're going!'

But Holly shook her head. She knew she was being unfair in not giving him the full story, but she wasn't about to tell him and she sure as hell wasn't staying in the dark, on the side of the road, unprotected and on her own. She slammed the car door shut and stood her ground. 'Tough!' she said. 'Because I'm coming!'

'You're not!' Kit countered, his patience failing.

'I bloody well am!' Holly snapped.

'Jesus!' Kit slammed his door shut and bent to lock it. Why did she always have to argue? 'You are the most impossible woman I have ever met!' He turned the collar of his coat up and dug his hands into his pockets. 'All right, have it your way, but don't moan if we have to walk four or five miles at least to find a phone box.'

'Four or five miles?' she echoed in disbelief.

Kit started off down the road. He didn't have the energy left to be sympathetic. 'At least!' he shouted over his shoulder. Holly jogged to catch him up.

'Four or five miles?' she said again, already breathless at having to keep pace.

Kit stopped and turned to her. 'Yes!' he snapped. Despite his resolve, his patience had finally evaporated. 'Now, do you want to continue or go back to the car?'

Holly turned away for a moment. The thought of what had happened earlier in the gallery made her suddenly shiver. 'I'll continue,' she said quietly and Kit saw her face.

He cursed himself for being so insensitive. Of course she was scared – who wouldn't be? He held out his hand. 'Come on then,' he said. 'Let's get going.'

Holly took it and Kit gripped her fingers tightly as he led her on down the uneven and unlit road.

They came to a phone box three miles on. It was on the side of the road by a bus stop, the only sign of human habitation they had seen the whole way.

'Thank God for that!' Holly said as they approached it.

'Keep your divine praise until we find out if it's working or not,' Kit answered. He went ahead and swung open the heavy glass-paned door. It was an old-fashioned phone box, red, with a door that shut tight. Kit glanced at the phone, intact and change-taking, then at the floor, clean. It must have been one of the few phone boxes left in the UK that no-one had urinated in. He called to Holly.

'It takes tens, twenties, fifties and one pound coins.'

'D'you have Jill's number?'

He shook his head. 'I worry about you sometimes, Holly, I really do. Of course I have Jill's number!' He pulled out his wallet and took the card Jill had given him. 'I've even got the right change.' He jangled his pocket. 'You stay here, I won't be long.'

Holly nodded and stared around her at the empty road. She felt nervous, miserable, cold and tired. She stamped her feet on the ground in an attempt to get them warm and took her hands out of her pockets, rubbing them furiously. Glancing up at the black, overcast sky, she shivered, and suddenly felt an icy drop of water on her face. It had started to rain.

Hurrying over to the box, she tapped on the glass door and yanked it open. 'It's bloody freezing out here,' she hissed. 'Can I come in?' Kit tutted, stopped dialling and moved aside to let her squeeze in. It was tight but she just made it. 'When you're ready,' he said wearily, 'I'll try again.'

'Sorry,' she muttered irritably, 'but there's no need to be so bloody grumpy! It is minus three out there, you know!'

Kit couldn't help himself. Here he was, squashed into a freezing phone box in the middle of Sussex at one in the morning and Holly couldn't even be civil. 'Well you should have stayed in the car then, if you wanted to be warm, shouldn't you?'

Holly glared at him 'If you're going to be so rude then you can stand outside and leave me to make the call!'

'I can, can I?'

'Yes!'

They glared at each other.

'Fine!' Kit finally growled. He shuffled to the right to squeeze past her, knocking the change off the ledge as he did so. Holly bent to retrieve it just as he shunted forward and they collided.

'Ouch!'

'Shit!'

They were stuck: Holly wedged firmly against the side of the box, Kit wedged firmly against Holly.

'Holly, stand up, for God's sake!'

'I can't!'

Kit edged forward.

'Ouch, stay still!' Holly was bent double, her bottom stuck against one side of the box, her head against the other. Kit was hemmed into the corner, pressed against the payphone.

He shuffled then bent his knees and painfully came down to Holly's level. 'Here, take my hands.'

She looked up and found herself face to face with him, his knees up around his chin, his body squeezed incredibly into about three foot of space. She took in his pained expression, his long legs doubled up, his back hunched and a look of sheer exasperation on his face. She couldn't help herself: she started to laugh.

'Jesus, Holly! I don't see what's so bloody funny!' Kit stared at her as she dissolved helplessly before his eyes.

It was relief, the stupidity of it all, and a sudden need for release. She felt her arms weaken and her legs begin to buckle as she snorted with uncontrollable laughter. She attempted to put her hand up to her eyes to wipe them and her whole stance collapsed. She fell forward, painfully, on top of Kit and, still laughing, felt herself heaved up into a standing position, her body wedged against his.

She hiccuped, fought to bring herself back under control and looked at his face. 'I'm sorry,' she mumbled, trying to keep a straight face, 'I just . . . you just looked so . . .' She felt the laughter bubble up again and bit her lip hard to stop it. 'You just looked so funny . . .'

Moments later she pulled back, away from a kiss that took her so completely by surprise that the laughter was instantly forgotten. 'Kit!' She stared at him. 'What was that for . . . ?'

He didn't answer. Instead, he placed his hands either side of her face, his fingertips over her eyes, forcing her to close them, and gently eased her mouth towards his. He kissed the outline of her lips, felt her shiver and parted her mouth with his tongue. He kissed her and she responded, in a way she had no control over. She tried to move her hands to stop him, to make some sort of protest, but she couldn't; she didn't want to.

Kit ran his hands down from her face along her spine to the hem of her skirt, lifting it and making her gasp. She pulled away from him.

'Kit? What . . . ?'

He silenced her with his mouth and slipped his fingers inside the thin lace of her underwear, tracing the curve of her bottom. Now he had touched her there was no going back; he couldn't have stopped if he'd wanted to. She felt her body being inched back, gently, until she was pressed hard against the door of the phone box, the glass icy and damp on her exposed skin. She could do nothing. There was no space; she had no will. Kit lifted her, very slightly, so that her feet were off the ground, and wrapped her legs around his. He unfastened his trousers, eased them down and cupped his hands hard around her hips, moving her up and back. Suddenly she cried out, the intense pleasure of him taking her breath away. She gripped his body with her thighs, throwing her head back, arching her spine and, slowly, Kit began to move inside her.

'Kit, you can't . . .' she whispered, losing her voice, desperate for him not to stop. 'You . . .' She held his waist, digging her nails into the muscled flesh of his arse, losing all sense of time and space. He felt her move with him, heard her moan as he pressed her body back into the freezing door to take him. She was no longer conscious of the noise that she made; it came from deep inside her, a cry of a pleasure she had all but forgotten. She closed her eyes, the eyelids flickering as the pace increased, her mouth parted. Kit clutched her thighs, never once taking his eyes from her face, loving the sight of her abandonment, her complete pleasure. He felt her shudder, her whole body begin to tense, and finally he let himself go. He too closed his eyes and saw the image of her face, loving him and wanting him, needing him. It was an image that had haunted him all the time he had been away.

It was over and they clung to each other, both breathless, both hot and damp with sweat in the icy night air. Kit rested his head on her shoulder and she moved her hands up to his hair, stroking the back of his neck where it curled onto his collar. They said nothing.

Finally, Kit moved. He disentangled his body from her and let her legs slip down to the ground. She stumbled momentarily on her feet, her knees weak, and smiled up at him.

'You have changed,' she said quietly as she adjusted her clothing in the three inches of space between them.

Kit reached out and brushed her hair off her face. 'Have I?'

Holly's smile broadened. 'In a phone box, Kit Thomas, on the side of the road . . .' She started to laugh. 'If I hadn't been here I would never have believed it!'

Kit smiled. He pulled her coat up around her ears and held the lapels. 'If you hadn't been here,' he said, 'I would never have done it.' He bent and kissed her mouth, then turned towards the phone. 'Jill,' he announced. 'We should get a move on.'

With difficulty, he retrieved the charge from the floor, then dialled the number. Glancing over his shoulder at Holly, he said quickly, 'Headache gone?' and smiling, she nodded. Seconds later, the pips went and he slotted the change into the machine.

An hour later, Holly sat in silence in the back of the Range Rover and stared out of the window. She could hear the murmur of Jill and Kit is conversation but she took nothing in. She was trying to work out exactly what had happened back there in the phone box and what to do next.

You stupid, stupid fool, she thought, biting her thumbnail. She'd been reckless, impulsive and bloody, bloody silly. Of course, her father had told her as much the day she'd given up Law, saying she never thought hard enough about anything. He was right. She was already in a bad enough mess, and now this – starting something she had no idea she could finish. Why had she done it? What on earth had possessed her? If only she'd held back, stopped herself. And Kit, what did it mean to him? God, she had no idea! He'd said nothing, not even, how was it for you? Just wham bam in the freezing bloody cold and then, it's time I got on with my call. Holly chewed on her nail even harder as an image of what had just happened flashed into her mind. She felt a hot flush envelop her entire body and leant forward to wind down the window. 'Shit,' she muttered under her breath, feeling thoroughly miserable. There was no way she could have held back; she knew that, just looking at the back of him in the car.

'You all right, Holly?' Kit glanced over his shoulder and she could have sworn she saw a glimmer of amusement in his eyes.

She nodded and looked away. Perhaps it was all a bit of fun for him, a trip down memory lane. Perhaps he'd just seen an opportunity, seen she was vulnerable, and taken advantage of it. She gave up chewing on one thumb and went on to the other. Shit, what a jerk she was! In the middle of all this chaos she had to add a bit of her own special brand.

She started as the car braked and Jill flipped on the indicator. The last thing she needed to do was dwell on it, she told herself. She had quite enough to think of already.

The wheels of the Range Rover crunched on the gravel drive of South Ridge Farm, and Holly saw Sophie standing in the porch. Again the peculiar resemblance to Sandy struck her – so like and yet unlike him that it mystified her. She forced a smile, waved and opened the door as the car swung to a stop in front of the house. Climbing down, Holly could see more clearly the exhaustion on Sophie's face. It was late, well after two am, but Holly had lost track of time. The day had seemed to somehow merge into one long, awful, suspended moment.

'Hello. You found them all right?' Sophie said.

Jill climbed out and slammed the door shut. 'Were you OK?'

Sophie shrugged. She was being brave; she'd been terrified left in the house on her own. Taking her arm, Jill gave her a quick hug and led the way into the house.

Kit waited for Holly at the front door. 'You OK?' he asked as she reached him. He went to take her fingers in his but the gesture was ignored and he had to let his hand drop. 'Holly, I . . .' She looked up at him, her face closed, and he suddenly lost his nerve. He had so much to tell her and yet he said nothing. 'Do you want to tell Jill what happened at the gallery?'

She shook her head. 'There's no point in making things worse.' Kit nodded. He stared at her for a few moments, wanting her to say something, anything, about what had just happened, but she didn't.

'Let's go in,' he said. Standing back, he let her enter the house first and followed her inside.

'A drink?'

Jill had taken her coat off and Kit noticed that she'd changed her clothes, replacing the cream wool and silk city outfit with pale canvas jeans and a cream cotton knit sweater. She looked just as stylish and classic, just as groomed, as she had done earlier and his heart went out to Holly, who, he realised, had noticed the same thing and kept her poncho on over her worn, and now grubby, clothes.

'Whisky, gin, wine?' From force of habit, Jill made it sound like a cocktail party, and Holly winced.

'A Scotch please, Jill,' Kit said, seeing the wince. 'Holly?'

'Oh, er, the same. Just as it comes.'

Jill nodded. 'D'you want to go into the kitchen? It's much warmer in there.'

They went through and Holly wondered why she hadn't noticed the details of the house before. It was beautiful, comfortable, warm and well cared for; it made her immeasurably sad. Kit pulled out a chair for her and they sat at the scrubbed oak table in silence.

'Whisky,' Jill announced, putting the bottle down on the table and handing a glass to Holly, then to Kit. She went to the fridge and poured herself a glass of wine, then turned as Sophie came into the room.

'D'you want tea or something?'

Sophie shook her head. 'What are we going to do?' She was nervous and upset; she wanted reassurance, answers, and she didn't want to waste any more time.

Kit opened the bottle of Scotch, poured a good measure into Holly's glass, then his own. 'Talk about what the police said, have a good look at what happened here today, then take it from there. How does that sound?'

Sophie glanced at Jill and Kit caught the look.

'Jill? Is something up?'

Jill stood where she was and took a gulp of wine. 'I didn't call the police,' she answered. 'I'm sorry, Kit, but if Alex is involved in all of this then I could lose everything. I can't afford to take that chance – I've got two children to bring up, I . . .' She stopped and took another gulp of wine. 'I thought it best,' she finished.

Kit shrugged; it was her decision, albeit a bad one in his view. 'Was there anything damaged, broken? Any mess? Anything that might give us a few clues to start with?'

'No, nothing,' Jill answered. 'The back door had been forced and things moved, particularly in Alex's study, but nothing else. I, er . . .' She hesitated, momentarily embarrassed. 'I guess it's my own fault; I forgot to put the alarm on this morning.'

Kit looked at Sophie again, still standing in the doorway, her hands clutched together in front of her, knuckles white with tension.

'Right then, Sophie,' he said. 'I think we should start by going through Alex's study, to see if we can find anything that someone might be looking for.'

She nodded, and he stood up. 'D'you want to show me where it is?'

'OK.'

'I'll come with you,' Holly said, uneasy at being left with Jill.

'You don't have to . . .' Kit stopped when he saw her face. 'Great,' he finished. 'The more help the better.'

She stood with him, and Jill, across the room, noticed the silent communication between them; she envied it.

Sophie looked at her stepmother. 'Jill?'

'Oh, I don't think I'd be any good,' Jill said hastily. 'I hardly knew anything about Alex's business; I rarely took any interest.' In truth it made her nervous, all this ferreting about, this unearthing of things. She was frightened of what she might discover, not sure that she could take much more than she already had.

'You knew where he kept things, though.'

Jill drank down the rest of her wine, looked at Sophie for a moment, then placed her glass down on the work surface. 'Yes, I did,' she admitted. She glanced at her watch. 'It's late, you know. Almost three.'

Sophie continued to look across at her.

'Oh, all right. I'm not tired anyway.' She walked across the room. And out into the hallway. 'They probably looked in Alex's study first, before they tried the sitting room and the bedroom.' Opening a heavy oak-panelled door, she led the way into a small, high-ceilinged room with a window seat, wall-to-wall shelving and a big old pine desk. It was a mess, with papers strewn all over the floor, books ripped off the shelves, and the chair overturned. Someone had obviously gone through it thoroughly.

Jill crossed to the window seat and threw the cushions onto the floor. Underneath, the seat top came up and she opened it to reveal five neat rows of labelled files and papers. 'Nothing secret,' she said over her shoulder as Kit came forward. 'Just practicality. I threw out those awful metal filing cabinets because I thought this was more visually appealing.' She turned and shrugged. 'Whoever it was didn't find it.'

'I had no idea!' Sophie said, walking across. 'It's dead clever!'

Jill shrugged again and moved away, busying herself with picking up the papers scattered over the floor. She glanced up at Holly, then quickly back at what she was doing. Holly's face was set in a grim expression of tolerance; it wasn't a successful cover-up.

'So, shall we start there, Sophie?' Kit asked.

'Yes, OK.'

Sophie looked across at Jill for permission and Jill said, 'You do that, Sophie, and I'll collect up what's on the floor and see if there's anything of interest there.'

Holly stood redundant by the door.

'Holly?' Kit had turned and saw her skulking, still in her poncho.

'I'll look through the shelves,' she said.

It wasn't a useful suggestion, but Kit didn't argue. He was too busy trying to muddle his way through the confusion in his head about what had just happened between them. He had no idea what to make of her attitude and couldn't understand why she was ignoring him, ignoring the fact they had just had amazing, euphoric, incredible sex. He simply couldn't tell if she was sorry, or embarrassed, or relieved – like he was – that very little had changed and that she still had the power to move him in a way no-one else on earth could. He watched her for a few moments as she ran her eyes over the titles, recognised the cataloguing system and then began to pick up books to put them back in the right order. Even at three in the morning, she amazed him with the sharpness of her brain. He turned away and looked down at his own task. Sophie had started on the A files, so he sat cross-legged on the floor beside her, and trying to put the complication of Holly as far to the back of his mind as he could, he started on the B's.

DCI Heeley walked into his office and chucked his mac across the back of his chair. He was soaked through, and thoroughly pissed off. It had been a lousy night, and he'd been out for most of it, standing in the pouring rain while the whole area had been sealed off, waiting for the scene of crime team and the bloody pathologist. Jesus, he hadn't even had a cup of coffee! He glanced at his desk as he reached for the phone to ring his wife. She worried if she knew he was out, so he would call and let the phone ring three times so she'd know he was back in. Daft old bat! But as he picked up the receiver, he saw DS Eames' note and his blood pressure rocketed. He slammed the phone down again, forgetting all about his wife, and stomped through to the outer office.

'Any one know DS Eames' home number?'

One of his officers looked up. 'It's half four, boss!'

'I didn't ask for a time check, Dobbo. You got his number?'

DC Dobson found his pocket diary and read out DS Eames' number. He exchanged glances with another officer as Heeley jotted it down and stormed back to his office. As soon as the boss's back was turned Dobbo drew a line across his neck with his fingertip.

'He asks for it, Dobbo,' his colleague said.

DC Dobson nodded. 'Let him do some legitimate overtime for a change.'

In his office, Heeley dialled DS Eames' number, let the line ring for some time and smiled with perverse satisfaction as he heard a muffled, sleepy voice. 'This is DCI Heeley,' he said. 'You wanted to talk to me, Detective Sergeant?'

Eames managed to focus on his watch and rubbed his hands wearily over his face. Bastard – it was half past bloody four!

'Yes, sir,' he answered, 'I've been waiting for you to ring.'

There was no way he was going to let Heeley have the advantage.

'Something urgent?' Heeley asked snidely.

'Yes, may very well be, sir,' Eames fired back. 'I've done some work on that Turner case, the form 584?'

Heeley swore under his breath. That was a name he didn't want to hear, not at the moment, not until the lab had done their bit.

'Go on.'

Eames sensed a change in Heeley's voice and realised he had his attention. 'There've been three break-ins connected with the case, sir – one at the flat Turner shared with Miss Grigson, one at the art gallery they ran together and one at a business he ran in the city, an investment business.'

'What was stolen?'

'That's the odd thing, sir. Nothing, well, certainly not in the first two cases. I'm not sure about the investment company; it was discovered only yesterday and I don't know the details yet.'

'You've been very diligent, DS Eames.'

It was a put-down but Eames ignored it. 'Thank you, sir. To my mind, the whole thing points to someone looking for something.'

'Not just a case of attention-seeking, perhaps?' Heeley didn't believe that for one instant, but he wanted to remind DS Eames why he was boss. 'Who reported the attempted burglaries? Was it Miss Grigson by any chance?'

'Yes, sir, the flat and the gallery, anyway.'

'And you're absolutely certain that it wasn't her way of keeping us on the case, keeping her situation fresh in our minds? Making up things to report?'

'Well yes! I mean . . .' Eames stopped. He hadn't looked at it like that. 'I don't think that's what it is, sir.'

'Well, it wouldn't be the first time, Detective Sergeant.'

'No, sir.' Eames recognised the technique; Heeley had let him know he was very much the superior officer and not only in rank.

'Was that all, DS Eames?'

'Yes, sir.'

Heeley rubbed his hands over his face and stared out at the main road below, just beginning to come to life with the dawn traffic. His victory was a shallow one. He'd been too harsh and he didn't feel good about it. 'You on early tomorrow?'

'Yes, sir.'

'Well, make sure you leave enough food out for the cat, because we've got a murder case on our patch and it's all overtime from here on in.'

'Right, sir. What sort of case?'

'Male IC1, shot in the back of the head. He was found about five hours ago.' Heeley could hear DS Eames' mind churning through the same motions as his own and he cut the conversation before he had a chance to ask. 'See you in about an hour or so.'

'Yes, sir,' Eames said. 'D'you think . . . ?' But he was talking to an empty line; DCI Heeley had hung up.

Kit closed the file he was reading and dropped it back into its allotted place in the system. He stood, stretched his arms behind his back and walked across to the window. He hated winter mornings. It was just after five, already the early morning, but there was no sign of life in the sky, just a pitch blackness that made him feel exhausted. He turned and saw Jill staring at him.

'Nothing,' he said.

She held her hands up. 'Me neither.'

Sophie glanced up from her file. Her small, pinched face was drained of all colour and dark shadows circled her eyes. She flicked a strand of hair off her forehead and closed the file. 'Everything seems completely normal,' she said. 'Investment portfolios with standard stocks, overseas investments, gilts, lots of correspondence; dear Michael, I am writing to let you know that ICI are proposing a rights issue blah, blah, blah . . .' She sighed heavily and rubbed her hands wearily over her face. 'God only knows what this person was looking for!'

Holly stepped forward, away from the bookshelf. 'It could have been this,' she said, holding a copy of the *Concise Oxford Dictionary*. They all turned to look at her. She walked over to the desk and put it down. Then she held up two pieces of paper. 'When I picked it up off the floor, this fell out.' She unfolded a piece of paper – a photocopy of a page of advertisements from the Yellow Pages. 'It fell out of the "I" section, presumably "I" for information. The ads are all for financial services, mortgage advice, investment, that sort of thing. I couldn't figure it out, so I glanced though the rest of the dictionary and found that this had been slipped into the "A's", under accounts.' She held out another piece of paper, a bill. 'There's no mention of receipt so I presume it's unpaid. It's for Ted Welsch, Financial Search. I think it could be some sort of investigative company, for assessing credit rating, that sort of thing. These companies can apparently find out almost anything from the amount of money in your pension plan to how many cheques you write in any one month.'

'You mean Alex had done a search on someone?'

'I would think so. The bill is for financial services, but the name of the company suggests it's not mortgage advice he was after.'

Kit came across and took the bill from Holly. 'Wouldn't this sort of thing be part of Alex's investment business, finding out if someone has the money to invest?' He glanced across at Jill.

She shrugged; she really had no idea. 'Can we ring? Find out what it was all about?' she asked.

'I don't see why not, particularly if the bill hasn't been paid. You could offer to pay it, as Mrs Turner.' Kit stopped short. He felt Holly flinch and cursed himself. Glancing at his watch, he said quickly, 'Why don't we stop for a rest? It's too early to ring now and I for one am exhausted.'

Jill smiled. 'Good idea. Shall I make some coffee and toast?'

'Hmmm, thanks. Holly?'

Holly nodded. She walked back to the bookshelf and picked up her poncho. 'If a search was done, then there'll be copy of it somewhere,' she said. 'It's obviously not here. D'you think that's what whoever broke in was looking for? Perhaps they found it.'

'They might have done.' Kit glanced around the room at the remaining mess. 'If they did, then the sooner we find out what it was all about the better. We need to know what we're up against.' He ran his hands through his hair and stretched. 'Come on,' he said, 'We all need a break.' And bending to pick his jumper off the floor, he turned and walked out of the study.

At eight thirty, with breakfast over, Kit returned to the study and sat at the desk, while Jill dialled the number on the bill. Holly and Sophie stayed in the kitchen. He fiddled with a pen and waited for Jill to speak; she was through quicker than he expected.

'Hello, may I speak to Ted Welsch please? Oh, it is, right, yes thanks. My name is Turner, Mrs Jill Turner. I'm calling about a bill you sent to my husband – I'd like to arrange payment for it.' Jill glanced at Kit. 'Yes, I'll hold.' She put her hand over the mouthpiece and whispered, 'He's just looking it up.'

They were silent for several minutes, then Jill said, 'Oh, right. Yes, of course. Do you have my number? Right. I'll hear from you in about five minutes then, thanks.' She hung up. 'He has to call me back,' she said. 'He can't find the file.'

Kit nodded but said nothing. He didn't like the sound of that one bit.

In a small, poky office in Soho, above a Chinese grocery store, Ted Welsch sat at his desk and stared at the Grigson file. He was sweating. It wasn't even nine am and already his blood pressure was through the roof.

He opened the file, glanced at the first page, then closed it again, instantly. Jeeze! This whole friggin' thing scared him shitless! He'd uncovered a whole lot of stuff that wasn't good for his health; Turner hadn't turned up with the cash payment; and now this. Who the hell was Mrs Turner? He'd never bloody heard of a Mrs Turner. Was she for real?

This job had been one giant headache from start to finish; he couldn't wait to be shot of it. Loosening his tie, he ran a handkerchief under his collar and brought it out damp and slightly grimy. He'd ring the lady back. If it was Turner's number then whoever she was she could have the information and good luck to her. He leant forward and dialled the number he had memorised.

'Hello? Mrs Turner? I have the file here. Sorry? . . .' Welsch's pulse pumped visibly in the side of his neck. What the hell was she playing at? How come she didn't know what the search was all about? He hesitated for a moment, then said, 'The Grigson Gallery.' There was a brief silence before she mentioned the name of the owner, Holly Grigson, and Welsch relaxed his grip on the receiver. He listened to what she had to say next and felt a whole lot better. 'Yes, that's right, he agreed to pay in cash.' He flicked through his diary. 'I'm just checking now. How about this morning?' He was desperate to be rid of the information. 'You can? Good.' He wiped again round the rim of his collar and made a note on his pad. 'I can meet you at Victoria,' he said, not wanting to take the risk of seeing her in the office. She could be anyone – it was better to meet in a public place, safer. 'I can be there at eleven, platform four. I'll have the file with me.'

He didn't write the time or place, just her name. 'Oh, yeah, of course. I'll be reading a paper, right by the platform entrance. Yes, thanks, Mrs Turner, I'll see you later.' He hung up, walked across the room and nervously put the file back in his safe.

Jill replaced the receiver and looked at Kit. She had been shaking all the time she was on the phone.

'You were right. He does want cash and he wants to hand the file on the Grigson Gallery over to me in person. He sounded uptight, very nervy.'

Kit touched her arm. 'Well done. You handled that well.' He stood and walked across to the window. 'A financial search on Holly's gallery,' he said, looking out at the garden in the drab, December morning. 'What the hell is that all about? If Alex was involved in the gallery then why in God's name do a search on it?' He turned. 'He would have known exactly what was going on. He had access to all the books; he did most of the business himself. Unless . . .' Kit shook his head, not really believing what he was about to say. 'Unless it wasn't Alex.'

Jill's stomach flipped. 'What d'you mean?'

'I don't know entirely . . .' Kit broke off and looked across the room. Holly stood just inside the door, her face drained of all colour. She had been standing there for some time. 'Why would Alex carry out a search on the gallery?' Kit asked her.

Holly shrugged. 'I have no idea,' she lied. She was exhausted, and very frightened. 'I have no idea about anything any more,' she murmured truthfully.

Kit watched her for a few moments and the temptation to go across and take her in his arms was so strong that he had to look away.

'This is a long shot,' he said. 'Probably totally ridiculous, but . . .' He turned back again and saw that Holly had composed herself. 'Is there any chance that Alex and Sandy Turner could have been two different men?'

Jill started. She looked down at her hands and fiddled with her rings.

'I know it sounds preposterous, but think about it. Holly's had these feelings that things didn't connect, that Sophie was so different to Sandy that it's almost unbelievable. We know that Alex or Sandy lived two completely different lives, with two completely different women; he ran two completely different businesses; and now we find that Alex was investigating the art side of the business, the side that Holly's Sandy ran. It doesn't make sense, does it?' He looked across to Holly. 'Does it?'

Holly was silent. Nothing made sense. She felt as if her whole life had been turned upside down – not even the days of the week made sense. 'Are you saying that my husband, Sandy Turner, was not Alexander Turner?' She narrowed her eyes. 'Despite his passport, his driving licence, and the fact that he looked the same as Alexander Turner?' She glanced across at Jill. 'You saw the photo, didn't you? You said it was Alex, and that you'd had an almost identical photo.'

Jill nodded.

'You did say that, didn't you?' Holly insisted.

'Yes, I did.'

'So how on earth could it have been a different man, Kit?'

Kit sat on the edge of the desk and sighed heavily. 'Forged documents, maybe?' he suggested. 'They would be easy enough to get hold of.'

'And what about the photo, the fact that these two men looked the same?'

'I don't know, Holly. I haven't got any answers, I'm just trying to think of some!'

Holly leant back against the wall and closed her eyes.

'Look,' Kit went on patiently, what if we start with the premise that these two men did look alike, maybe knew each other even . . .'

'Wait!' Jill stood, her body suddenly tense. 'There is someone! Someone who looks like Alex! They were partners – remember I told you? His name was Hugo Blandford. They had been friends since university, but Hugo went off the scene a couple of years ago, and I've not heard much of him since then. What if it's him? What if . . .'

Jill stopped and followed Kit's gaze towards the door. Holly had moved aside and Sophie was in the doorway, a uniformed policeman behind her.

'Jill, it's the Sergeant from Brighton Police Station.' She stepped forward and the officer came into the room.

'Sorry to call so early, Mrs Turner, but I've got some bad news for you, I'm afraid.' He removed his cap and held it, glancing down at it briefly to get his nerve. 'A body has been found, Mrs Turner, in the London area, a murder victim.' He coughed to clear his throat. 'Would you be able to accompany me up there to to identify it?'

Jill held onto the edge of the desk, her knuckles white with tension. The Sergeant looked at the space above her head.

'I'm afraid we have reason to believe it is your husband,' he said.

27 DECEMBER 1993

Chapter Twelve

The weasel waited down in the lobby of the hotel. He was out of place in the rich cream and gold interior and he knew it. He was uncomfortable, sweating heavily as he stood by the phones, half hidden by a white marble pillar but still within view of the desk clerk who watched him suspiciously. He smoked, cupping his grubby fingers over the cigarette and flicking the hot ash furtively onto the carpet. His eyes darted nervously towards the phones. Moments later, in the booth closest to him, the line rang. He dropped the butt of his cigarette into the nearest ashtray and took the lift up to the first floor.

The door was ajar as he approached it but he tapped lightly on it before walking in. The man who paid him stood at the window. He couldn't see his face but he could smell him – he could always smell him, the same expensive smell.

'I got what you wanted,' he said, 'and a little extra.'

The man didn't turn.

'I'll leave it on the table for you then.' The weasel stepped forward and dropped the package and a brown envelope onto the coffee table. He began to sweat again.

'What else?'

The weasel shuffled from foot to foot. He didn't work like this usually; he liked at least to know who the fuck he was dealing with. He waited a few moments, but the man kept his back to him, so he went on: 'Grigson made several calls at the gallery; she noted 'em down; and the Turner woman has contacted some sort of financial services guy, someone we've not heard of before.'

'Get him out of the way,' came the reply. 'I don't care how, just do it.'

The weasel felt a bead of sweat trickle down the side of his face and he wiped it on the sleeve of his jacket. The man flicked the blind, peering out at the street below. He said nothing further and the weasel edged back towards the door. The meeting was over.

'I'll be in touch then,' he said. There was no answer. 'I'll let you know.' But he was wasting his breath. He realised it and shuffled backwards out of the door. Once in the corridor, he leant against the wall and closed his eyes. Christ, that bastard got to him! He should never have taken the job; it was really beginning to put the shits up him. Straightening, he took out a dirty handkerchief, wiped his face and neck, then fumbled in his pockets for his cigarettes. He lit up, inhaled deeply and felt better. Smoking, but still uneasy, he made his way back to the lifts to get out of there as fast as he damn well could.

Inside the suite, the man turned and took the envelope off the table. He slipped the contents out, a set of black-and-white photographs, and glanced at the top one, a close-up of a woman's face. He realised with a jolt that she was in mid-orgasm and a familiar excitement flared as he shuffled through the rest. They were all of the same thing, a man and a woman having sex in a phone box, but they were clever, expertly shot, and as he ran his fingers across the images, his breathing quickened.

'You OK?'

He jerked round suddenly and saw the girl standing in the doorway to the bedroom. She was naked. 'I heard the bloke go and you didn't come back so . . .' Her voice trailed off as she looked at his face. 'Sorry, I . . .'

'Come here.'

She clenched her fist behind her back and dug her nails into the palm of her hand, but she moved forward, her fear carefully concealed. As she got to within inches of him, she held her breath, but he reached forward gently to touch her hair and she relaxed slightly. Suddenly he grabbed the back of her neck and dug his fingers viciously into the flesh. He forced her down hard onto her knees and she cried out.

'Do it!' he spat, fumbling with his trousers. He still held the photograph in his hand and she moved her eyes to it, her head locked rigid in his grip. 'Do it like she does!'

The girl opened her mouth and shut her mind. As long as he didn't hurt her too badly she could handle it. The money was good, but it was only because of that fact that she could handle any of it at all.

It was five minutes past eleven and Ted Welsch stood on platform four at Victoria Station with a copy of *The Times* held up over the lower part of his face, his briefcase gripped tightly in his right hand. His palms were sweating and he watched the crowd anxiously, checking his watch every fifteen seconds or so. Where the hell was she? He'd said eleven, for Christ's sake! He turned briefly to look over his shoulder at the platform and saw a train approaching. Shit, that was all he needed! The train was packed and some idiots had already started to jump down onto the platform despite the fact that it was still moving. He shuffled away from the exit and lowered the paper. A whistle blew and the train ground to a halt, near to where he was standing. Twenty seconds later, hundreds of people began to alight, swarming all over the platform like flies.

'Hey! Watch it, will you?' he called out as a man pushed past him, sending him staggering to one side. 'Jesus!' It took him several seconds to regain his balance. Moments later he felt a shove from behind – a definite hand in the centre of his back – and he stumbled forward, knocking into the stream of people filing through the exit.

'Whoa!'

'Watch it, mate!'

He put his hand out to stop his fall and dropped his case. There was a scuffle, he lost his balance completely and fell into the crowd.

'Oh shit! Sorry . . . I . . .'

A football supporter helped to right him. 'You all right, mate?'

Welsch spun round and searched the ground for his case, his heart thudding in his chest. 'Oh Christ . . .' There was no sign of it, just his newspaper, scattered all over the platform and trampled on. His eyes darted across the faces around him – day trippers, shoppers – but he saw nothing. He ran the length of the train, pushing through the crowd. Nothing.

Turning back towards the exit, he glanced up at the announcement board. It was then that he saw it. The glint of a gun on the roof of the building behind the platform. The arm moved; the gun took aim. He froze.

In the midst of the moving crowd he stood perfectly still and felt the hard throb of his pulse. Bodies jostled past him, and he was shunted forward a few inches. For a moment he closed his eyes. Then a woman knocked into him.

'Oh, I'm so sorry,' she said, touching his arm. He opened his eyes and looked at her. She was blind.

'Not at all,' he said quickly. 'Please, it was my fault. Would you like a hand off the platform?'

'Oh, how kind! I've got my daughter meeting me outside but I feel a little disorientated; it's the crowd.' She smiled. 'You sound in a hurry, you don't mind?'

Welsch took her arm. He glanced up at the roof top but it was clear. Whoever it was had gone.

'No, I don't mind at all. It's my pleasure.' He led her towards the exit.

Five minutes later, he was in a taxi and heading back to his office in Soho. He had a bundle of cash there that the tax man didn't know about and he was going to pick it up and scarper. He was really in trouble this time. He didn't have the nerve for this sort of thing. He was an ordinary bloke, for Christ's sake, doing an ordinary job. All right, he did the odd illegal scam to get the information he wanted, but who didn't nowadays? Jeeze! He took out his handkerchief and wiped his face. He was sweating, worse than he had ever sweated in his life before.

God help Turner, he thought, if he's still alive. And huddling down in the seat, below the window, he thanked God for his small but timely piece of intervention.

Holly sat with Jill in the back of the police car and held onto the grip above the door as it swung into the concrete car park at the back of the morgue. She was tense and exhausted, and a low, sick feeling churned in the pit of her stomach. The car stopped and DS Robert Eames turned to look over his shoulder.

'Are you both all right?'

Holly nodded and Jill said, 'Yes, thank you,' her voice high and tight.

'Right, let's go.' He climbed out and opened the door for Jill, while the Sergeant who'd been driving did the same for Holly. All four headed for the entrance and Holly felt an overwhelming urge to turn and flee. She glanced at an approaching bus on the main road and had to pinch the flesh on her wrist to stop herself from darting out and running as fast as she could away from what lay ahead.

DS Eames pulled open the glass door and stood there waiting for them all to go in. He touched Holly's arm to reassure her and Holly nodded. Inside, the reception area was much the same as in any other government building, neat and tidy and grey, with an arrangement of flaccid silk flowers on the counter.

A young man took their names and came around the desk to show them to a small side waiting room. 'They are just preparing the body now, it won't be a long wait,' he told them. Holly shuddered.

The waiting room had a couple of magazines in, two low office armchairs and a side table. It looked as if the same flaccid flowers had moved with them. Jill sat down but Holly stood by the door as if ready to make a quick escape. She watched Jill flick through an ancient copy of *Good Housekeeping* and wondered if anyone ever noted down recipes to use for the wake. This thought made her smile.

'I'd better explain the procedure before the coroner arrives,' DS Eames said. 'It's the quickest, and I hope the least upsetting, way to do this.' He saw Jill's hands tremble and took a deep breath. God, this was a gruesome part of his job. 'What will happen is that you will be taken to a viewing room and will view the deceased from behind a screen. He will be in a chapel of rest, in a shroud.' He felt uncomfortable; he'd never been able to stomach this as well as his colleagues. 'Unfortunately, the body is already four days old and we will have to use photographs of certain distinguishing marks – the scar on the left side of the neck, for example. You can, of course, go in and see the body, if you so wish . . .' He broke off and glanced at the door as a middle-aged, grey-suited man came in. He looked more like a banker than a coroner.

'Good morning. I'm the district coroner, Mike Petersham,' he said. He neither smiled nor frowned, his face oddly expressionless. 'If you're ready, I can show you through to the viewing room.'

Holly moved away from the wall. She had prepared herself for this, telling herself all the way up here that it wasn't going to be Sandy. She had convinced herself that Kit was right: there were two men; she had been married to someone else. But now she started to shake. She waited until the room had emptied and tagged on the end of the little group, clasping her hands tightly together to stop them trembling. She was the last to go into the viewing room, deliberately, but she felt herself being shuffled forward to stand by Jill in front of the screen.

'The body of the deceased is approximately four days old,' the coroner said. 'And is as a result, reasonably decomposed. It has been in a shallow grave and the low temperatures have helped to keep it from rapid deterioration, but I must warn you not to expect the face of the one you remember and love.' He pressed a button and the curtains opened electrically. Holly thought she would remember the sickening whir of it for the rest of her life. She closed her eyes for a moment and when she opened them she saw Sandy, not clearly, not the way she had last seen him, obviously, but it was definitely him. She nodded and put her hand up to her mouth, biting the knuckles.

'Can you identify this body?' DS Eames asked.

Jill nodded. She was completely still, an expression of such pain and grief on her face that Holly momentarily forgot her own nausea and shock. She put her arm out in the dark cramped space and felt for Jill's hand, holding it tight. Jill's fingers were like ice.

'Holly?' DS Eames looked away from the body.

Holly nodded. 'Yes, as far as I can tell.'

Kit had been wrong. There weren't two men; there had been just one – one miserable, dishonest bastard. Christ, what a god-awful mess! She stared at the body, sickened by it.

'That's Sandy Turner,' she said. And in the deathly, stifling silence, Jill began to sob.

Chapter Thirteen

The incident room was makeshift. It was an old locker room somewhere off one of the rambling corridors of the Victorian station. All the junk had been cleared, a row of ancient tin lockers had been shoved to one side and the space was now filled with flip charts, banks of photographs on portable screens, action boards, telephones, desks and all the other paraphernalia of a murder investigation.

DCI Heeley sat at the front, on the edge of the desk, and waited for his team to assemble. He had ten officers working on overtime, putting in near on sixteen hours a day, and so far they had got nowhere. He was strung out, and the boss wanted a result.

He stood and took his hands out of his pockets. 'Right. Everyone here?' He scanned the room for faces as the men and women settled. 'Good. Let's make a start.' Over by one of the action boards DS Eames shifted on his feet.

'Good morning, ladies and gents, thanks for all cutting into your rest time to be here. I know it's early and I know you're all tired. It's been a long week but sadly it's not been a very productive one. We've been working on this now for over six days, there's a lot of money going into it, and to be bloody frank, we're getting nowhere!' There was a murmur and he held up his hands. 'Yes, I know, it's Christmas, and that's made it doubly difficult to get answers, but we do need a result.' Heeley moved away from the desk. 'So, let's go over exactly what we've got, just to refresh your memories.' He walked across to the photographs and wheeled the screen round so that everyone had a clear view.

'Alex Turner, male IC1, forty-five, shot at point-blank range through the back of the head sometime on the fifteenth of this month. Right, from the position of death – kneeling, hands and ankles bound – it looks pretty well like a nice, clean, professional job, but the pathologist's report and my gut feeling say different.'

Heeley took the piece of paper that DS Eames handed to him. 'OK, according to the lab, the bullet in the back of the head was the second one; the first went in through the shoulder, here . . .' He pointed to a photograph. '. . . punctured the right lung and came out the other side, here. It was found embedded in an oak tree near to where the body was buried in Walsam Copse – here and here.' Heeley pointed to the photos of the crime scene then moved up to the shots above.

'There's more. This discolouration here is from a massive blow to the back of the neck – not fatal, but enough to knock the victim unconscious. Not at all like cold-blooded murder, more like a bit of a bodge job.' He pointed to another photo. 'My guess is that our murderer has gone to a great deal of trouble to set this up. He more than likely knows the lie of a professional job – certainly the position of death is a classic trademark of one, and the weapon is almost definitely from an armourer, and untraceable. But our man slipped up. First, he lost his nerve . . .' Heeley broke off at this point and glanced across at DS Eames. 'Or, to be politically correct, *her* nerve. Our man could very well be a woman.' He smiled briefly.

'Whichever, as a result he or she knocked the victim unconscious to make the whole thing less painful, then shot him. Also, there's the question of the spent bullet. A professional never misses, that's what you pay him for. This person did and we've got the bullet down in ballistics to prove it. So . . .' DCI Heeley moved back to the desk and perched on the edge of it, facing his officers. 'Who wanted Alex Turner out of the way and who would be able to reconstruct a professional hit with such detail?' He glanced a second time at DS Eames. 'Can we just run through the action board and check the leads, Bob?' Heeley couldn't say he liked Eames but the man was tenacious and he got results. He reminded Heeley of a stubborn terrier.

Robert Eames nodded and picked up a marker pen. No-one shortened his name, except Heeley, but Heeley had been reasonably civilised the past week, so he let it go. It still irritated the hell out of him, though. 'Business leads,' he began. 'Alex Turner Investments and the Grigson Gallery.' He glanced at the name on the board under that heading. 'DC Dobson, what have you got?'

Three hours on, the incident room was thick with smoke. The meeting was about to wrap up and DCI Heeley stood at the front, ready to finalise the action. He was pleased. It had been a bugger of a morning, but he had something to show for it.

'Right, everyone clear on what they've got to do?' There was a murmur of assent. 'Let's run through it one more time, shall we?' The shuffling of chairs and papers stopped and DCI Heeley felt the strain in the room. 'Yeah, I know, it's been a long morning and it's only . . .' He glanced at his watch. '. . . ten o'clock.' He shrugged apologetically and the tension eased. 'OK, DC Dobson and team: up to the City. Go back to the Stock Exchange, the futures market, the commodities market, bars, pubs and ask around again. I want any gossip, hearsay, or scandal on Alex Turner or this one-time partner of his, Hugo Blandford. I want any whiff of a rumour that might give us something to go on.' Heeley glanced across at the action board. 'Anything relevant, DS Eames will follow on. You don't need to re-interview anyone we've already talked to; DS Eames will be doing that. DC Newman: door-to-door enquiries in Notting Hill. Anything on Holly Grigson, the Grigson Gallery or Sandy Turner, and report to DS Henson on that. DS Henson: Sotheby's, Christie's, any of bigger galleries in Cork Street or Albemarle Street. See how well known the Grigson Gallery was, what they specialised in, their reputation, et cetera. You might want to see if they've shown any artists at some of the bigger exhibitions this year. There must be a circuit that these galleries do to get their artists into the limelight; look it up.

'DS Eames, talk to your contact in the fraud office, but keep it low key at the moment. Also, get on to the Stock Exchange, the futures market and commodities market and find out if they keep any record of what business their members do and apply for a court order, or at least get the wheels in motion. We might want to look at the bank accounts for both businesses in the very near future.'

DCI Heeley ran his tongue over his lips and reached for his coffee. It was stone-cold, but he drank it anyway; he'd done too much talking and his mouth was as dry as hell. 'Right, that's it. Remember, everybody, that this is beginning to look like more than a murder investigation. It could be drugs, it could be fraud, it could be theft on a major scale. Whatever Alex Turner was into, someone wanted him out of the way and it looks like that someone is looking for something he left behind. Tread carefully. Right, off you go and thanks for your time.'

He turned and collected his papers together as the quiet in the room was broken by scraping chairs and the hubbub of conversation.

'Sir?'

He glanced up at DS Eames. 'It went well, Bob. Thanks for your input.'

DS Eames smiled. Heeley was not the sort of man to admit he'd ever been in the wrong but he'd gone a fair way to making up for his earlier animosity. 'Sir, I was wondering if it would be any good to bring Holly Grigson in again for questioning.'

Heeley raised an eyebrow.

'I've been going over the tapes of her interview,' Eames went on, 'just after Turner's body was found, and there's an edge there. She's not telling the truth, I'm convinced of it.'

Heeley picked up his file and tucked it under his arm. 'D'you think she's involved in the murder, or in whatever else is going on here?'

'I don't know, I haven't worked it out yet.'

Heeley thought for a moment. A terrier was a good description for DS Eames. 'I think we need to get some idea of what's been going on before we haul her in again for questioning. I don't want to panic her into clamping up. Let's leave her, find out a bit more and, if we've got something to go on, then maybe put her under surveillance.'

'Surveillance?' DS Eames was surprised; Heeley was talking big sums of money if he was contemplating surveillance.

'Yeah, it's a possibility.' Heeley nodded to another officer to let him know he'd be free to talk in a moment. 'Let's wait and see what we've got, shall we?'

DS Eames nodded. He was about to ask Heeley something more when his superior smiled and turned to move off. The conversation was over. Whatever ideas Heeley had up his sleeve, he wasn't about to share them with him.

Kit sat at the desk in his father's study with a pad of paper in front of him, idly scribbling with a pen, making patterns, writing the odd word. He had some work to do – his office in New York had faxed it through – but he couldn't get his head together sufficiently to tackle it. He listened to the sounds of the house, on the last day of the Christmas holiday: his mother shouting to his father to bring more wine up from the cellar for lunch and his father ignoring her, with the stereo on full blast, his Christmas CD blaring out Mozart.

Kit dropped his pen and rested his chin in his hands, staring at the paper. He'd written Holly's name and the words, break-in, mugging and suspicious circumstances. He couldn't stop thinking about Holly and the whole damn mess. She'd taken off, of course, in typical Holly style, just after identifying the body. She had upped and gone to some rented cottage in deepest Cornwall with no explanation or contact number, just a postcard from the village she was staying in. And Kit worried. He worried all over Christmas that she was alone, he worried when it snowed and he worried that whoever had broken into the gallery might still be after something that Holly had. Most of all he worried that despite nearly two years in New York, several lengthy phone calls to his so-called steady girlfriend, a good job, an entire life without Holly, one moment of intense passion had shattered everything. He was back to square one, wanting her in the same impossible way he always had, from the moment he first set eyes on her, eating an ice cream in the hot afternoon sun and licking her fingers as it melted all over her hands.

He walked across to the window and looked out across the lawn to the bleak Northumberland landscape beyond. The predomiant colours were grey and dull, dark green, with outcrops of rock on the barren, snow-scattered hills. It was a desolate scene, wild and forlorn, but it exhilarated him, and somehow put life into perspective. He turned round and walked back to the desk. Picking up the phone, he flicked through his diary for the number he wanted and then pressed the buttons. Moments later, the line rang.

'Hello?'

'Hello, Jill, it's Kit Thomas.'

Jill had been on her way from the sitting room to the kitchen to fetch a drink for herself and Harry when the phone rang in the hall. She was shocked when she heard Kit's voice on the other end of the line said.

'What can I do for you, Kit?' There was no warmth in her voice. She didn't want any more involvement in Alex's murder: it was in police hands now, and that was how it should be left.

'I wondered if you'd heard from Holly,' he said.

'Holly?' Jill didn't bother to conceal her surprise. Why Holly Grigson should be in touch she had no idea. After walking out of the morgue, they'd said goodbye to each other, and to be frank, she'd been relieved. 'No, I've not heard from Holly. It's been a very quiet Christmas and we've needed the time to recover, to try to restore some normality to our lives.' She hadn't meant it to sound as cold as it had but she was unable to keep the edge out of her voice. She didn't want any more reminders of the pain and grief.

'I see.' Kit understood but he had to go on, he couldn't stop himself. 'Jill, I wondered if I might come down and see you. I'm worried. I can't get this thing out of my mind and I need to talk.'

'Where's Holly? Shouldn't you talk to her?'

'All I know is that she's in Cornwall, in a village called Wynnerton, but I've no idea where she's staying, or if she's all right even.'

Jill said nothing; she didn't want to be drawn in.

'Jill, please, I really think we need to talk this through. I'm sure that something very peculiar is going on.'

Through the open door, Jill could see Harry in the sitting room, munching on chocolates, watching the television. It was the first time he had been anything like his old self for days. She felt sympathy for Kit and for Holly and she wanted to say yes, but she wouldn't let herself do so. Christmas had been awful, lonely and painful, watching Alex's children try to come to terms with their grief and confusion, let alone coping with her own. She couldn't face any more; she had to think about her son. What good would it do her anyway, to get involved? If there was anything to be found, the police would find it, so why rake up all the pain and confusion? She didn't need it; Sophie and Harry didn't need it.

'Jill?'

Jill turned as the front door opened and Sophie came in from her walk. She glanced briefly at her stepdaughter and said, 'No, I'm sorry. I need time to get over this; we all need time.' And without another word, she hung up.

Sophie took her coat off and bent to untie her boots. 'Who was that?'

Jill watched her for a moment. She was wearing jeans and a shirt which was open at the neck, and her collarbone poked painfully through the taut skin. She had lost so much weight it was beginning to worry Jill. 'It was Kit Thomas,' she answered.

Sophie immediately straightened. 'What did he want?'

Jill hesitated. Sophie had been so withdrawn, so low and depressed, that she was loath to say anything at all about the call. She seemed to have had the spark knocked out of her; she didn't need any more blows.

'He, er . . .'

Sophie waited, her face brighter than it had been for days. She didn't want her father's murder brushed under the carpet, just forgotten. As far as she was concerned, as long as the whole question of what had happened was alive, then he was alive.

'He wanted to come down and talk to me,' Jill said finally. 'He's not happy about what's happened. He wants to . . .'

'When's he coming?' Sophie interrupted and Jill saw a flicker of hope in her eyes. It made her wince.

'He's not,' she answered. 'I told him I didn't want to get involved.' But the moment she said it, she regretted it. The hope in Sophie's eyes died and her expression closed. She kicked her boots off, not looking at Jill, and bent to pick them up. Without a word, she walked past Jill and up the stairs in her socks.

'Sophie?'

She turned halfway up and Jill saw such desolation in her face that it wrenched her. She about to try and explain, to say something that might comfort, but she realised there was no point. There was a moment's silence, then Sophie shrugged and carried on up to her room.

Slumping back against the wall, Jill put her hands up to her face. Was she really thinking about Harry, about both Alex's children? Or was it herself she was trying to protect? She didn't know, and as she closed her eyes, she saw Sophie's face, the dejection and the kind of hurt that cut deep to the core. Opening her eyes again, she wiped her sweating palms on her trousers and hunted in the drawer in the hall table for her address book. She found the yellow Post-it she had stuck on the front with Kit's home number on it and dialled.

'Kit, it's Jill,' she said. 'I'm sorry, I was being selfish. Please come, any time you want.' She glanced at her reflection in the mirror above the table and thought how much she had aged in two weeks. 'You're right. We need to sort this out. We need to find Holly.'

Kit replaced the receiver and closed the notepad he had been scribbling on, feeling relieved, excited, nervous. He went through to the kitchen of the big, draughty old Northumberland farm-house and found his mother counting a stack of plates on the kitchen table.

'Mum, I've got something to tell you,' he said, standing with his hands in his pockets and his head down, like a small boy. 'I'm sorry, but I'm . . .'

'You're going to have to leave today,' Alison Thomas finished for him, 'despite the fact that your two sisters, your brother and his wife and family are trekking all the way up here to see you and that I've got two joints of lamb for lunch, enough for twelve people.' She looked up. She wasn't smiling but Kit knew she wasn't cross. 'Eleven plates, then,' she said, taking one off the pile.

'You don't mind?'

She raised an eyebrow. 'No, of course I don't mind. Your father and I were only saying this morning that we were sick of you.' She did smile this time and Kit smiled back.

'You weren't?'

'Oh yes, and the fact that you're a terrible drain on resources. You eat too much, drink too much wine; we get through double the quantity of loo paper . . .' They both started to laugh. Kit was the oldest and possibly the most precious of Alison's children, although she would never have admitted it. 'And you take an awful lot of showers. It must be a habit you picked up in America. I've a good mind to charge you meterage for the water.'

Still laughing, Kit crossed and embraced her. Alison's other children never hugged her spontaneously and she blushed, unused to it.

'I suppose it has something to do with Holly Grigson,' she said.

Kit stood back. 'How did you . . . ?'

'Your father and I may look stupid, Kit, but I can assure you that we're not.' She did frown now. She worried about his involvement with Holly. 'You'd have to be on planet Mars not to notice your preoccupation with her this Christmas.'

Kit shrugged and Alison touched him gently on the arm. She liked Holly – she had spirit, she was feisty and independent – but by God she was in a mess. Kit didn't need that; he'd only just sorted himself out from the last tangle.

'You sure you know what you're doing?' Alison picked up the spare plate and carried it over to the cupboard. She wanted the question to appear more casual than it was.

'No, I'm not sure about anything where Holly is concerned.'

Alison stopped and looked back at him, surprised by his honesty. 'Then why go?'

'Because I have to.' He knew it didn't make much sense. 'She won't ever ask for help and if I'm not there to give it when she needs it then I've missed my chance.'

Alison stood by the cupboard with a dinner plate in her hands and felt for a moment almost forty years younger. It could have been her husband speaking. Kit was so like his father that it took her breath away.

'You understand, don't you?'

She nodded. It had taken Kit's father four years to convince her to marry him, even though she loved him, and once she'd done it she had known he was right; there could never have been anyone else. 'I understand all right.' She smiled. 'Go on then, push off.' She bent down to put the extra plate away.

Kit smiled at her eccentricity and silently left the room.

It was a long drive but the roads were clear. Most people were leaving the great Christmas trek home until that night or even the following morning. Kit stopped once, for petrol, then continued on his way with a can of drink and a chocolate bar for lunch. He was eager to get there. Once he'd made up his mind, even if it was on the spur of the moment, he wanted to get on with things. He was a man of action and hated wasting time.

Pulling off the motorway onto the A roads was a relief. It was mid-afternoon, and the light was rapidly fading. Kit followed the route he had planned and arrived at Jill's without losing his way, something that wouldn't have been possible with Holly in the car.

Jill was waiting for him.

She came out and stood in the porch to greet him as he slowed and stopped in front of the house. He looked at her for a moment before climbing out – immaculately dressed and made up, with a set smile on her face – and suddenly he felt terribly sad. For the first time he could see quite clearly that the image held her together and he understood it. Slamming the car door shut behind him, he walked across to her and kissed her cheek, taking her hand in his.

'Thanks,' he said. 'I'm sure this is the right thing. I'm sure it'll help if we have some answers.'

Jill nodded. She wasn't convinced but she attempted a smile anyway. 'Sophie's inside waiting for you,' she said. They turned and went into the house together.

*   *   *

An hour later, Sophie looked across at Kit in the warm, lamplit sitting room and hugged her arms tight around her knees to stop herself from physically shaking. Her cheeks burnt with two high spots of colour as the anxious excitement coursed through her body. She waited for Jill to answer.

'Think about it,' Kit said again. 'Just think about what I'm saying, Jill.' He leant forward on the sofa. 'Let's say that your husband Alex was in trouble. He knew something was going on, something illegal, sinister even; he knew perhaps that another man was impersonating him at the Grigson Gallery. He tried to find out what was happening and he was found out. A suicide was set up to cover the tracks of his murder. This other man, Holly's husband, disappeared.' Kit found himself more and more convinced of it as he talked it through. 'I just can't believe it's the same man,' he insisted. 'I just can't . . .'

'But I saw him!' Jill suddenly cried. 'Holly saw him! We both identified the same man.' She was upset. They had been going round and round in circles for the past half an hour, getting nowhere.

'You saw what you thought was him,' Kit said, as gently as he could.

'No!' Jill said. 'We saw Alexander Turner! They showed us photographs of his scar, the same scar we had both mentioned on the missing persons form. It was him, Kit! I know it was him.' She stood up and paced the floor 'I don't know what else to say to convince you,' she said desperately. 'Look at Harry, our son. He has the same thing as his father – a mole on his neck where his collar is. He'll have to have it removed, just like Alex did, in the next year or so; same age, same problem!' She turned and stared at Kit. 'Holly confirmed that Sandy had a scar there for exactly the same reason. It was definitely Alex, I know it was!'

'Sophie? What do you think?' Kit asked. But Sophie was silent. She didn't know what to say. Kit might well be right – her instinct told her he was – and yet Jill had all the evidence.

When she didn't answer, Kit went on. 'I hear what you're saying, Jill. But why was Alex murdered? It has something to do with the gallery, I'm sure it has, or with his business. Why was the office broken into, and why was there a break-in here? Then there's this man, Ted Welsch. You never picked up the file, we never heard from him, but we do know that Alex was investigating the Grigson Gallery. Why would he do that if he ran the place? I'm absolutely sure that he knew something dangerous about someone. What exactly did this Welsch man have? What was the Grigson file?'

'Stop it!' Jill suddenly shouted. 'All these questions, I can't stand it!' She put her hands up to her face.

Kit hung his head. 'I'm sorry,' he murmured.

'Yes, I'm sorry too!' Jill cried. 'I can't go on like this. All these questions, questions, questions and no bloody answers! I haven't got any, nor have you. Why do we have to keep torturing ourselves like this?'

Sophie spoke up. 'But Jill, we have to . . .'

'No!' Jill interrupted. 'We don't have to do anything. Nothing like this has ever happened to me before, and I don't know how to cope with it. I haven't got the intelligence, and I haven't got the nerve!'

'But shouldn't we give it a chance?' Sophie pleaded. 'Please, Jill, just listen to Kit, try to see his point of . . .'

'No.' Jill shook her head. She was close to tears, suddenly exhausted by the whole thing. 'I can't do this,' she said quietly. 'I'm sorry, Kit, but I just can't.' She dropped her hands lifelessly down by her side and her whole body seemed to slump. 'Please go now, Kit. Leave us alone.' Without looking at either Sophie or Kit, she walked silently out of the room and along the hall to Alex's study, closing the door behind her.

The study had been tidied – not by Jill, she couldn't face it, but by her cleaning lady. She sat at Alex's desk and stared around her at the books, the pictures, the faded old rag rug Sophie had made in needlework at school. She was dimly aware of a murmur of voices in the hall, then the sound of Kit's car leaving as she fingered the things in front of her: the blotter; the pen holder made out of an old biscuit tin, gruesomely painted by Harry; a stone paperweight, just an ordinary clump of rock picked up on the beach one year from a deserted spot where she and Alex had made love. The whole room was suffused with a feeling of her dead husband but it was a good feeling, one of warmth and familiarity. She held the rock for a moment, remembering, thinking that in a hundred other lifetimes she couldn't have been happier than she had been, then she laid her head down on the desk and closed her eyes.

Perhaps Kit was right. Perhaps Alex did deserve the right to questions, however painful. Could he really have married Holly, deceived Jill like that, deceived both of them, his family, the children he loved so much? Jill stood up and walked across to the bookshelves, comforted by the sight of the books that Alex had loved. Victorian classics steeped in morality – George Eliot, Trollope – Aesop, Plato, but nothing on art. No, there was one: Kenneth Clark's *Civilisation*.

Moving on, she saw the huge *Concise Oxford Dictionary* and took it down from the shelf. She flicked through the pages, remembering Holly and what she'd found there. Jill stopped, the book open in her hands and thought hard. If Alex had known something then he would have had a file on it, notes of some kind; he had notes on virtually everything he had ever come across. And if a file did exist and it wasn't here in the study, then it had to be somewhere else. Her mind went through certain possibilities, but she dismissed them almost as soon as she had thought of them. Then she went back to the dictionary as Holly had done and thought of a word: secret. She went to S and looked it up; there was nothing. Disappointed, she tried hidden, then treasure, but again found nothing. She closed the book and went to put it back. Cache! she suddenly thought, grabbing the book again; hidden treasure! She turned to the C's, ran her finger hurriedly down the page, flipped it over and found the word. Her heart stopped for a moment. There it was! Cache, with a tiny pencilled note in the right-hand column alongside it that said: See A. Jill's hands began to shake. She flicked back to A and began to scan the pages. Her finger ran down the words: Abacus, aesthete, answer, Arabic, atone. She turned the page. Attic! She stood perfectly still, the dictionary in her hands, staring down at the word and the tiny pencilled asterisk by the side of it. Then she snapped it shut and ran out of the study.

'Sophie!' she hollered. She ran up the stairs, still carrying the book. 'Sophie! Come quickly!'

Both Sophie and Harry appeared at the top of the stairs.

'What?' Sophie looked frightened. 'What's the matter?'

'This!' Jill cried, thrusting the book towards her. 'Look! Under A, attic.'

Sophie opened the dictionary and fumbled through the pages.

'There's a reference to attic by cache, hidden treasure. If there is a file, if there's anything that Alex wanted us to know, he hid it, up there!' Jill pointed to the ceiling. 'In the attic.'

Sophie's face flushed as she found the reference. She looked up and her eyes were bright with excitement. Jill had already moved across to the airing cupboard where the rod for the loft hatch was kept.

'Harry, can you go down and make some tea for us, darling?' she called over her shoulder. She turned. 'Yes, I know it's a bore, but we'll only be up there for a few minutes.' She pulled a face. 'Please?'

Harry shrugged his shoulders and started for the stairs.

'Here!' Jill announced, finding the rod and carrying it over to the loft hatch in the middle of the landing. She hooked it into the handle and pushed up, releasing the catch, thus lowering the hatch with its concealed ladder. She reached up, pulled the ladder down to ground level and put her foot on the first rung.

'You coming up?' she asked Sophie.

Sophie nodded. Jill clambered up the steep steps, fumbled in the dark and found the light switch. She climbed into the loft space and looked around her. Sophie followed a few seconds after.

'Heavens! Where do we start?' Jill said.

Sophie stared at the boxes, old suitcases and general household rubbish. Then she spied a small leather suitcase marked with Alex's father's initials. 'Here,' she answered, trusting her instinct. She walked across to it, knelt down and looked at the lock. 'It's open, I think.' She tried it and it flipped up. Turning, she looked back at Jill. 'Come on, have a look.'

Jill walked over, her pulse racing, and feeling slightly sick. She knelt beside her stepdaughter and waited as Sophie lifted the top of the case. Inside was a single file, full of handwritten notes. The Grigson Gallery, it said on the front, in Alex's handwriting, and Jill felt her eyes well up.

'You were wrong,' Sophie said, taking the file out and opening it.

'I was?' Jill had turned her face away and hurriedly wiped her tears on the back of her hand. She sniffed. 'What about?'

Sophie handed her the file. 'You do have the intelligence,' she answered, 'and incredible nerve.' Then she smiled. 'I think you have just found the first answer.'

It was a long drive to Cornwall. By the time that Kit pulled off the motorway at the sign for Torverton, his eyes were bloodshot and he had backache. Although he had only been in the car for three hours, it felt more like days. He pulled into a lay-by and cut the engine of his hire car, then switched on the central light and reached for his map. He had marked the route in fluorescent marker pen and glanced at it again now, to make sure of the next thirty miles. He made a mental note of the road numbers and the villages he would go through, then he started the engine. It was getting late and he didn't want to waste time. He knew the name of the small fishing village Holly had escaped to but that was all; once there he'd have to nose around until he found a clue as to where she might be staying.

The day had passed into evening by the time he reached the lane that led to the sea. The signpost was one of the old wooden ones, black and white, virtually impossible to see clearly, and Kit nearly turned back twice, sure he must have got it wrong. He drove slowly, up over the hill, the road banked high on either side with shorn hedgerows, the sky overcast and dark grey with no hint of a moon. But at the top of the incline he suddenly saw the village, a small cluster of lights, white and orange set out against the shoreline, then the sea, a dense, inky blue, only just darker than the sky. He stopped for a moment and smiled. If he'd had to picture the kind of place that Holly would escape to, he would have imagined somewhere like this, and for the first time since he'd set foot back in the UK he felt a glimmer of hope. Perhaps things weren't as unpredictable as he'd imagined.

Driving on, he came down into the main street, with its collection of whitewashed fishing cottages, crooked, uneven cob set against the straight stone of later and wealthier houses. He passed the post office and general store, the greengrocer's and a florist, and at the end of the street, facing the small harbour, he found the pub. This was a double-fronted building, white and unadorned, a single coach lamp revealing its sign swaying in the night wind. He drew into one of the three parking spaces and climbed out. The whole place smelt salty and damp, the wind had the faint taste of sea water and the air was heavy with winter. Kit stretched and took several deep breaths before reaching into the dashboard for his wallet and then heading into the pub.

The warm, conversation-filled room fell silent as he appeared in the doorway. 'Good evening.' He strode across to the bar, the heels of his shoes tapping lightly on the stone floor. 'A pint of . . .' He glanced up at the board. 'Quinton's ale, please.' The patter of conversation started up again.

'A good choice, sir,' the barman said, relieved that Kit hadn't ordered a pint of Heineken. 'You holidaying round here?'

'No, I'm not actually,' Kit answered, digging in his pocket for some change. 'I've driven down from London to see a friend who's renting a cottage here.'

'Really?' the barman stared at him, as if looking for something in his face

Kit took a sip of the frothing, murky liquid and placed his glass on the bar. 'Hmmm. Good ale this.' He wiped his mouth on his handkerchief. 'She's called Holly Grigson. You don't know her, do you?'

The barman ignored the question and pulled himself half a pint of the same ale. 'She a good friend of yours?'

Kit looked him in the eye. 'A very good friend.'

'I see.' The barman drained the glass in one. 'You'll know where to find her then,' he said.

'Well actually, no, I don't.' Kit drank again. 'To be honest with you she ran out on me before Christmas and all I got was a postcard – "Greetings from Wynnerton".' He put his glass down. 'I was pretty upset.'

'I see.' The barman pulled himself another half glass of beer.

'You don't know where she's staying, do you?' Kit asked, digging in his pocket again. 'Here, let me get that.'

'Very kind,' the barman said. He drank most of it, then looked Kit over a second time, as if making his mind up about something. Kit waited and finally the man said, 'As a matter of fact, I do. It's a small village, this. There's not much I don't know.'

'I'm sure.'

'Yes, well, she's renting the beach cottage off my sister-in-law.

It's down along the harbour and turn right. Last house on the lane. Mind you,' he said, leaning forward conspiratorially, 'you's the second one that's been asking today. At lunchtime a bloke came in with the same question.'

'Really?' Kit felt a moment of alarm. 'Did he say who he was?'

'No, not local, though. London accent. Drank vodka and Coke.' The barman's lip curled disdainfully. He finished his drink, then said, 'You need somewhere to stay?'

'I might,' Kit said. Who the hell knew Holly was here? 'This bloke at lunchtime, d'you remember what he looked like?'

The barman smiled. 'A rival?'

Kit shrugged. 'Sort of.' He saw the barman's hand go for the ale pump again. 'I'll get that,' he said. 'Have a pint this time.'

'Thanks, don't mind if I do.' The drink was poured and sipped, then the barman said, 'Short, dark-haired and a bit shifty.' He glanced around the bar. 'Pasty-looking, a townee.'

Kit nodded and finished his drink. He had begun to worry about Holly's safety. 'He still around?'

'No, I saw him leave. I've been watching out for Holly, young woman on her own like that.'

Kit put his glass back on the bar. 'Thanks, I appreciate that. Down along the harbour, you say?'

'Yes. Can't miss it, it's a pink cottage, tucked away like.'

'Thanks.' Kit nodded and smiled. 'Might see you again.' And acting more casual than he felt, he strolled out of the pub.

Kit drove the short distance the barman had directed him and found Holly's cottage exactly as it had been described. There was a single light on in the front room, the faint glow of which Kit could just make out behind thick curtains covering the small latticed window. He parked the car on the lane and walked along the short track to the cottage. Standing still, he listened for sounds within, heard the quiet strains of Radio Three, then knocked and waited. Moments later, the light went out and he tensed. Looking around him, he could just make out the shape of the front garden in the darkness but little else. He moved towards the shadow of a tree, his whole body wound like a spring, and watched the house. It was still, the radio had been turned off and the sound of the sea two hundred yards away was audible as a faint murmur on the wind. He stood immobile for several moments, straining to listen for a sound, scrutinising the darkness for any movement, then he heard the rustle of a bush to his right and spun round. He glimpsed a figure dart out from the side of the house and lunged forward.

'Whoa! Got you!'

'Help! Ahhhhhh . . . Get off me! *Help!*'

'Holly?' He released his arm lock and sprung back.

'Kit?' Holly turned on him, her eyes blazing. 'What the bloody hell are you doing here?' She shook her head, instantly furious. 'Christ! You nearly scared me to death! What in God's name do you mean jumping out at me like that? God, you could have given me a heart attack!' She was shouting and her whole body was trembling. 'You stupid, stupid fool! What if I'd clubbed you with this?' She held up a heavy brass candlestick and waved it menacingly at him. 'I would have, you know, after this afternoon. I would have walloped you with . . .' Suddenly she turned away and put her other hand up to her face. The candlestick dropped to the ground with a thud and Kit winced.

Squatting to pick it up, he said, 'Come on, don't get upset. I'm sorry, I didn't mean to scare you.' He wanted to touch her, to comfort her, but he didn't dare, even though he now held the weapon.

'Didn't mean to scare me! God, Kit Thomas, you're insufferable!' She had stopped crying and wiped her face on the sleeve of her coat, then sniffed loudly. 'There was a man here,' she said, 'snooping round this afternoon. I wasn't here, I was on the beach, walking, and I came back to see a light on and the window latch had been broken. I hid out here, terrified, for half an hour and then I saw him leave the house.' She took the candlestick from Kit and held it tightly. 'The only person who knows I'm in Cornwall is you. And not even you knew where I was staying.'

'There was a man in the pub this afternoon, asking after you,' Kit told her. 'I was in there a few minutes ago; the barman told me where you were staying.'

'What man? Who was he?' Holly's voice rose in panic.

'I don't know.' Kit took her arm. 'Look, is there somewhere we can talk, somewhere else?'

'What's wrong with the cottage?'

'I don't know. I'm not happy with the idea of being there.'

'We can walk on the beach, then maybe go for a drink at the pub.' Holly looked at her watch. 'There's plenty of time; last orders are eleven.'

'OK, let's go.' Kit's mind had been churning as he stood there. The only person he had told about Holly was Jill, when he'd spoken to her on the phone that morning. He tried to tell himself the idea was ridiculous, but he was well aware that listening devices were commonplace. Christ, this whole thing was becoming sinister!

'Kit?' Holly sat on a rock and watched Kit at the water's edge, skimming pebbles across the surface of the waves. He had his back to her and had said nothing for the past ten minutes. She bit the inside of her lip and tried again; his silence unnerved her. 'Kit?' He turned round. 'So?' She was nervous, impatient with him. 'What do you think?'

She had just explained what had really happened at the gallery that night: how the books were stolen, what she'd found in them, and how she was convinced that someone had tried to kill her. She'd told him she'd been frightened and confused – that was why she'd fled – but she didn't tell him now that she still was.

Kit threw the last pebble, then dug his hands deep into his pockets. 'I think,' he said slowly, 'that you and Jill could be part of something very big and very dangerous.' He walked across and sat on the rock beside her. 'But at the moment, I can only speculate. There isn't any evidence to prove my theory.'

'Which is?'

Again Kit hesitated before answering. He didn't want to scare Holly and he wasn't entirely sure of what he was saying. 'Money laundering,' he said finally. He turned to look at her.

'Money laundering?' She shook her head, unable to take it in. 'Like drug money, money from prostitution, that sort of thing?'

'Yes.'

Holly was appalled at the very idea. 'You can't be serious?' She stopped and stared out at the sea for a few moments, then turned back to him. 'Can you?'

Kit nodded.

'But how, and who for?'

Again Kit took his time to answer. He wanted to explain it properly, so she would his idea a chance. 'You've just told me that the books contained figures that didn't seem to make sense to you, right? Huge sums of money were being paid for works by this artist Marcus, yes?'

'Yes.'

'Sums of money that were almost unbelievable, that's what you said.'

'Yes, but who's to put a value on a piece of art? It's down to individual taste and what a buyer's prepared to pay. Just look at recent sales of Impressionist art – some works have sold for millions more than expected and shocked the art world.'

'Exactly.'

'What d'you mean, exactly?'

'If you wanted to legitimise a large sum of money, let's say half a million, money from illegal sources, wouldn't it be a clever way of doing it? You'd set up the sale of a painting, perhaps the work of a new artist, who has already had a myth created about him, and put it through the Grigson Gallery, say, to a bogus client somewhere, in the States or the Middle East. The money is transferred legitimately for a "work of art" whose value is simply a matter of taste and demand. It's impossible to trace, but once it's registered in the UK, it's clean and it's been paid legally, with the duty, tax or whatever, for a painting. You could move huge amounts of dirty cash around the world like that, cleaning it up in the process.'

Kit had warmed to his explanation. 'You said that when you tried to ring a couple of the appointments in the diary before Christmas, the clients didn't seem to exist. You were sure it wasn't a coincidence then. Well, perhaps it wasn't. Maybe these clients don't exist, maybe they're just a front. What about this artist? Have you ever met him or done an exhibition for him?'

Holly shook her head, bewildered.

'And you said that Sotheby's hadn't even heard of him, or Sandy Turner for that matter. Another front, maybe? All part of the myth . . .'

'Whoa! Wait a minute, Kit!' Holly stood up abruptly, feeling the need to make some kind of movement. She walked several paces away, then turned to face him. 'You're suggesting that Sandy was involved in some kind of money laundering, using the gallery as a front?'

Kit stared at her for a few moments, holding her gaze. Finally, he nodded. 'So how does this fit in with Sandy's suicide?' she asked. 'Or with Jill, Alex Turner, and the business in London? It seems to me that we have two completely different situations. I don't understand.' Her voice faltered slightly and she hugged her arms around her. 'This is all so bizarre . . .' she murmured.

Kit walked across the wet sand, stood in front of her and gently held her arms. 'Holly, you remember the idea Jill had, before they found the body?'

She shook her head.

'It was a flash of inspiration,' he went on quietly, 'but it was instantly forgotten when the policeman arrived that morning.' He paused as Holly looked at him. 'Jill said that Alex Turner had a partner, and that they looked very alike, or had done in their youth, remember?'

'Yes, I remember.'

'Well, what if we are talking about two different men here, one impersonating the other? What if the man you were married to only posed as Sandy Turner, used the identity while he needed it, then disappeared, killing off the real Alex Turner and covering the murder with a suicide? What if . . .' Kit stopped and stepped back. Holly was smiling at him, shaking her head as if he'd just said something funny. 'What are you smiling at?' he demanded.

'You!' Holly answered. 'I'm smiling at you, because this is all so far-fetched and unbelievable and because you've been reading too many thrillers, Kit!' The smile had vanished, replaced by a flash of anger. 'Money laundering, murder, false identities! This whole thing is ludicrous!' She turned and walked away from him, suddenly furious.

'Why were the books stolen then?' Kit called after her. 'And why did someone try to scare the hell out of you? They didn't try to kill you, Holly. Believe me, if they'd wanted to do that you'd be dead by now.'

She spun round and Kit saw a very real fear in her face.

'Explain the huge sums of money from clients you can't trace,' he went on. 'Or why Alex Turner ran a financial search on the Grigson Gallery and why he was murdered. Explain why the gallery was broken into, why your flat's been searched, as well as Jill's house and Alex Turner's business.' He couldn't stop now; he had to make her face up to it. 'If you can't see the connection, Holly, if you can't see that someone wants to make sure you don't know or find out anything, then you must be blind, or stupid, and from what I remember of you, you're certainly not that.'

Holly stood perfectly still and stared at him. 'You really believe all this, don't you?'

'I don't know,' Kit answered truthfully. 'I think so, but I need to find out more.'

Holly continued to stare at him. 'And you really think it's some kind of organised crime, on a big scale, don't you?'

Kit was silent, avoiding her eyes.

'Don't you?' she insisted.

He shrugged, still unable to face her.

She walked back to him. '*Don't you?*' she said once more, her voice hard and cold.

Kit nodded. 'Yes, I do think it's some kind of organised crime ring. Who or what I have no idea, but I suspect it's a highly professional organisation.'

Holly closed her eyes as an image flashed into her mind. She felt the thud on the back of her neck, the hot, tight, suffocating space, her struggle to breathe. She gasped for air.

'Holly? Are you all right?'

Her eyes snapped open as Kit shook her. 'Yes, I . . .' She shivered and struggled to compose herself. 'Is that why you wouldn't talk in the house – you think it's bugged?'

'I don't know, but I'm not sure anywhere is safe. I keep wondering how the hell they traced you down here, unless it was from my call to Jill this morning.'

Holly shook her head. 'You think Jill's phone is bugged?'

'It might be. Bugging devices are very common. It could be the reason for the break-ins.'

Holly moved over to the rock and sat down. She slumped forward and dropped her head in her hands. 'I'm frightened, Kit,' she said quietly, 'and very confused.'

He stood looking down at her. 'We need some more answers. More information.'

She glanced up. 'Like?'

'Bank statements – they'll confirm the cash book. And maybe we should contact this artist Marcus, talk to him, see what deals Sandy did with him.'

Holly nodded.

'And we need to go over as much as you can remember about Sandy, the fine details, to see if there isn't something that might just give us a clue about his true identity . . .' Kit broke off at the sight of Holly's face. 'Or confirm that he was who he said he was,' he finished.

Again Holly nodded, feeling drained and lacking the energy to answer him.

He held out his hand. 'D'you want to go for a drink?'

'Is there still time?'

Kit looked at his watch. 'It's ten past ten. Come on, I think we could both do with a large whisky.'

Holly took the proffered hand and he pulled her up. 'You OK?'

'I think so,' she said, then she smiled. 'Frozen, but better at the thought of a large glass of J & B.' She dropped her hand away from his now that she was standing and tucked her fingers down into the pockets of her coat. 'Here,' she said, nodding towards the sandbanks. 'We can walk through the dunes up to the harbour.'

Without waiting for Kit, she headed off along the beach and he had to stride out to catch up with her.

They sat by the fire in the pub. The crowd that had been in there earlier had drifted away and now there was just a handful of people, elderly locals nursing what looked like the same drinks they'd had all evening and staring at Kit in the same intrusive manner. It was out of season for holiday folk and even when it wasn't, strangers were only just tolerated.

Holly drank her first whisky down in one and felt a rush of blood to her head. Kit got her another, and as she sipped it, feeling warmer and more at ease than on the beach, she opened up to him, talking about Sandy in more detail than she'd imagined she would remember or even want to.

'So he approached you then?' Kit asked, after she'd told him about putting an offer in for the gallery and meeting Sandy standing outside it,

'Yes, we got chatting about art. He asked me about the lease and my plans for it and said he thought I was very brave to start a new business venture in the middle of a recession.' She had been skimming over the past two years, picking out odd incidents, things she'd noticed about Sandy, but Kit had asked her to start at the beginning and go over exactly how they'd met. He wanted to know what Sandy was like then, and to follow the development of their relationship, to establish when she had realised that perhaps she didn't know the man she had married. Holly went on.

'He asked me out for a drink and as I'd been lonely and depressed, I accepted. It wasn't something I'd normally have done. He was an attractive man, but he was a stranger.' She shrugged. 'I thought, what the hell. He was interesting, he knew a lot about the art market, and . . .' She laughed. 'He was really quite pathetic, with this bandage on his neck, feeling immensely sorry for himself.'

'Bandage?'

'Yes. He'd just been into hospital to have his mole removed. It left a small scar.' She frowned. 'Jill identified the same scar, remember?' Holly put her drink down. 'Kit? Are you listening to me?'

Suddenly Kit stood up. 'Holly, you're sure about this, the fact that he had just had the mole removed?'

'Positive. Why?'

'Finish your drink.' He hopped from foot to foot impatiently. 'Come on, drink it down! We have to phone Jill.'

Holly looked up at him as if he'd gone bananas, but she drained her glass and stood up. Kit took her hand and literally dragged her out of the pub.

'What's all this about?' she said, as the cold air hit her face and sobered her up sharply. She was half walking, half running to keep up with Kit.

He stopped halfway down the main street and faced her. 'Jill told me this afternoon that Alex had his mole removed at ten or eleven years old.' Holly looked momentarily puzzled. 'That's the clue. That's it, don't you see?' She narrowed her eyes. Kit took a deep breath. 'We were talking about the body you both identified in the mortuary, and she cited the scar as proof that it was Alex and Sandy, the fact that you'd both identified the scar. She said her son Harry had the same problem as his father, that he'd have to have the mole removed at roughly the same age his father had.'

'So you're saying it couldn't have been the same man because it wasn't the same scar?'

'Yes!' Kit rushed on, in a great hurry to make her understand. 'The man who impersonated Alex Turner even had a scar made on his neck in the same place, for authenticity. Who's to say it was a mole he had removed? He might have cut himself and had it stitched; anything to produce a distinguishing mark, the same distinguishing mark as Alex Turner!'

Holly stood still. It made sense and yet she couldn't quite grasp it. 'Do you really think . . . ?'

'Yes!' Kit interrupted. 'I do! This was one hell of a professional operation. It was serious money, and whoever Sandy Turner was, he was working for the big boys. He wasn't taking any chances; he'd got every angle covered!' He took her hand again. 'Come on, before we get too carried away, let's phone Jill, and just confirm what she told me this morning.'

He started for the phone box, dragging Holly along in his wake. 'I'll ask her to ring the coroner first thing in the morning and get him to date the scar. If he dates it to fit with what Jill said then we have one of our answers.'

Holly stopped short, forcing Kit to do the same. He turned

round impatiently, then pulled himself up short on seeing her face. It was stricken, deathly pale under the sickly orange glare of the street lamp.

'And if it was two different men,' she said, her voice suddenly small and frightened, 'then who the hell was I married to?'

Chapter Fourteen

Jill was unable to sleep. It was eleven, she was exhausted and she should have been in bed, but instead she sat up in the kitchen in semi-darkness, her hands cradling a mug of tea. Her fingers felt numb and despite the heating, the aga and two sweaters, she felt cold inside, and very frightened. She stared out at the night sky, not really seeing it, with Alex's file open in front of her and Sophie's photograph of her father, the same one she had shown to Holly, in its frame to her right. The house was deathly quiet. Sophie was listening to her Walkman in her room, Harry was asleep, and the tick of the kitchen clock was the only thing that broke the stifling hush.

Then the phone rang.

For a few moments it didn't register. The shrill bleep echoed in the hall until finally it pierced Jill's consciousness. Instantly, panic rose in her chest. Standing up, she scraped her chair back and hurried out to answer it. Her hand hovered by the receiver for a second then she picked it up. There were a few seconds' silence while money was slotted into the machine, then she heard Kit's voice. The relief was almost overwhelming.

'Hello, Jill, it's Kit. Don't say anything, all right?'

'Yes, OK.' The feeling of panic came again and she slumped down on the nearby chair.

'Jill, you have my home number, don't you?'

'Yes.' Kit's voice was tight with tension and he sounded distant; it was a bad line.

'Can you go down to the phone box or use a neighbour's phone to ring my parents for my number? I don't want to give it to you on this line and we need to talk. I have to ask you something.'

'Why, what's . . .' Jill's voice trailed off as she understood what he was saying. She glanced down at the receiver with shock. 'I'll do it now.'

'Thanks, Jill.' Without another word, he hung up.

Ten minutes later, Jill knocked on the door of South Ridge Cottage and asked if she could use the phone. 'Mine's on the blink,' she said. 'Would you mind?'

'Of course not, dear, come on in.' Mrs Birch ushered Jill inside and along to the phone. 'There you are.' She hovered by the door as Jill picked up the receiver, but Jill turned and hesitated before dialling, making it clear she wanted some privacy. 'Oh, yes, right,' Mrs Birch said. 'I'll, um, leave you to it then, dear.' She retreated and closed the door of the small study quietly.

Jill dialled Kit's home, wrote down the number that he had rung through to his mother and then dialled Cornwall. Kit answered the call immediately.

'Kit! What's going on?'

'Jill, thanks for calling back so quickly. I need to ask you about Alex's scar, the one on his neck that you mentioned earlier.'

'OK.'

'Are you sure that he had a mole removed as a young boy?'

'Yes, why?'

'He didn't have any further surgery on it, a couple of years ago?'

'No, not to my knowledge. It was an old scar, very faded. Why on earth . . . ?'

'Jill, Holly tells me that when she met Sandy two years ago he'd just had the mole removed. He was wearing a bandage and the scar was new.'

'That's impossible, it can't have been! Alex had always had the scar. Even when I first met him, sixteen years ago, he . . .' Jill stopped. The realisation of what was being said hit her with a jolt. 'It's not the same man, is it? That's what you're saying?' For a moment she felt dizzy with emotion. She took a deep breath.

'I think that's what I'm saying. We need verification from the coroner; he'll be able to date the scar. You need to ring him first thing in the morning, but not from home. Can you do that?'

'Yes, I . . .' Jill had to hold onto the edge of the desk for support. Her legs had buckled under her and she thought for a moment she was going to faint.

'Jill? Are you all right?'

Her head swum and she tried to breathe deeply. 'Yes, Kit, I'm all right . . . Sorry, it's just the shock, I . . .' She broke off again, breathing deeply. 'Are you saying that someone impersonated my husband and . . .' She swallowed hard; she hadn't used the word husband since the whole thing had started. 'Sorry, this person, you think they had a scar made on their neck?'

'Possibly, for authenticity. I don't know, we need the coroner's report.'

'Of course . . .' Her voice trailed away.

'Jill, is everything all right your end?' Kit was worried; Jill sounded very peculiar.

'Yes, fine. I . . .' Jill shook herself, suddenly remembering the file. 'God, Kit, I nearly forgot! We found Alex's file, this evening, after you'd left. It must be what whoever broke in was looking for. It's full of Alex's notes and figures on deals in the commodities market, dates, commissions, things I don't really understand, and it's got a list of names – clients, presumably. It looks perfectly harmless and I'd never have known what it was except that it's got Grigson Gallery written on the front. There's no information on the gallery but there is a note of that man Welsch, along with his number. I got the feeling that the information on the gallery was the next step.'

'Christ! Jill, that's amazing, well done!'

Jill heard the sound of muffled voices. Obviously Kit was explaining to Holly what she'd just said. She hung on and glanced out of the window, across at her own house. It was lit up and the alarm was on, but Sophie and Harry were alone and she suddenly shivered with fear. 'Kit, I'd better go. I've left the children alone,' she said quickly. 'What do you want me to do tomorrow? Shall I ring you on this number?'

Kit hesitated. 'No, I think I'll come back to London. Can I call into Sussex on the way?' He was hoping to persuade Holly to come with him but he didn't say that.

'Yes, whenever you like. Look, I really must go.' She was starting to panic. It was becoming a familiar sensation: suddenly she would find herself totally overwhelmed with fear. 'I'll see you tomorrow, Kit.' Without waiting for him to answer, she hung up.

'All right, dear?' Mrs Birch was miraculously just outside the door as Jill left the room.

'Fine, thanks,' Jill said, hurrying towards the front door. 'Let me know how much I owe you.' She yanked it open and dashed out into the night. 'Bye!'

'Mind how you . . .' Mrs Birch's voice trailed off and she didn't finish her sentence. She switched the porch light on but it was too late. Jill had run off down the lane towards South Ridge Farm and disappeared from view.

Ted Welsch sat under the neon sign of a beach bar in Fuengirola on the Costa del Sol and sipped a warm gin and tonic. It was raining and the place was sodden and deserted. The neon above his head spluttered and buzzed every now and then as the water leaked into its electrics, and the sound of Spanish radio blared in the background, weather interference breaking into the mindless, foreign beat of the pop song.

Welsch felt miserable. Not just because of the rain, but because of the constant strain of looking over his shoulder every time he moved; the tired, listless atmosphere of an out of season resort, complete with litter, drab buildings, a smelly, pathetic beach and high prices; and the inevitable Spanish tummy. Welsch wished to God he'd never set foot in the place.

It was hardly the sun-drenched paradise he'd imagined – girls in bikinis, fast cars and hedonistic freedom. He missed the cat, decent bacon, milk that tasted fresh, and he missed his beer. Moreover, he felt like a rat in a hole, and however much he tried to ignore it, he couldn't escape the fact that he was hiding, snivelling in fear in the back end of Marbella. He hated himself for it. Every day that he got up, looked out at the bleak grey skies and put on another short-sleeved shirt and his lightweight trousers, he lost a little bit more of his self-respect. He shouldn't be here, he knew that. He wasn't a hero, but he wasn't a cop-out merchant either. He should have told the Turner woman about the file, explained how dangerous the whole thing was and who she was dealing with, and he couldn't get her voice out of his head. If something had happened to her he'd never forgive himself, and he couldn't get that out of his head either.

Standing up, he left the money for his drink on the table and walked out of the bar. No-one paid the slightest bit of attention to him – not like the local in Soho. Here he was just another faceless tourist. The rain had stopped so he walked along the promenade and then hopped down onto the beach, the wet sand quickly staining the canvas above the rubber sole of his shoes. He walked past the rows of coconut rush umbrellas and upturned sunbeds that some hopeful entrepreneur had kept out for the Christmas trade and down towards the sea. Bending down to pick a pale pink shell out of the sand, he turned its smooth, attractive shape over in the palm of his hand, then had to leap back as a wave washed up suddenly over his shoes, soaking his feet.

'Oh Christ!' He sighed irritably, squelched back up the beach, turned a sunbed over and sat on its edge to untie the plimsolls and peel off his wet socks.

'Eh, signor?'

Welsch looked up as he wrung his socks out.

'You pay for zis bed.' A young man wearing torn jeans and a tee-shirt stood over him.

'I'm sorry?' he said.

'You seet'ere, you pay for zis bed. You give me a thousand pesetas now.'

Welsch stood up. He was shorter than the youth, lighter and altogether a much smaller man, but that didn't stop him. He looked up at the Spaniard, his temper only just intact. 'It's half past eleven at night,' he growled, 'and you want me to pay for a sodding sunbed!' He leant forward menacingly, his face level with the boy's chest, and snapped, 'Bugger off!' He shoved the boy backwards, with one finger in the middle of his chest. 'Go on,' he shouted, 'bugger off! If you think I'm paying for this then you'd better bloody think again!' He bent and snatched up his shoes. This was somehow the last straw.

'Jesus! Foreigners! They're all the fucking same!' he snarled, walking barefoot up towards the promenade. 'The sooner I get out of this place the better.' He climbed up onto the pavement just as it started to rain again.

'That's it!' he announced, looking up at the sky. 'I've had it!' And chucking his wet summer shoes and socks into an overflowing rubbish bin, he walked barefoot back to his hotel to pack.

It was nearly midnight and Holly stood by the door of the pub while Kit made arrangements at the bar for his room. They had officially closed but several drinkers still sat around and sipped on pints obviously pulled after last orders, the fire was roaring and the atmosphere was warm and comfortable. Holly felt miserable. She dreaded going back to her cottage, and she wanted Kit to stay in Cornwall or to go back with him to London, but her pride wouldn't let her admit it. He hadn't offered and she hadn't asked; she wouldn't lower herself.

'OK, that's settled.' Kit had crossed the bar and stood in front of her. 'Come on, let's go.' He opened the door for her and she followed him out into the cold air. 'It's this way,' he said.

'What d'you mean?' She stood still and he turned. 'What's this way?'

'The room,' he answered. 'We go in the back way to the guest bedroom and bathroom.'

Holly stared at him. 'We?'

'Yes, I booked the room for two people. You're staying here tonight with me and tomorrow we'll pack your things and I'm taking you back to Jill's.' He said it as a statement of fact, with far more conviction than he actually felt. He had decided, in the past ten minutes or so, that the only way to handle the situation was not to give Holly the choice. 'Come on, it's starting to rain.'

But Holly stood her ground. One half of her, the independent half, was furious at having arrangements made for her; the other half, the half that was scared and lonely and confused, was flooded with relief. She didn't know what to do. 'The room's only got one bed,' she said, 'I know because I stayed here the first few days, before I found the cottage.'

Kit shrugged. 'So?'

'So, er, where do I sleep?' She wasn't being coy; she was genuinely nervous. The last thing she needed now was the confusion she had suffered several days ago.

'You sleep in the bed,' Kit answered. He hesitated for a few moments, staring at her face. He had thought there might be a glimmer there, a flicker of memory of the other night, but there wasn't. She simply looked sad and anxious. 'And I sleep in the easy chair,' he finished. 'The publican's wife is bringing up extra blankets.'

Holly nodded. 'OK, thanks.'

Kit turned away. 'Come on then,' he called over his shoulder. He made off in the direction of the pub's back yard and stopped at the gate to hold it for her.

Watching her go ahead, he felt relief that she'd agreed without her customary fight but also an aching disappointment that there was no recognition of the other night, not even the smallest sign that Holly had felt any way near the way that he had.

Chapter Fifteen

The Weasel went straight up to the suite; it was the first time he hadn't been kept waiting. He stubbed his cigarette out on the sole of his shoe and dropped it into his pocket before knocking on the door and waiting for an answer. Moments later he walked in.

The man was by the window, with his back to the room, and the Weasel realised that he had never properly seen his face. He'd know him anywhere, though – it was the scent; he'd never be able to smell it again without breaking out into a sweat. He took his hands out of his pockets and ran his tongue over small, sharp teeth, swallowing uncomfortably.

'Holly Grigson's done a runner from Cornwall,' he said. 'She upped and left this morning. And there was a call last night to Sussex, from that bloke Thomas. He told the Turner woman not to use the phone.' He stopped but the man said nothing and he wiped damp palms on his trousers before continuing. 'Which means the phone's been sussed as well.' Beads of perspiration stuck to his greasy fringe and made his forehead itch. 'They know something – maybe that I'm following them, maybe more than that.' He ran his tongue over his teeth again, his mouth bone-dry with anxiety.

'You know where they are now?'

'Sussex.'

'Can you listen in to the house?'

'No, I didn't think it was necessary, not in the beginning, not . . .'

'Then watch it,' the man snapped. 'Watch everything they do and ring me the minute anything happens. If Holly Grigson leaves let me know.' He still didn't turn but he didn't need to. The menace in his voice was enough.

The Weasel edged back towards the door, not wanting to turn his back on the man but eager to get out of there. 'Anything else?' he ventured.

Ignoring him, the man moved away from the window and walked across to the bedroom, then disappeared, clicking the door shut behind him.

The Weasel took the opportunity to flee, hurrying out of the suite, down the corridor and along to the staircase. So anxious was he to get away that he didn't even consider waiting for the lift.

In the bedroom, the man stood for a few moments looking down at the sleeping figure in the bed, then he yanked back the bedclothes. 'Get up,' he said. The girl rolled over and lifted an arm up over her head in a stretch. He walked to the window, pulled back the drapes and switched on the overhead light. 'Now!' he snapped. The girl sat up.

'Why? What's happened?' She was naked, sleepy and confused. She saw him walk towards the wardrobe. 'Hey! Did I do something wrong?'

The man took her clothes out of the cupboard, ripped off the dry cleaning plastic, and chucked them on the bed along with her boots and handbag. 'You're leaving,' he said. 'Now.' He turned and looked at her briefly but no emotion registered on his face. She was a tart; she'd been lucky to last this long. Going to the wardrobe safe, he tapped in the number and opened it, taking out a roll of cash. He peeled off a handful of notes and counted them. 'Two weeks,' he said, 'and a bonus.'

The girl was already out of bed and half dressed; she glanced up and nodded. She wouldn't have put it past him not to have paid her at all and she sure as hell wouldn't have argued about it. He was a perverse bastard and he frightened her; not many men did that. He was charm laced with menace and she wasn't sorry to be out of there.

He threw the money at her and she just caught it. She pulled on her boots, ran a hand through her hair and shoved the money into her handbag. Seconds later she walked towards the door, then stopped as he called her back. She turned nervously and saw him smiling at her. She smiled back, her face set, her whole body straining to leave.

'I don't know your name,' he said politely.

The girl shrugged. She hesitated for a moment then said, 'Call me anything you like.' And with her high-heeled boots leaving small indentations in the thick cream carpet, she hurried to the door and before he could answer her she had gone.

The man sat down on the unmade bed. His head throbbed and he felt sick; stress did that to him nowadays. Pulling open the bedside drawer, he took out a small packet and emptied a tiny amount of cocaine onto the bedside table. He knelt, cut the coke and did a line, quickly and expertly; instantly the hit relieved him. He looked up and sat back on his heels. Holly Grigson. The image of her face came straight into his mind. He had never seen her, but by now he knew every inch of her flesh, every expression of her face. The camera never lies. He knew Holly Grigson and he wanted her, but that would come later. First he had to sort out the mess he'd been left with. She knew too much, but exactly how much he had to find out.

Standing up, he touched the empty bed. The indentation of the girl's body was in the shape that she slept, small and tight, curled up as if protecting herself, and the bed was still warm. The man hardened instantly, momentarily wishing her back. But he moved away towards the sitting room, blanking it out. He didn't have time for that now; he had other things to do. She'd been good for the money – she had satisfied a need, but that particular need had now been replaced by another. Another more pressing need, he thought, taking up the phone and dialling the Weasel's mobile number. And a far more dangerous one at that.

Kit pulled into the drive of South Ridge Farm and stopped in a space to the right of Jill's Range Rover. He could feel Holly bracing herself beside him, already tense, and wished he could do something to ease the way she felt. But he didn't want to risk rejection, and he didn't want to complicate things – for Holly or for himself. So he ignored his emotions and climbed out of the car. 'You all right?' he asked briefly and Holly nodded. She too climbed out, just as Jill came towards them.

'I rang the coroner,' Jill said excitedly, unable to contain the information. 'You were right. The scar isn't new, it's old skin tissue! He wasn't able to date it exactly, but he said it was definitely over ten years old. He said he'd send off to the lab for further tests. I can't believe you thought of it, I . . .' She suddenly broke off and smiled. 'Sorry, how rude of me! Please, come in.' She led the way into the house and through to the kitchen. Sophie stood up as they entered and Jill put her arm briefly around her stepdaughter's shoulders. 'Would you like tea or coffee? Sophie, how about you?'

'I'll do it,' Sophie said.

Kit walked into the warm, saffron-coloured room and pulled out a chair from the kitchen table. He sat down, but Holly stood tensely by the door. She could see a clear difference in both Jill and Sophie, and it made her feel intensely jealous. Jill had lost her pallor, her haunted look, and had gained in confidence – not outwardly, but it was there, beneath the surface, Holly could see it. It insulated her, making her surer, easier. And Sophie had changed, too. The barrier was down, that invisible screen that she had used to keep her stepmother at a distance; she moved around the house now as if she belonged. Holly recognised the feeling in the house and she begrudged it. It was relief. The whole place was suffused with a sense of relief – that Holly had played no part in their lives, that their image of Alex was untarnished, that a woman they had neither liked nor understood had no claim to a man they had both loved. Holly understood it but she also envied it. It set her apart and, for the first time in her life, she felt a victim. It was a very lonely feeling.

Sophie placed a tray of tea on the table and Jill set the mugs out, pouring milk, acutely aware of Holly's unease as she stood by the door. To break the tension, she looked up and said, 'Shall we take this into the sitting room? Sophie's made a fire.' It wasn't a customary gesture for Jill. Three weeks ago she might have registered someone else's unease but she certainly wouldn't have interfered. She had always been one to keep her distance. Now she led the way through the hall, set the tray down and poured the tea. Holly, she noticed, had taken her coat off and sat staring at the fire.

'So, Kit,' she began, dispensing with the small talk, 'what does this all mean?' She handed out the tea and sat back on her heels, anxious to get things clear in her mind; frightened, if she was honest with herself. She wanted to know what they were involved in, and how dangerous it was. 'Why would someone impersonate Alex and why go to such enormous lengths to do it? Have you any clearer idea of what was going on at Holly's gallery?'

Kit sat forward. 'The answer to the last question is yes and no,' he said. 'And as for the others, I think it's all connected.' He took a sip of his tea, then placed the mug on the floor by his feet. 'I think – and I'm not at all sure of this, it's only speculation – I *think* that Holly's husband was laundering money through the art market, using Holly's gallery as a front, and, if that's the case, then we're talking major sums of money and very probably organised crime.' He paused to take breath. 'As far as the impersonation is concerned, it was a cover-up. It had to be foolproof, and my guess is it was expertly planned to boot. Holly was very probably targeted

– she fitted the bill and . . .' He broke off and looked up as Holly left the room. He was silent for a few moments, looking down at his hands, then he said, 'Excuse me, I'll just go and see if she's all right.' He got up and walked out after her.

'Holly?'

Holly stood at the sink in the kitchen and buried herself in filling a mug from the tap. She didn't turn.

'Are you OK?'

She drank down half a mugful, giving herself a few precious seconds to compose herself, then she glanced over her shoulder. 'Yes, fine. I just needed a drink, that's all. It's hot by the fire.' Her voice wavered as she spoke but she covered it with a small smile and turned back to refill the mug. There was a time when she would have told Kit how she felt, when she would have wanted and needed the comfort his friendship offered. Now she was too confused and upset even to begin to explain. Her whole life was a sham. She had been used, made a fool of, involved in something dangerous and illegal by a man she trusted, a man she had married, for God's sake! Everything she had believed in – the gallery, her marriage, her entire life for the past eighteen months – had been a complete waste. Bigamy had been hard enough to come to terms with, but this, the fact that she had been targeted as Kit said, and had been so blind that she couldn't see it, so stupid that she had no idea of what had been going on . . . It was unendurable. Holly drank down a second mug of water and faced Kit.

'Sorry,' she said. 'I'm fine, honestly. I'll come through in a minute.'

Kit nodded. He would have said, 'I'll wait,' but something in her face deterred him. Without a word, he turned and left the room.

Holly watched him go, feeling lower than she could ever remember, but she didn't call out. What good would it do? The last thing she needed was another mistake. How the hell could she trust herself, or anyone, after this? Rinsing the mug, she left it on the draining board and went back through to the sitting room.

'So what now?' Jill asked, as Holly came in and took her place again by the fire. 'Presumably we ring the police and hand it all over to them.'

Kit said nothing. He glanced at Holly, who also kept quiet.

'We must go to the police!' Jill insisted. 'From what you've told us, this whole thing is extremely dangerous. We could be in serious trouble if we . . .'

'There's something else, isn't there?' Sophie interrupted, looking directly at Kit.

Kit gave and her quick glance at Holly, then said, 'Holly is implicated in all of this. The gallery is in her name; she is a director of the business; she countersigned all the papers, cheques and deals. The fact that she knew nothing at all would be very hard to prove once the police become involved.' He turned to Jill. 'And we have no evidence that the man Holly was married to was not your husband. As far as the police, fraud squad, or whoever investigated this would be concerned, there would be no reason to look further than Alex Turner. They might even explain his murder as a part of the whole situation, saying, for example, that he stepped out of line, got greedy, or was redundant.'

Jill stared at him, then shook her head. 'I don't believe it,' she murmured. 'All this leads to nothing, is that what you're saying?'

'No, not exactly.' Kit hesitated, then said, 'What we need is some clear answers, some facts. We need . . .'

'Evidence,' Holly finished for him. 'We need to find out who I was married to, and if he's still alive.'

'Still alive?' Jill was shocked. 'Is that what you think, that he's . . .'

Holly cut her short. 'I don't know,' she said. 'He could well be. It could even be him who's been rifling through my flat, and your house, looking to see if there's anything to incriminate him.'

She said all of this without emotion, as if trying to scare Jill. 'He might have murdered your husband and disappeared, using the suicide – the murder – as a cover. He may be prepared to murder again if we find out too much, or know something that endangers his plans.'

'Whoa! Hang on a minute, Holly, one step at a time!' Kit had seen the horror on Jill's face. She might look together, but Kit reckoned her confidence was brittle, and he didn't think it would take much to shatter it. 'We don't know any of that,' he said. 'We don't anything at all for certain, do we?'

Holly stared at the fire for a moment. 'No, I guess not,' she answered finally.

'Right, then I suggest that we start by trying to think through Sandy Turner's true identity.' He looked at Holly and begrudgingly, she nodded. 'You said some time ago, Jill, that Alex had a partner, d'you remember?'

'Yes, Hugo Blandford. I suggested him when we talked through this before, when it was just a theory. He and Alex were at university together. They looked so alike in those days that people thought they were brothers.' She looked across at Sophie. 'You remember him, don't you, Sophie? He used to come sailing with us up until a few years ago – do you remember that?'

Sophie nodded. She didn't have a clear picture of Hugo in her head and she couldn't think how anyone could mistake him for her father. There was only one Alex Turner in her mind; it just didn't seem feasible.

'D'you have any photographs of him, Jill?'

'You really think it might be him?'

'I don't know, it's worth a try.'

Jill stood up and went across to the bureau to open it, then suddenly stopped and turned, her face flushed. 'I don't have any photos,' she said in a small voice. 'I've just remembered, I . . .'

'We cleared them all out,' Sophie said, 'just after all this happened. We couldn't face having them in the house.' She spoke with her chin tilted defiantly, daring Kit to question her.

He didn't. 'Shit! I'd been banking on you having a photo somewhere.'

Sophie looked down at the floor. She had an album under her bed, one she'd managed to save on the day of Jill's madness. She blushed but said nothing, then glancing up, she saw Holly watching her and remembered a moment of sympathy, the touch of Holly's hand on her arm and the comfort it had given her. 'Actually I have got a photo album,' she said. She cleared her throat as Jill glanced across at her, startled. 'It's in my room. It's one of yours, Jill, one Dad did for you. I'll go and get it.' She stood up and hurried over to the door. 'I'm sorry,' she murmured, looking briefly over her shoulder at her stepmother, but Jill just shrugged; the apology wasn't necessary.

Within moments Sophie was back. She held the album out and Jill took it, one of the old leather style that Alex had loved, with stiff black pages and photo corners. Jill opened it, glanced down at the first page, then stood up and moved across to Holly. 'I'll go through it with you,' she said. 'See if you can pick out Hugo or at least recognise him.' Holly nodded and tensed as Jill sat on the arm of the chair, pointing at the first snap. It was black and white, two young men in rowing blazers, very alike. 'Hugo and Alex,' Jill announced, 'twenty odd years ago.'

Holly stared at the snap, then pointed to one of the men. 'That's him,' she said.

Jill nodded and turned the page with a heavy sense of foreboding; Holly had just identified Alex.

Twenty minutes later, Holly sat with her head in her hands while Kit flicked through the album. It hadn't taken long for Holly to go through it and for them to realise that she couldn't tell the difference between Alex and Hugo; the photos were too dated and the exercise had amounted to nothing. Kit could see a vague difference but then he wasn't emotionally involved and under pressure. He felt for Holly; she looked thoroughly miserable.

'That needn't be the end of it,' he said optimistically. 'We could always . . .'

'We could always what?' Holly snapped, jerking her head up. 'Put an ad in the personal column of *The Times*?'

Kit ignored her outburst. 'We could ferret around for a more recent picture,' he said. 'There must be one of Hugo Blandford somewhere, or Alex, for that matter.'

Jill shook her head. 'I'm afraid not,' she said miserably. Like Holly, she was beginning to feel helpless. 'I'm sorry, I blame myself,' she went on. 'If I hadn't acted so rashly, been such a fool, then we wouldn't be in this situation now. All we've got left is that one picture of Alex that Holly's already seen. The one you said you have on your . . .'

'Wait!' Sophie jumped up from the floor. 'That picture!' she cried, smacking her palm against her forehead. 'Oh God, why didn't I think of it before?' She ran out of the room, leaving the three of them staring bewildered after her. Minutes later she was back, clutching the photo frame and a holiday snap of her father. 'This picture of Dad . . .' she mumbled, fiddling with the back of the frame, her fingers clumsy in her panic to get it off. She prized the clips up and pulled the back free. 'It's folded in half! It's of Dad and Hugo, sailing, about five years ago.' She unfolded the photo and held it up. 'Look!'

Jill jumped up and grabbed it, glaring down at the image. 'That's definitely Hugo,' she said. 'There's no mistaking the difference.' Then she held out the picture to Holly and waited, her heart pounding in her chest.

Holly looked down. The snap was of the two men on a boat, the one half of which she already had – the half with Alex in it, in profile. Hugo, beside him, was facing the camera, and although he was very like his friend, with the two men juxtaposed, in brilliant sunshine, there was a definite difference. She stared, the image blurred and she blinked several times, a small tear falling onto the glossy picture. Finally, after what seemed like forever to the three other people in the room, she said, 'The man in profile could easily be mistaken for my husband, a few years ago, tanned, on holiday.' She stopped and held the photo out to Kit. 'But it isn't.' She swallowed. 'I was married to the man on the right, the one without the scar on his neck.'

Kit took the snap and looked down. Alex Turner was wearing a tee-shirt, his scar very apparent, just a small dash of pinkish white against his dark tanned skin; while Hugo Blandford was bare-chested, his head thrown back slightly as he laughed and the whole of his neck visible, showing perfectly tanned, evenly brown skin. There was no sign of a scar.

'Hugo Blandford,' he said, and Holly put her hands up to her face and began to cry.

Kit slammed the door of the hire car shut and bent to speak to Holly through the window. She had the keys in the ignition, ready. 'Are you sure you feel up to going?' he asked.

Holly nodded. 'We need to know what's in the bank statements,' she said wearily. In truth she didn't feel up to anything, except lying down in a darkened room and crying her heart out. 'And I'm the only one who can speak to this artist, Marcus – if I can get hold of him, that is.'

'You sure you don't want me to come with you?' Kit knew the answer but he had to ask, just in case.

'No, thanks.' Holly started the engine and Kit stood back. 'I'd far rather you went to Brighton and found out if that bastard left in one piece,' she called out of the window.

Kit nodded. Her voice had taken on a hard, bitter edge, and although he understood, it worried him. He wasn't at all sure this was the right thing to do, to leave Holly alone in her fragile state of mind, but he kept that to himself. She didn't invite his sympathy or his help and she didn't want his confidence.

Holly shifted the car into gear and moved off. She could see Kit in the mirror, frowning, his hands in the pockets of his cords, and for a moment the need to turn back and hold him was so strong that she had to stop and take a breath. She saw him staring after her and she waved at him then continued on slowly down the drive. What a mess, she thought, pulling out into the main road, what a bloody mess!

Jill stood in the hallway with her coat on as Kit came back into the house. She was rifling through the drawer in the hall table for Alex's car keys. Glancing up, she said, 'Is Holly all right, do you think?'

Kit shrugged. 'Are any of us?' He turned as Sophie came down the stairs with her rucksack over her shoulder and her coat in her hands.

'Harry!' Jill called up the stairs. 'Come on, we're off to Granny's!' She looked back at Kit. 'You want me to try and contact this Welsch man again, yes?'

'Yes.' He chewed his lip for a moment. 'I still think it's pretty odd that he didn't ring after you failed to show up at Victoria ten days ago. You said he sounded edgy when you rang, as if he couldn't wait to get shot of whatever it was he had.'

Jill turned to face him. 'He did, but perhaps, like me, he just wanted to forget this whole thing.'

Kit thought it highly unlikely. He was worried that something sinister might have happened to Welsch but he said nothing, not wanting to scare Jill.

'So, let me get this straight,' Jill said, reaching for her coat. 'I'm to get my mother-in-law to leave a message with her number but not her name, right?'

'Yes.' Chances were that if Welsch was still alive he was also being watched, and his phone was very probably bugged.

'And if I do get hold of him, I'm to arrange to meet him and collect the file he prepared for Alex?'

'If possible, yes.'

Jill picked up her handbag. 'Right. What time will you both be back?'

'No later than five this afternoon.'

Jill kissed Sophie on the forehead. 'I'd really rather you came to Granny's with us,' she said, but Sophie didn't answer and she knew better than to argue. Alex's daughter needed to be involved; she realised that now.

'Right then, we'll see you here later, for tea.' She watched Harry bounce down the stairs, then ushered him straight out of the door.

Kit and Sophie followed, then Jill keyed in the alarm and slammed the front door shut. She handed Kit Alex's keys and opened the back door of the Range Rover for Harry to jump in. The police had brought Alex's car back last week and she watched Kit open it up for Sophie, then go round to the driver's side and climb in himself. It made her feel peculiar and she determined to sell it, as soon as she possibly could.

Climbing up into the Range Rover, she started the engine and shifted into gear. 'Don't belt up yet,' she said to Harry over her shoulder. 'Gate please!'

She pulled over onto the grass verge just beyond the drive, waved as Sophie and Kit drove past her, then waited for Harry to jump out and close the gate. Seconds later, he got back in, fastened his seat belt and Jill accelerated off.

'What's this all about, Mum?' he asked, before he flipped on his Game Boy.

Jill looked at his pale, anxious face in the rear-view mirror. 'I don't honestly know yet,' she answered, glancing nervously over her shoulder back at the house. She heard the electronic bleep from the back seat as the computer came to life and indicated to turn down Little Hill. 'I only wish I did,' she murmured. 'I only wish I did.'

Kit parked Alex's car in one of the voucher spaces in John Street, a few hundred yards up from Brighton Police Station, and Sophie jumped out to read the notice. 'We've got about four hours,' she said, popping her head inside the car as Kit switched off the engine. 'That should be enough.'

'Right.' Kit climbed out of the car and locked up, tucking the keys in his pocket. 'I hope you know your way round, Sophie, because I haven't got a clue where I am. Which way's the sea?'

Sophie smiled. She stopped, looked behind her and pointed. 'The sea is somewhere over there,' she answered, waving vaguely over the buildings. 'OK?'

'OK.' He smiled back. 'Come on then, police station first. You never know, something new might have turned up.' He began to walk off. 'It's as good a place as any to start and we'll do the seafront after that. Come on!' Sophie had to half run to catch him up.

Inside the station, Kit left Sophie by the door to look at the notice board while he went over to the duty desk and asked the officer sitting there if it was possible to speak to anyone in CID.

'What's the problem, sir? Can I help at all?'

Kit was taken aback; he hadn't expected such a user-friendly approach. 'Er, I don't know but I don't think so. I'm making enquiries about a suspected suicide here, two weeks ago, on the seventeenth of December. Alex Turner – his clothes were found on the beach. I'm here with his daughter Sophie, and we were wondering if any new information might have turned up at all – a witness, or something like that?'

The Sergeant glanced behind Kit at the young woman hovering by the notice board. He remembered the case. It had been the talk of the nick – the bigamist, a fake suicide, then the body turns up in London and it's a murder enquiry transferred to the Met. 'I'm afraid there's no-one available in CID at the moment, sir,' he said truthfully. 'And I wouldn't be in a position to be able to discuss that sort of information with you. I'm afraid we're pretty pushed as we've our own murder enquiry on our hands.'

'I see.'

'Can I take your name and address and perhaps get someone to contact you?'

'No, thanks, but don't worry. I can call back another . . .' Kit stopped to let a young WPC carrying a stack of paper talk to the Sergeant.

'Who're these going out with?' she asked, struggling under the weight of the pile.

'Give them to Charlie, he'll distribute them. Oh, and put a few up round here, will you?'

The WPC nodded, lifted the partition of the desk and walked past Kit with her leaflets.

'Sorry, sir, you were saying?' the Sergeant asked Kit.

'It doesn't matter,' Kit answered. 'Thanks for your time.'

He turned away and walked across to Sophie at the notice board. She was chatting to a young man but Kit ignored the conversation and waited for the right moment to interrupt. He was anxious to be off; they had a lot to do.

'I'm sure they'll find out what happened,' Sophie said to the young man. 'You'd probably be best to go off home and wait there for someone to call you. It might be some time before any news comes in.'

Kit tuned into the conversation and glanced down at the person she was talking to. He was sitting opposite the desk, in full Salvation Army uniform, pale and upset, probably no more than Sophie's age.

'I just can't believe it,' he said, dropping his head into his hands.

'I couldn't when she disappeared. I knew something like this had happened, I just knew it!' He looked up at Sophie. 'I've no idea what she was doing in that area. She told her mum she was going for a walk by the sea, half past two it was. She went in her uniform.'

Kit touched Sophie's arm. She had been drawn into this young man's plight and he could see it was upsetting her. 'Sophie,' he said gently, 'we really ought to go.'

Sophie nodded. 'I'm sorry,' she said to the young man. 'I really hope you find out what happened.'

The young man shrugged hopelessly and Kit glanced above his head at the poster the WPC had just put up. The man's girlfriend had disappeared on the same day as the suicide, the seventeenth of December, and her body had been found last night, in the Kemp Town area. A 999 distress call had been recorded at three pm that day from a public phone box in the same area and the police were appealing for any witnesses who might have seen the woman to come forward. So that was why CID were busy, he thought, moving towards the door. He waited for Sophie to join him, opened the doors for her and then followed her out into the cold, damp December afternoon.

'It's awful, isn't it?' Sophie said, pulling her coat in tight.

Kit shook his head. 'There's nothing we can do,' he answered. They had enough awfulness of their own to contend with. 'Come on, let's get going.'

Together they walked off in the direction of the Brighton Pavilion and the scene of the faked suicide: the grey, forbidding sea.

Two hours later, they sat in a café overlooking the ocean at the tail end of the seafront, where the respectable hotels gave way to the shabby, run-down guest houses used by the social security to accommodate the victims of the housing shortage. Kit was feeling glum. He put the photo of Hugo Blandford on the table between them and every now and then picked it up, tapping it on the

Formica surface. They had run up another dead end: no-one had seen or recognised the man in the photo. They had tried every big hotel and, as far as Brighton was concerned, he hadn't even been there.

Sophie sipped her cappuccino and watched Kit. She had an opinion but she wasn't at all sure about voicing it; she didn't have the confidence. Suddenly Kit glanced up and caught her staring. 'OK,' he said. 'What's your view?'

'How did you . . . ?'

'Practice. Lawyers notice everything, they have to. You have to know if your client is being entirely honest with you, or if they're holding something back, and you have to watch the opposition, pick up on even the minutest clue as to what they're thinking. Well, good ones do anyway.'

'Are you a good lawyer then?'

'Shit hot!' Kit said, and they both smiled.

'Well . . .' Sophie put down her cup. 'If you're so convinced that he would have stayed here . . .'

'It makes sense, doesn't it? He'd have to watch the beach for a day or so, to check the quietest times. He wouldn't want someone coming to try to save him, would he? And he'd need somewhere to stay to be able to do that.'

'OK, accepted, but if it were me, I wouldn't stay anywhere high profile, would you? I'd lie low, especially if I were on the run. I'd choose somewhere very out of the way, in Kemp Town probably, somewhere a bit run-down and seedy where I could pay in cash and no-one would notice me.'

Kit sat upright. 'Hey! That's a pretty smart idea. If this were business, I'd steal it from you and peddle it as my own.'

Sophie smiled.

'So where's Kemp Town?'

'It's where that poor girl was found, a bit of a way up from here.'

Kit stood up, dug around in his pocket and put a couple of pound coins down on the table for the coffee. Sophie picked them up, looked at the till receipt on the saucer and took out her purse. She counted out the exact sum, put it on the table and handed Kit back his money as she stood. 'You owe me seventy pence,' she said. 'I wasn't going to leave them a sixty pence tip.'

Kit smiled, he couldn't help himself. He'd forgotten what it was like to be adolescent, hard up and a student. 'Thanks, I'll give it to you when I get some change.' He helped her on with her coat, then waited for her to lead the way out of the café and on towards Kemp Town.

'So you've never seen this man before?' Kit said again, laying the photo of Hugo Blandford on the top of the reception desk.

'I told you,' the man said, 'never.'

Kit nodded and glanced back at Sophie. She was staring at the man behind the desk, her mouth slightly open as he reapplied his lipstick and twisted a curl at the front of his shoulder-length blond wig with a long pink fingernail. She took the hint and moved off to look at the murky tropical fish tank set into the wall, one ear intent on the conversation at the desk.

The man smiled at Kit and pulled his tight pink sweater down, straightening the hem and drawing attention to his large false bust. Kit put his hand inside his jacket and took out his wallet. He extracted two twenty-pound notes and laid them on top of the photo.

'You're absolutely sure?' he asked a third time. He had a feeling about this place, about this man. Just then the man put his hand over Kit's, on top of the money, and Kit felt the unnatural softness of his skin.

'You're not the old bill, are you?'

Kit held down his repulsion. 'No. Why?'

The man ran his tongue over full, pink lips. 'They've been sniffing round here this morning,' he said, his camp voice lowered to a seductive whisper. 'It's the murder of that little lassie. Poor girl, but it's bad for business. I don't want to get involved with the police. I told them, I know nothing.'

'Of course not,' Kit said, easing his hand away. 'But you have seen this man, haven't you?'

The man nodded. He made to pick up the cash but Kit stopped him, taking hold of his wrist. 'Details,' he said.

The man gasped effeminately. 'Before Christmas.' He fluttered his other hand dismissively in the air. 'It was my busy period, I don't remember the date.'

Kit held the man's wrist and tightened his grip, twisting slightly. 'Try,' he said.

'The same day that girl disappeared,' the man stammered, 'I remember it because I said to Billy that it was a coincidence. I said . . .'

'How long did he stay?'

'One night. He arrived the day before, in the morning, and paid cash for two nights. He left the following afternoon, in a bit of a hurry, about three thirty.'

Kit released the man's wrist and turned away as the man rubbed his inflamed skin. As he turned back he saw that his action had aroused the man: his face was flushed and he smiled, his pink lips pouting.

'You remember anything else?' Kit asked.

The man shrugged. 'He carried a suitcase, and he had a bunch of French francs in his room. The cleaner found them by accident, she . . .'

'Yeah,' Kit interrupted. He didn't want to listen to pointless lies. Picking up the photo, he left the cash where it was. 'Thanks,' he said.

The man smiled and tucked the money down under the desk.

'Any time, sweetie,' he said. 'I'm all yours!' And he laughed as Kit collected Sophie and strode out of the guest house.

'Bingo!' Kit said on the pavement outside. 'That's our man and chances are he's still alive.'

Sophie turned and looked back at the guest house. 'God, what a dump!'

Kit followed her gaze. 'Like you said, perfect if you're lying low. There's no way any of that information would reach the police. The place is as good as a gay brothel, perfect cover.'

Sophie turned back to Kit. 'So, what now?'

'Now we check the nearest ferry port . . .'

'Newhaven,' Sophie filled in for him.

'Right, Newhaven. He apparently had French francs in his room so it looks like he was planning to cross the Channel. We'll see if there's anyone there who remembers him. It's a long shot, but you never know.'

Sophie slung her bag over her shoulder and fell into step with him. 'You know, there's something about this Salvation Army murder that's been bothering me,' she said.

'Try to put it out of your head,' Kit answered. 'I know the young man upset you, but . . . Sophie?' He stopped and turned to look back at her. She had suddenly stopped dead on the pavement.

'What is it? What's the matter?'

Kit walked back to her and placed his hands on her shoulders. 'Sophie? You OK?'

She looked up at him. 'This girl – her boyfriend told me she'd gone down to the beach for a walk, around two thirty, right? Let's say she's walking and she sees a man or the beach trying to commit suicide – he's taken his clothes off and maybe gone into the water – so she runs up the beach and past the seafront to a phone box. The nearest one is not far from here. She makes a 999 call but she never gets to speak to the police. Hugo didn't want any witnesses. It was essential that no-one saw him; you said so earlier. If it'd been

228

reported as it happened then they would have found the body, only there wasn't one, was there? So he sees the girl, follows her, finds her in the phone box and silences her – he doesn't have any choice. He dumps the body near his hotel and leaves in a hurry; the man in there said so. He . . .'

'Stop!' Kit suddenly shouted. 'Sophie, this is crazy! Calm down!' He squeezed her arms and held her still in front of him. 'You can't possibly believe all of this. Your imagination is running wild.'

She stared up at him. 'Is it?'

Kit held her gaze for some time, then dropped his hands away from her arms. 'Yes, I think it is.'

'Well, answer me this then,' she said. 'If you were in serious trouble, and I mean serious trouble, if you'd just murdered someone and covered it up, would you take the chance of being caught out?'

Kit felt his instinct take over. He shook his head. 'No,' he agreed, 'probably not.'

'I don't think there's any "probably" in it,' Sophie said, her eyes blazing. 'Because if you've murdered once, then you can murder again.'

Kit looked at her face, suddenly recognising the truth.

'And again,' she said, and she shivered in the chill winter wind.

Chapter Sixteen

Ted Welsch paid the cabbie and glanced up at his office above the Chinese grocer's. He smiled, sniffing the carbon monoxide in the air, and waved at the Wongs, who ran the shop. Christ, it was good to be back.

Unlocking the door, he shoved it open, stooped to pick up a stack of letters and circulars from the mat, tucked them under his arm and climbed the steep, narrow stairs to the first floor and his office. He could smell stale cigarette smoke in the air and the faint aroma of spices that wafted up from the shop below, familiar smells that made him feel at home. He dumped his case in the passage, put the key in the lock and peered in through the frosted glass panel as he opened the door. His office was exactly as he'd left it: an ashtray full of cigarette butts; a mug of half-finished coffee with mould on the top; and a litter of papers and rubbish on the desk, the filing cabinet and every spare inch of space in the room. Welsch crossed to his desk and sat down. He's made the right decision, he was sure of that now.

Leaning forward, he lifted a pile of papers to look for a notepad and pen; he wanted to go through the post. As he did so, he saw two of the files he'd been working on that he'd abandoned in his haste to leave. He dragged one out from under the pile and flicked through it, stopping twice to double-check the order of the papers. Welsch worked in a mess, he lived in a mess, but his files were always in immaculate order. He put down the file, flicked through the second one and then stood, carefully taking in every inch of the space around him. He had been mistaken; his office wasn't exactly as he'd left it. Someone had been there.

Crossing to the safe, he unlocked it and glanced inside. There wasn't much in there – he'd taken all the cash two weeks ago and he kept his copies of the files on disk at home – but he had an almost photographic memory and he could see immediately that what was in there had been moved. They were looking for copies of the Grigson file, no doubt about it. He walked back to the desk and picked up the phone, then thought better of it. If they hadn't found a copy – and he was certain they hadn't – then they'd still be looking. He reached for his letter opener, slipped it into the join in the receiver and flipped the phone apart. Carefully he pulled out a small electronic chip from the mouthpiece and examined it. Christ, these things were becoming so complex! He held it between his forefinger and thumb for a few moments, pleased with himself, then he flicked it up in the air and dropped it into the mouldy coffee. He clipped the phone back together, pressed the message button on the answermachine and sat down to listen.

Cold call, he wrote on the pad, fast forwarding the first message, then B.O., which stood for bottled out, a message enquiry with no name and number to follow up, then two new clients. He scribbled down their names and numbers with D.C. by the side, initials for divorce case, and fast forwarded the second cold call, from the same office equipment salesman. He stopped the machine halfway through the next message, listened, made a note of the number, then rewound and played it again. He leant forward, straining to pick up any clue in the voice, then cut the message short and grabbed the telephone directory off the floor. He ran his finger down the pages of national codes and spotted the code he'd just jotted down: Henfield. He reached for his road atlas, on top of a pile of papers on the filling cabinet, looked up Henfield in the index and turned to the appropriate page. Henfield was near Eastham; it was a hunch but it felt right.

Welsch tore the piece of paper off the pad, thrust it down into his jacket pocket and headed for the door. He'd phone from the pub. He needed a drink and it was safer there: if the phone was bugged, the office might be as well. Locking the door behind him, he headed for the stairs, stepping over his suitcase and leaving it where it was. Nothing in there to steal, he thought, hurrying down, except some cheap Spanish brandy and a bunch of damp summer shirts. He walked out into the street, double locked the main door and set off to investigate what he was pretty sure was a call from Jill Turner.

Holly sat in the bank manager's office in Chelsea, a swish, high-tech affair with chrome and leather chairs and a black ash desk, and stared at the mass of papers spread out in front of her. She was numb with shock. How could she explain her utter stupidity? She had had no idea what had been going on. She had trusted the running of the business to Sandy and never questioned or even looked at the cash books or bank statements. Why had she done it? Why, with all her education and intelligence, had she chosen to ignore all this?

She picked up the August and September statements. The amount of money coming into the account was phenomenal, much more than she'd been led to believe, and the money going out was even more staggering. It all looked quite legitimate, of course; Sandy had been selling works of art in the Middle East and loading the proceeds into various offshore accounts. Presumably, knowing what she did now, these accounts had already been set up for him; it was all part of the system. She dropped the two statements and picked up those for November and December. In November there had been three major deals, worth almost two million pounds; in December the entire amount had been transferred into a numbered Swiss bank account. Holly's signature was on the withdrawal slip, along with Sandy's. Holly picked up this withdrawal slip and studied it; her signature wasn't perfect but it was a damn good forgery.

'Of course, you do have an overdraft facility to cover the expenses, Miss Grigson, and I'd be happy to extend that to whatever you think you might need.'

Holly nodded blankly.

'Your business is important to us. We've watched you grow over the past two years, and keeping clients is one of the bank's main concerns.'

Again Holly nodded.

'But I would need some sort of confirmation from you as to when funds would be forthcoming. Of course there's no hurry, but . . .'

Holly looked up. 'I'm sorry, you were saying?'

'The funds to cover the overdraft? Perhaps you could give me some kind of time frame? A loose one even?'

Holly's stomach started to churn. 'I don't understand,' she said. 'What about our commission account, the instant savings one, held in joint names?' They had two accounts: one for everyday business and one for the commission, the gallery's profit from the deals. The commission was drawn off the cheque account at the end of every month and transferred. Holly knew this because she always saw those statements; she made sure she did. That account was the measure of the business's success.

The manager opened the brown card file in front of him and flipped through the correspondence in it. 'Here,' he answered, holding out a letter typed on Grigson Gallery paper. 'You instructed us to close that account last month, Miss Grigson. We gave your husband a banker's draft for the amount, as per your instructions.'

Holly looked down at the letter and her hand trembled. It had been printed out on her desk jet – she recognised the type – and it was her signature on the bottom, along with a handwritten note.

'I see,' she murmured, her face ashen. 'May I have a copy of this?'

'Of course. Are you all right, Miss Grigson? Can we get you a glass of water?'

'No, thank you, I'm fine.' Holly closed her eyes for a moment and took a deep breath. When she had recovered, the manager handed her a copy of the letter, which she tucked into her pocket, then she sat for a few moments trying to muster the strength to stand up. 'Can I get back to you on the overdraft?' she asked when she finally managed to get to her feet.

'Yes, of course!' The bank manager was round the desk and by her side within seconds. He was a young man, too young, she thought, as he took her arm. He smelt strongly of expensive citrus aftershave and the scent of it momentarily revived her.

She stood straight, drew on the last of her energy and hooked her bag over her shoulder. 'Thank you for your time this afternoon,' she said, holding out her hand.

'My pleasure, Miss Grigson.' He shook her hand. 'My secretary will show you out.'

'Yes, thanks.' Before all this, with her energy and confidence, Holly might have needled the young man; he was self-important and irritating. But she wasn't at all her former self. She wasn't anything like the Holly Grigson of two weeks ago; she was a shadow, fast losing track of what was happening to her and what she was doing.

Wordlessly, she followed the secretary out into the main part of the bank and left the building. Climbing into a taxi, she gave her address and let her head fall back against the seat. What was the point? she thought. Who was she anyway? And as the cab pulled off into the London traffic she stopped trying to think any more and gave herself up to the feeling of hopelessness that swamped her.

Guy Ferreira sat in his hire car outside Holly's flat, watching the building. He had tried the buzzer but there had been no reply, so all he could do was to sit and wait. He had been there quite some time when a black cab pulled up.

He sat forward and saw Holly climb out, hand some money over and walk towards the building. She stopped at the door and scrabbled fruitlessly in her bag for her keys. Slipping it off her shoulder, she dropped it to the ground, knelt on the cold concrete and ferreted about until she found them. Guy Ferreira watched her, expecting her to go on into the building, but she suddenly started, as if she had just realised something unpleasant, and then swore loudly. She put her hands up to her face and her shoulders sagged. Before she could do anything else, he hurriedly climbed out of the car. By the time he had walked across to the building, Holly was sitting on the steps and, with her head in her hands, she had begun to sob.

'Hello? Excuse me, hello?' Guy called up, standing below her. Holly ignored him but the sobbing stopped. She kept her head down, covered with her hands, and prayed that he'd go away. He didn't. 'I'm sorry, but I'm looking for Holly Grigson,' he said. 'I was wondering if you might know . . .'

Holly lifted her head. She wiped her face hurriedly on the back of her hand and looked at the man in front of her. 'I'm Holly Grigson,' she said. 'Who wants her?'

'Guy Ferreira. I'm a friend of your husband's and . . .'

With that, Holly started to cry again.

'Good Lord! Are you all right?' Guy moved forward, carefully, so as not to intrude. 'God, you're really upset. Is there anything I can do?'

Holly shook her head, keeping it firmly buried in her hands. She recognised the name, remembering his phone calls. Why the hell couldn't he stop interfering and just go away?

'Can I drive you somewhere to get some help? I have my car . . .'

For the second time, Holly looked up. 'I don't need a car,' she snapped. 'I had a bloody car and I've left it in bloody Chelsea, on a parking meter that ran out an hour ago!' Fresh tears welled up as she spoke, angry, useless, hopeless tears. Suddenly she jumped up and stomped off down the steps, then turned round, her face stricken. 'I don't know what I'm doing half the time. I'm making stupid mistakes and errors of judgement, and nothing, nothing at all is right. Everything is wrong! Everything! My whole life is a bloody mess and I can't even remember that I was driving a sodding hire car! I get in a taxi, completely oblivious to the fact that . . .' A sob escaped her and her face collapsed. 'I'm sorry,' she mumbled through her tears, and then turned and fled down the street.

Guy stood where he was for a moment, then set off after her. 'No, wait!' He caught up with her and held her arm, stopping her. Holly was too upset to resist. 'Do you have the car keys?'

She nodded. 'Right, then I'll drive you to the car to collect it.' He kept hold of her arm. 'If there's a fine or a clamp or something then I'll take care of it; I've got cash on me. All right?'

Holly stared at him, the tears streaming down her face, then Guy eased her round, his grip on her arm firm and insistent, and walked her the twenty yards back to his car. He opened it, helped her into the passenger seat and then climbed in himself. 'Where did you leave the car?' he asked, starting up.

'On the King's Road,' Holly answered flatly.

'Right,' Guy said. He pulled out without another word, and Holly sat dumbstruck beside him, wondering how he had just managed to solve a problem that a few moments ago had seemed insurmountable.

Following Holly's directions, Guy drove directly to the hire car, parked a few spaces down and climbed out with her. He had been silent on the journey across, and he was silent now. Holly checked her windscreen for a ticket, but thankfully there was none. She unlocked the driver's door, then turned and looked at him fully for the first time.

'Thank you,' she said, 'I appreciate your help.' He was a good-looking man, elegant and distinguished in his dark suit and immaculate shirt and tie. He didn't look British, but his accent and mannerisms placed him as a public school, Establishment type. It was one Holly was used to. She thought briefly how attractive he was, then focused back on her misery. 'Look, I'm sorry, I'm not usually so out of control. It was just the last straw in what's been a pretty bloody rotten day.'

'Please,' he said, 'it was my pleasure. I certainly couldn't leave you there on the pavement in tears, now could I?'

Holly shook her head and he smiled. 'I never could resist a damsel in distress. Besides, you might have flooded the street.'

Holly smiled back at him. 'Well, thanks again, I appreciate it.' He shrugged. 'When did you last see Sandy?' she suddenly asked. She felt a moment of doubt about him; he was almost too good for words.

But Guy answered the question with ease. 'Gosh, I don't know. It must have been several months ago, I should think. We have a pretty casual friendship – the odd dinner when I'm in town, that kind of thing, you know?'

'Yes, I know.' She pulled open the door and threw her bag across the seat. 'Where did you meet again?'

'On a plane, going to the Middle East.' Guy smiled. 'I liked Sandy straight away; he was very easy to talk to.'

'Yes, he was.' Holly said. She had thought almost the same thing herself when she'd first met him.

'Oh well.' Guy turned to leave.

'Yes. I must get going.' Thanks again; it was really kind of you to rescue me.'

'Not at all.' He shrugged again and set off towards his car, then glanced back over his shoulder at her and waved.

So he wasn't a good friend of Sandy's, Holly thought. He certainly didn't seem to have any idea of what had happened. He really was very attractive. She waved back and watched him for a few moments, wondering how on earth she had got so out of control about forgetting the car, then smiled to herself and climbed in. She started the engine, switched on the lights and sat there, thinking. It really was extremely kind of him, and he'd handled it with the minimum of fuss. She didn't feel nearly as stupid as she might have done and she had put him out without even asking if it was all right. Suddenly, she swung open her door and climbed half out of the car.

'Hello? Excuse me?' she shouted. She'd had an idea. Maybe Guy knew something she didn't. Perhaps, if they talked a bit about Hugo, or Sandy as Guy knew him, she might just be able to glean something from him that she hadn't thought of.

Guy turned round from unlocking his car. 'Yes?' he called back.

'Hang on!' Holly bent inside the car to switch off the engine, then walked along to his car. 'I'm sorry,' she said. 'You must think me terribly rude. You've been so kind, I wondered if maybe I could buy you a drink to say thank you?'

Guy stared at her face for a few moments, then said, 'That's awfully sweet but no, thanks. You look exhausted and you really don't need to thank me – it was a pleasure, honestly. You should get yourself home.' He flashed her a smile. 'Another time maybe.'

He was right – she was tired, another time would be better – but now she'd thought of it, she had to do it. Holly smiled; he was so polite, so terribly English. He reminded her of her brother and she liked his concern for her; it reassured her even further. 'I'm tired,' she said, 'but not exhausted. I'd like to, if you would.' All it would take would be one comment in a conversation, one stray remark, and she could be a hell of a lot closer to solving this whole bloody problem.

Guy glanced at his watch. 'I tell you what, Holly. You buy me a drink and I'll buy you supper. Despite what you say, you look shattered, and I'm worried that if we don't get some food inside you you might collapse on me.'

Holly smiled once more. Why had she been so suspicious of this man? 'It's a deal,' she said.

The restaurant was a small rustic Italian place in a back street of Chelsea. It was well known and expensive, but not smart or pretentious – all terracotta tile, pale cream and Tuscan pottery, dimly lit and packed, the air thick with loud conversation, cigarette smoke and the smell of olive oil and garlic. The food was superb, although Holly didn't taste much of it. By the time the main course arrived she had downed a bottle and a half of good Chianti Special Reserve and nibbled on a lone piece of ciabatta dipped in chilli-infused olive oil. She spoke quickly, slurring her words every now and then, smoked Guy's cigarettes almost continuously, and completely lost track of what she had said to him and why. Holly was drunk. She had forgotten that she hadn't eaten properly for two days. Over the past few hours Guy had continually filled and refilled her glass so that it had never once been empty and she had no idea how much she had downed. Not that it mattered, of course. Guy was the perfect gentleman – courteous, pleasant, understanding. Hell, he had even been at the same school as her brother! He was an old Seftonian, ex-Cambridge too – a completely different college to her and Kit, and older of course, before their time, but still a Cambridge man, and, frankly, that made her feel very comfortable.

And the more comfortable Holly felt, the more she relaxed and the more she lost track of the wine. It loosened her tongue; it made her want to talk; and talk she did. She opened up with amazing ease, feeling, under a haze of wine-induced relief, that she was conversing with someone who really understood. She talked about Sandy and kept muddling his name up, calling him Hugo or Alex. She told Guy about the gallery, the accounts, the bugging of Jill's phone, the fact that her husband wasn't her husband, wasn't even the man he had said he was, and she divulged Kit's idea of money laundering and an involvement in organised crime. She told him everything and he listened, carefully and sensitively, saying very little, showing he understood the way she felt by the odd touch of his hand, a look, or a comment. Holly would never have unburdened herself if she had been sober, but she wasn't sober. She was under the alcoholic illusion that she was safe – with a man whom she had thought two weeks earlier might be involved in something sinister.

'So you see what a bloody mess I'm in?' She sat, her chin propped up by both hands, a plate of untouched pasta with smoked salmon and vodka sauce pushed to one side, a cigarette smoking in the ashtray in front of her. 'That's why I flipped about the car!' She shook her head, reaching for her wine and slopping it over the tablecloth. 'The car,' she slurred, 'was the last thing, the last thing I could cope with . . . the last thing . . .' Holly picked up the cigarette and stubbed it out, then took another from the box, gesticulating with it. 'I tell you, Guy, I couldn't have taken much more, I . . .' She leant forward to the candle, lit the cigarette, singed her hair and narrowly missed setting it on fire. 'Whaddayou think, huh? Isn't it terrible? Huh?'

Guy nodded. He had somehow managed to indicate that he wanted his bill without Holly seeing him move. A waiter materialised by his side and Holly looked up, amazed – not that she could see the waiter particularly clearly, or Guy for that matter.

'Where'd he come from?' she said, smiling lopsidedly. 'Pooof! Magic!' She clicked her fingers, dropped the cigarette and burnt a small hole in the cream linen tablecloth. 'Whoops, thilly me!' Sitting up straight, she took another sip of wine and wondered, in a flash of rational thought, how she had gone from reasonably tipsy to pretty damn drunk in so short a space of time. 'I think we'd bedda go . . .' she murmured. The room was hazy and Guy's face swam slightly out of focus across the table from her. Holly stood, held onto the table for support and breathed a sigh of relief as Guy appeared almost instantly by her side. 'You,' she said, poking him in the chest. 'You are sooo wonderful . . .' He held her arm and smiled, guiding her expertly out through the maze of tables. 'And you shmell delicious. Hmmmm!' She nuzzled his neck. 'Floris!' she announced. 'Know it anywhere . . .'

Holly waved and smiled at several diners staring at her. 'Byeee,' she called to a table she knocked into. 'Soo sorry . . .' Minutes later she was safely outside the door.

'Right,' Guy said. 'Home.'

But Holly couldn't answer him. The icy air had hit her full force and she swayed precariously, suddenly very drunk indeed. She let Guy lead her along the road to his car, slumped against it while he opened the door, and then collapsed onto the front seat, her head falling forward. Guy clipped in her seat belt, leant across her to lock the door and finally switched on the engine. He glanced at her, saw she was asleep and relaxed for the first time all evening.

Clipping in his own seat belt, he shifted into gear and pulled out, switching on the headlamps as he went. He glanced sidelong at Holly, snoring lightly in the passenger seat, and amusement flickered in his eyes. He smiled, then looked ahead and focused on the road. 'Here's to us,' he said. 'And a very productive friendship.'

Holly heard something but couldn't quite focus her brain. She kept her eyes shut and drifted in and out of consciousness for a minute or so. She rolled over, pulled the duvet up around her ears and let the images in her mind soothe her back to sleep.

Ten minutes later, she sat bolt upright in bed.

'Oh shit!'

Holding down the urge to retch, she put one hand up to her throbbing temple and fumbled blindly in the dark for the telephone with the other. Eventually she grabbed it, her hand trembling, her whole body in a state of acute alcoholic shock, and croaked down the line. 'Hello . . . ?'

'Holly? Is that you?' It was Kit; he sounded frantic.

'Yes . . .'

'Where the hell have you been? It's three am! Christ, I've been worried sick! What happened? Are you all right?'

Holly dropped back on the pillows, closed her eyes for a moment, and a vision of the evening with Guy flashed before them. She groaned and snapped them open again. 'Where are you?'

'I'm in Sussex. Holly, what's . . .'

'I'll ring you back!' Seconds later, she leant over the side of the bed, grabbed the plant pot and was violently sick.

Crawling out of bed, she staggered to the bathroom, held her head over the basin and was sick again. She retched for ten minutes. Exhausted, she ran the taps until the sink was clean, and then went back to the bedroom to clear up the mess. That done, she returned to the bathroom and ran the shower. She was wearing just her bra and pants – she had no idea how she had got undressed or into bed. She could only thank God that she was still in one piece. Stripping off, she dropped her underwear on the floor and stepped under the shower. Feeling the hot water pour down over her, she scrubbed herself with a soapy loofah, shampooed her hair, scrubbed again, then switched the water to cold. She gritted her teeth and stood under the powerful jet for a minute or so, then climbed out, reached for a towel and wrapped herself up. She sat on the edge of the bath shivering while bits of the evening flooded back to her, filled with remorse.

What the hell had she done? She must have been out of her mind. She had gone out to dinner with a man she had never met before, got blind drunk, told him everything, put herself in danger, perhaps even put Kit and Jill in danger. She had no real idea of who Guy Ferreira was. Sure, he was at school with her brother – did he say he was at Cambridge? She couldn't quite remember. But what connection did he have to Sandy; where did he come from? And, if he worked in New York, then what was he doing in London? Christ, she hadn't even asked!

She went to the airing cupboard and found a pair of floral winceyette pyjamas. Dropping the towel on the floor, she put them on, then added a pair of clean socks from the laundry basket, a cardigan and a clean towel for her hair. Going through to the hallway, she found her bag and took out her diary, which contained Jill's number. She was about to pick up the phone when she saw a handwritten note propped up against the lamp.

She sat on the chair in the hall and opened the envelope. 'Dear Holly,' it said, 'I delivered you home and helped you into bed, in case you are wondering how it all happened, and I am off to collect your car now. I will drop the keys through the letter box and get a taxi back to where I am staying. I enclose one of my business cards, the number of my accommodation is on the back. Please ring and let me know that you are all right or I shall worry. Yours with affection, Guy.' The writing was small and looped, a neat script, very proper.

Holly looked at the card for a few moments, unsure of what to make of it all, then she replaced the note in its envelope and dropped it on the hall table. She dialled Sussex and spoke to Kit but said nothing about her evening, nothing about Guy, just that she would see him in the morning, once she had tried to call Marcus. She apologised for worrying him, made some feeble excuse about fatigue and needing to be alone, then hung up.

Still holding the card, she wandered through to the sitting room and slumped down onto the sofa. She felt hungover, exhausted and sick, in the pit of her stomach – sick of the whole damn mess and her own stupidity. She would ring Guy Ferreira in the morning, thank him for his concern and leave it at that. She had made another huge mistake, but she would clear it up as best she could and try to forget it.

Chances were that he was a perfectly decent man, she thought. He did after all get her home and care enough to make sure she was all right. The problem was, she had been blind drunk, made a ghastly fool of herself and said far too much. That made her vulnerable and she was exposed enough as it was.

Curling up and hugging a cushion, Holly went over what she would say to Guy Ferreira. She would be pleasant and cool, but would make it quite clear that last night was a one-off. She would keep it polite, tell it to him straight, and hopefully, that would be the end of it.

Outside in the street the Weasel watched the light in the second-floor flat go out. He watched for any other sign of movement, then, satisfied that Holly had gone back to bed, he took out his mobile and dialled.

The man shifted position slightly and reached for the phone. He was naked; the girl he had just hired was underneath him, kneeling on all fours, her firm, oiled buttocks pressed hard against his groin, her full breasts swinging forward over the edge of the bed. She moaned as he twisted to answer the call, but held perfectly still so that he didn't need to withdraw.

'It's me,' the Weasel said. 'It's all quiet, she's . . .'

'Yes,' the man interrupted. He held the phone in the crook of his shoulder and moved his hands down to the girl's hips. She was small and dark, lithe, as alike as the agency could manage. He ground into her, making her gasp, and smiled. 'Tell me something I don't know,' he said into the phone. Then without another word, he hung up.

Chapter Seventeen

At seven am the following morning, Holly sat propped up against a pile of cushions on the sofa in the sitting room and nursed a hot, sweet cup of tea. She had swallowed back two aspirins half an hour earlier and managed to keep them down, so now she was attempting the tea. She felt lousy. She had slept for only an hour since the phone call from Kit, and on waking her head ached even worse, her stomach churned, she was shaky and depressed, and to cap it all, she looked as dreadful as she felt. Her hair was a frizz from not blow-drying it, her face was blotchy and puffy, her eyes bloodshot, and the fingers on her right hand reeked of stale tobacco, a smell so stubborn that no amount of scented soap could shift it. Miserably, she waited for the tea to warm her and for her symptoms to work their way through her system. She had things to do, calls to make, but none of it could be done while she felt like death.

Staring at the wall, Holly tried to think of anything but the previous night, only, no matter how strenuous her efforts, she couldn't help herself. The whole evening kept whirring round and round in her head: what she'd said, what she hadn't said; what she could and couldn't remember. It was a mess, and the sooner she cleared it up the better.

Finishing her tea, she gingerly walked back to the kitchen and reached up into the cupboard for a plain biscuit. It she could keep the tea down then a biscuit was the next move. If the biscuit stayed put, then she could get on with calling the States without the threat of throwing up halfway through the call. She nibbled, found she was actually able to swallow, then bit a chunk of biscuit, chewed and got that down. She refilled the kettle for more tea, finished the biscuit and took two more out of the tin. At this rate she might just make the call before the end of the day. Feeling slightly cheered, she made a second cup of tea and took it through to the sitting room.

An hour later, Holly was dressed. She didn't feel well but at least she didn't feel as ill as she had done. She looked up Marcus's telephone number in her diary, where she had copied it from the book in the office. She knew New York was five hours behind but she didn't care – at three o'clock in the morning she reckoned she had more chance of catching him, even if it was in bed. She dialled the number, waited for the second or so it took for the international line to connect, then heard a ringing tone. Three rings and an answerphone clicked on. At least that's better than nothing, she thought, then she felt a rush of blood to her face.

'Hi there! You've dialled Day Fresh Cosmetics. We're sorry but there's no-one here to take your call at the moment. Our opening hours are between eight am and six pm, but if you'd like to leave your name and telephone number, one of our operators will ring you right back. Thank you for your call – and please speak after the beep.'

Holly hung up, checked her number and dialled a second time. There were three rings and the same answerphone clicked on. She hung up again.

'Oh shit!' She recognised the pattern; it was sickeningly familiar. Dialling international directory enquiries, she gave Marcus's full name and address, as she had copied them down, and was asked to wait. Fifteen seconds later, the operator came back on the line.

'I'm unable to trace any persons listed under that name and

address, madam. Would you like me to ask the operator in the States to have a go?'

'Yes, please.' Holly sat on the chair in the hall and waited. She already knew the answer. A minute later, the operator was back on the line. 'There is no-one listed under that name and address, madam.'

'I see,' Holly said. 'Thanks.'

She hung up and dropped her head in her hands. Of course there was no Marcus! Of course there was no New York studio address, no listed number for him – he didn't exist! Why should he? Nothing else was real in this whole bloody mess, so why should he be? She massaged the ache in her temples for a few moments, then picked up the note from Guy Ferreira. She dialled the number on the back of his card, asked for his suite and was told the line was busy.

'Do you wish to hold?' the receptionist asked.

Holly sighed. If she didn't hold then she'd probably bottle out, the way she felt at the moment. 'Yes,' she answered, feeling horribly sick again. 'I'll hold.'

Moments later Guy came on the line.

Holly instantly prickled at the sound of his voice. She was nervous, but anxious not to let it show.

'Hello? Guy Ferreira?' She tried to sound relaxed.

'Holly!' Guy took out a cigarette and lit it. 'Good morning! How are you feeling?'

'Fine,' she answered tightly, thrown by his warmth. 'Thanks for, er . . .' She flushed as she spoke. 'For last night and helping me home. I'm sorry about . . .'

Guy cut her short. 'Forget it. You're under pressure; last night was a safety valve. No harm done.'

'Look, Guy . . .'

'Look, Holly . . .'

They both spoke simultaneously. Holly laughed nervously. 'Sorry,' she said. 'You first.'

'OK. Well, I was going to say that I think we need to talk.'

Holly tensed. 'Really?' She swallowed, her throat dry. 'What about?'

Guy paused. 'Did you get through to that artist chap you were talking about last night?'

Holly closed her eyes for a moment. She couldn't remember even mentioning Marcus. 'Artist?' she murmured.

'Back at the flat,' Guy answered quickly, 'you said . . .'

'Oh, I see.' Of course she couldn't remember. She had been so drunk by the time they'd got back to the flat that she couldn't even remember how she had ended up in bed, let alone the conversation leading up to it. 'As a matter of fact, no, I didn't.'

'I had a funny feeling you were going to say that,' he said.

Holly tensed again. 'You did?'

'Yes.' Guy paused, just long enough to add resonance to his next sentence. 'Holly, I'm worried about all this, about what you told me, and I'm not sure, but I think I can help.'

Holly said nothing. She had been so ready to take the initiative, to cut things dead, and so practised in her lines, that she wasn't prepared for this. Guy had the upper hand and she was momentarily lost for words.

'You don't have to make any decision now but I think we should at least talk. Can we meet for lunch?'

Holly hesitated.

'All right, not lunch then, a cup of coffee, and just listen to what I've got to say?'

She was flummoxed.

'Please, Holly, I'm worried for you.'

The edge of sympathy and understanding to his voice was what did it. 'All right,' she agreed. 'Let's meet in the coffee room at the Savoy. I can be there in an hour.'

Guy smiled on the other end of the line. 'Good, I'll see you then.'

'Yes, see you then.' She hesitated. 'Oh, and thanks,' she added. His smile widened. Without another word, he hung up.

Kit drove slowly along Pleasant Place Road in Merton while Jill counted off the numbers of the houses; they were looking for forty-two. At fifty, Kit spotted a parking space. He manoeuvred Alex's car expertly into the slot, switched off the engine and looked at Jill.

'It's three houses down, on the right,' he said. Jill nodded, looking back at the mile or so of identical mock-Tudor semis they had driven past, all with immaculate front gardens, pruned roses and winter bedding plants. She opened the door and climbed out.

'Are they all the same?' she asked.

Kit glanced across at her, unsure if she was taking the piss. 'Pretty much,' he answered. 'Come on.' He locked the car and led the way along to number forty-two.

Ted Welsch opened the door as they came up the front path to let a large man wearing outsize jeans and a black ZZ Top tee-shirt out of the house. The fat man was carrying headphones, along with what looked like a metal detector, and he was sweating, despite his tee-shirt in the icy January weather. Welsch smiled.

'Mrs Turner?'

'Yes.'

He stepped forward and held out his hand. 'Ted Welsch,' he said, moving in closer. The smell of his aftershave was overpowering. 'Nice to meet you, very nice. This is a friend of mine, Garth.' He spoke quickly and nodded towards the fat man.

Jill smiled but the fat man looked at her impassively, without speaking, so she shook Welsch's hand, introduced Kit and tried to ignore him.

'Come on in,' Welsch said. 'Garth's just leaving, he's been doing a small job for me. Cheers, Garth, mate, I'll catch up with you later, awright?'

Garth nodded but still said nothing. Both Kit and Jill stepped aside to let him down the path.

'Was that a metal detector?' Kit asked, following Jill inside the house.

'No.' Welsch led them through to the front room. 'A machine to detect bugging devices. It's very complicated and I can't for the life of me remember what it's called, but Garth is an expert. Doesn't look it, mind you . . .'

'You think the place was bugged?' Kit interrupted.

'I know it was.' Welsch pointed to the huge tropical fish tank he'd had set into the wall and both Jill and Kit turned to look at it. 'Have a look, see if you can spot 'em.'

'Kit smiled. He walked across and looked into the water, where he saw two tiny electronic chips, one settled on a shell, the other in amongst the long, floating leaves of an aquatic plant.

'They won't be able to hear much from this house now. Drink?' Welsch nodded towards a mock Hawaiian bar in the corner of the room, complete with rattan bar stools and pictures of palm trees. 'Or coffee?'

Jill saw the bar and her mouth dropped open. She took in the cocktail glass on the top with its collection of small pink and purple paper parasols, the huge full-colour photo of a topless Hawaiian girl in grass skirt and floral garland on the wall behind, the rows of gruesome-looking bottles of spirits and liqueurs and the six matching plastic coconut shells with detachable lids for cocktails. She heard Kit cough politely behind her and swung round. 'Oh, er, coffee,' she answered quickly. 'Please.'

Welsch smiled. 'You like it, eh?'

'What?' Jill followed his gaze. 'Oh, yes! it's very, er, authentic!'

Welsch's smile warmed. 'Yeah, it is, isn't it? Made it myself, after a trip out there, to Honolulu, 'seventy-nine, I think it was, or 'eighty. Fantastic place! Ever been?'

'No, I haven't. Have you, Kit?'

Kit shook his head. 'You travel much with your work?' he asked.

The question brought Welsch back to the purpose of the visit. 'Nah, not much. Come on into the kitchen and I'll put the kettle on. I use the back room there as my office.' He led the way through an arch into the back room and the kitchen tucked off the side.

Jill smelt cats, looked down just in time and narrowly missed walking into the cat litter tray.

'Oh, mind the cat's toilet,' Welsch said. He picked it up and slid it inside a kitchen cupboard, then turned to wash his hands in washing-up liquid, squelching them together with the thick green liquid and rinsing them vigorously under the tap. 'Don't mind cats,' he said, 'but I wish they'd shit outside!'

Jill couldn't help herself; she smiled.

Welsch made coffee, offered chocolate biscuits round then led the way back into what had been the dining room and was now his home office. He switched on his computer, turned the desk chair upside down and slipped his hand inside a split in the material underneath. He pulled out a disk.

'As I already told you on the phone, the hard copy of this got taken, but I keep the important files on disk, and this one,' he held it up to the light, 'is shit hot!'

Upturning the chair again, Welsch sat down and slotted the disk into his machine. Within seconds the screen was filled with lines of figures and dates.

'The Grigson file, 1991, we called it,' he said, 'courtesy of your husband, Mrs Turner. It's a list of trades in commodities futures, trades put through the market by his partner Hugo Blandford.' Kit leant forward to look at the screen and Welsch reached across the table for a couple of swivel chairs. 'Here,' he said, 'have a better look.' He pushed his own chair back and Kit sat one side, Jill the other. They stared at the screen.

'See how a lot of the money comes from a bank in the Cayman

Islands?' Welsch pointed out several figures. 'Here and here and here . . .' Kit nodded. 'That was when Alex Turner got suspicious. A Cayman Island bank could have meant that the money was dodgy, and that, along with the huge sums Blandford was throwing into the market, started ringing alarm bells.'

'Why is a Cayman Island bank dodgy?' Jill asked.

'Well it isn't, not always, but it is a known way of hiding dirty money and it's a good way of getting partially washed money into the country. It's semi-legit, so to speak. Once an operator like Blandford puts it into the market it's virtually impossible to trace. There's no documentation, and providing the clearing house isn't concerned about credit – which presumably they weren't, because there was plenty of cash – then Blandford could push as much money as he liked into the market. He was a sharp dealer, he made hundreds of trades, and the money got "lost". When he took his profit, which he invariably did, playing the market as well as he did, then that profit was clean.'

'Jesus, it's complicated!' Kit said.

Welsch smiled. 'Not really. All you need to remember is that before the Criminal Justice Act of 'ninety-three, which well and truly put a spanner in the works, no-one really cared where the money came from, and once into the market it was untraceable. That's why they brought in the money laundering regulations. It was too friggin' easy!'

'So why didn't Alex go to the police then, if he thought Hugo was doing something illegal?' Jill had always seen life in terms of black and white, right and wrong; she found grey areas very hard to comprehend.

'Maybe he was scared. We're not talking small money here or small-time crime. Hugo Blandford was in it right up to his neck. Maybe your husband was frightened for you as well – it's not unheard of for . . .'

'So what did happen?' Kit asked quickly. The last thing Jill needed was a résumé from Welsch on the violence of an organised crime ring.

'Things went quiet,' Welsch said, disappointed not to be able to go into gruesome detail. He moved on to the next page in his file. 'Blandford stopped dealing such large amounts. My guess is that the big boys had had the tip-off about the regulations and he started looking for another route for the money.'

'The gallery,' Kit said.

'Right.'

'But why was Alex involved?' Jill asked. 'Why couldn't he have left it alone? I mean, if Hugo wasn't using the business any longer?'

Welsch glanced sidelong at her. She was a hell of a looker and if it'd been him he'd have got the hell out of there, taken the wife and the family and disappeared. He shrugged. 'Your husband thought Blandford might be impersonating him and he wanted to know what the hell he was up to.'

'That's when he contacted you?'

'No, a bit later on, in the middle of last year. He let things lie for a while, watched Blandford to make sure there was something there, then he decided that he needed to find out more, so he called me.'

'And commissioned a financial search on Hugo Blandford?' Kit asked.

Welsch sucked his cheeks in and ran his tongue over his top teeth. 'Not exactly,' he answered. 'This was a bit more than that. He, er, paid me in cash for most of the work. It was more of an investigation, really.' He glanced up. 'But I did put through one account for financial search, to keep the Inland Revenue happy.'

'The one we found.'

'Yeah, that's it.'

'What sort of investigation?' Jill asked tensely.

Welsch sighed. 'It started as a general enquiry but once I got going I knew there was more. I shouldn't have got involved myself really but it kind of spiralled.' Again he ran his tongue over his top teeth; it was a nervous habit of his. 'I looked into Hugo Blandford, found out what he was doing in the art market and with the Grigson Gallery, then I went higher up and tried to suss out the organisation behind him.'

'And?'

Welsch clicked the mouse on, flipped through the file and pages of notes flicked across the screen. 'You know about the art deals?'

Kit nodded as he watched the screen. Welsch seemed to have everything there; it was beginning to scare him.

'And you know presumably that Blandford planned to do a runner when the time came with a whole lot of money? Or that's my guess, anyroad.'

Kit nodded. 'He did it,' he said. 'Three million transferred into a numbered Swiss bank account.' Holly had told him what had happened at the bank during their phone conversation the previous night.

'Jesus!' Welsch looked round and shook his head. 'And he's disappeared, yeah?'

'Yes.'

'Well, that explains a hell of a lot of what you told me on the phone – the bugging, the break-ins. If Blandford's ripped off his employers then there's going to be one very pissed off set of thugs on the loose.' He went back to the screen and continued to click the pages of his file on. 'Jesus!' he said again, shaking his head. 'When did you find this out?'

'Last night.'

Welsch carried on searching. 'Here,' he said finally, 'this is where I got to.' A police-type dossier came up: a photograph had been scanned in and personal details typed underneath it. 'The middle man,' Welsch announced. 'He's one of the runners and someone Blandford took his instructions from. He knew where the money was and where to set the deals up.' Welsch clicked the mouse and another page came up, this time showing two photos of the middle man, conferring with some other men.

'Who's that?' Kit asked, pointing to a figure in the shot. The photo was slightly blurred due to the distance and the other man had his back to the camera, but Kit had a feeling about him. He had an aura of power about him, even from a distance and in black-and-white print.

'Dunno,' Welsch answered. 'Might be important, our middle man looks as if he's about to kiss his ass!' He smiled. 'Nice suit too, designer label.'

'You've no idea?'

'Nah.' Welsch flicked another picture up onto the screen. 'There's two or three I can't name, probably yes-men like our friend, all reporting to someone else.' He forgot Jill was in the room for a moment and scratched his crutch. Glancing up, he saw her staring at him and nervously lubricated his teeth with his tongue. 'They run the whole thing like some sort of huge multinational corporation, area managers reporting to, say, an MD for Europe. The higher up they are, the more qualifications they have; people like bankers, international lawyers. It's bloody smooth and it's bloody professional.' He sat back. 'It's what I'd call slick,' he said finally, summing it up.

Kit leant forward. 'Go back a page, would you?'

Welsch did as he was asked.

'Are you absolutely sure you don't know who that is?' Kit asked, pointing to the man seen from behind.

'No idea. He could be the top man but I really couldn't say. That's the baby I'm missing and without him . . .' Welsch held his hands up helplessly.

Kit stared at the shot, then turned away. 'Yes,' he murmured, 'understood. So what next? What are you going to do with all this?'

Welsch snorted. 'What am I going to do?' He shook his head. 'It isn't up to me, mate; you're as involved as I am!' He tapped his neck. 'We're in it up to here,' he said, thinking back to the day at the station. 'Christ, I've already nearly . . .' He broke off as Jill abruptly stood up. Perhaps it wouldn't do to say too much about the attempt on his life in front of the lady. 'You awright?' he called out.

Jill had opened the back door and stood in the freezing air looking out at the unashamed mess that was Welsch's back garden. She hugged her arms in to her body and shivered. What the hell am I doing? she thought. How the hell did I get involved in all this? An image of Alex's body on the slab flashed before her eyes and she caught her breath at the intensity of it.

'You all right, Jill?'

Kit stood behind her but kept his distance. She nodded, unable to speak. Was she all right? Or was she out of her mind? She turned round. 'Who killed Alex?'

Kit took a deep breath. 'I don't know,' he answered honestly, 'not for certain, but I think it was Blandford.' He glanced behind him and saw Welsch watching him. 'What do you think?'

'It wasn't a professional job,' Welsch said. 'They'd never have found the body if it had been.'

Jill shuddered. 'So what now? You know all this . . . no, correction, *we* know all this, and where the hell does it lead us?'

'It leads us to the only possible conclusion,' Welsch said.

'Which is?'

'Find Blandford.'

Jill shook her head. 'You must be joking!' she exclaimed. 'Why on earth should we . . .'

Welsch held up his hands to interrupt her. 'We aren't playing parts in some Hollywood movie here, Mrs T – this is for real and I don't think we got much choice. This whole situation's beginning to look bloody dangerous. We know too much, you understand that?' He stopped to make sure she was taking in what he was

saying, then went on. 'You asked me what next, Mrs T. I'm telling
you. We gotta find Blandford and leave the trail wide open.'

'You really think that's the thing to do?' Kit asked.

Welsch shrugged. 'Yeah, I think it's the thing to do. In fact I think
it's the only thing to do.' He looked from Kit to Jill, then turned back
to his screen and stared at the picture of the man for a few moments.
Without looking up, he said, 'We gotta find Hugo Blandford. It's as
simple as that.'

'Find Hugo Blandford?' Holly sat back astounded. 'I see. It's as
simple as that, is it?'

Guy held up his hands in protest. 'Whoa! I never said it was
simple. I just said that as far as I can see you haven't got much
choice.'

'I haven't?'

'No. This Blandford could be dangerous, not to mention the
people who will be looking to get their money back. In my opinion
it's a question of finding him before he – or they, for that matter –
find you.'

'In your opinion? It is only an opinion then?'

'Yes, it's my opinion. I'm not telling you to do anything, Holly.'
Guy shrugged. 'You should have realised that by now.' He
motioned for the waiter, ordered more coffee, then lit a cigarette.

Holly watched him turn away and glance around the coffee
room, giving her time to make up her mind about what he'd said.
He didn't push, or cajole, he simply stated what he thought and
left her to it. Holly liked that; it credited her with intelligence.

Of course, she'd been suspicious at first. She had arrived at their
meeting with her lines rehearsed and her mind made up. But Guy
was convincing and, despite her resolve, she had listened to what
he had to say. Now, looking across at him, Holly realised that a
great deal of it made sense. If it wasn't Sandy going through her flat,
Alex Turner's house, his office and the gallery, then it was someone

who wanted him or information on him, and if they couldn't get Sandy, would she be the next best thing? Holly closed her eyes for a moment and the recurrent image of her body tied and taped up flashed into her mind. She shivered, with a very real fear of the memory. Perhaps Guy was right. Perhaps she should trust him, trust her own instincts? She really didn't know. Certainly she had nothing to lose by going along with him, for a while at least.

'OK,' she said, waiting for Guy to turn his attention back to her. 'Supposing I haven't got any choice and I agree with what you've said. Here's my next question for your precise legal mind. How? How the hell do I find Hugo Blandford?'

Guy stubbed out his cigarette and poured them both another coffee before answering her. 'Now that is what I, we, still have to work out.' He spooned some sugar into his cup and stirred, slowly. 'But much of it, of course, depends on you.'

Holly put down her cup. 'Me?'

He smiled. 'Don't look so surprised. Yes, you. Before we decide anything at all, Holly, you have to make up your mind about me.'

'Make up my mind?'

Guy narrowed his eyes. 'Yes, about whether I'm legitimate or not.' He took a sip of coffee, carefully placed the cup on the saucer and looked straight at her. Holly wondered for a moment if he could read her mind. 'I've told you who I am and who I work for in New York, but I get the feeling you still don't believe me. Certainly I don't think you trust me, probably quite rightly, after what you've just been through. But,' he paused a moment, 'I'm afraid I think this whole thing is far too risky for you not to have worked it through, properly and carefully. I want you to be sure before we go any further.'

Holly was surprised. There was no macho posturing here. Guy had given her her own space, not tried to push or dictate his terms.

'What if I decide that I don't trust you?' she asked.

Guy shrugged. He finished his coffee and said, 'I leave well alone. I don't want to get involved in something like this just for the sake of it. I will finish my legal business in the UK, get on the next plane and you will never see me again.'

Holly stared at him. 'So why get involved anyway?' He looked away and reached for his cigarettes. He had been waiting for this moment. Fumbling slightly, he lit up, then turned back to her. She waited.

'Because I like you,' he answered finally. 'I like you an awful lot more than most of the people I've met before.'

Holly caught her breath. She lowered her eyes, suddenly embarrassed. His words were very powerful in their honesty and simplicity.

'And I want to help you, Holly,' he added.

She looked up and met his gaze. For a moment she was stunned by the sheer physical beauty of him, then out of nowhere Kit popped into her mind and she glanced down again.

'So?' Guy asked gently.

Holly hesitated, still unsure, then she took a deep breath and went with her instinct. 'OK. So tell me, how do I find Hugo Blandford?'

'How?' DS Eames asked. 'How on earth do you expect me to find Hugo Blandford?' He sat back and rubbed his hands wearily over his face. 'Supposing, of course, that he can answer our questions, which I sincerely doubt!' He shoved the pile of photocopies he had been working on to one side. 'I don't see what he can tell us that this stack here can't.'

DCI Heeley offered his pack of cigarettes and Eames took one, lit it and handed the lighter across the desk. He was sitting directly opposite Heeley and had occupied the same seat for over seven hours now. He was tired, and he couldn't grasp Heeley's point at all.

'Look,' Heeley said, 'data from the London Commodity Exchange says that Alex Turner Investments were putting through one hell of a lot of trades in 'ninety-one, shortly before the Criminal Justice Act of 'ninety-three that cleared the market of dodgy deals. We're talking large amounts of money that suddenly dry up post the Act. Don't you think that's some kind of massive coincidence?'

Eames shrugged. 'Perhaps they lost a major client?'

'Too bloody right they did. The big boys don't take stupid risks. Once the market regulations looked set to go, they got out. They moved on to easier things.' He reached across the desk for the Grigson Gallery bank statements. 'Nice work, by the way. How did you manage to get the court order through so quickly?'

'Judge Wilcox wanted me in and out so he could get back to his festivities. I think we rather interrupted things.' Eames raised an eyebrow. 'He was half-cut, full of . . .' He imitated the elderly judge: '". . . rather splendid roast beef, lad!"'

Heeley smiled. 'Well, you got what we wanted and these statements here tell us that whatever Alex Turner was selling at that gallery, he was making an awful lot of dosh from it. Then he was piling that dosh into offshore accounts. The trouble is, the statements don't tell us any more than that. We're not fraud squad – which reminds me, did you speak to your mate over there?'

Eames nodded. 'He's keeping an eye on things. He'll let us know if he comes up with anything.'

'Good. So, why find Hugo Blandford?' Heeley finished his cigarette and immediately lit another one. 'OK, so far all we've got is a bunch of figures that might or might not be suspicious, right? Blandford disappeared in early 'ninety-two, just after the big deals stop and just before the whole art thing starts. My guess is that he knew exactly what was going on at Alex Turner Investments and was scared off. I will also hazard a guess that he knew about the gallery as well.'

Eames nodded. 'Well, whatever was going on,' he said, glancing through the pile of data from the Stock Exchange, the Commodities Exchange and the Futures Exchange, 'Turner was certainly a very busy man.' He ran his finger down a list of trades on the Stock Exchange. 'In February this year, Alex Turner was not only doing a brisk business in finance . . .' He cross-checked with a bank statement for the gallery, '. . . but he was also selling a hell of a lot of paintings. In fact . . .' He suddenly stopped, glanced back and double-checked the date. Then he looked up at Heeley. 'According to this, sir, he was in two different places at exactly the same time!'

'What?' DCI Heeley jumped up and went across to Eames' side of the desk. He was holding a statement for the bank's own credit card. 'Look, here, Turner must have been in Beirut – there's the transactions he did there, two dinners, one purchase in duty free – and yet here . . .' Eames held his finger under the appropriate line on the computer sheet. 'He also bought three thousand shares in ICI, three thousand in Hanson . . .' He trailed his finger down the list. 'And the rest . . .' He looked at Heeley. 'All dated while he was in Beirut and all done in London.' He shook his head. 'I knew it! I bloody knew it. Holly Grigson! He couldn't have done this alone, unless he's a bloody magician! He must have had someone else in on it.' Eames stood up, too agitated to sit. 'Jesus! We should have had her in again. I knew she wasn't telling me everything, I knew it right from the . . .'

Heeley held up his hands. 'Whoa! Hang on a minute!' He continued to look through the data for a few moments. 'It could be the other one, you know, the legit wife.'

'Jill Turner? No, no way!'

Heeley sat on the edge of the desk. 'Any reason why not?'

'Yes! God, tons of reasons! She's not up to it, she's, God, I don't know, too ineffectual, too . . .'

'All right, I take your point.' Heeley moved back round to his side of the desk. He searched under the pile of papers for the file on Holly Grigson. 'You think we should get her back in?' He found the file, opened it and glanced over the details. 'Not much here to go on. We're going to need a pretty good reason to haul her in a second time for questioning.'

Eames didn't answer. He lit another cigarette, then moved across to the window. 'You did mention surveillance,' he said, looking over his shoulder at Heeley. 'Is that still an option?'

'Might be, if there's a good enough reason and we can justify the expense.'

'Well, if Holly Grigson is involved,' Eames said, 'then sooner or later, and my guess is sooner, whoever she is working for is going to get in touch. Turner was murdered for a reason – more than likely lining his own pocket, I should think – and the big boys are going to want their money back.'

'So?'

'So when they do, if we've got her on surveillance . . .' Eames reached across, ground out his cigarette in the ashtray and turned his full glare on Heeley. 'Then we're ready for them,' he said.

Chapter Eighteen

It was five o'clock in the afternoon by the time Holly reached the gallery. She had stayed for lunch with Guy in the end, talking through every detail of his idea, and had left the Savoy meaning to go home; only she hadn't. The temptation to go to the gallery, to try to think things through, had been too great. So she had hopped on the tube and crossed London to Notting Hill, then walked to the gallery from the station, enjoying the familiarity of the streets and buildings, feeling in many ways pleased to be back. She arrived there with her cheeks flushed from the cold air and the vigorous exercise.

Wanting to be alone, she slipped past the Patels' shop, quietly unlocked the gallery and went inside, turning on only the desk lamp at the far end. She put the kettle on in the back and made herself a coffee. Then she wandered through, holding her mug, and stopped in front of the first painting hung on the wall. It was a litho, a strong, four-colour print by a young artist from the Slade. It was impressive, dark and majestic, and Holly knew the young man was doing well. Shortly before Christmas, she had read an article about him in one of the colour supplements, and perhaps, if she had tried a little harder, pushed more herself, then she might have made a go of selling him. She might have become more involved in the gallery – her gallery. She sighed, ran her finger over the frame and moved on to the next work. Maybe Guy was right, she thought, looking at the pale winter landscape. Maybe she did have the talent to really do it . . . Suddenly Holly swung round.

Kit stood in the doorway, half in shadow, and the sight of him startled her. She caught her breath, surprised by his impact on her, then he moved fully into the light and she quickly looked away. In that moment she knew fully how she felt about him and her heart sank. Not now, she thought, please God, not this, not now.

Kit closed the door behind him and stood just inside the gallery with his coat still on. He had tried to call Holly repeatedly, both before and after the visit to Welsch, and hearing nothing but a constant ringing tone, he had panicked and driven up from Sussex at breakneck speed. Holly was the most important thing in his life. If he hadn't known it before, he knew it now – just looking at her across the room, he knew there would never be anyone else.

'You promised to call me this morning, when you got up.' He didn't mean it to sound like an accusation but the relief in seeing her suddenly brought out his aggression. 'Where've you been? What are you playing at, going off like that, in this situation, and not telling me where you are, not keeping in touch . . .' Kit stopped, aware of his tone. He hated himself for it, but he'd been worried sick; he couldn't help it.

Holly stared at the floor. She understood why he was acting this way, but he made her feel small and stupid and she didn't like that; in fact she didn't like the way Kit handled things at all. 'Look, Kit, I'm sorry, but something important's happened . . .' She glanced up and saw his face. 'Don't look at me like that!' she cried. 'Why do you always have to make me feel as if I need to apologise for everything I do?'

Kit glared at her for a few moments, then turned away. Christ, was that the way he came across? 'OK,' he mumbled, 'point taken.' They stood there silently for a couple of minutes, then Kit said, 'What is it that's happened? You said something important . . .'

'Yes.' Holly walked back to the desk. 'Look, come and sit down, we need to talk.'

Kit nodded and crossed the gallery. He perched on the edge of a chair and unbuttoned his coat. Everything about his stance was unyielding and defensive and Holly sighed.

'Kit, I've been thinking,' she started. 'And I've met someone who has helped me sort things out a bit in my own mind, helped me come to a decision about all this . . . this mess.'

Kit bristled at the phrase 'met someone' but he said nothing, waiting for her to go on.

'I met a friend of Sandy's . . .' She stopped. 'I mean Hugo's – well, not really a friend, a business acquaintance – he rang me before. You might remember; his name is Guy Ferreira.'

'Guy Ferreira? No, I don't remember.' But that was a lie. Kit did remember him; he remembered Holly's paranoia about the man, her conviction that he might have been involved in all this, and he remembered the messages on the answerphone and the precise time the clock had been broken and had stopped. Still, he said nothing. He was beginning to get angry.

'Anyway,' Holly went on, 'that's not important. What is important is what he said to me and what I've decided to do.'

Kit gritted his teeth. 'Which is?'

'To find Hugo Blandford,' Holly announced, sounding far more confident than she felt. 'Guy came up with an idea and I've decided to run with it. I think it might work. If I can find Blandford then I can retrieve the money and get out of this awful bloody mess.'

Suddenly Kit stood up. He had spent most of the morning with Welsch trying to think through ways of tracing Blandford, but they were all too damn risky. This wasn't a game; it wasn't a case of experimenting to see what might work.

Holly looked up at him. 'Kit! What's the matter?'

'I'll tell you what's the matter,' he snapped. 'Your whole damn attitude is the matter, Holly! This isn't a game, you know! And what are you going to say to Hugo Blandford when you find him? Eh? Please, Hugo, Sandy, whoever, may I have the money back that you stole from the people you were working for? Jesus!' He turned and walked away, really irritated by her simplistic and naïve view. A few paces away, he swung round. 'And how the hell are you going to find him? To quote you a few days ago – "put an ad in the personal column of *The Times*"?' He shook his head. 'This whole thing is absolutely ludicrous!'

'Oh is it?' Holly stood up. 'You haven't even heard me out and you go spouting off your opinions, dismissing what I've said! You always know bloody best, don't you?' She glared at him. 'All you want to do is muscle in and take control . . . All you want . . .' She broke off and looked away, too upset to continue.

Kit watched her and his heart ached. Why did it always have to end up like this? Why couldn't she see that he was frightened for her, that he loved her, for God's sake? Despite his better judgement, he said wearily, 'All right, I'm sorry. Tell me what you think you can do. Tell me what this Guy Ferreira suggested.' He walked back to the desk and sat down opposite her. 'I'm listening, OK?'

Holly sank down onto her chair, suddenly exhausted. She wasn't sure she had the energy to explain. She took a deep breath to calm herself and stared down at her hands. Perhaps Kit was right – perhaps this was lunacy? She had been so sure and now she just didn't know. 'It's all to do with the gallery,' she said eventually. 'And this artist Marcus, who Sandy, I mean Hugo Blandford, was using as a cover for the deals.' She didn't mention that she hadn't been able to trace Marcus, not wanting to add to Kit's scepticism. 'If I can get him to agree, then the idea is to try and create a market for his work. He's good – no, he's actually quite brilliant; I think that's why Hugo used him in the first place. Anyway, if I can do it, over the next few months, with intense publicity, exhibitions, attracting the critics, perhaps even invent a few wealthy patrons, then it could well lure Hugo right into my hands.'

Kit looked at her. She had started off a little shakily but the more she spoke, the more her confidence grew. He could see the excitement in her eyes, the thrill of the challenge.

'I don't understand,' he said. 'How will it "lure" Blandford?'

Holly drew breath then forged on. 'Hugo is almost certain to have paid for commissions in advance. That's the way it works: the artist is usually paid an advance, to keep him or her going, and it seals the agreement to deliver the finished work. Well, disappearing as he did, the commissions won't have been fulfilled, and Hugo will be owed work, yes?'

Kit nodded.

'And if the market for the work he's owed suddenly escalates, genuinely rocketing the value of that work, then he'll want his paintings, won't he?' She ran her tongue over her lips, her mouth dry from talking so much. 'I'll have the paintings and that's the trap. Simple! The best ideas often are.'

Kit was silent for a few moments. He had to be careful what he said next; he didn't want another row. 'You think that with all the money he has and the enormous risk of losing it that Hugo would endanger himself to contact you and claim a few paintings?'

'Yes!' Holly's face was flushed, her chin set determinedly. 'It's not about money, it's about art – collecting it and the enormous kudos involved in that. Blandford won't be able to resist it, I know he won't! If he's owed a work that's potentially highly valuable – the equivalent, in twenty years' time, of a painting by Lucien Freud, say, or Francis Bacon – then he's going to want to call in his debt. What does he have to fear from me anyway?'

'And you think you can, what did you say, create a market for the paintings, in just a few months? I thought it took years for artists to really make it.' Kit tried hard to keep the sarcasm out of his voice but failed. It crept in and gave his words a hard edge that Holly immediately picked up on and resented. She frowned.

'A bona fide market, no,' she answered, 'but a combination of false clients, a few well-placed articles, a couple of critics on my side, and yes, I could probably create the image of a young artist about to hit the big time. I think I could hype it up very nicely thank you.'

Kit was silent. It was a good, strong idea but that was the way it should stay: an idea. It was ridiculously ambitious, and moreover it was bloody dangerous. Did Holly really think that she could handle a man who had killed not once but possibly twice to save himself? He hadn't told her about the Salvation Army girl – he hadn't told anyone, nor had Sophie. Perhaps he *should* tell her, scare her senseless . . .

'You don't think it'll work, do you?' Holly asked, interrupting his thoughts. Kit glanced up and saw her staring at him. He shrugged.

'Please, be honest enough to tell me what you think,' she said.

'All right. I think you're insane. I think the whole thing is a flight of fancy and thoroughly dangerous. I think . . .'

'You think I can't do it without you!' Holly snapped. 'You don't like the way I've worked it out on my own and haven't consulted you or asked for your help and you don't like the way I've been helped by Guy . . .'

'Guy, Guy! Who the hell is this Guy Ferreira?' Kit snapped back. 'It's nothing to do with him and you and your little friendship; it's to do with the fact that this whole thing is dangerous! Think about it, Holly. Who is this chap? What do you know about him? Did you check him out before you started involving him in something that could get him and you and all of us killed?' Kit stopped, conscious of the fact that he had lost his temper, but he could see that he'd shaken Holly up, so it wasn't for nothing.

'He's a lawyer, with a British firm in New York,' Holly said. 'He was at Sefton College with my brother.' This wasn't strictly true; he had been at Sefton College, but several years before Holly's brother, a fact Holly didn't care to admit. 'And then he went to Cambridge. He told me the name of his law firm, I . . .'

'Did you ring them?'

'No! I . . .' Holly stopped. 'Look, Kit,' she said after a few moments, 'he's legit, honestly, I'm sure of it. He hasn't seen Hugo, or Sandy as he knows him, for months. God, he's been as worried as I have . . .'

'You're sure he's not involved?'

'Yes! They met on a plane. Guy only knew Sandy eighteen months or so . . .' She broke off a second time as Kit picked up the telephone.

'Call his law firm,' he said, dialling the international directory. 'Just check it out.' He spoke to the operator: 'Yes, hang on a moment, it's . . .'

'New York,' Holly said, 'Wiseman, Beech and Decker, Attorneys at Law.'

Kit repeated what she'd said to the operator and fifteen seconds later the number came back. He jotted it down, hung up and looked at his watch.

'Ring them,' he said, 'it's mid-morning there.' He held the receiver for her and Holly took it and dialled the number.

'Good morning. I'm trying to contact one of your lawyers, Mr Guy Ferreira?' The receptionist asked her to hold, then a few seconds later said she would put Holly through to his office. Holly let out a breath. This was at least making some sense.

'Yes, hello, I hope you can. May I speak to Guy Ferreira?' She listened to the reply, then said, 'Oh I see. In London? And you don't know when he'll be back . . .' There was a pause, then Holly said, 'Oh, right. Thank you, no, no message. Goodbye.' She hung up.

'I just spoke to his secretary; she said he's in London on business. He told me this morning that he had rung the office last night and extended his stay and his secretary just told me she had expected him back in a week or so but he's had to extend his stay. She didn't know for how long.' The relief in her voice was apparent – for once things seemed to fit. 'Satisfied?' she asked.

Kit shook his head. 'It's not a question of being satisfied, of you win, I lose.' She was being childish and he only just stopped himself from telling her as much. 'It's a question of us getting involved in something I don't trust, in something risky and uncertain.'

Holly looked at him. Sitting this close she could easily reach out and touch his hair, run her finger along the line of his jaw to his mouth, trace the outline of his lips. She felt a sharp, involuntary ache in the pit of her stomach at the thought of it and caught her breath. She sat still for a moment, then she did exactly that: she reached out and touched his hair. She felt him start as she trailed the tip of her finger down his face to his lips. She held it there and waited, watching his face.

Kit swallowed and his whole body tensed. He felt an instant excitement at the smallest contact with her. He had been longing for her to touch him, for just the brush of her hand, anything, only now it had happened he was confused, unsure of himself. One minute they were arguing, the next this happened, and his mind was spinning. What the hell did she want from him? Was it love, or just reassurance? He shifted uncomfortably on his seat, slightly out of her reach, and her hand dropped away. That wasn't what he had intended and he quickly looked up at her, but Holly had turned away.

'Holly, I . . .'

She stared at the wall for a few seconds, her face blank, and Kit didn't know what to do. He wanted to say, 'Holly, hold on for a moment, talk to me, explain things to me, give it time.' But he couldn't, not now he had shunned her caress.

'Holly, should we really get involved in all this, I mean . . .'

'*We?*' she suddenly questioned.

Kit blinked rapidly. 'Yes, I . . .'

Holly was smarting. She had been rejected and that hurt. At that moment she had needed him and wanted him more than she could ever remember. 'You are assuming that I intend to include you in all this,' she said coldly.

'No! I mean, well, yes, I . . .' Kit broke off a second time. She was right; it was what he had assumed. They were in this together, weren't they? 'You asked for my help and you took it when you needed it,' he countered.

'And what if I don't need it any more?'

Kit stared at her. So, it had been reassurance she'd wanted just then, nothing more – just a kiss or an embrace, the feeling that good old Kit was there no matter what. There to tell her he loved her, to make her feel good. He clenched his jaw; he wasn't about to start playing games. Either she wanted him or she didn't.

'Well?' He continued to stare. 'Do you need my help, Holly?'

Holly looked away for what seemed like forever and Kit waited If only he could have gone back three minutes, handled it differently, said what he'd felt, followed his heart instead of his pride. 'No,' she said finally, 'I want to do this on my own.'

'With Guy?' It was out before he could stop it.

'Yes, with Guy!' she snapped. 'Just Guy!' But as soon as she'd said it Holly wished she hadn't. It wasn't what she meant at all; he had goaded her into saying something stupid.

Kit stood up. He had told Holly a few weeks back that he wouldn't give up on her, but looking at her now he realised that he didn't have any choice. He had made a mistake, read the wrong signals. He had said it when he thought there was hope; he knew now that there wasn't. She had used him, taken advantage of his love for her. 'You like this chap Guy Ferreira?' he asked.

Holly shrugged. As attractive as he was, she didn't like him, not in the way Kit meant, but how could she explain all that? It was

271

too involved; it would drag up too much that she didn't want to admit. So she stared down at the ground without replying.

Kit couldn't stand the silence; it was all the answer he needed. Unable to take any more, he turned and walked towards the door.

'Kit?'

He glanced back.

'Where're you going?' There was real fear in Holly's voice.

'Back to my hotel to pack.'

'*Pack?*'

'If you don't need me, Holly, then there's no point in staying.' He stood where he was for a minute or so and gave her the chance to contradict him, but she didn't. She felt completely helpless. Why did he have to choose now to want answers? Why did he have to put her under pressure in this way?

Kit dragged his eyes away from her face and opened the door.

'Kit?' Holly leapt to her feet, suddenly panic-stricken.

But he didn't respond. He had had enough. Stepping out into the cold air, he buttoned up his coat, dug his hands in his pockets and, oblivious to her cry of pain, walked away.

'Kit, wait!' Holly ran to the door and flung it open, then dashed out into the freezing night and started up the street after him. '*Kit!*' she yelled.

He ignored her. Increasing his pace, he strode off, his figure lit intermittently by the street lamps, his footsteps sharp for a while, then fading into the noise of the traffic. Seconds later, he turned the corner and Holly stopped, her heart pounding so hard in her chest that she had to gasp for air. She slumped against the wall of a shop and dropped her head in her hands.

'Oh no,' she murmured. 'Please God, no . . .'

Looking up at the empty street, she knew she had just watched Kit Thomas walk out of her life for the second and last time. She closed her eyes again and turned her face to the cold brick wall. She was too numb and too bereft to cry.

Kit stood on the pavement outside the office of T. Welsch Financial Services and looked up at the windows above the Chinese grocer's. They were dark and there was no sign of life. He wondered briefly about leaving a message, then decided against it, and set off along the street, stopping at the first pub he came to. It was early evening and the place was packed.

Shoving his way to the bar, Kit ordered a double whisky. Ignoring the people either side of him, he drank it down in one when it arrived, then ordered a second and handed over a tenner. Turning to find a seat, he caught sight of Welsch, propping the bar up at the far end and gesticulating at him, shouting something inaudible above the roar of the crowd. Kit made his way over.

'You celebrating?' Welsch asked. He'd seen Kit down the first whisky.

Kit smiled half-heartedly and shook his head. 'You talk to Jill?'

Welsch motioned to the barman. 'Yup,' he answered. 'Bloody madness but it's her choice.'

Holly had rung Jill after Kit left. They had talked at length, then Jill had discussed Holly's idea with Sophie. Finally she had called Kit. She was prepared to back Holly up, she said, despite Kit's reservations, and as a last resort he had told her to call Welsch.

'You couldn't convince her?'

'Nah.' Welsch had ordered another whisky for Kit and a gin martini for himself. He handed Kit his drink and said, 'I don't try to tell people what to do. It's up to them in my business.'

Kit nodded.

'I'll watch it, though, keep in touch. That's what you came to ask me, right?'

Kit was surprised; he had thought Welsch insensitive.

'And you? Where're you going back to?'

273

'New York,' Kit said. He didn't remember ever telling Welsch he had come 'from' anywhere.

'You got a number? In case I need to call you.' Kit pulled out his wallet and handed Welsch a business card.

'You've got mine,' Welsch said. 'I don't have cards.'

'No, quite.' Kit watched Welsch drink the gin martini, then pop the cherry into his mouth. He burped, rubbed his chest and said, 'Pardon me.' Then he dropped down off the bar stool and reached for his coat. 'Be lucky,' he said, zipping up the fake leather bomber jacket. 'Ring if you need to.' And without saying goodbye, he shoved his way through the noisy crowd.

Kit lost sight of him almost immediately. He finished his own drink, then the one Welsch had bought for him in quick succession and turned to leave.

He was pretty drunk now, but it would hit him even harder later – three double Scotches on an empty stomach. He wove his way through the throng and out onto the pavement, breathing deeply in the clearer air after the thick smog of cigarette smoke. He glanced up at the pub, saw it sway momentarily, then turned towards the road to look for a taxi. Better drunk than sober, he thought, as he headed off in the direction of Leicester Square in search of a cab, better to numb the pain. And walking as best he could, he concentrated on scanning the traffic for his taxi. A few minutes later, he spotted one, whistled for it and climbed inside.

That night Kit made an airline reservation, then threw his belongings into a suitcase. He fell asleep in his clothes and by seven am the following morning he had boarded the BA flight from London Heathrow to JFK New York.

By the time Holly woke up that day, he had gone.

7 JANUARY 1994

Chapter Nineteen

There was a palpable tension in the room as Holly sat cross-legged on the floor of the gallery, three address files and two notebooks open in front of her and her head in her hands. They had been working flat out for a week and could find nothing on the artist Marcus – no notes or reference to any dealings with him, no mention of his work; in fact not one thing to suggest that he had even existed. There were just ten working days to go before Art '94, the major London exhibition. Holly had taken a hell of a risk and booked into it, paying out a large deposit and organising a private view. Now she was in a state of high anxiety, convinced that she was about to lose her savings and her reputation. At a loss for what to do next, she decided to try a route they had already been down.

'Can you look up degree shows again?' she asked, looking across at Jill. 'We might have missed something the first time.' Jill swivelled her chair round and studied the computer screen. It was hardly likely – they had been through it all in meticulous detail. Holly was clutching at straws, but she didn't say so.

'What shall I look under?' she asked. 'I've got finals from 'eighty-nine through to 'ninety-three – would it be one of those?'

'Finals 'ninety,' Holly said. 'I think there's a list of artists we liked at each show.'

'Got it. Any show in particular this time?'

'Try the RCA.'

Jill searched while Holly flipped through the address book on her lap one more time. She could hear the flick of paper as Sophie worked her way patiently through a mountain of art magazines to see if she could spot any reference to Marcus. It was a long shot, but at this late hour they all thought anything was worth a try.

'No, nothing,' Jill said, breaking the anxious silence. Both Holly and Sophie looked up.

'You?'

Sophie shook her head.

'Me neither,' Holly said. She uncrossed her legs and stood up. 'Kit was right,' she announced miserably. 'This whole bloody idea was insane! What on earth possessed me to think I could do it?' She stomped over to the desk and slumped down in a chair opposite Jill. 'I don't know what to do next,' she said, on the brink of tears. 'I don't know why I ever imagined . . .'

'Because you had to!' Jill interrupted, a little more sharply than she'd intended. 'And because there wasn't much choice, remember, not for you or for any of . . .'

The phone rang. Holly looked up.

'Are you going to answer it?' Jill asked.

Holly hesitated. 'I don't know,' she murmured. 'It'll be Sally Holland from the exhibition, she'll . . .'

Jill had picked up the receiver. 'Hello, Grigson Gallery.' Holly held her breath. 'No, I'm sorry,' Jill said, 'but she's not here at the moment, can I take a message?' There was a short silence, then Jill said, 'Oh, right, I see . . .' Her voice trailed off. 'Yes, thanks, I will.' She glanced across at Holly. 'Yes, goodbye.' She hung up.

'Is it bad?'

Jill shrugged. 'It wasn't Sally Holland; it was her assistant. They want the slide and lists for the catalogue by the end of the day because they go to print this evening. If they don't have confirmation of who we're showing, then they'll have to let the stand go to someone else who's ready. Apparently they have a wait-ing list.'

'Shit,' Holly said.

'Exactly.' Jill perched on the edge of the desk and folded her arms across her chest. There was a long, anxious silence.

'Well, that's it then,' Holly announced, her voice wavering.

'Not necessarily,' Jill remarked.

'Not necessarily!' Holly exploded, throwing her hands up in the air. 'Not necessarily! How can you say that? It's over. There's not a hope in hell of finding bloody Marcus and getting him exhibited now, and without that we might as well forget it! It's three months until the Chicago Art Fair, by which time we'll probably all be dead anyway, and if we're not . . .'

'That's enough!' Jill snapped, jerking her head round and glaring at Holly. 'Stop all this nonsense right now! It's not over until tonight, so let's just forget the dramatics and get on with it. You were the one who wanted to do this, you and Sophie, so let's do it. All right?'

Holly's mouth dropped open and both she and Sophie stared at Jill. 'And I don't know why you're looking at me as if I just stepped off another planet!' Jill went on. 'I'm only stating the obvious.' She stood up and smoothed the trousers of her suit. 'Look, we all need a drink, so I'm going to pop next door to the Patels' for a bottle of wine, OK?'

Holly and Sophie nodded, almost in unison, as Jill put on her jacket, ran a hand through her hair and walked across the gallery. Opening the door, she stepped outside, closed it behind her and set off towards the corner shop.

Three doors down, she stopped, leant against a shop front and took a huge gulp of air. She was shaking. It had taken every ounce of her nerve back there to assume that air of calmness and to cover her fast mounting panic. It left her suddenly exhausted.

Kit was right, she thought, closing her eyes. I should have

listened to him; I should never have let Holly talk me into this. What the hell am I doing? This thing is far too dangerous to afford mistakes. The longer we stall, the more we put ourselves at risk. She put her hands up and rubbed them wearily over her face. At risk. The terrible image of Alex, face up on the mortuary slab, flashed into her mind and she shivered, opening her eyes and moving quickly away from the wall.

She threw her shoulders back and took a deep breath. She had to get a grip. No matter how desperate she felt, she couldn't let it show, not right now. She carried on to the Patels', bought a bottle of wine and made her way back to the gallery. Outside, she stood for a moment or so to compose herself, knowing that it was up to her to support Holly and Sophie, at least for the time being, then she pushed open the door and walked back inside.

'Right,' she said, heading straight for the back in search of a bottle opener, 'let's have a drink!' She pulled the cork, poured three glasses and carried them through.

'If at first you don't succeed . . .' she toasted, holding her glass aloft and masking her own unease and lack of confidence with a determined smile. 'Right?'

'Right!' Sophie agreed.

'Right, Holly?'

Holly shrugged and sighed heavily. She took a large gulp of wine then looked across at Jill. 'Yes, I guess so.'

Jill drank, then placed the glass down on the desk. 'Where was I?' she murmured, sitting down at the computer to carry on with her search. She had changed almost beyond recognition in the past few weeks. The time of thinking only of herself had gone.

Holly stood where she was and held her glass, drinking steadily, unsure of what to do next. She watched Jill for a while, aware of the change in her, relieved, if she was honest with herself, that someone else had the strength to move things along at that moment. She finished her wine in one last big gulp and crossed the gallery to pour herself another glass. The alcohol taken on an empty stomach made her feel slightly woozy. Stopping suddenly, she felt in the pockets of her jacket, seemingly searching for something, and both Jill and Sophie looked up. Then Holly threw her hands up in the air and cried, 'Why the hell did I ever give up smoking?' She stormed over to her bag and rummaged furiously in it. 'Bloody Polos,' she muttered darkly, 'I can never find them. They're in here somewhere . . .'

Sophie exchanged glances with Jill. They kept quiet.

'Bloody hell! Where are they?' Impatiently, Holly grabbed her bag, squatted on the floor and tipped it upside down, emptying the entire contents over the pale ashwood floor.

'Oh dear me,' she exclaimed, staring down at the mess. She sighed hopelessly, then began to sort through the pile, discarding old lipsticks, panty liners, pens, scraps of paper, old receipts, a broken string of beads and a mascara brush she was reluctantly pleased to retrieve. There were postcards, a purse, keys, cheque books, cheque book stubs, three hairbrushes, several horrid-looking packets of sweets, empty sweet wrappers, packs of travel tissues and baby wipes; the assortment was weird and wonderful.

Sophie walked across to Holly and crouched down beside her, marvelling at the jumble of items. She rummaged, scattering the mess even further across the floor, and moments later, said, 'Aha! Polos!' She picked up a packet – only three or so mints left on the roll, the top sweet distinctly grimy – and handed it to Holly.

'Thanks,' Holly said, peeling the wrapper down and taking the mint underneath. She held them up to offer them around but Jill smiled her refusal, while Sophie was busy retrieving the contents of Holly's bag and trying to scoop them up into some sort of order. She found another pack of Polos, stuck to a postcard, and pared the card away from the sweets.

'This is nice,' she said, turning the card over. It was a business card, a print of some artist's painting on one side, illustrating his work, with his name and address on the back. 'It's really powerful! Have a look at this, Holly, it's pretty good. I wonder who this chap is?'

Holly glanced up. She had been chewing her mint frantically, deep in morbid concentration, and she gave Sophie only a cursory look. She had no further interest in the contents of her bag.

Seconds later, she sprang to her feet.

'My God!' Snatching the card from Sophie's hands, she stared down at it, momentarily stunned. 'I don't believe it! Where was this?'

'Stuck to a packet of Polos, at the bottom of your bag.' Sophie was puzzled. 'Why? What is it?'

'It's only a painting by bloody Marcus!' Holly cried.

Jill stood up and hurried round the desk.

'Are you sure?'

'Yes! Positive!' Holly continued to stare at the print of one of Marcus' paintings. 'It's a calling card – a number of artists and illustrators use them. It reminds you of their work on the one side and has a contact number and address on the back.' She turned it over. 'Adrian White?' She gave it to Jill. 'But I thought . . .' She broke off. Another deception, another of Sandy's lies. 'He wasn't called Marcus at all; he's called Adrian White. Sandy must have made the name up!' She shook her head miserably. 'God, I should have thought, I should have realised sooner . . . How stupid of me!'

Jill placed a reassuring hand on Holly's arm. 'It doesn't matter,' she said kindly. She turned the card over. 'Ring him, Holly. Let's get this thing moving!'

Holly took the card and tapped it against her palm, thinking for a moment. For some reason she was suddenly nervous. 'I don't know. Maybe we should leave it a bit, mull it over for a while . . .'

Jill took the card back. 'There's no need to think about it; we have to ring – now!' She walked back to the desk and picked up the telephone. 'D'you want to ring, Holly, or shall I?'

Holly hesitated and saw Jill begin to punch in the number. 'OK, OK!' She hurried over to Jill and smiled begrudgingly. 'Point taken, I'll ring now.' Jill finished dialling and Holly held the receiver to her ear. The gallery was suddenly anxiously silent.

'Hello?' she said. 'Is it possible to speak to Adrian White, please?' She waited – the anxiety deepened. 'Who wants to know? Oh, er, my name's Holly Grigson, from the Grigson Gallery. Have I got the right number?'

Sophie dropped her head down, unable to stand the tension any longer. Another dead end, she thought bitterly. No Marcus, no show . . .

'Yes, OK, that's fine. Yes, I've got the address. How about right now?'

Sophie jerked her head up.

'He's there . . .' Holly hissed, her hand over the mouthpiece. 'Someone's just yelling out to him to check it's OK if we go over . . .' She held her crossed fingers up. 'Yes, I'm still here. Great! Yes, as soon as I can. Thanks.' She smiled at Jill, the first real smile for days. 'Bye.' She hung up.

'We're on,' she announced. 'If he's the right man, then he's there in Camberwell and we're to go right over to the studio.' She laughed. 'I can't believe it!' Glancing down at the card on the desk, she said, 'How on earth did this get into my bag? It's weird – it seems to have popped up just at the right moment. I don't understand it, I . . .' Suddenly she broke off and smacked her palm against her forehead. 'Of course! Before all this started, the night Kit arrived at the gallery! There was a young artist; he asked me to take a look at his work, then Kit came and interrupted and well . . .' Holly frowned. 'I wonder why he didn't say that Sandy had bought his work before?' She thought for a few moments, trying to remember the details of that night, but the only thing she could see in her mind's eye was an image of Kit. She shrugged. 'I guess he thought he ought to get the hell out of here before the place exploded and gave me his card as he left. I just dropped it in my bag, didn't think twice about it. God, I might never have seen it if . . .'

'You hadn't given up smoking!' Sophie quipped.

Holly laughed again. 'Right,' she said excitedly, 'grab your things and let's go!' She hurried towards the back for her poncho and bag. 'Jill? Can you drive? I think I might be over the limit, all that wine on an empty . . .'

At that moment the phone rang and all three turned to look at it. There was a short, painful silence, then Jill said, 'Shall I answer it?'

Holly hesitated. For some instinctive reason the shrill bleeping unnerved her. It was a bad omen, she was convinced of it. 'I don't know,' she said. Her joyous mood had instantly evaporated and she bit her thumbnail nervously. 'No, leave it,' she decided.

Jill raised an eyebrow but Holly stuck to her decision. 'Come on, let's get going, there's no time to waste.'

She led the way out onto the street, leaving the shrill bleep of the phone echoing in the dark, empty gallery.

The man sat with the receiver in his hand and listened to the line ring, on and on and on, each second it was left unanswered making him angrier. He left it for fifteen minutes in all – fifteen minutes with him knowing that she was there, listening to it, letting it ring – before he slammed it down and stood up. He crossed the room and lit a cigarette. Holly Grigson was giving him the slip, and he didn't like that one little bit. The idea of it filled him with fury.

He stood in the centre of the room, his body tight and hard with a powerful feeling of violence, and the hand holding the cigarette shook. It was the same violence the girls he hired were scared of, the same violence the Weasel knew. It was sudden, explosive and sadistic – his trademark.

Suddenly he felt an agonising pain in his fingers. He jerked his hand up and dropped the cigarette down onto the floor where it smouldered on the carpet. It had burnt down and singed the skin around his nails. 'Shit! Fucking woman!' he snarled. Walking through to the bathroom, he ran the cold tap over his fingers. He closed his eyes and saw the same recurring image of Holly, her head thrown back against the glass, abandoned, helpless, beautiful, and the sudden need to hit out was so strong that it almost overwhelmed him. He snapped his eyes open again, wrenched his hand away from the tap and walked back into the bedroom.

He sat down on the bed, took a hotel message slip out of his jacket pocket and stared at it for a few moments before opening the bedside drawer. 'Chicago called', it read, underneath which was the time, then: 'No message.' He placed it with the other three notes and closed the drawer. He knew what that call meant. He was running out of time.

Glancing down at his hand, he saw a red blister had begun to swell on the skin of his index finger. Bracing himself, he put it to his mouth and bit it, the instant pain almost comforting. That was what you had to do with things – control them, no matter what the price. He reached for the phone and dialled his contact. He couldn't wait any longer. She had to be brought under control. Like a dog, he would bring her to heel.

The line was answered and he glanced at his watch.

'I want you to frighten her,' he said. 'Tonight, at nine; exactly nine.' He listened for a few moments, then cut the Weasel short. 'I don't care,' he interrupted. 'Just be thorough.' And with that he hung up.

Crossing to the safe, he tapped in his code and the electronic lock whirred, then clicked open. He swung the door back and glanced inside, reaching for the small cellophane packet of cocaine he kept there. As he did so, his fingers brushed over the pile of photographs and, unable to help himself, he pulled them out and dropped them onto his lap. He stared down at the top one, an image so intensely sexual that it made him shudder with revulsion and lust. He wanted Holly Grigson; he wanted her so badly that it hurt every time he thought about her. But he didn't like her. He hated her, the same as he hated all the women he wanted.

He flicked through the snaps, his fingers tracing the curve of her body, rubbing parts of it, imagining, exciting himself, then abruptly he shoved them back into the safe and stood up. He didn't have time for that now; it would have to wait. He took the packet of coke, emptied a small amount onto a pocket mirror, then replaced the packet in the safe. He walked into the bathroom to get himself ready and quietly locked the door behind him.

Jill parked the Range Rover opposite the building Holly had directed her to and left the engine running while Holly double-checked the address.

'Yup, that's it,' she said, peering up at the three storeys of slick glass and concrete. 'Looks a bit odd for a studio. Oh well.' She opened the door and jumped out onto the pavement.

'Strange,' Sophie commented, as Holly led the way over the road and swung open the big double doors. 'Looks more like a block of offices.' Her voice echoed in the large, draughty lobby area.

'That's because it is,' a voice said from behind a reception desk. Seconds later the head and shoulders of a tall young man emerged and he stood smiling, with a piece of card in his hand. 'The council built it in the late eighties, just before the property crash, and rather than leave it empty in this very salubrious area, they now rent it to a group of us for a nominal fee to use as studios.' He came round the desk, his thin figure clad in paint-splashed farm overalls.

'Adrian White,' he said, looking directly at Holly.

'Hello, I'm Holly Grigson.' She stepped forward, her hand outstretched.

'I remember you from the gallery,' he said, smiling and giving her the piece of card. Holly looked quizzically down at it. 'Oh,' she murmured, and Adrian White, realising only then that she had meant for him to shake her hand, flushed deep red.

'It's for the car,' he stammered. 'So your hubcaps and stereo don't get nicked.'

'Does it work?' Jill asked in a small voice.

'A hundred percent,' Adrian said. 'We've got one or two pretty heavy dudes on the project here and everyone knows it. They don't dare mess with cars attached to here.'

'Glad to hear it,' Jill murmured, not quite convinced.

'I'll put it on the dashboard,' Sophie volunteered.

Adrian turned to look at her for the first time. 'Thanks,' he said, smiling.

Now it was Sophie's turn to flush. Her pale skin suddenly flooded with colour and she grabbed the card, hurrying out of the doors with it. Holly watched Jill watch Adrian watch Sophie as she darted across the road. It was a tense triangle.

'This is Jill Turner,' Holly said loudly.

Adrian started and tore his gaze away from outside. 'Hi, Jill,' he smiled.

'And Sophie across the road there is Jill's daughter,' Holly went on, wanting no confusion at this early stage.

'Right,' Adrian said. He glanced again at Sophie as she came back into the building and the two of them exchanged another smile.

Holly felt the smallest tinge of dismay. There was something in the way he looked at Sophie that reminded her of . . . She broke off her train of thought, not quite able to put her finger on it. 'Adrian,' she said, focusing hard on the present. 'Is there somewhere we can talk?'

Adrian turned away from Sophie and missed Jill's irritated sigh.

This is all I bloody need, Jill thought angrily. I hope Sophie shows a little sense.

'Yes, sure,' he answered. 'My studio.' He fumbled in his pocket for a key and unlocked the connecting doors. 'There's a lift shaft but no lift,' he said, noticing Holly's eyes stray to the elevator. 'It's the stairs, I'm afraid, three flights of them.' He held open the doors, the three women went through, and he relocked them before leading the way up to his studio.

'Is it always this noisy?' Jill called above the racket of banging, hammering, several different radio stations, chat, the odd shout and what sounded like a scene from *The Texas Chainsaw Massacre*. She had one hand over her ear and strained for his reply, frowning distastefully.

'Always,' Adrian stated quite categorically. He smiled, held open the doors at the top for his guests and followed them through, taking the lead again, up along a maze of small studios sectioned off from each other by makeshift walls of plasterboard. 'Here,' he announced finally. 'My humble studio.'

Holly walked in first, saw the huge bank of glass windows, and then Adrian's painting in progress, a six foot by six foot canvas flooded with colour and warmth that completely took her breath away. She stood absolutely still and felt a rush of pure joy through her whole body.

'Wow!' Sophie breathed behind her. 'That's . . .'

'Amazing,' Jill finished.

Holly turned, surprised. 'You like it, Jill?'

Jill nodded. 'I love it,' she murmured. Then she looked at Holly and raised an eyebrow. 'Just don't ask me to explain it.' They both smiled.

'Adrian, this is wonderful!' Holly exclaimed. 'Is it nearly finished?'

'I'm not sure,' Adrian answered. 'I haven't made up my mind yet. I'm waiting for the painting to tell me.'

Jill laughed, then belatedly realised it wasn't a joke.

'Have you any other recent work we can see?' Holly asked.

Adrian folded his arms. 'A bit,' he said warily. 'Can I ask why the interest?'

Holly spun round. 'Oh God! Yes, of course! I should have said straight away, I'm sorry . . .' She dug in her pockets, nervously searching for her Polos; she couldn't find them. 'It's, er . . .' She had planned exactly what she was going to say, had spent the whole journey across London thinking it through, only there was something very disarming about Adrian White and his easy, honest, unassuming manner, and now she wasn't at all sure of her saleswoman patter. 'D'you want to sit down?' she said.

Adrian shook his head.

'OK, right.' Holly took a deep breath. 'Well, Adrian,' she began. 'The thing is, you know, obviously, that my, er . . .' She hesitated, winced and managed the word, 'My, er, husband, Sandy Turner, has sold a number of your paintings over the last year and I've been very impressed with the response.' She paused and glanced at the canvas leaning against the wall. 'And, recently, we've had several enquiries about your work from various collectors,' she lied. 'Not surprisingly, I can see it is absolutely stunning.' That, at least, was truthful.

'Thank you,' Adrian said, flushing.

Holly nodded, thrown for a moment by such modesty. 'Where was I? Oh, yes, er, well, Adrian, to be frank with you, I really think you have a very bright future indeed.' She let that fact sink in, then went on; 'I would like to manage that future, Adrian, or at least help get it well and truly underway. I have a space at Art 'ninety-four and I'd like to exhibit you – if, that is, you are interested.'

'Interested!' Adrian exclaimed, amazed. 'My God! This is the chance of a lifetime. Of course I'm bloody interested!' The atmosphere in the small space instantly relaxed.

'Great!' Holly said. 'I'm delighted.'

'Just tell me what I have to do and I'm all yours!' He was grinning, hopping from foot to foot, too excited to stop still.

'Well, first I need to see your work and we have to make a few choices. I need a slide – you've got some, presumably?'

He nodded.

'Brilliant! I've decided to put one of your works in the catalogue . . .'

'You're kidding?'

Holly felt her confidence slip again at the sight of such earnest delight. 'No, not at all,' she went on, trying to conceal her anxiety. 'But we need to move fast. I have to get a slide off to the exhibition organisers literally right now!' She smiled briefly. 'Can we sort out the slides first, then perhaps tomorrow you'd like to see the space I've hired at the show so you'll have an idea of light and position and what would hang well there?'

'Yeah, great!' Adrian hurried across to a big black filing cabinet in the corner of the studio and unlocked it. He pulled open the top drawer and lifted out a sheet of slides. 'Here,' he said, holding them up to the light and glancing briefly through them, 'this is my most recent work.' He handed the sheet to Holly. 'Did you change your mind about someone else then?'

Holly was scanning the slides. 'Change my mind?' she asked vaguely, deep in concentration.

'Yes, for the catalogue? Or did someone drop out?'

Holly lowered the sheet. She looked at Adrian, suddenly realised what he was saying and blushed. 'Someone dropped out,' she murmured, lifting the slides back up to the light to cover her face. She was an appalling liar when confronted, always had been.

'Ms Grigson?'

Sophie held her breath. She knew what was coming. Holly was transparent; the lie had been too obvious.

'Hmmm?'

Adrian moved forward and lifted the sheet of slides out of her hands. 'Why me for the catalogue?'

Holly glanced at her watch. 'Look, never mind that now, we can talk about it over a drink later!' she said quickly. She dug in her bag for her mobile telephone and walked across the studio to the window, turning her back on them all. 'I'll just ring the exhibition and let them know we're on our way with the slide,' she said over her shoulder. 'You choose, Adrian, just pick what you think is one of your best.' She dialled, held the phone up to her ear and waited for the line to be answered. Moments later, the phone was taken out of her hands.

'No call and no slides until you tell me what's going on,' Adrian said. He switched off the phone. 'You're not being straight with me and I don't like it.'

Holly turned to face him and ignored the last comment. She was ready to lie. 'What do you want to know?' she asked.

Adrian, disarmed by her approach, hesitated for a few seconds, then said, 'OK, first, who else is exhibiting?'

'Who else?'

'Yes, that's right.'

Holly swallowed hard. She couldn't fudge this. She took a deep breath and answered him. 'No-one,' she said.

Adrian blinked. 'You mean I'm the only exhibitor?'

'Yes.' Holly met his gaze. 'You are the only artist I plan to exhibit.'

'But how come? You must have lots of other people just as good on your books. You'd want a balanced show to give the best impression of the gallery, surely?'

Holly tucked her hair behind her ears and stalled for time to think through her answer. 'No, not exactly,' she began. 'That isn't what I had planned, not for this year anyway.' She moved across the room to the canvas and stared at it for a few moments, then she turned round to face him.

'Adrian, your work is the best I have seen for a very long time and I am being completely honest when I say that I think that you could have a brilliant future. But . . .'

Jill caught Sophie's eye. She knew Holly was about to create a web of lies to cover them all and she wasn't sure she could take it. She saw Sophie was gritting her teeth and looked away, staring down at the ground.

'In reality,' Holly went on, 'in order to achieve that future you're going to need an almighty push. It's not a question of leaving it to chance, I'm afraid, in the hope that you'll be discovered. We have to go out there and stun the art world, take them by the balls, if you'll pardon the expression; and to do that I have to concentrate on you completely. If we want to make an impact then the show has to be you and you alone. It's a hell of a risk, but one I think is worth taking.'

Adrian stood silent for a minute, then he looked straight at Holly. 'Why?' he asked.

Holly flinched and tried to cover her instinctive movement with surprise. 'Why what?'

'Why is it suddenly a risk worth taking?' Adrian enquired coolly. 'Sure, Mr Turner bought heaps of stuff off me, but I've never been exhibited by the gallery before and you've never represented me yourself – we've really only just met – so why the sudden urgent interest? It doesn't add up as far as I can see. Sorry, Holly, but I just don't buy it.'

Holly swallowed hard. 'Of course it adds up,' she stammered. 'Your work is the only explanation I need. Just look at it, I . . .'

'No, stop right there! You aren't being at all straight with me, Holly Grigson,' he cut in.

Holly dropped her head down and stared at the ground.

'Are you?' he insisted.

She remained silent and Adrian looked across at Jill. 'Could you give us a few minutes in private?' he asked.

Jill bit her lip and stood where she was, at a loss for what to do. 'It's ten to four,' she said to Holly.

Holly glanced up. 'Just give us a couple of minutes?'

'All right, but we're running out of time.' Jill moved towards the entrance. 'Sophie? Come on, we'll have a look round.'

'Thanks.' Adrian waited for them to leave, then leant against the wall, his arms folded across his body, and stared at Holly. 'OK,' he said, 'talk. I'm not stupid, Ms Grigson. I don't know what the hell you think you're playing at, coming here and making all sorts of ridiculous promises, but I do know that no gallery in their right mind would want to exhibit an artist they've never met before, never even exhibited before, unless there was a major problem, or a fiddle, or something pretty odd going on.'

'Like what?' Holly pleaded.

'I don't know, you tell me.'

Holly sighed and walked across to the window. There was a long, uncomfortable silence, then Adrian said, 'You haven't been honest with me and I resent that.' He spoke to her back and she didn't have the nerve to turn around. 'It would have been much better if you'd just been straight with me, and now I think it would be better if you left.' He walked across to his table and began to clean his brushes, ready for work.

But Holly stood where she was. It would have been better if I'd been straight with everyone, she thought miserably, looking down at the deserted street below – if I'd been honest with myself above all. If I had been honest two years ago then I would never have been in this situation now. If I had faced up to my feelings then I wouldn't have made such a God almighty mess of my life. She wrapped her arms around herself, suddenly very cold, and pressed her head against the window. 'What time is it?' she asked quietly, her breath frosting up the glass.

'Four o'clock,' Adrian replied.

She turned round. 'It's too late anyway,' she said hopelessly. 'I would never have got the slide there in time.'

'Probably not.'

'I'd better go.'

'Yes.' He watched her, her small frame silhouetted against the window. She moved away into the studio and it was then that he caught it – the terrible shadow of fear and despair in her eyes – and he stared, consumed with a memory that was so painful it made him flinch.

Holly picked up her bag in silence and made to leave. Adrian felt himself caught in a suspended moment, a moment that seemed to last forever. He had the chance to call her back, to ask her why, maybe to stop the suffering in a way he had never been able to with his brother, but he couldn't speak. His hand shook as he held his brush.

Moments later he dropped the brush. As he lunged for it, he knocked his paint table, and a bottle of turps crashed to the floor. The sound of splintering glass seemed to catapult him back to reality. Holly spun round.

'Look . . . er, Holly, perhaps we should talk?'

She stared at him.

'Do you want to explain? I don't know, maybe it would make a difference. I might be able to help if I knew . . .'

She tensed. 'Knew what?'

'What you were scared of.' He'd said it; it was out. She would tell him to bugger off, of course, but at least he had done something this time.

Holly didn't answer. She leant against the plasterboard partition and dropped her head in her hands, then she slid down the wall to the floor and slumped there. Adrian said nothing. He left the mess on the floor, took a bottle out of his paint box and wiped the inside of a tin mug on his hanky.

'Here.' He held the mug out to her, and as she looked up and took it, he poured from the bottle.

'What is it? Meths?'

He smiled. 'None left; it's all on the floor. It's whisky, emergency supplies.'

Holly drunk it down in one. 'Thanks.'

Adrian shrugged. 'I had a brother,' he said, 'younger than me, seventeen. He died a year ago this Christmas.'

'I'm sorry.'

'Yeah, me too.' Adrian took a swig from the bottle, then went on. 'He came to me for help, the week before he died. He was in trouble, only he wouldn't say what. He wanted money, as usual, but I wouldn't give him any. I didn't have any, to be honest, but I could've got hold of some, if I'd really wanted to. He looked like you do – frightened, helpless – and it pissed me off. He'd always had it easy, been the baby, and he'd fucked up, wasted himself on drugs and drink, pissing away his education. I told him to clear off and a week later he was dead.' Adrian took another gulp of whisky. 'He fell out of a window, ten floors up. Apparently he owed money to some low life on the estate for drugs. They said his death was an accident.' He snorted derisively. 'Fat chance. It was a warning, to the other poor bastards like him. Pay or die.'

'I'm sorry,' Holly said again.

'Yeah, me too,' Adrian repeated. 'I should have done something.' He offered her more whisky and she held the mug out.

'I'm in trouble,' Holly murmured, looking into the mug. 'I'm in very big trouble and you were my only hope – if by some crazy chance it had worked.'

Adrian squatted down on the floor. 'Tell me,' he said.

She looked at him.

'If you want to, that is.'

Drinking down the second cup of whisky, Holly waited for the familiar warmth to hit her stomach. It was all too late. What did she have to lose?

'All right.'

She leant her head back against the wall, a feeling of complete hopelessness washing over her, and began to talk. She was only going to give him a few brief details, but once she had started, she was unable to stop. The whole awful tale unravelled itself and Adrian listened with a sinking sense of pity and dread.

Jill led the way up the stairs back to the third floor, held open the doors for Sophie and followed her stepdaughter along the maze of passages towards Adrian White's studio. She was tired and anxious. They had been walking round the other studios on the first and second floors for over forty minutes, unsure of what to do, waiting for they didn't really know what. As they approached the small space at the far side, Jill felt her stomach knot. It was way after four. If Holly hadn't left for the exhibition offices with the slides and a list of works then the whole thing was over – she would have missed the deadline. Turning the corner, she heard Holly's voice and stopped dead in her tracks. The disappointment was crippling.

'Jill?' Sophie placed her hand on Jill's arm. 'It might not be that bad.'

Jill placed her own hand over Sophie's and squeezed it reassuringly. 'No,' she murmured, 'it might not.' But she was wholly unconvinced.

Holly and Adrian were sitting on the floor with the empty bottle of whisky between them when Jill and Sophie walked in. They were silent and a heavy feeling of despair hung in the air; Jill could feel it like a blanket of choking smog.

Holly looked up.

'You all right?' Jill asked.

Holly shrugged, then glanced away; Jill could see she'd been crying. 'I'm sorry,' she murmured; she didn't know what else to say.

Holly got to her feet. 'I told Adrian what happened,' she said wearily. 'All of it.'

Jill made no comment. Despite the sickening despair that swamped her, she could feel a sharp needle of anger. What the hell did Holly think she was doing? Her jaw tensed and she walked across the room to the window before she said something she might regret.

'Was that wise? That's what you're thinking, isn't it?' Adrian said.

Jill turned slowly to look down at him. 'Yes, it is exactly what I'm thinking,' she answered tersely.

Adrian glanced at Holly. 'It's not connected, but my brother was thrown out of a window,' he said bluntly. 'Ten storeys up. He couldn't pay his drugs bill.'

'I'm sorry,' Jill said automatically.

'Yeah, well I'm more than that.' He got to his feet, walked across to the table and picked up the sheet of slides. 'I won't ever get the bastards that did it but I can do something. Maybe it might stop some other helpless kid wasting his life.' He held the slides out to her. 'Tell me what you think of these,' he said.

Jill stood where she was for a moment. She didn't understand – was he ridiculing her?

'Go on.'

She took the slides and stared at him. 'But I don't know the first thing about art!'

'No? Well look at them anyway and tell me what you think.'

'Why?' Jill wanted to know.

'Because sometimes you just have to trust your instinct.' And with that, Adrian picked Holly's mobile up off the floor and pressed the redial button.

'Sally Holland,' he said. 'Yes, you can, it's *Art Review* magazine.' All three women stared at him.

'Sally Holland? Hi, I'm Jake Yates, assistant editor of the *Art* . . . ah, you have? It's nice to know someone reads me. Thanks, I'm very flattered!' Holly's mouth dropped open. 'Yup, you can. I'm ringing to let you know we're doing a special on one of the galleries exhibiting at Art 'ninety-four, the Grigson Gallery? Yes, that's right, Notting Hill. Yup, they've got a big new name, a very exciting young painter, Adrian White . . .' He paused. 'Oh, good lord, is that right? They haven't? . . . No, to be honest, sweetheart, it doesn't surprise me. Apparently after Paris he's been a bit of a prima donna, keeps messing them around.' He laughed. 'Oh I know! Tell me about it, Sally, most creatives are!' He rolled his eyes at Sophie and she smiled.

'Well, it's a diary piece with three or four plates and a bit of a hype for Art 'ninety-four, his first showing since Paris . . .' He stopped, listened, then smiled. 'Ooh, could you? Yes, I would if I were you. Ring them right now, get them to do an addendum, with illustration. You mustn't miss the piccies, they are quite fabulous!' Another pause. 'Oh, absolutely, not to be missed! Yup, when we've got the copy I'll fax it over to you. No, no problem at all.' He smiled again. 'And you, Sally, cheers! Bye bye.' He switched the phone off and looked at Holly.

'You've still got your space,' he said. Then he turned and looked at Jill. 'So you'd better get going on those slides. They'll want one for the addendum and a list of paintings exhibited, OK?'

'Yes, er . . .' Jill broke off. 'Fine,' she murmured, then she looked across at Holly, who burst into floods of tears.

Chapter Twenty

It was early evening, dark and gloomy, when Holly and Jill left the studio. They crossed to the car, Holly carrying a stack of unframed canvases under her arm, Jill a bulging portfolio of drawings, prints and sketches. Jill dropped the portfolio down by the boot of the car, checked her hubcaps and unlocked the door. 'Still intact,' she said grimly. Holly smiled.

Opening the driver's side, Jill glanced over her shoulder and said. 'Shall I run back with the card?' Her gaze travelled up to the third floor of the building and Holly guessed what she was thinking. They had left Sophie to go through the remainder of the work with Adrian; Jill would pick her up later that night.

'No,' Holly answered, 'we can hang onto it. We'll need it in the morning anyway.'

'Oh, right.'

Holly saw Jill hesitate and glance behind her again. It was obvious she didn't want to leave.

'She'll be fine, Jill, honestly,' Holly said, placing the canvases and portfolio carefully in the boot. She opened her door and climbed in. 'She's got a good eye; she knows what she's doing.'

Jill got into the driver's seat. 'Does she?' She started the engine and Holly put her hand on Jill's arm. Jill was referring to the obvious attraction between Sophie and Adrian, an attraction they would have had to be blind not to see.

'I think she does,' Holly said gently. 'And if she doesn't, then she has to make her own mistakes.'

'Like you?' Jill snapped suddenly.

Holly flushed. She removed her hand and locked her fingers together, looking down at them in her lap.

'Holly, I'm sorry, I shouldn't have said that,' Jill stammered. 'It was unkind . . .'

'No, it wasn't unkind, it was honest. You were right, I've made far too many mistakes and I'm not even sure I've learnt anything from them.'

Jill put the car into gear and pulled off. She honestly didn't think that there was anything more to say.

Half an hour later, Jill swung right into Bishop's Road and followed Holly's directions, stopping halfway down, outside a red brick Victorian building.

'Thanks, Jill,' Holly said. 'What bloody awful weather!' She peered out at the torrential rain. 'You will drive carefully, won't you?'

Jill switched on her hazard lights. 'Yes, dear.'

They both smiled. In the past week Holly, Jill and Sophie had become a team. They looked out for each other; they had to. 'And you're sure you're all right on your own?' Jill asked.

'Yes, fine, thanks, Jill.' Holly leant across to the back for her bag. 'I'm going to have a large drink . . .'

'Another one?' Jill interrupted.

Holly smiled. 'Yes, another large drink, and then sort out my hit list of journalists for tomorrow.' She was making light of something that was monumentally important; finding Adrian and setting up the exhibition had been just the beginning.

'Have you decided what you're going to say yet?'

Holly frowned. 'No, but I will, by tomorrow morning.' She opened the car door and jumped out. 'See you tomorrow. I'll be at Adrian's studio around lunchtime.' She slammed the door shut, went to the boot for the paintings and made a dash for the building. Depositing the work inside the hall, she went back for the drawings, ran through the rain with them and laid the portfolio against the wall just inside the door. She turned and waved.

Jill waited for her to go inside before shifting into gear. It was a false confidence, she thought, watching Holly. A great deal depended on her – too much – and despite the relief at getting off the starting blocks, Jill was under no illusions. It was make or break in the next few days, and break didn't even bear thinking about.

Pulling away, Jill switched the wipers onto speed and slowed as a sudden burst of rain pelted the windscreen. She glanced to her left, spotted a lone figure on the pavement battling against the downpour, and felt a momentary dart of panic. He hadn't been there a few minutes ago; it seemed he had just appeared out of nowhere. She changed gear and held her foot tensely over the accelerator, her heart thumping in her chest. She quickly glanced behind her at Holly's building to check Holly had gone inside. She had; the street was deserted apart from this one man. She stared at him, holding her breath. He was hardly dressed for a storm: his bomber jacket was drenched and the newspaper he held over his head was sodden. Jill continued to stare as she drove past. There was something vaguely familiar about his gait and she couldn't help feeling she'd seen him before. It scared her but she forced herself to look more closely. Adjusting her rear-view mirror slightly, she slowed right down and took a good look behind her. It was the way he walked; the shoes, two-tone black and tan brogues; the flared slacks. She peered for a few seconds longer, decided she was being silly, imagining things, and with one last glance, put her foot down on the accelerator. At that moment he looked up.

'Ted Welsch!' Jill uttered. 'Good Lord! What the hell is he doing here?' She stopped, yanked on the handbrake and put the window down. 'Ted? Mr Welsch? Hello? Mr Welsch?'

Welsch dropped the newspaper and squinted at the lady in the car. It was dark, the rain obscured his vision and he hadn't a clue who this was. He carried on walking and dropped the newspaper a bit lower to cover his face. He was nervous; he didn't know anyone in this area.

'Mr Welsch? It's Jill Turner!' Jill called. 'Remember? We met a couple of weeks ago!'

Welsch turned round and looked at the woman in the silk floral headscarf, trying to connect her to the tall, slim blonde who'd come to his house. He wasn't sure; there was something familiar about her face. Slowly he approached the car, one eye on her, one eye on the rest of the street. He wasn't taking any chances.

'Ted Welsch?' Jill smiled and pushed the scarf back off her hair. 'What a coincidence! What on earth are you doing here?'

'Hello, Mrs T.' Ted removed the newspaper and tucked it under his arm. He looked uncomfortable, and avoided her eye. 'Awright?'

'Yes, fine thanks. D'you have business in the . . .' Jill broke off. It had suddenly occurred to her why Ted Welsch might be in Bishop's Road. 'You'd better get in,' she said, 'and tell me why you're watching Holly's flat.'

Welsch considered what she'd said, then shrugged, dropped the paper on the ground and walked round to the passenger side of the car. He waited for Jill to press the central locking switch and opened the door.

'You got a plastic bag?' he asked.

'A plastic bag?'

'Yeah, for the seat. I don't wanna drip all over your nice upholstery.'

Jill shook her head. He really did have the most extraordinary manner. 'I don't know,' she answered. 'Have a look in the back.'

Welsch opened the rear door, scrabbled about on the floor under the seat for a minute or so and came up with a Tesco's carrier bag. 'Here,' he said, 'I'll use this.' He tore along the join and opened it out, placing it carefully over the front seat, then climbed in.

'You mind if I smoke?' He shifted on the plastic, attempting to stretch it out under his thighs as a small wet stain started to seep onto the seat. The whole car was filled with the sharp scent of his aftershave.

'Yes, sorry, but I do mind.' Jills eyes were smarting and she wondered if smoke might be preferable.

'Oh, right.' Welsch unzipped the bomber jacket and shook the water off his sleeves as he did so. He found a bubble gum in his inside pocket, unwrapped it and kneaded it between his forefinger and thumb a few times to soften it before stuffing it into his mouth.

'So?' Jill said. She had pulled into the side of the road and switched off the engine. She wound the window down a crack to clear the air.

'So what?'

'So what are you doing here?' she asked. 'You're not visiting clients, are you?'

'No. I've been keeping my eye on Holly Grigson's flat.'

'Oh, really?'

Welsch shrugged; the sarcasm went over his head. 'Yeah.'

'Can I ask why?'

'You need to?'

Jill lost her patience. The truth was, she was pretty unnerved by Welsch's appearance. 'Yes, I need to!' she snapped. 'Please, just tell me what is going on.'

Welsch took the bubble gum out of his mouth. 'It's like I said before, Mrs T. This isn't some sort of game you're playing. You could be in a lotta trouble and I'm just making sure that you don't get me involved in something I don't know about first.'

'You?'

'Yeah, me. I got a file that someone wants, remember? And that makes me a target, if they find out I got it.'

'Does Holly know you've been watching the flat?'

'No. She doesn't know I've been watching the gallery either.'

'Did you see anything suspicious?'

Welsch put the gum back in his mouth and chewed for a few seconds. 'Not a sausage,' he answered.

Jill let her breath out silently.

'It won't get any easier, you know,' Welsch said. 'You're gonna get more and more scared the longer this thing goes on and the closer you get to finding Blandford.'

'I didn't say anything about being scared,' Jill countered.

Welsch reached over and took her wrist. He held it for a minute, his finger over the pulse. 'You're scared, Mrs T,' he said. He looked at her. 'You'd be a pretty queer fish if you weren't.'

Jill stared down at her lap. There was a long silence in the car, then Welsch asked, 'You awright, Mrs T?'

Jill nodded. 'It's Jill,' she said.

'What's Jill?'

Jill looked up. 'Me!' she exclaimed. 'Me, I'm Jill, not Mrs T. Please, call me . . .' She broke off and saw that Welsch was smiling.

'Jill,' he said, 'call you Jill. Right, Mrs T, I mean, Jill.'

She smiled back. 'Are you always this irksome?'

He chewed for a moment, thought about the question, then said, 'Always. What does irksome mean?'

Jill grinned. 'Very funny, Mr Welsch.'

'It's Ted, please, call me Ted. What does it mean?'

'Never mind,' Jill answered. 'I'll tell you some other time. Can I give you a lift back to your office?'

Welsch cleared a small area of the steamed-up window with his hand and peered out at the rain. 'I don't want to put you out at all,' he murmured, 'but . . .'

Jill shifted into gear. 'You will put me out, a great deal,' she said. He looked at her. 'But . . .' They both smiled. Indicating, Jill glanced over her shoulder, pulled out and set off in the direction of Soho.

'We've got a positive ID, Sarge!' DC Dobson came into the incident room carrying a slip of fax paper. 'Ted Welsch – private investigator, formerly CID, Metropolitan Police, Bromley.'

Robert Eames looked up from what he was doing. 'Jesus! That's all we bloody need, a bent copper! Get on to Bromley, will you, Dobbo, see if you can trace one of his mates. He must still be in touch with someone. Let's get some kind of background on him.' He stubbed out his cigarette and picked up the phone. DCI Heeley was at home, getting some long overdue rest time.

'Sir? It's Robert. Sorry, you weren't asleep, were you?'

DCI Heeley had been. 'Sorry, sir,' Eames said again. 'It's just that we've got a positive ID on our man, sir, ex-CID, in the Met. I'm not sure how to proceed.' He held for a few moments, then said, 'Right, yes, I've done that already, sir.' He reached for his cigarettes. 'Thanks, yes, I have.' He lit up, coughed behind his hand and fiddled with his lighter while Heeley spoke. 'OK, sir, I'll do that. Yup, no problem. See you later then.' He hung up.

'As soon as you get someone, Dobbo,' he called across the office, 'let me know. I want to fix up a meeting.' Dobson was already on the phone and gave Eames the thumbs-up to show he'd heard.

Eames was pleased at this latest development: at least it was something to go on. He stood up and stretched, then picked up the phone once more to dial.

'DS Eames,' he said, getting straight through. 'Just Bishop's Road again, we've had a positive ID on suspect four. We're onto it.' He smiled as one of the surveillance team on the other end cracked a joke about the boredom factor. 'Yeah, well you're not in it for entertainment value, Dave!' And laughing at the reply, Eames hung up.

Dave was right though, he thought, walking along to the coffee machine. Up to now, surveillance, at his suggestion and costing more than he liked to think about, had been producing bugger all results. Nothing, sweet FA, except Holly Grigson getting on with her job, and that made for very unexciting watching.

Eames slotted his coins in and pressed coffee, black with sugar. He took the cup after it had filled and sipped. Boy did he need this lift! Ted Welsch. Whoever the hell he was they'd know about it soon enough.

'So what happens next?' Welsch asked, topping his glass up with the remainder of lemonade and stirring the drink with his swizzle stick. 'You've found the bloke, talked him into showing his paintings, so where does that get you?'

Jill stared down at what had been the garnish on Welsch's Malibu and lemonade – a chewed bit of orange peel and half a cocktail cherry, lying discarded in the ashtray. He had talked her into a drink at his local and she sat there, opposite his small, steaming figure, wondering what the hell she was doing and amazed that she was actually enjoying doing it. 'It is supposed to get us Blandford,' she said, not at all sure of that fact. 'If this thing works, if the exhibition goes well, then the press hype Adrian White up, we put ads out for the gallery as his sole representatives, rumours start about the prices and . . .' Jill shrugged. 'You know the rest – presumably Kit told you.'

'You think it'll work?'

'Holly seems to think so. It's not about money, apparently; it's about art, collecting it, the kudos involved . . .' She stopped, suddenly conscious of the fact that she was quoting Holly. 'I'm sure Kit explained most of it,' she finished.

'Yeah, he did.' Welsch tapped his fingers on the table top. 'So, then what happens?'

'What d'you mean, then what happens?' Jill was taken aback by the question. 'With any luck it leads Blandford to Holly and we've got him.'

'Yeah, but then what happens? What happens after you've got him?'

Jill stared at Welsch.

'Is Holly going to ask him nicely for the money back?'

'For God's sake, we're not that stupid,' she answered sharply. 'I don't know exactly what will happen, but I do know that whoever wants Blandford will be watching us to see if we lead them to him and once we do, it's out of our hands.'

'And you believe that?'

'Yes! I . . .' Jill broke off. 'You don't,' she said. She dropped her gaze and looked at her hands. 'It isn't over till the fat lady sings, is that what you're saying?'

Welsch smiled. 'Nice expression. Yeah, that's what I'm saying.'

'And that's why you're watching Holly, because you think we've underestimated the danger.'

'I think,' Welsch said, looking at Jill's face, 'that it's highly unlikely, knowing as much as you all do, that you're going to be allowed to get away with it. You don't fuck with these boys, Jill, I tried to tell you that before.'

Jill sat perfectly still and felt the sharp twist of panic in the pit of her stomach. But he was the one who had told her they had to find Blandford; he was the one who had said . . .

'You awright?'

'Do you really think that, Ted?' Jill swallowed. 'I mean, you think we could be killed?' She looked up. 'Even after finding Blandford?'

Welsch reached forward, picked up the other half of the cocktail cherry and chewed on it for a few seconds. A cigarette would have been better, if he'd been allowed to smoke.

'I don't know,' he answered. That was the truth. 'What you know, what I know, is pointless without names, and for that we need Blandford. If someone else gets to him first, then maybe they won't bother with you, or me for that matter.' Jill's face had drained of all colour and Welsch worried for a moment that she might faint. 'They took a shot at me,' he said, 'but they never came back. The only thing I can think is they didn't reckon it was worth it. What I know is useless without Blandford. I haven't got any names, not the ones that matter anyroad, and without them I got nothing.'

Jill picked up her glass with shaking hands.

'I shouldn't have told you all that,' Welsch said grimly. 'I've scared you.' He took her glass and held it up, catching the barmaid's eye. He pointed at it and mouthed brandy. A couple of minutes later a drink arrived.

'Here.' He handed it across to Jill.

'I can't, I'm driving. I'll be over the limit.' She reached for her coat. 'Besides, I have to go and pick up Sophie. She's at a studio in Camberwell; I shouldn't have left her. I wasn't thinking, I realise that now, it's far too dangerous. I should have . . .'

'Drink it,' Welsch ordered. 'You need it and you've only had three or four sips of wine, barely half a glass, it won't take you over the limit.' He nudged the glass towards her with his finger. 'Sophie is with someone, isn't she?'

Jill nodded.

'She'll be OK then, for the moment. Go on, it'll dull the fear a bit.'

She did as he said. As soon as she had swallowed down the cognac she felt some kind of feeling come back to her body.

'So what the hell do we do?' Jill put the glass down on the table and clutched her hands together. Her fingers were icy. 'There's no way out, is there?'

Welsch hesitated, then shook his head. 'No, not that I can see.' He finished his drink. 'The only thing you gotta do is be bloody careful. Think about every little thing that doesn't seem right, every move you make, analyse every newounce . . .'

'Newounce?'

'Yeah, it's French for . . .'

'Nuance,' Jill murmured. 'You mean nuance?'

The correction went right over Welsch's head. 'Yeah, that's the one. Take it in, and call me if anything don't feel right.' He stood up, glass in hand, and Jill watched him. Despite all her reservations, she liked him. He was caring, funny and smart, and she realised, for the first time in her life, that was all that really mattered.

'You want to get going, don't you?' he said.

Jill had tried not to look agitated but she'd failed. 'Yes, sorry, if you don't mind.' The thought of driving across London alone suddenly frightened her. 'I just want to collect Sophie and get home.'

'Not surprising.'

Jill reached behind her for her coat and bag. 'I'd better go then.'

He nodded. He liked the way she didn't overdramatise things. In fact he liked Jill Turner more than he'd liked anyone since Macie left. Putting his glass down on the table, he slipped his bomber jacket off the back of the chair. 'I'll see you to the car,' he said.

Jill stood. 'There's no need, honestly.'

'No, well, I'll do it anyway.' He helped her on with her coat. 'Nice cloth that.'

She glanced over her shoulder at him. 'Thanks.' She smiled; it was an odd compliment.

As they left the pub, Welsch waved at several people. 'D'you spend much time in here?' she asked.

He shrugged but didn't answer her. They walked in silence to the car. Standing aside as she unlocked it, he said, 'Tell me why you got mixed up in all this? Considering the risk, that is.'

Jill was surprised at the question. She turned and looked at him for a moment. 'Because of Sophie, because she needed to find out what happened to her father, and because of Alex, of finding out the truth. I felt I owed it to him.'

'Yeah, but . . .'

'No buts. Have you ever been married, Ted?'

He was about to answer no, the same as he always did, but hesitated. 'Once,' he said, 'when I was eighteen. Macie Green, Miss Butlins, Ayre, 1960.' He dug his hands in his pockets. 'She ran off with my brother; they went to Australia.'

'I'm sorry,' Jill said.

'I was too. The marriage lasted six months but it was the best six months of my life.'

Jill placed her hand on his arm and he stared at it. She quickly removed it, thinking she'd overstepped the mark.

'I never told anyone,' he said. 'There didn't seem any point.'

'No, I can understand that.' They were silent for several moments, then Jill opened the car door and climbed into the Range Rover. She didn't know what else to say, if anything at all, so she just thanked him for the drink and started the engine.

'You got my number?' he called.

She nodded.

'Ring me if you need to.' He stepped back onto the pavement as she pulled off and held his hand up in a wave. He stood and watched her drive off, round the corner into Romily Street, before moving back into the pub. He hadn't meant to get involved in all this; he'd meant to keep an eye on it from a distance and be shot of it if things got out of hand. Sighing heavily, he made his way to the bar, ordered himself another Malibu and sat down at the table he'd shared with Jill.

He picked up her glass, looked at the lipstick mark, a light natural pink, and remembered the shape of her mouth. He hadn't meant to even get to know any of them; he'd planned to keep it strictly impersonal. He wiped her glass, transferring the lipstick onto his clean white handkerchief, and tucked it away in his pocket. All that was ruined now. Not only did he know Jill Turner, he liked her too. He patted the pocket where the handkerchief sat and glanced down at the sleeve of his jacket where she'd placed her hand. He liked her a lot, and whether he wanted to be or not, he was involved. No matter what happened now, getting shot of it just didn't seem an option any more.

It was after nine when Jill parked the car up on the kerb right outside Adrian's building in Camberwell and climbed out, looking up to see if any of the lights were on in the studios. There were four or five still burning so she pushed open the doors and pressed the buzzer, shivering in the dark, empty lobby. She waited three or four minutes, then pressed the buzzer again. A young woman appeared.

'Yes?'

'I've come to see Adrian White. Is he still here?'

The girl walked into the lobby, bent behind the desk and opened what looked like a school exercise book. 'He's not signed out yet, so I assume so.' She glanced up. 'Come on in.'

Leading the way, she locked the doors to the stairway after them and said, 'You know where you're going?'

'Third floor, I think.'

'Right. End studio, on the corner, lucky bugger.' She smiled and disappeared off through the door to the ground-floor studios.

Jill made her way up the stairs, pressing the timed lighting on each level, her shoes clicking on the concrete flooring. At the third floor, she followed the passage between the partitioned studios, the whole place in partial darkness, lit only by the sickly orange glow from the street lamps outside. It was deserted. She could hear no conversation or noise and the hush unnerved her. Perhaps Adrian and Sophie had left without signing out. At the end of the passage, she turned the corner and knocked on the wall of Adrian's studio space, calling out. Then she walked right in, thinking it must be empty.

'Oh! Oh Lord, I'm sorry, I . . .' She took a pace back as two figures suddenly moved apart in a tangle of clothes and limbs on the floor. 'I'm so sorry . . .' she stammered. 'I didn't think . . .' As she moved back again, she stumbled and knocked the light switch with her shoulder. The whole space was flooded by the neon strip overhead.

'Sophie! My God! What on earth are you . . .'

'Jill!' Sophie clutched at the cape she had round her shoulders in an attempt to cover her bare chest. Her face was aflame.

'What the bloody hell is going on here?' Jill shouted. Her anger was sudden and intense. All the fear she'd felt for Sophie exploded in one terrible bout of fury. 'My God! What the hell were you thinking, child?'

'I'm not a child!' Sophie cried.

'Well you're bloody acting like one! For Christ's sake, Sophie! Couldn't you show a little sense for once?'

'She was posing for me,' Adrian interjected. He had moved to Sophie's side and held the cape round her. 'I wanted to draw her, in shadow, I thought . . .'

'I know only too well what you thought, young man!' Jill snapped. 'Get dressed, Sophie!'

'Jill! Please . . .' Sophie's eyes filled with tears. 'Don't talk to me like that. I'm not a child and we were only . . .'

Jill cut her off. 'I know exactly what you were doing! I know . . .' Her voice faltered and for one awful moment she thought she was going to cry. Her head swam and she had to put her hand out to the wall to steady herself. In the face of all the danger, of the fact that they might all end up dead and buried before it was over, Sophie was here, half-naked with someone she hardly knew! The sight of such intimacy infuriated Jill. What time was there for intimacy? For Christ's sake, how did she have the nerve?

She bent down and hurriedly gathered Sophie's clothes together, throwing them in a bundle at her stepdaughter. 'Get dressed now!' she shouted. 'I'll wait for you in the car!' Turning on her heel, she stormed out of the studio, and down to the car.

Sophie followed her down five minutes later. She had wanted to stay but Adrian had dissuaded her. He didn't know what the hell was going on but he did know that leaving a rift only made it harder to heal and he liked Sophie too much to see her hurt unnecessarily. Sophie got into the car without a word to Jill, clicked in her seat belt and stared out of the window, her face pale, her skin stained with the streaks of her tears. How could Jill do that to her? After everything they had shared in the past few weeks, how could she revert to type and treat her so insensitively? Sophie gripped the seat, the urge to burst into sobs of anger and humiliation almost overwhelming. She saw the reflection of her stepmother's face in her own window, her profile set in a dark expression of fury, and she closed her eyes, to avoid looking at it.

They drove to Sussex, in grim silence all the way

Chapter Twenty-One

At the same time, in Chelsea, Holly too was staring at a reflection in the window. It was the reflection of a young woman, tired, frightened and alone; she barely recognised it as her own.

On the desk in front of the window, she had scattered the slides of Adrian's work. The desk lamp faced the wall and she had been holding each transparency up to the light, discovering that his paintings in all their wonderful colour and emotion were as vibrant on film as they were in real life. She had been thrilled, filled with hope and daunted, each in turn. Now she was simply depressed.

How could she do this? How could she involve this incredibly talented young artist in the mess her life had become? If things went badly wrong she could ruin his reputation, sink him without a trace; she could even put him in serious danger. If things went right she could still put him in serious danger. Was he really aware of that? And even if he was, what right did she have to let him take that risk? What right did she have to let Jill or Sophie take that risk, for that matter?

Holly dropped her head in her hands and she too closed her eyes on a reflection she didn't want to see. She wasn't sure now that she had the courage to see this through. She felt hopeless and alone, and for the first time since he had left, she thought about Kit. She put her head down on the desk, ignored the answerphone as it clicked on and wondered where he was, what he was doing and if he ever spared a moment in his life to think about her.

Seconds later, she jerked her head up. Her message finished and she heard the caller come onto the tape. It was Guy Ferreira, for the second time that night.

'Hello, Holly, I'm ringing from my car. I realise that you probably didn't get my first message and that you're probably still out but I'm on my way back from a client in Chelsea Harbour and I thought I'd drop by. Just in case you get back in time, that would be in about ten or so minutes. Hope to see you. If not I'll be in touch. Bye, bye.' The line went dead, and the machine clicked off then started to rewind. Holly sat where she was and listened to the tape whirring, very unsure of what to do. The last thing she wanted was to see Guy. He had been very kind but she just didn't need that sort of complication, not right now, not on top of everything else. So she walked across to the phone and unplugged it, then she went to the window, glanced down at the street and reached up to draw the curtains. She would switch the lights off and ignore the buzzer; that way Guy would think she was out.

But just as she reached up she heard a crash of glass in the kitchen. She jumped, and then froze. All the lights in the flat fused and she was plunged into darkness. Trembling, she left the curtains open and hurriedly fumbled her way to the bureau for a torch. She knelt, scrabbled around frantically in the drawer, then stopped dead still as she heard the whisper of a voice. Suddenly the flat was filled with a horrible roaring.

'Oh my God . . .' Holly jumped up but it was too late. A fist came at her and she took the blow full on the shoulder. She fell back. Before she could open her lungs a body was on top of her, pressing the breath out of her, forcing her down. Kicking and punching for her life, she closed her eyes and began to scream.

Guy sat in his hire car opposite Holly's building and watched the second-floor window. He saw the lights go out, the vague outline of Holly's figure in shadow, and glanced at his watch: it was five past nine. When he looked up again her figure had disappeared. He climbed out of the car, crossed the road and approached the building. He could hear the screaming fifty yards away. Breaking into a run, he sprinted through the main door, up the stairs and into her flat. He sprang from out of nowhere, roaring and flaying his arms, lunging at the man on Holly, dragging him off and cracking his head down violently against the table. There was a struggle, Guy lashed out, took several blows to the head and finally hit the floor. As Holly knelt screaming, the two men took one last crack at him, then fled. She started to sob.

'Jesus!' Guy struggled to his knees and held his head for a few moments. He looked up. 'My God, Holly! Are you all right?' He moved across to her and hugged her in close. 'Sssh, it's OK, sssh, come on, don't cry . . .' He rocked her gently for several minutes, oblivious to the fact that he was bleeding from an open wound on the side of his head, and finally she began to quieten. He held her for a while longer, then released her and looked at her face. 'Are you all right?'

She nodded. Reaching up, she touched the skin under his cut. He flinched. 'Here, wait.' She took her scarf off and put it up to stop the flow of blood. 'I'll get something to clean it with.'

She made to stand but Guy held onto her arm. 'Take it easy,' he said. 'There's no rush, I'm not going to bleed to death.' She dropped to her knees again, relieved not to have to move.

'What on earth happened?' Guy asked. 'Did they take anything?'

'I don't know, I . . .' Holly shook her head. 'I don't think they were burglars, I think . . .' She broke off again as her voice failed her.

'You think what, Holly?' Guy sat back on his heels. 'Wait, we need some light on the matter.' He stood up and rubbed his back where he'd been kicked, then felt his way to the door. 'Where's the fuse box?'

'Kitchen,' Holly answered. She watched him disappear and within minutes the room was flooded with light again. She caught her breath, relief swamping her, then stood to close the curtains.

'OK?'

Holly looked up at him as he stood in the doorway. 'Yes, I think so.'

He crossed to her and held out his hand. She took it and he led her towards the sofa. 'Come and sit down, I'll get you a drink.' He turned. 'Where d'you keep the strong stuff?'

She nodded to a bottle of whisky on the bureau. 'Glasses are down in the cupboard underneath,' she said. Guy bent, found two and poured them both a drink.

'Here.' He handed her a glass and stood with his own. 'Now, I want the truth. Who were these men? You sounded just then as if you knew.'

Holly stared at her glass. 'I don't know, not for sure, but I think they were after me, not my possessions. I think, that if you hadn't have come, they might have killed . . .' A sob caught in her throat. 'I'm sorry, I . . .'

He squeezed her hand. 'I did come,' he said softly, 'that's all that matters.'

She nodded and they were silent for some time. Holly sipped her whisky, not really wanting it, a terrible sickness in the pit of her stomach.

Then Guy stood up. 'Holly, I think we have to talk.' She stared up at him blankly, and he went on. 'Things seem to have moved on since we last spoke. I think that things are getting out of hand.'

Holly looked down.

'Will you let me help you?'

She continued to stare at her lap.

'Will you at least talk to me, sort some things out?' He held his glass and swirled the whisky round and round.

'I don't know. I don't see what there is to sort out,' she said.

'There's the fact that if I hadn't come round here this evening, purely by chance, I might add, then you might well not be sitting here now. Had you thought of that?'

'Of course I've thought of that!' Holly cried. 'I've thought of nothing else since you . . . since you . . .' She couldn't finish. She put her hand up to her mouth to stop herself from crying again and Guy walked over to the fireplace, turning away from her and leaning against the mantelpiece. He watched her in the mirror overhead but glanced away as she looked up.

'Then you have to act,' he said, facing her. 'You have to take this thing into your own hands. How long to go before the Art 'ninety-four exhibition?'

'Ten working days.'

'Can you wait that long?'

She swallowed. 'I don't know. I don't see that I have any choice.'

'What if it doesn't work?'

'I can't think about that. It has to work . . .' She broke off and shrugged helplessly. 'It just has to.'

Guy sighed heavily. He walked back and sat on the arm of the sofa, looking down at his drink. 'I have an idea,' he said. 'I've been thinking about it for some time now and I wasn't going to mention it – I thought you had things pretty well under control – but now I think I have to. I think it would be irresponsible of me not to.'

He looked at her. 'Do you want to hear it?'

Again Holly shrugged. She didn't know what she wanted to hear; she was too confused and frightened to think clearly.

Guy hesitated; his timing was crucial. 'OK, well, I'll run it past you anyway.' He finished his whisky and placed the glass carefully on the floor. 'I was wondering, Holly, about moving this whole thing to Paris.'

Holly almost smiled. 'Paris! What on earth would I do in Paris?'

Guy stood and began to pace up and down. She got the impression he was thinking on his feet. 'Don't jump on it,' he said. 'Let me explain. It's not as crazy as you think. Hear me out, all right?'

'All right,' she agreed.

'Well, the way I see it, is that you've got ten more days to go before the Art 'ninety-four exhibition here, and that's a long way away. Anything could happen in that time. Do you agree?'

She nodded.

'What if we were to set things up in Paris in the next couple of days, arrange a gallery viewing for Adrian White, put some ads out, invite the press and get this whole thing off the ground? Now! It looks as if you've got most of the work here – certainly enough to put on a show. It would get you out of London, to somewhere safer, and you could create a storm across the Channel. Then, if that didn't work you'd still have a shot at the art expo here . . .' Guy stopped. Holly was smiling and he felt the smallest twist of anger in his chest. 'What's so funny?'

'I'm sorry,' Holly replied. 'It's just that it's a nice idea but totally unrealisable. My knowledge of the French art market is scant, I don't speak the language and there is no way on earth I could arrange a private view, press, advertising in just a couple of days, if at all for that matter.' She shook her head. 'Thanks for thinking of me, but it really would be impossible.'

It was Guy's turn to smile. 'That's where you're wrong,' he said. 'It's not impossible at all; I've already looked into it.'

Holly narrowed her eyes. 'You have?' This conversation was verging on the ridiculous, she decided.

'I rang a colleague of mine, a public relations professional; she handles all the top people in Paris. She can fix anything from a restaurant opening to a movie premiere and she can do it in twenty-four hours if she has to. She rules the press and knows everyone who's anyone up and down the country. She started looking into this a couple of days ago and all she's waiting for is the word from me.'

Holly sat speechless. On the one hand this was so preposterous that she had an overwhelming urge to laugh hysterically, and yet on the other she felt a glimmer of hope, the tiniest spark of light at the end of the tunnel. She watched him for a few moments. He was absolutely serious, of that she was convinced, but he couldn't have thought it through properly. He couldn't possibly have realised that she didn't have the sort of money . . .

He interrupted her thoughts. 'You're wondering how you could afford to finance all this, aren't you?'

'Yes! I . . .' She stared at him. It was as if he could read her mind, then pre-empt her questions with the right answers.

'I have money, Holly. I have enough money to last my lifetime and to spare – a trust fund, to be precise – only I've never had anyone to spend it on. Not until now, that is.'

Holly dropped her gaze. 'What you're saying is that you'd be prepared to set this whole thing up and then to finance it all for me?'

Guy paused to add weight to his answer. 'Yes.'

Holly shook her head again. 'I don't believe it.'

'Why not?' Guy thought for a few moments. 'OK,' he went on, 'if you're not entirely happy about that, then we could set up some sort of arrangement that says I take a percentage of the artist's earnings if you manage to make a success of him into the bargain. A business deal.'

Holly looked up. 'But why? Why get involved, why waste your money on someone you hardly know? I don't understand, Guy, you must be insane! Why me, for God's sake?'

He turned away. 'You really have to ask?'

There was a silence which seemed to Holly to last for ages and all she could focus on was the rapid beating of her heart. She twisted her hands in her lap, knotting her fingers tightly together. Could Guy really do all this for her? He was like some kind of charm, always appearing at exactly the right moment with the right words and the right solutions. He was the white knight and for a few moments she was dazzled by him. Then reality struck.

'I couldn't possibly let you offer all this,' she said sadly. 'There is no guarantee it would work; it could involve you in something potentially very dangerous and I can't take your money, Guy, it wouldn't be right.'

'Of course it would be right!' Guy exclaimed. 'For God's sake, Holly, it could save your life! Good Lord, I'd never forgive myself if something happened to you. If tonight wasn't warning enough for you then it was for me. I keep thinking what might have happened if I hadn't come here, if I'd been five minutes later, if . . .' He swallowed back his fear and squatted down in front of her, taking both her hands in his. 'Holly, listen to me, please, just think it through. Blandford's in France, right? If you operate in Paris then you're in a far better position to attract him. We can put an ad in the national press, in all the papers. He'd be bound to see it, and he wouldn't be able to resist it – the international showing of the new David Hockney, an artist who still owes him five, six, maybe even ten or more canvases. Think of it, Holly. By this time next week it could all be over, you'd be safe, this whole nightmare . . .'

'No! Stop all this!' Holly snatched her hands away and abruptly stood up. Guy sat back on his heels and stared up at her. 'You don't know that! What if it didn't work, what if Blandford didn't turn up?'

'Then what would you have lost? Nothing. You come back to London and do the Art 'ninety-four exhibition.'

'And who would organise that in my absence in Paris?'

'Let one of the others do it, what's her name?'

'Jill?'

'Yes, or her daughter . . .'

'Sophie?'

'Yes, why not? Just get them to come over to Paris for one day to pose as clients and the rest of the time they spend here, organising Art 'ninety-four.'

'But Jill doesn't know any of the journalists. How could we . . .'

'Invite them to Paris, all expenses paid. They'll come – most journos will to a freebie that's prestigious enough. Once they've done Paris, if he's as good as you say he is, then they'll want to do London – even if he's not they'll owe you one. My lady in Paris can handle it. Lord, she could even get HRH to a barbecue in Pinner if she had to.'

Despite the sudden churning in her stomach, Holly smiled; she couldn't help herself.

'That's better,' Guy said. 'I like it when you smile.'

Holly flushed. She turned away and fiddled with the small Elisabeth Frink bronze, running her finger along the smooth, sleek line of the figure, thinking hard. What had seemed ludicrous half an hour ago now seemed just incredible. It had gone from total fantasy to possible reality, and Holly wasn't sure how. Perhaps he was right. It might just work. She turned and looked at him. He was staring down at his hands, nervously tapping his fingers in a rhythm against his leg.

'And if I agreed with this crazy, insane idea,' she said quietly, 'how would I ever repay you, Guy?'

He looked up at her, holding her gaze for several moments, then he shrugged. 'Let's just take one step at a time, shall we?'

Holly nodded and they were silent, looking at each other. Finally she asked, 'When would you want to get started?'

He glanced at his watch. 'There's a plane that leaves for Paris at six thirty am.'

'Can I think about it?'

Guy shrugged again, then stood. 'How long d'you need to make up your mind about something that seems to me to be inevitable?'

'I don't know,' she answered. 'I just think I need some time alone – an hour maybe?'

'Fine, an hour.' Then he smiled. 'Take all the time you need, Holly, I'll be at my hotel.'

As she watched him move towards the door, Holly suddenly said, 'Your face, I should dress that cut, it . . .'

'It's nothing,' Guy interrupted, 'honestly.' He went through to the hall and stepped over the broken glass on the carpet. At the door he stopped and looked back at her. 'You'll ring?'

'I'll ring,' she answered. And with that, he was gone.

Down in the street, Guy leant against the wall, took his handkerchief out of his pocket and put it to the cut on his head. What a fucking fiasco! He flinched as he wiped some of the blood away. He was stiff and sore, it had been a hard night and he still hadn't convinced her.

Standing straight, he pushed the handkerchief down into his pocket and walked across the road to his car. He opened the door, climbed inside and started the engine. He was tired, he hurt and he was angry. He didn't bother to look behind him, and he didn't see the camera or the man who watched him.

'Hello, sir, thanks for coming in so quickly.'

'Evening, Bob.' DCI Heeley dropped his mac over the back of his chair and came round to Eames' side of the desk. The fact that Robert Eames winced every time he was called Bob completely bypassed Heeley.

'It's gone frigging haywire,' Eames said. 'Something's happened to stir things up and I can't think what.'

323

'This the report from surveillance?'

'Yes.'

DCI Heeley started to read. 'The prints ready yet?'

DS Eames glanced at his watch. 'Half an hour. They just came into the lab.'

'Let me get this right,' Heeley said, over the top of the report. 'At five minutes past nine a car pulls up. Good, you got the reg. Have you traced it yet?'

'Hire car. Dobbo's onto it now.'

'The lights in the suspect's flat go out, there's a struggle inside, a male IC1 gets out of the car, runs into the building and joins the struggle? Yes?'

Eames nodded.

'They got this on infrared camera?'

'Yeah, the boys are just going over the tapes now. We can see them in a minute.'

'Good. Then the lights go on and the curtains are drawn, but you think there's some kind of dialogue with this man. Any idea who he is?'

'No, not yet. It could be Welsch, it could be anyone; surveillance couldn't make out much in the dark. The pictures will tell us more.'

'Right, as soon as we get them up let's start on our IC1 male.' Heeley glanced down at the report again. 'The men in the assault, did they get away?'

'Out the back, sir, no-one saw them.'

'Has the incident been reported?'

Eames shook his head. He reached for his cigarettes and offered one to Heeley, who took it and then answered the phone.

'Hensen,' Heeley called out as he replaced the receiver. 'Run down and collect the prints, will you?' He turned to Eames and took the offered lighter.

'Come on,' he said. 'Let's get a move on with those tapes.' He lit his cigarette and dropped the lighter back on the desk. 'So Holly Grigson gets assaulted in her own home and doesn't report it,' he said, leading the way out of the incident room and along the corridor to a makeshift viewing area. 'Very interesting.' He held the door for Eames. 'Women can't be trusted,' he remarked. Eames glanced over his shoulder, but he saw that Heeley was smiling.

The man walked into the suite, slammed the door shut and hurried across to the bar. He poured a badly needed Scotch, then headed for the bedroom and the small packet of cocaine he kept in the safe. Halfway across the room he suddenly stopped.

'Where you been?' The voice was Colombian, thick and heavily accented. The man knew it instantly and spun round.

'My God! Paulo!' He attempted to smile. 'Christ, you gave me a scare!' He extended his hand as he walked across the suite, then quickly dropped it by his side when it was ignored. 'It's good to see you, Paulo. I'm sorry I wasn't here, I've been taking care of a bit of business. I . . .'

'You been here a long time, what the fuck you playing at?'

'I've got it under control. I know what I'm doing, I just need a little more time. These things can't be done in a day, you know that, I . . .'

'Save it. You got three days to finish it. The boss wants his money back; he don't care about nothing else, you understand?'

'Three days?' The man had started to sweat. 'Look, come on, Paulo, I need a week at least. One more week – that's not a lot to ask, is it? Surely you could arrange it for . . .'

'I ain't arranging shit. You got three days and I don't want to hear nothing about this, you understand? I want a result, so don't fuck up.' The door of the suite was opened and the Colombian stepped out into the corridor. The two men waiting outside silently flanked their boss and closed the door behind him. The man was left staring at the empty room.

'He's on his own,' the Colombian said, outside the hotel. 'He's a fucking mess; he don't know what he's doin'.' He took his coat and hung it over his arm 'It stops with him; he's the last link. Anyone above him is safe. You understand what I'm saying?'

The bigger of the two men nodded.

'Good.' Climbing into a waiting taxi, the Colombian leant forward on the seat and beckoned both men closer. 'Then you know what to do,' he said. He sat back, the door was closed for him and the cab moved off.

The man stood alone in the suite, still holding the glass of whisky. He loosened his tie, unfastened his collar and drank it down in one. He was sweating heavily. Back at the bar he poured himself another, drank that as well, then he went through to the bedroom. He took the packet of cocaine from the safe and stared at it for a few moments. He knew what he was doing to himself but he couldn't stop; he had never been able to stop, that was his problem. He was in deep shit; he'd lost his nerve and if he didn't get it back he was about to lose an awful lot more than that. He took the cocaine across to the bedside table, knelt and carefully cut a line – bigger than he was used to, but he needed it. He bent, laid his face flat against the wood and snorted. Then he stood, felt the beginnings of a massive hit and took several quick deep breaths. His nerve began to strengthen.

Three days, he thought, walking back through to the sitting room of the suite for his cigarettes. If things worked out then he might just do it. He lit up and inhaled deeply. His hands stopped shaking.

It had never occurred to him that Blandford might not show up. He knew how greedy the bastard was and he knew the lure of the trap. Blandford's ego was too big to turn down an opportunity like this. Besides, what did he have to fear? Holly Grigson? The man smiled. She was easy bait. He moved across to the bar. It would make Blandford's day to think he'd got away with all that and more. He'd have to come back for the paintings. It would be the ultimate scam: several million dollars and a collection of prestigious contemporary works that he had unwittingly discovered.

Pouring himself a third Scotch, the man took it over to the sofa and sat down. He dropped his head back and closed his eyes. 'As long as Holly Grigson comes through,' he murmured under his breath, the now familiar image of her forming in his mind as he went over and over the photographs. He let his body relax for the first time in several hours. 'She'll come through,' he said aloud. 'She'll do it for me.'

Suddenly the phone rang.

Blinking rapidly, the man tried to focus on the room. His vision swam. Covering his eyes with his hands, he put his head between his legs and took several deep breaths, exhaling each one slowly, with control. Gradually, he felt better. He picked up the phone.

'Yes.'

'It's me.' The Weasel's voice was sharp with panic. 'Holly Grigson's being watched.'

The man sat forward. 'Christ! What do you mean? Who the fuck . '

'I don't know! I think it's the police, but I don't know for sure. It's friggin' slick, whoever it is. They'll have got you clocked by now. They were there tonight; I just caught sight of them.'

'Did they see you?'

'Nah, I don't think so, but I don't like it. There must be something pretty big goin' down for them to do surveillance. It's put the shits up me. I want out. I can't afford to be involved; I gotta . . .'

'Shut up!' the man snarled. 'You do as I tell you, that's what I pay you for.' He rubbed his hands over his face, his mind already in overdrive. His pulse was racing and his brain was trying to cope with the rush of blood.

'Get over there,' he snapped. 'Now. When she leaves make sure they follow you.'

'How the hell am I supposed to . . . ?'

'I don't give a fuck how the hell!' the man suddenly shouted. 'Just do it!' And he slammed down the phone.

Chapter Twenty-Two

It was nearing midnight. Guy had been gone for over an hour, and Holly had rung an emergency glazier, swept up the glass in the kitchen and generally tidied up. Now, not knowing what else to do with herself, she paced the flat, tracing a route from the bedroom to the kitchen to the sitting room and back. It calmed her but it didn't help her to think; nothing could do that. Her head was a mess and she couldn't get it straight. There was one phrase that kept going round and round in her brain – Blandford is in France – four simple words that Guy had said, four simple words that didn't make any sense to her at all. Holly stopped, stood in the centre of the sitting room and stared at her face in the mirror above the fireplace as if looking for clues.

'I never told him that,' she said to her reflection, 'I'm sure I didn't.' She chewed her lip and tried to think back to every conversation she had had in the past week. It was impossible. The words somersaulted, tripped over each other; situations merged; faces blurred; and the harder she tried the less she could remember. Standing there in the centre of the room, she realised that she had no clear recollection of who had said what or when, and yet the awful sense of unease she had just wouldn't budge. She didn't know what to do. Paris might be the way out, but she couldn't decide. She was locked in an endless circle of confusion.

329

Suddenly she started. The main door buzzer had sounded and she snapped back to the present, hurrying into the hall.

'H & D Emergency Glaziers,' a voice said over the intercom.

'Wait a moment.' She darted through to the window, looked down at the street and saw their van parked opposite her building. Back at the intercom, she pressed the door release. 'Come on up, second floor,' she said. She waited, heard footsteps on the stairs and clenched her fists. With the chain on the door, she opened it and peered through the crack. The two young men were in overalls and carried a tool bag each. She unchained the door and opened it.

'You alright, luv?' one of them said.

She nodded. 'A bit nervous,' she answered. 'I was here when they broke in.'

'Bad luck.' He put his tool bag down and took out a tape measure. 'We'll measure up then go and get a pane from the van.'

'Right.' Holly moved aside and wandered into the sitting room. The men went downstairs and she hovered by the window, watching for them. She saw them cross to the van to take out a sheet of glass. A couple of minutes later they were back.

'Will you be long?' she asked.

The one obviously in charge glanced up at her from rummaging in his bag for a tub of putty. ''Bout twenty minutes. Why, d'you need to go out?'

'No, I . . .' She stopped. Now that he'd mentioned it, perhaps she should go out. She could simply go across to Guy's hotel and ask him when she had spoken to him about Blandford being in France. If she asked him face to face, she would be able to see if there was anything odd in the way he answered, and she would know if he was lying.

'Yes,' she said suddenly. 'I am going out. Can I write a cheque now and leave you to get on with it?'

The man had prized the lid off the putty. He stood, tub in hand.

'Don't see why not. You're not worried about leaving the Chubb lock off?'

'No.' The only thing Holly was worried about at that moment was trying to get this thing sorted. 'You can bang the door shut when you've finished.' She dumped her bag on the hall table and scrabbled in it for her cheque book. Another time, she probably wouldn't have left two complete strangers in her house unattended but she really couldn't think about that now. She scribbled out a cheque, grabbed her coat from the stand, stuffed a hat on her head and threw her bag over her shoulder.

'Thanks a lot.' She squeezed past them and headed for the stairs. 'Leave me a note if there're any problems.' And waving over her shoulder, she hurried down the stairs and had gone before either of the men could say goodbye.

'Oscar Foxtrot four. Target leaving the building, approaching her car, a red Volkswagen Beetle, registration Lima, Victor, X-ray, eight one one Hotel. Driving off in the direction of the King's Road.'

'Tommy Echo three, we've got her.'

Holly pulled out into the traffic of the King's Road and behind her a red Fiat swung out from a parking space.

'Tommy Echo three, target heading north up the King's Road, towards Sloane Square. Following in the vehicle.'

The driver of the red Fiat braked suddenly as a blue Ford transit van pulled out from a side road fifty yards up. 'Shit! Frigging rust bucket!' He leant his head out of the window and attempted to peer round the van. 'I can only just see her. Jesus! Sodding van!' His passenger picked up the handset. 'I'll radio up ahead.'

The driver swung out sharply, then back into the stream of traffic. 'No, it's OK, I've got her, two cars up.' They followed, slowed at the traffic lights and stopped on red. The driver drummed his fingers on the steering wheel, waiting for the change. 'OK, we're off.' He revved as the lights changed to let the van know he was in a hurry. As the Volkswagen Beetle at the head of the traffic moved off, the transit van followed for five yards or so, then stopped suddenly, in the middle of the intersection. Several cars turning right had to slam on their brakes and the red Fiat behind just missed the van's back bumper. A small, pinched-faced man with lank hair jumped out of the driver's seat and hurried to the bonnet of the van. He lifted it and bent in to the engine.

'Fucking asshole!' The driver of the red Fiat picked up the handset. 'Tommy Echo three, target moved off the traffic lights, heading down . . .' He leant out of the window but he couldn't see round the van's bonnet up in the air. 'We think she's heading north up the King's Road towards Sloane Square. We've lost contact.' He slammed the handset down on the dashboard and swore.

His partner chewed a fingernail. 'We got anyone up that end?'

The driver shrugged, then shook his head. 'Bugger it!' he said.

At Sloane Square Holly turned left into Sloane Street, heading for Piccadilly and Guy's hotel. Twenty minutes later she was there and nobody knew where she had gone.

Guy Ferreira was standing by the window in the sitting room of his suite when the phone rang. He had been staring down at the traffic below, trying to keep his mind focused, and he'd been smoking heavily. The room was thick with the smell and taste of stale tobacco. Moving across to the telephone, he took several quick breaths, then picked it up. 'Yes.' He listened to the voice on reception. 'Yes, please,' he said, 'thank you.' And lighting up another cigarette, he smoothed his hair off his forehead, opened the window and stood where he was to wait for her.

'Hi.' Holly stood nervously in the corridor, her coat over her arm. 'I'm sorry, I know it's late. I hope you weren't in bed or anything, but I had to talk to you.'

Guy opened the door wide. 'No I wasn't, I was working, so don't

332

worry, please. Come in.' He stood aside as she entered and closed
the door behind them. Holly walked into the suite, smelt the air
heavy with smoke and saw the ashtray, the scattered ash, the heap
of cigarette stubs, the empty glass. Guy looked dishevelled, and the
situation wasn't at all what she'd expected. It felt grubby, and she
was out of place, as if she'd encroached on something private. She
realised that she really didn't know this man very well and waited
tensely for him to speak.

'D'you want a drink?'

'No, thanks. I, er, just came to talk to you. I wanted to ask you
something.'

'Do you mind if I sit?' He assumed a relaxed pose on the sofa but
he was picking up bad vibes. He smiled, inwardly bracing himself,
then leant forward, suddenly concerned. 'What is it, Holly? You
look upset. My God, they didn't come back?'

'No, nothing like that.' She glanced down. 'Thanks though, for
being concerned.' She was beginning to think she was mad. She
shouldn't have come.

'Holly?'

She looked up. 'Sorry,' she said. 'Look, I probably shouldn't
even be asking you this; it's just that I can't remember telling you
about Blandford being in France. I mean, obviously I must have, or
you wouldn't have known, but I really can't remember ever talking
about it.' She frowned. 'When did I mention it?'

Guy's brain went into overdrive. He had slipped up. She hadn't
told him about Blandford; he'd found that out through his own
means. He felt the uncomfortable prickle of sweat on the back of
his neck and reached for a cigarette to give himself time. 'To be
honest,' he said casually, 'I'm not sure I can remember either.' He
lit up, inhaled, then said, 'It was a few days ago, I think. I called
you at the gallery and we had a brief conversation. You were busy,
sounded muddled.' He smiled. 'A bit uptight, to be honest. It was
right in the middle of trying to find your artist. I think you said

the gallery was chaos, everything was out and I'd caught you at a bad time.' If he played on her confusion and anxiety he might just be able to convince her.

Holly remembered the call. She remembered saying that but she had been concentrating so hard on searching through the computer records that she couldn't remember saying much else.

'I think I said, "How's it going?", or something like that, and you said, "It's chaos". Then I asked if you'd had any leads at all and you told me Blandford was in France; that was as far as you'd got.'

Holly narrowed her eyes. 'I did?' She honestly couldn't remember.

'Yes, I think so. You could always ring your friend, check with her.' He was calling her bluff.

'God, no, I believe you.' He had to be right, didn't he? 'It's just that I couldn't remember.' The relief was clearly written on her face. She half smiled. 'I'm sorry, you must think me very foolish.'

'Not at all. Now, can I get you a drink?'

'OK then. But something soft, mineral water, or tonic.' She was beginning to feel a bit more relaxed. He seemed nonchalant about it, and that convinced her that she must have been working herself up into a frenzy over nothing. It was obviously just her state of mind. Only, as she watched him move across the room to the bar, she sensed something different about him, something that didn't quite fit. She tried not to stare but she couldn't help herself. His movements seemed studied, as if he were concentrating very hard on making them look relaxed, and it began to unnerve her. 'Guy?'

He looked round, a moment too quickly, and she caught a glimpse of something she didn't recognise. Was it panic, or worse, malice? 'Yes?'

Holly shrugged. 'Nothing.' She stared round the room. 'Nice suite.'

'It is, isn't it?' He brought her drink over and held it out to her, standing just a little too close. Holly tensed. 'Have you thought any more about my idea, Holly?' His hands were shaking, the index finger on his right one stained a brownish yellow.

'Yes, I mean, no. I, er . . .' Holly dropped her gaze, embarrassed. Guy was very close. She could smell his breath, hot and acrid. 'I don't know.' She stared down at the glass for a few moments, then finally up at him.

Guy looked at her face. It was a face he knew so well and yet not at all. It was a face he despised and yet wanted so much that it hurt, a deep, physical ache down in the pit of his stomach. 'You must,' he whispered. He reached out and touched her hair, winding a strand of it round his finger, holding her captive. He couldn't help himself; he was desperate. He had to make her see sense, see that she needed Paris, needed it like he did. His hold tightened and Holly winced. It hurt. She held very still but she had started to panic. 'You have to come,' he murmured, his lips almost touching her cheek. 'You have to, Holly, I need you.'

Holly swallowed hard and lifted her face away from his, tilting her head back slightly, out of reach. Guy stared at her. For one split second his fantasy became reality, the photographs came to life, and he grabbed the back of her neck, jerking her head in towards his, pinching the flesh violently with his fingertips, forcing her mouth onto his, viciously biting her lips. Holly gasped and cried out. Reality struck.

'Oh Christ!' Instantly the grip relaxed and Guy dropped his hand. He shook his head for a second as if dispelling his thoughts and Holly backed away from him. 'Holly, God, I'm sorry, I . . .'

But Holly was near to tears, her pulse racing, the sudden shock of his assault making her breathless and faint. She could taste blood on her lips. 'I'm sorry,' she stammered, 'I have to go to the bathroom, I . . .' She glanced over her shoulder, saw a door behind her and fled.

Moments later Guy was left staring at an empty space. 'Fuck!'

he muttered under his breath. He dropped his head in his hands and closed his eyes on his own drugged stupidity.

Alone in the bedroom, Holly staggered to the bed and collapsed onto it, thinking for one terrible moment that she might be sick. She sat huddled there for quite some time, frightened, shocked, unable to stop shaking. It was the most awful, consuming fear she had ever experienced. Then, finally, she stood up. She needed the bathroom; she needed to be able to lock the door.

Looking around the room, she saw the door to the bathroom on the far side and moved towards it. But in her hurry to get across the room, she knocked into the open wardrobe door with her hip. She stopped, only just suppressing a cry at the pain, and held onto the door for support. As she did so, she glanced down into the cupboard and saw the safe, still open, the photographs on the top of it. She stared, unable to make out the image for several seconds, then she recognised the shape of two bodies joined together and stared harder. It was pornographic but there was something about it, something odd, something . . . Suddenly Holly sprung back. It was a phone box – she could just make out the panes of glass – the couple was in a phone box. She froze for what must have been a minute or so, unable to move at all, then she felt an enormous rush of blood through her entire body. She grabbed the pictures and flicked through them, her heart pounding and her face burning with indignation and shock. It was her and Kit, there was no doubt; there was even a close-up of her face.

Shaking, Holly bent down and rummaged frantically through the safe. After a quick glance over her shoulder at the door, she pulled out a plastic bag containing the gallery's books, all of them, accounts, records, files – everything that had been taken. She held them for a moment to her chest, then threw them back in the safe. She saw the packet of cocaine, and a huge amount of cash, neatly stacked. She dropped the photographs on top of the safe, shut the wardrobe door and turned away. As calmly as she could manage, she crossed to the bathroom, closed the door behind her and locked it.

Holly sank down on the cold marble floor and put her hands up to her face. She began to whimper. Rocking herself back and forth, she tried to calm herself, but she couldn't stop trembling. She was in trouble, deep trouble. Whoever Guy Ferreira was, he was a sick, evil bastard and he was out to get her. She held her breath to stop herself from crying out. What was going to happen to her? 'What am I going to do?' she murmured.

A sudden jolt of realisation ran through her: it wasn't only her at risk; it was Jill and Sophie and Kit as well. Through her own stupidity she had endangered the lives of three other people, people she had talked into helping her, people who trusted her. Holly squeezed her eyes shut and rested her head on her knees. 'Oh God,' she whispered, over and over again, too terrified to move. 'Oh God . . .'

Guy stood by the door to the bedroom, one hand on the handle, his palms sweating. He felt weird, disorientated. He began to panic. He knew what he'd just done but it didn't seem real; he'd been on a huge high. The whole thing had happened in seconds – the physical need of her, the image of her like that; his body had taken over. He put his ear to the door and listened hard. What the hell was she doing in there?

Inching the door open, he peered inside. There was no sign of her. Silently he slipped into the room and across to the bathroom. He could hear nothing. Putting his face close to the door, he said, 'Holly? Are you all right?' And holding his breath, he waited for the answer.

Behind the door, Holly froze. She tried to control her shaking, to breathe evenly. She knew she had to answer him, had to act normally, at least until she got out of there. She swallowed and pulled herself to her feet. Running the taps, she said, 'I'm fine, I'll be out in a minute.' The noise of the water covered the tremor in her voice and outside Guy relaxed slightly. He stood there for a few moments longer, unsure of what to do, and finally said, 'Holly, about just now, I'm sorry, I rushed things.' The door between them helped. 'I'm overtired and I've had a few drinks; they went straight to my head.' He listened hard for any sound in the bathroom.

'Holly?'

She looked up and saw her face in the mirror. 'Yes?'

'It won't ever happen again. I really am sorry.'

Gripping the sink, she forced herself to answer. 'All right, Guy.' She listened for his footsteps, then slowly let out the breath she was holding. She hung her head and stayed like that for some time.

It was quite a while before Holly had the courage to look up again or to let go of the sink. She didn't know how long she had been there but her arms ached with the force of her grip and her fingers were colourless, drained of blood. She brought them up to her chest and made fists with them, trying to restore the circulation, then she ran the hot tap. She splashed her face with water, soaped her hands and dried herself with a warm towel. But as she reached up to put it back she knocked Guy's washbag over and the contents spilt out onto the marble sink top.

She sprang away and stared at his things. Then, very carefully, she picked up a small silver spoon and looked at it. She placed it back on the sink beside a compact mirror and a razor blade and slowly began to line all the things up. Her hands were shaking as she handled the eye drops, the nasal spray, the bottle of tranquillisers, the spoon, the mirror and the razor blade. She stood back. For some reason the packet of white powder in the safe hadn't registered back then, but it did now, and so did everything else. Guy was a drug addict; cocaine, she guessed. Her hands still shaking, she reached forward for the washbag and carefully searched it, unzipping the side pockets, shuffling the remainder of the contents. There were no needles or syringes;

her guess was more than likely right. She replaced the bag on the sink, put back all its contents, then sank down on the edge of the bath and dropped her head in her hands.

Who the hell was Guy Ferreira? She pressed her fingers hard against her temples, trying to work it out. He had to be connected to Blandford, she was pretty sure of that. He had appeared when Sandy had disappeared. He wanted to be involved – it had been his idea to find Blandford. And he knew exactly what was going on, he always had. He'd even known Blandford was in France. Holly suddenly sat straight. She hadn't told him, she was sure of that now. She could even remember the phone conversation they'd had; it came back to her with astonishing clarity. She had said nothing of any note; she had been too busy, too preoccupied. Suddenly it all connected. She stood up and took several deep breaths to calm herself. It must have been Guy who had been bugging the phones, who was responsible for the break-ins, the attempt on her life! It had to be – how else could he know so damn much?

Holly continued to breathe deeply, fighting the panic that threatened to rise up and swamp her. She had to think this through, if she was going to survive. She had to get it straight in her head, know what she was up against. Obviously Blandford was working for Ferreira, laundering money. Ferreira was part of this organisation Kit kept talking about; that much had to be right. But why did Guy Ferreira need to know where Blandford was? Why hadn't he organised someone else to find Blandford and then dispose of Holly, once he'd found out how much she knew? What was it Kit had said? If they had meant to kill her she'd be dead by now, no question. She shivered, but the intense fear was beginning to subside as a very basic instinct to survive took hold. She thought hard.

No, Guy Ferreira was keeping tabs on Holly because he needed to. He wanted her alive and he wanted to know exactly what she was doing. Suddenly Holly stood up. 'He doesn't know where Blandford is!' she burst out. 'And he wants me to find him.' She glanced back at the washbag. Guy Ferreira was out of control, the drugs had made him negligent, and because of that he'd lost millions. The millions Blandford had stolen. Holly stared at the marble sink top, not really seeing it, her mind racing, the adrenaline beginning to pump through her veins. But it wasn't Ferreira's money to lose. He had fouled up and had been sent to sort it out. She put her hands up to her face and massaged her temples. That had to be it. And Ferreira was still negligent, she thought – the safe left open, the photographs – only he was more out of control than ever and that had made him desperate. She looked at her reflection long and hard in the mirror and made a sudden decision. Then she turned and unlocked the bathroom door.

Desperate men were dangerous, she knew that – Blandford was proof of it. But desperate men were also careless, and that thought gave her the first real glimmer of hope she'd experienced since the whole awful nightmare had begun. One more mistake could change everything. He had already made one – he had just given himself away in one stupid, reckless moment – and he was bound to make another. Holly wasn't sure of much but she did know that, at least. He would make another mistake.

She glanced back at the washbag, staring at all the tools of the drug user, then she stood straight, took a deep breath and opened the door. Knowing full well what she might have to face, she walked out.

'Guy?'

He was standing by the bar, a drink in his hand. He turned as Holly came into the room and she saw clearly now how stoned he was. He smiled easily, he covered it brilliantly, but then he lived with it; he was used to handling it.

'Holly. Are you all right?'

She nodded and smiled.

'I'm sorry, I . . .'

She held up her hands to silence him. 'There's no need to apologise, honestly.' The tone of her voice relaxed him and she wanted that. She wanted him as much off his guard as she could manage.

'Guy, I . . .'

'Holly, I . . .'

They both spoke at once, and both smiled.

'Please, you first,' he said. Perhaps he had got it wrong. He stared at her face for a few moments but she gave no hint of distress. With relief, he swallowed down his Scotch.

'Guy, I've been thinking about Paris, about all the things you said.' She stared down at her hands. She had always been an atrocious liar but she was surprising herself; it was far easier than she had thought. 'Tell me honestly, do you really think it will work? Can you really do all you promised?'

Guy walked across to stand in front of her, staring down into her face. She was vulnerable, she needed him; he could see it in her eyes. 'I can do all that and more, I promise you.'

Holly lowered her gaze. His voice was calm and smooth, perfectly modulated, his manner easy, suave and believable. Only she could sense the paranoia. It lay beneath the surface, artfully concealed, but there nonetheless. It gave her an edge over him, and it was this that finally decided her. She looked back up at him. 'What time does the next flight for Paris leave?'

Guy felt relief, then the small, sharp thrill of power. He was still in control; he could make things happen. Glancing briefly at his watch, he answered, 'Six thirty am. Do you want me to book it?'

Holly hesitated for a moment. If she'd had a choice before, she didn't now. She knew there was only one way out of this and that was to go with it. Guy would make a mistake. She would watch him like a hawk, stay right beside him every inch of the way, and she'd wait for that mistake. It was her only chance. Finally she nodded.

'You're sure?'

She was sure. For once in her life she had made a decision not based exclusively on herself. She thought for a second about Jill and Sophie and Kit. If she went now, simply disappeared with no explanation, then she would either win this or lose it, but she would do it alone. 'Yes, I'm sure,' she said.

'And the others, shall I book for all of you?'

Holly tensed slightly; she hadn't been expecting this. 'Yes, I should think so,' she lied.

'Do you want to ring them, let them know?'

Holly looked at her watch. It was nearly one am, and with any luck Jill would be in bed with the answerphone on. 'OK.' She tried to sound relaxed but her heart was thumping in her chest. She managed a smile and walked across to pick up her bag. Guy was already at the telephone. 'Shall I dial?'

'Let me find the number first.' Holly found her diary in her bag and crossed to him. 'Here, let me,' she said.

Guy handed her the receiver. She was suddenly edgy, he could sense it.

Walking back to the bar, he poured himself another drink. He could feel the paranoia working itself up again and took a deep breath to relax himself. Sipping his drink, he kept his back to her and listened suspiciously to her call.

Holly dialled Jill's number, heard the five rings, then the answerphone click on. She knew she had to speak quickly while the message played and guessed that she had about twenty-five seconds.

'Hi, Jill,' she said across the message. 'It's me. Yes, fine. Look, I'm sorry to rush you but something's come up, something very important, and basically, I think we need to go to Paris. It's too complicated to explain now, I haven't got time, but Guy Ferreira has had this idea to move the whole thing over there and I really think it could work. I can explain it all when I see you but we need to know if we should book the flights. Will you trust me on this one?'

The tape bleeped for her to leave a message and she knew she had to be careful now; what she said next would be recorded. She didn't want Jill to know anything about this; she just wanted to disappear without a trace. It was safer that way. 'Yes, I know it's a shock. Yes I have, I've thought of nothing else since he mentioned it.' Holly paused for effect. With any luck she'd run out of tape. After several seconds, she smiled. 'You will? Thanks, Jill, I'm sure it's the right thing to do. Right, yes, give me two days to get things organised then you, Sophie and Adrian can join us on Monday.' She looked across at Guy as he turned, and held her thumb up. 'Right, I will, I'll have them sent here. Yes, I'll be careful, I promise.' Then she stared down, suddenly tearful. She swallowed hard and said, 'You take care, Jill, and look after Sophie. Thanks for everything.' She took a deep breath. 'Goodbye.' And with that, she hung up.

'They'll come on Monday, like you suggested,' she said.

Guy nodded. Something was wrong. Holly was acting strangely. 'Are you all right, Holly?'

She shrugged, then suddenly said, 'Actually, no, I'm very nervous. I hope to God I'm doing the right thing.'

Guy put his drink down. 'That's understandable. So am I.'

Holly turned away, unable to conceal her anger. 'I suppose I'd better go and pack.' She glanced at her watch. 'We'll need to leave for Heathrow at what, four?'

'Yes, round about then. Shall I collect you in a cab at quarter past?'

She had to look back to answer and took a few moments to compose her expression before doing so. 'Yes, fine,' she replied eventually, smiling at him.

Guy picked up her coat and walked over to her. 'Here.' He held out the coat. 'Let me help you.'

'Thanks.'

He held her gaze. 'Trust me, Holly,' he said.

Holly let him place the coat around her shoulders and then moved away to open the door of the suite. As she stepped out into the corridor she glanced back at him and it took all of her courage to lie. 'Yes,' she answered, 'I do.' And she left him staring after her as she walked alone down to the lifts.

At South Ridge Farm, Jill walked into the hall from the sitting room, carrying her cup, and glanced at the telephone on her way to the kitchen. She saw the red message light flashing. 'Damn!' she muttered, hurrying over. 'I must have left the bloody thing on.' She pressed the play button and reached for the lamp, then realised she had turned the volume down and had to fiddle with the side of the phone to find the right button. Holly's voice came on just as she switched the light on.

'Yes, I know it's a shock. Yes I have, I've thought of nothing else since he mentioned it. You will? Thanks, Jill, I'm sure it's the right thing to do. Right, yes, give me two days to get things organised then you, Sophie and Adrian can join us on Monday.' Jill glanced behind her as Sophie appeared at the top of the stairs. She came down and stood beside Jill to listen to the message. 'Yes, I'll be careful, I promise,' it went on. 'You take care, Jill, and look after Sophie. Thanks for everything.' Jill pressed the button to rewind the tape. She looked at Sophie. 'Is it my imagination, or is that a really odd message?'

'No, it's just that the tape missed half of it, that's all.' Sophie sighed irritably and raised her eyes skyward. Then she folded her arms across her chest and walked on into the kitchen. What Jill had done earlier was unforgivable in her eyes; she just didn't understand and Sophie wondered if she ever would.

'Sophie? Wait!' Jill followed her and stood in the doorway. 'Sophie, I'm sure you're not right; it sounds really odd to me. Listen.' She moved back and stopped the tape. 'It's one half of a conversation – she sounds as if she's talking to me. And here, does she sound tearful to you? Listen . . .'

Holly's voice filled the hallway. 'You take care, Jill, and look after Sophie.'

'It's as if she's saying goodbye.' Jill frowned. 'What do you think, Sophie?'

Sophie had come to stand in the hall. 'I think she's off some-where and she'll ring us when she gets there. For God's sake, Jill! Why do you have to make such a drama out of everything?'

Jill clenched her jaw. 'I'm not making a drama out of anything,' she said tightly, pointedly ignoring the inference to the incident with Adrian. 'I think there happens to be something wrong here.'

Sophie turned her back on Jill and headed towards the stairs. In truth she was inclined to agree, but she wasn't going to admit it. 'It's nothing, Jill, leave it. She's gone somewhere and will ring us later.'

'But where could she have gone?'

Sophie shrugged. 'I don't know and I don't care.'

Jill held down a flash of anger; the last thing they needed was a row. Perhaps she was overreacting. She was frightened, after her conversation with Ted. She went to rewind the tape again, but as her hand hit the button, the phone rang. She stopped the machine and picked up the receiver.

'Hello?' There was silence on the other end. 'Hello? Holly? Is that you?' Nothing. She heard a faint click and the caller hung up.

'Sophie? Sophie, I just got a funny call!' Jill called up the stairs.

Sophie appeared at the top. 'It's nothing, Jill,' she snapped. 'God, just forget it, can't you? Go to bed!' Hiding her own sense of unease, she stomped off to bed.

But Jill couldn't forget it. She rang Holly's flat, then the gallery, and got no reply from either. Unplugging the phone, she took it upstairs with her. She would try again later. She wasn't happy about this and she knew she would try all night if she had to.

Guy put down the phone and reached across his body to massage his right shoulder. Christ, he was feeling tense! He should trust his instincts. Holly had telephoned Jill – he had checked with BT, then dialled the number that came back to him. It was the Turner woman, all right; he recognised her voice from the phone tapes.

Picking up the receiver again, Guy dialled reception. 'I need two first-class tickets for the early morning flight to Paris. Yes, this morning. No, I don't have a preference, any airline will do. Certainly, Mr Guy Ferreira and Ms Holly Grigson. Yes, there is, I want three more tickets, economy, for the morning flight out on Monday. For Mrs J. Turner, Miss S. Turner and Mr A. White. Yes, to Paris. Yes I will be, in about an hour. Can you send someone up for my bags?' He went to hang up. 'No, there are no return dates,' he said impatiently, 'I would have said if there were. All five tickets are one-way. Thank you.' And he replaced the receiver, then went into the bedroom to pack.

Kit put his key in the lock and turned as Lauren reached up and touched his hair. He smiled, took her hand and led her into the apartment. Just inside the door he pulled her towards him and kissed her, leaning back against the wall, pressing her tight into his body.

'I missed you while you were away,' she whispered as he caressed her neck with his lips, making her shiver and catch her breath. 'I thought you might never come back. I thought there might be someone in London . . .'

Kit pulled away.

'What's the matter? Did I say something?'

He attempted a smile. 'No, of course not.' He was lying – just the mention of London made him weak with longing for Holly. 'Let's go and get comfortable,' he said gently. 'It's chilly out here.'

Lauren smiled up at him. 'Are you OK, Kit? You seem a bit, well, distracted.'

'I'm fine, honestly.' He put his arm round her. 'Come on.'

They went through to the living space: one long room with a dark wood floor, three arched windows and a fifteen-foot ceiling. At the far end there was a single canvas, unframed, by Elisabeth Frink. It had been bought as a birthday present for Holly years ago, only Kit had left England before he'd had the chance to give it to her. At the other end two bleached cotton sofas stood opposite each other. There was a bookcase reaching from floor to ceiling, stuffed with books, and more books were stacked on the floor, along with piles of magazines: art magazines, law magazines, the *Spectator* and the *New York Times Review*.

Lauren wriggled away from Kit and walked across to one of the sofas. His apartment always made her feel sexy. It was sparse and masculine but it had a lot of style and Lauren liked style. She sank down and curled her feet up under her, picking up one of the law magazines from a pile on the floor and flicking through it. She was a petite woman, slim and blond, but her stature belied her personality. She was a ruthless corporate finance lawyer and although she kept it well disguised, she was as tough as old boots. Looking across at Kit, she dropped the magazine down on the sofa and said, 'What are you waiting for? Come over here, I want to show you how much I've missed you.'

Kit hesitated. Holly never said things like that. With Holly it was always impulsive, they were never able to help themselves; it just somehow happened. But Holly isn't here, he thought, loosening his tie and slipping off his jacket, so you might as well just forget her. She's never going to be here and Lauren is.

He kicked off his shoes and walked across to Lauren. Kneeling down, he uncurled one of her legs and held it, running his hand up her shin to her thigh. He unclipped her suspender, back and front, and slowly peeled the fine black stocking down her leg, running his lips over her bare skin as he did so. She smiled and leant her head back as he took her other leg and stripped it. She could feel the soft, sensuous touch of his lips as he worked his way back up her bare leg again, from her toes to her inner thigh, then his tongue, licking her skin, so close to the lace edge of her underwear that it sent a spasm of anticipation through her body. She relaxed back, unbuttoned her shirt to reveal a sheer lace bra over her very expensive designer breasts and closed her eyes.

Moments later, she snapped them open.

'Kit?' She sat forward. 'What are you doing?'

Kit glanced up. He had been kissing her leg and his eye had caught the headline on the front page of the *Legal Review* on the sofa beside her. He picked the magazine up and flicked to the relevant article.

'Kit?'

'Hmmmm . . .' He sat back on his heels and read the first paragraph.

'Kit?'

'Wiseman, Beech and Decker,' he muttered. 'Wiseman, Beech and Decker. Why do I know that name? Where have I . . .' Suddenly he jumped up. 'Oh shit! Oh Jesus Christ!'

Lauren sat up. 'Kit! What the hell's going on?'

Kit had already moved away from her, carrying the magazine. He turned round. 'Oh God, sorry, Lauren. Look, er, this is important, can you hang on a bit?' He gave her a quick glance and hurried off in the direction of the bedroom. At the door he turned again. 'Sorry,' he said and Lauren sighed. She was cross but she was all revved up and in the mood for sex. She could wait, for a while anyway. She watched him disappear and slowly buttoned her shirt again.

Kit sat down at his computer and switched it on. He tapped in his password, logged onto the Internet, then went into information mode and brought up the magazine file. He looked through it for references to Wiseman, Beech and Decker, found three and recalled them. Wiseman, Beech and Decker, he read, had been suspended from practising law; they were currently under investigation by the CIA for fraud and connections with the Mafia. All three articles repeated what the *Legal Review* had said; the chances were that this law firm had been working for the mob.

Kit sat back and stared at the screen. He remembered where he had heard the name before; he remembered the connection; and he felt a stab of fear. It was Guy Ferreira's law firm, and Ferreira was heavily involved with Holly.

He didn't know how long he had sat like that but it must have been some time, because when he looked up, Lauren stood in the doorway. She had her coat on.

'I'm going home,' she said.

Kit began to stand up but she held up her hand to stop him.

'I don't know who she is, Kit, but you'd better sort it out before you call me again. I don't like to play second fiddle.' She fastened her coat and turned to leave. 'Thanks for dinner.' And without a smile, she left.

Kit heard the front door slam and went back to the screen. He didn't know what to do next. Make some notes was the only thing that came to mind, and pulling open the drawer, he rummaged around in it for a pencil and some paper. But under a pile of old bank statements he saw the small silver clock that he had pocketed at Holly's flat and the whole scene that night came back to him with startling precision. Of course Ferreira was involved! He had dialled the flat just minutes before it had been broken into; he had been checking that Holly wasn't there. Why hadn't Kit realised that at the time, or acted on it? Why hadn't he checked this Ferreira himself? He should have done it right at the beginning, before the bastard got his grip on Holly.

Kit cursed himself for being so careless, for letting Holly talk him out of going to the police, for leaving her alone in London. He swore at his blatant stupidity, then he picked up the telephone and dialled Holly's flat. He left the line ringing for five or six minutes and felt his blood pressure escalate. On the off chance that she might be at the gallery, he dialled that number too, but there was no reply. He paced the floor for a while and tried the flat again. Still no reply. Then, desperate to get through to her, he typed a fax message and sent it through to the gallery. At least it was there now, in black and white; she would get it in the morning. Finally, he rang the airline and he booked a ticket to London, then called his boss to explain.

He had to go to London for Holly. There was no decision to be made, it was the only thing he could do. He threw a bag on the bed and began to pack. In his rush he didn't even think about Lauren. She had gone and he just didn't have time to worry about it.

There was an air of heavy, almost stultifying tension in the incident room. There was no conversation, no banter, just a stiff, anticipatory silence. The phone lines were quiet; the only sound in the room was the click of the keyboard.

DS Robert Eames sat with his head in his hands. It was five am, he had been in that room for fifteen hours, and he felt exhausted. He had made a mistake. They didn't know what it had cost in terms of time – maybe nothing, maybe the whole damn case – and he was humiliated by it, angry with himself for not doing the job properly. If there was one thing he had over the other officers it was the fact that he had always done the job immaculately; it was his trademark.

He should have been off duty but he couldn't face going home. DCI Heeley came into the room and Eames looked up.

'All quiet?'

There was an affirmative silence. 'Right.' He stood just inside the door with a sheaf of papers in his hand. 'Fraud squad boys are on overtime as well – I just got this through.' He held up the sheets of fax paper. 'It's like we thought. The pattern of deals set up by the gallery is a familiar one. They've seen it before in other situations – money laundering on a grand scale, very neat, very clever and very professional. The sum of money that was withdrawn several weeks back has gone missing and is virtually untraceable – not a big surprise to any of us. In other words, it's been nicked.' There was a faint smile on several faces in the room. Heeley looked across at DC Dobson. 'Dobbo, your boys come back to you with any more on this man Ferreira yet?'

They had drawn a blank on Ferreira's details from the hire car firm. 'No, not yet, still waiting.'

'Hensen?'

Hensen shook his head. 'Nothing on computer, sir.'

'Any more on Welsch?'

'You've had all we know so far, sir.'

'Right. And still no word from surveillance?'

Both men shrugged and glanced across at DS Eames. 'It's all quiet, sir,' he said. 'The suspect returned to her flat at two am and there's been no movement since.'

Heeley nodded and turned towards the door. 'Bob, can I have a quick word? Outside.'

Eames nodded, then stood, and followed Heeley out into the corridor. Heeley closed the door of the incident room.

'You're off duty as of now,' Heeley said.

'But sir, I . . .'

Heeley cut in. 'Don't argue, just get your coat and go home for some sleep.'

Eames stood where he was. 'Is this because I fucked up?'

Heeley shrugged. 'It's because you're knackered, Bob, any idiot can see that, and you're no frigging good to anyone in that state. So you missed a figure in the gallery's books, a sum of money that didn't reappear; don't beat yourself over it.' Heeley smiled and patted Eames on the shoulder. 'Just go home, eh?'

And for the first time since he'd met his superior officer, DS Eames reckoned that Heeley might be human after all.

Holly stood by the front door and listened to the phone ringing. Her bag was packed and ready by her feet, and she had left instructions on what to do with the flat and the gallery, in case anything happened to her. She tried to block out the constant, shrill bleep, but she didn't answer it, thinking it might be Jill. It was up to her now: she had started all this mess and she had to finish it, no matter what happened. She was more scared than she had ever been before but she knew what she had to do. There was no other way out, not his time. This time she had to face up to her mistakes and sort them out. It might cost her life but thank God it wouldn't cost anyone else's. It was that thought and that thought alone that kept her going.

She started as a car horn tooted down in the street and hurried to the window to see if it was Guy. It was. Opening the front door, she picked up her small case, then all the canvases, and carried them down to the hall, finally going back for the portfolio. As she closed the door and locked it, the telephone rang on and she thought momentarily about Kit. She wondered what he would say if he knew that she was at last doing something that was not entirely for herself. 'Probably "about time too"!' she said aloud and, despite the awfulness of her situation, she felt strangely reassured by that thought.

'Sir!'

Heeley was halfway up the corridor when Robert Eames shouted to him just seconds after they'd finished their conversation. He stopped and swung round.

'Surveillance have radioed in! The suspect's on the move. She

352

just left the building and got into a taxi with Ferreira. They're being followed in the vehicle.'

Heeley hurried back to the incident room. 'They seem to be heading west, towards the M4,' Eames said, opening out a street map of London on the desk. 'Grigson was carrying a suitcase and a large portfolio.'

'Heathrow,' Heeley said. 'Bugger!' He listened to the next radio message and put his finger straight on their location. 'It's got to be Heathrow. Bob, get onto passport control. Hensen, call surveillance and find out what they're going to do if it is Heathrow. And, Dobson, as soon as you find out where Ferreira was staying, get onto them and see if he left any onward address.' Heeley glanced over his shoulder at DS Eames. 'Sorry, Bob, you can forget looking for your car keys – you're back on duty until further notice.'

Eames looked up. 'It's not my car keys I'm looking for,' he said, still scrabbling in his drawer. 'It's this!' He pulled out his passport. 'It runs out at the end of the month; I was about to send it off for a new one.'

Heeley stared at Eames holding the passport aloft, then rubbed his hands over his face to give himself a moment to think. DS Eames was a bloody good copper but it was clear he was shattered. Heeley couldn't afford to make a mistake, not even one. He dropped his hands and shrugged.

'It's not my decision, Bob. We have to let surveillance handle it.'

'And if they're not prepared to follow Grigson abroad, what then? Grigson just disappears and we lose the entire case!'

'It's a chance I have to take. It's out of my jurisdiction.'

'Is it?'

'I'll ignore that remark, Bob.' Heeley felt a moment of intense frustration. Eames could be such a prat. But he let it go – they were all tired, tense. This was a hell of a blow. 'You know as well as I do that the final decision has to be made by surveillance! Now, get on and ring passport control, will you?' He offered a smile but it wasn't returned. 'We can at least then have some idea of where they are headed, even if we can't follow them.'

Chapter Twenty-Three

At six am, Jill finally got up. She had tried Holly's flat and the gallery every hour or so through the night and now she was worried sick. She pulled on a dressing gown, padded downstairs and went into the kitchen. Standing by the aga, she warmed her hands while the kettle boiled and thought about what to do next. There was something wrong, no matter what Sophie said. Jill was convinced. Holly was in trouble, and she had to do something. She made herself a cup of tea, carried it into the hall, found the number she wanted in her diary and dialled.

'Hello? Ted? It's Jill Turner, I'm sorry to ring you so early but I think we're in trouble.' Now she had said it out loud she was more certain than ever. 'I think Holly's gone missing,' she went on, 'and I don't know what to do.'

An hour later Jill was dressed and ready to go. She stood waiting for Sophie in the kitchen. Ted Welsch was meeting them at Adrian's studio – on Ted's suggestion Sophie had rung him to see if Holly was with him, and he had immediately wanted to be involved. Begrudgingly Jill had agreed. They needed his help and it was a genuine offer, she had to admit that. She tapped her fingers on the table top, looked at her watch and went to the bottom of the stairs.

'Sophie!'

Sophie appeared at the top and looked down at Jill over the banister. She had spent the past hour in the bathroom and with newly washed hair, mascara, eyeliner, a pair of black jeans and a fine lawn Indian shirt, she was finally ready. The sight of such preparation irritated Jill. This was serious; it wasn't a date.

'You're ready, are you?' she said as Sophie hurried down. Sophie ignored the sarcasm and went to the cupboard for her coat.

'Right, let's go.'

As Jill hurried across to the Range Rover, the phone began to ring inside the house, but she didn't hear it. She started the engine, swung the car round and drove off, the gravel flying up under the spin of the wheels.

The phone rang on, for several minutes. Finally, in New York, Kit hung up.

Adrian put the kettle on and spooned coffee into the three mugs he had borrowed from a painter in the next-door studio. He dropped a tea bag into his own tin cup, added a hefty spoonful of sugar and opened the carton of milk. As he did all this he glanced sidelong at Sophie, caught her eye and smiled. He felt good about Sophie. Something worthwhile had just come into his life and after what had happened to his brother, he was relieved. He had been down for too long.

Jill saw the small, secret smile and tensed. She had been talking to Ted about what to do next and she couldn't help but catch the current of emotion that ran through the room. She glanced away, out of the window, and Ted watched her for a few moments, feeling immensely sorry for her. There was a short silence, then he said, 'So, there's nothing else for it, I think I'm gonna have to break in.'

'Break in?' Jill turned back to him. 'You can't do that, Ted. It's illegal . . .' She stopped, realising how stupid that sounded and looked at him. 'D'you think you can?'

'The flat's easy; the gallery will almost certainly be wired up but I'm pretty sure it won't be anything elaborate.' He flicked his thumbnail against his tooth. 'You still can't think where this Ferreira bloke came from? I'm pretty sure he's the man Holly was referring to, the other person in the "us" you're supposed to join.'

Jill shrugged. 'I just can't remember Holly ever telling me where he was staying. Sophie, can you?'

'No.' Sophie was still punishing Jill for the previous night, answering only in monosyllables, if at all. Jill felt another flash of irritation.

'I don't think I even know his first name,' she said. 'I'm sorry, Ted, I feel pathetic, not knowing this in such a dangerous situation.'

Welsch shrugged. 'I think it would be wise to try the gallery first. I don't feel right 'bout snooping round her flat.' Welsch had never met Holly. He zipped up his bomber jacket. 'You know anything about the alarm there, Jill?'

Jill nodded. 'I think I can remember where the code panel is; Holly had it updated after the gallery was broken into . . .' She stopped and suddenly smacked her palm against her forehead. 'And she left a key with the Patels next door! Just in case anything like that happened again. God, I'm stupid – why didn't I think of that first thing this morning?' She bent and picked her bag up off the floor. 'Come on, let's get over there! I know the Patels, they'll more than likely give the key to me.' She dug in her bag for the car keys. 'Sophie, if you stay here with Adrian to try to sort some work for the exhibition out of what's left.' She looked up. 'Sophie?'

Sophie didn't answer, but kept her head down, picking at a loose cotton on her shirt. Jill looked at her for a few moments, then she turned to leave. 'Ted, are you ready?'

Ted had been watching the two of them. 'Yup, I'm ready. Why don't you go down to the car and I'll catch up.'

Jill looked quizzically at him, then shrugged and slung her bag over her shoulder. Without another word, she left the studio and went down to the car alone.

Welsch took a packet of cigarettes out of his pocket and offered them around. Finding no takers, he lit up, inhaled and said, 'The last one this morning as I'm in the company of your stepmother, Soph.'

Sophie nodded.

'Look,' he said, 'I hope you don't mind me saying this but . . .' He broke off to flick his ash into the palm of his hand. 'The thing is, I detect a bit of an atmosphere and I don't think it's gonna do anyone any good.' He saw Sophie bristle and glance sidelong at Adrian. 'I don't know what's goin' on but I thought I should tell you that your stepmum's scared, Sophie; she's scared out of her wits, quite rightly so, and she's trying bloody hard not to let it show.'

Sophie stared down at the floor.

'I reckon that you two probably got a bit of a thing going.' Sophie glanced up and blushed as Adrian moved forward, placing his hand on her shoulder. Welsch smiled and she smiled back. 'I'm pleased for you,' he said. He paused. 'But your stepmum's just lost the man she loved.' He didn't need to say any more. He saw Sophie's eyes fill with tears and turned to go.

'Did Jill put you up to this?' Sophie called.

Welsch looked back. 'Nah. She don't know I've said any of it and she don't wanna know either.' He took a last drag of his cigarette, lifted the heel of his shoe and ground it out against the leather sole. He dropped the butt into his pocket. 'I thought your stepmum was a bit stuck up when I first met her,' he said. 'But she isn't. She's one hell of a nice lady and she's worried about you.' With a smile and a shrug, he turned and walked out.

'You were a long time,' Jill said as Welsch climbed into the Range Rover. She sniffed. 'You had a smoke, right?'

He smiled. 'Right.' Jill shifted into gear and pulled out into the traffic. 'That's a very fine nose you got there, Mrs T,' he said and Jill smiled. But it was the last time she was to do so that day.

The Patels did remember Jill. They gave her the key to the gallery and she let herself and Ted in, dashing through to the back to find the code panel. She hoped there might be a key or something to stop the alarm from going off but when she found the small electronic box hidden in a cupboard she saw immediately that it needed a code. Just under the panel, taped to the wall, she saw 'My birthday' written in large black letters on a piece of paper. Jill thought for a moment, then tapped in the numbers and the bleeping stopped.

'We're safe!' she called out. Closing the cupboard, she walked back into the gallery to find Welsch.

'Ted?' He didn't answer. He was standing by the telephone reading a fax that had come through on the machine. 'Ted, what's that?'

'This,' he said, picking up the two sheets and holding them out to her, 'is serious trouble.'

Jill looked at his face, then down at the fax. She read it and her stomach flipped over. 'I don't understand,' she murmured. 'Is Kit saying that this man, this Guy Ferreira, is involved with the Mafia?'

Welsch said nothing.

'How can he be? Holly said he gave her the idea of going for the exhibition, of using the artist to try to find Hugo. He told her . . .' Suddenly Jill looked up. She caught the expression on Welsch's face and closed her eyes for a second, feeling sick. She sat on the edge of the desk and dropped her head down. Welsch picked up the telephone and dialled a number. He listened silently, then hung up after a minute or so. Jill swallowed and faced him. 'This Ferreira set the whole thing up, didn't he?'

Welsch hesitated, then shrugged.

'He set Holly and me up to find Hugo Blandford for him, and then what – he'd get rid of us all?'

Still Welsch didn't answer.

'But something's gone wrong and he's had to speed things up a bit. Maybe it's this investigation by the CIA; maybe it's that he thinks he'll be found out, so he's taken Holly off somewhere and . . .'

'Whoa! Hold on a minute!' Welsch held up his hands to stop her. 'That's speculation,' he said. 'Stick to what we know.'

'Which is?' Jill was scared and it made her snappy.

Welsch took a big breath, unzipped his jacket and took it off. 'Which is, that we know Guy Ferreira is involved with the Mafia in some way and from that we can deduct . . .'

'Deduce,' Jill interrupted.

'Yeah, that too, we can figure that he more than likely set Holly up. Which means,' Welsch was beginning to get into his stride, 'now I'm speculating here, but it probably means that he doesn't know any more than we do about Blandford, otherwise he would have gone it alone.' He began to pace up and down.

'But he's not a hit man, I'm pretty sure of that. If he was, the job would have been done by now. Those blokes are shit hot professionals. So, who is he? Where does he fit in?' Welsch brought his cigarettes out of his pocket, took one out and put it between his lips. He stopped, looked at Jill and said, 'It's OK, I'm not gonna light it, it just helps me think.' He continued pacing, the unlit cigarette hanging out of the side of his mouth. Every now and then he took it out, twiddled it between his finger and thumb and then replaced it. He stopped a second time. 'You remember when all this started – someone turned the gallery over, your husband's office, your house, Holly's flat, my office?'

'Your office as well?'

'Yeah, well, that was Ferreira, I'm sure of it. He wanted to know how much you'd found out.' Welsch chewed on the end of the cigarette. 'But I reckon Holly must have confided in him. Did she tell you she had?'

Jill shook her head.

'No, she wouldn't, but that's the only reason I can think that he wanted you all involved, because you know too much.' Welsch began to pace again. 'This changes everything.'

Jill was starting to feel giddy, watching him pace from one wall to the other, turning and retracing his steps. 'How?' she cried finally. 'For God's sake, stop still, Ted!'

He halted.

'How does it change everything?'

Welsch shrugged. 'I don't honestly know, I haven't worked it out yet.'

Jill stood up. 'I don't understand any of this,' she wailed. 'All I know is that Holly's gone off with someone very dangerous and Kit's arriving, what time . . . ?' She picked up the fax. 'At five pm to add to this mess!'

'He's working alone,' Welsch said suddenly. 'That's why it doesn't add up – he's on his own!'

Jill sighed, exasperated. 'Ted, were you listening to anything I said?'

Welsch crossed to her. 'No, but wait. Listen, Jill! This whole thing has been one big fuck-up. It's uncharacteristic of everything I know about organised crime and that's what's been throwing me.'

Jill shook her head. 'I don't understand.'

'Blandford did a bunk with millions belonging to some sort of organised crime ring, yeah?'

Jill nodded.

'Well, that sort of thing just doesn't happen. They watch too closely; they're too careful, Jill, much too careful. Whoever was in charge of this side of the operation – 'scuse my French – fucked up and someone's been sent to sort it out. You see?'

'I don't know, I think so.'

'That someone is this bloke Ferreira. He's been dumped in London and told to clear up this mess, only he's not very good at it. You've found out a whole load more than you should and chances are he's running out of time.'

Jill slumped back against the desk. Her head was full of cotton wool; she couldn't seem to get it clear. 'How do you know all this? How can you make all these guesses?'

'I've done it for a long time now, Jill, fitting bits together, adding two and two to make five.' Welsch shrugged. 'Mainly grubby divorce cases, to be honest, debt collections, rotten references. But I got a knack, and I think I'm right on this one.'

Jill was silent a moment, then she said, 'So, if Ferreira is running out of time, where's he gone with Holly?'

Welsch took the cigarette out of his mouth and put it in the ashtray on the desk. 'That, I can't answer. I think we need to go through the flat.'

'You don't think Hugo Blandford's made contact and they've gone to meet him?'

Welsch shook his head. 'Doubtful.' He saw Jill didn't believe him. 'Why would Blandford make contact now, out of the blue? It's pretty unlikely, seeing the amount of trouble Ferreira has taken to set things up to lure him.' He took up his cigarette again and twiddled it between his fingers.

'For God's sake, light the bloody thing!' Jill suddenly burst out. 'I can't bear to see you fiddle with it any longer!'

'Oh, right.' Welsch took his lighter out and lit up. He smoked for a minute or so then stubbed out the cigarette. He saw Jill look at him, then the ashtray. 'I didn't fancy it after all that,' he said.

Jill stood up and walked into the back of the gallery. She took the kettle and filled it at the sink. Welsch followed her and stood in the doorway.

'You awright?'

She kept her back to him. 'I don't know,' she answered truthfully. 'Every time I think we've gone one step forward we end up three steps back.' She turned round. 'I'm scared, Ted, very scared.'

'I know,' he said gently, 'I know.' He came across and put his arms around her, folding her into a clumsy embrace. Jill was four inches taller than him but she laid her head on his shoulder, relieved at the physical comfort.

'What are we going to do?' she whispered.

'Find Holly,' he answered. 'And put an end to this agony.'

Kit walked through the green channel and straight out into the arrivals lounge at Heathrow at five forty-five that evening. His plane had landed on time and he had only one bag that he'd carried as hand luggage. He didn't bother to look at the waiting crowd, not expecting anyone to meet him, but halfway along the row of faces he looked up.

'Kit?'

It was Jill Turner. She waved, unsmiling, and moved away from the throng to meet him. Greeting him at the end of the walkway, she said, 'We got the fax this morning.'

'Is Holly OK?'

She didn't answer him. 'The car's this way,' she said. 'I've got Ted Welsch waiting for you.'

She walked off but Kit grabbed her arm. 'Jill? Where's Holly? What did she say about the fax?'

Jill faced him. 'Holly's disappeared,' she said, 'last night, before she knew about Guy Ferreira. We think she's gone with him.'

'Jesus Christ!' Kit stood dead still and the traffic of the airport had to walk around him. 'Where the hell is she?'

Jill shrugged. 'We don't know,' she answered. 'We have absolutely no idea.'

* * *

Heading up the M4 back into London, Kit sat in the rear of the Range Rover, filled with self-recrimination. He blamed himself for having left Holly alone, for not stamping on this whole thing right at the beginning and handing it over to the police. He shouldn't have listened to her; he should never have started investigating it, helping her along, pushing her towards danger. He listened to what Welsch had to say and it chilled his blood. It made sense. He was no expert on organised crime but he did know that this didn't look like a professional job – it was too haphazard, too personal. He leant forward, towards Welsch and said, 'D'you think this Guy Ferreira knows what he's doing?'

'I don't know. I'd say he was pretty clued up but nervous. If we're right, if he's been told to sort things out, then he'll only get one chance and if he cocks it up then he won't have a face left, let alone a job.'

Kit saw Jill flinch. She stared straight ahead at the road but he noticed it. She was frightened, and not only for herself.

Ted went on, 'He'll know that; he won't be under any delusions.'

'Illusions,' Jill said.

'Yeah, those as well. They'll cut him off without a second glance and dispose of him. They may do it even if he finds Blandford and the money.'

Kit shuddered. 'And you think he's gone off with Holly, following a lead on Blandford, to bring things to a head?'

'Probably.'

'And Holly doesn't know all this?'

Welsch shrugged. 'I've got the answerphone tape, you wanna listen to it? Tell me what you think?'

He passed a Dictaphone over his shoulder and Kit pressed the play button. Holly's voice filled the car. They listened in silence for the minute or so that she spoke, then Kit rewound the tape. 'This is really odd!' he exclaimed. 'She wants it to sound as if she's having a conversation with you, Jill – is that what you thought?'

Jill nodded and Kit went on, 'There must be someone else in the room with her; Ferreira more than likely. Perhaps she wanted him to think that she was talking to you in person.'

'Maybe that's why I got only the end of the conversation,' Jill said. 'She had to talk while the message was playing to make it sound realistic.'

'Yes, very possibly.' He played the tape again. 'It sounds to me like Holly is trying to hide something. She doesn't give any information away, does she?'

'No, but I just assumed that was because the tape wasn't recording.'

'Holly would have known she wasn't being taped, Jill, I'm sure she would.' Kit handed the machine back to Welsch. 'She's far from stupid and I can't help thinking she did it on purpose.'

Jill glanced in the mirror at Kit. 'Why would she do that?'

'Maybe she doesn't want you involved, Jill. Maybe she knows it's dangerous and she doesn't want you to take that sort of risk.'

Jill indicated and pulled off the motorway down towards the Shepherd's Bush roundabout. 'But we're in this together!'

'Not any more, you're not,' Kit countered.

They were all silent for a while, then Jill said, 'I'm sick of speculating, we don't know any of this for sure! We've got to find Holly, that's the most important thing!' She approached the roundabout. 'Where to? What are we going to do now?'

'You've tried all the big hotels?' Kit asked.

'All of 'em.'

'Who did you ask for?'

'Guy Ferreira or Holly Grigson.'

Kit thought for a moment. 'Wait a minute, play that last bit of tape again, will you?'

Welsch rewound the machine, then switched to play.

'Yes, that bit, just then.' Kit sat forward. 'I'll have them sent here, she says – well, what sent here? It must be plane tickets or train tickets or some sort of travel documents, surely? And "here" must mean the place she was ringing from, presumably Ferreira's hotel, right?'

'Yeah, right!' Welsch turned in his seat to look at Kit. 'So, what, you think there's a packet somewhere in Jill's name? Is that what you're saying?'

'That's exactly what I'm saying!' Kit reached for his bag, opened it and took out his portable computer. He switched it on, logged onto the Internet, then looked in the directory under hotels and found the electronic travel agent file. He accessed it and read down the list. 'OK, let's do the Dorchester, the Park Lane Hotel, the Ritz, the Hyde Park Hotel, the Hilton Park Lane . . . any other suggestions?'

'The Savoy and the Inn on the Park,' Jill said.

'Fine. You OK to drive, Jill?' Jill nodded. They were heading up Notting Hill towards Marble Arch. 'I suggest we leave the car and do the three on Park Lane first, then Knightsbridge, then down to Green Park and the Ritz.'

'Fine,' Kit said again. He switched off his machine and closed it, placing it back in his bag. 'We'll split up, shall we?'

'No, let's stick together. Jill can park as near as she can get to the hotels, I'll stay in the car, you two go and check it out, awright?'

'Yes, fine,' Kit said for the third time. He looked out of the window as Jill indicated, went round Hyde Park Corner and swung into Park Lane. But it was far from fine; it was the worst possible scenario he could think of and he was dreading what they might or might not find.

An hour later, Jill turned into a side road off Piccadilly and swung the Range Rover up on the kerb behind a row of parked cars. She was sick of driving, the traffic was appalling and the search had been futile. It was beginning to look hopeless.

Climbing out, she waited for Kit to come round the side of the car and said, 'I don't hold out much hope.'

'You never know,' he answered, but he felt much the same way. It was already after nine, Holly had been missing for twenty or more hours and the anxiety was grinding him down. 'Come on,' he said with as much conviction as he could muster. 'You never know.'

They crossed the road, entered the hotel and Kit stood in the lobby, while Jill went to reception. He watched her ask for the package, saw the receptionist look down, probably glancing over a list, then shake her head. She said something to Jill who nodded, obviously thanking her, and turned to leave. Kit headed back towards the doors, then abruptly turned as someone called Jill's name.

'Mrs Turner?'

Jill stopped. She glanced back and another desk clerk held up a British Airways travel wallet in the air. She hurried over to the desk.

'Sorry, Mrs Turner, Mr Ferreira had this delivered here for you but my colleague was looking under room messages.' The young man handed the wallet across. 'Lucky I overheard, or you might never have got these.' He smiled.

'Yes, er, thank you.' Jill felt she ought to smile back but the shock of finding the packet had thrown her. She turned away, looked across at Kit and walked towards the doors. 'British Airways,' she said, following him out.

'Then it must be abroad,' he replied. They crossed the road and Jill waved the wallet in the air as they approached the car. Welsch jumped out.

'You got something?'

'This.' She opened it. 'Reservations for the Queen Elizabeth Hotel and airline tickets, for . . .'

'Look at them in the car,' Welsch instructed. Jill glanced up. He looked edgy, so she did as he asked.

'There're three of them,' she said as Welsch climbed in beside her. 'For me, Sophie and Adrian. They're for Paris.' She continued to look at the tickets, then she turned and stared at Kit in the back. 'And they're all one-way.'

Kit leant forward to peer at the screen as Welsch brought up the next page of the file.

'You see what I mean?' Welsch swivelled on his chair to look at Kit. 'I done a line chart and all contacts stop there.' He pointed at the blank line at the top of the page. 'The head of European Operations, I call him, but you can't get no further, it's impossible.'

'And you think that blank line should read Guy Ferreira?'

'Yeah. It makes sense, doesn't it?'

Jill was standing behind them, looking over Welsch's shoulder. 'So what does that mean?' she asked.

'It means,' Kit answered, 'that the likelihood of him working on his own is strong. Whoever is behind him has covered themselves – there's no way we can get to them – so if one man fouls up then the operation is intact. It's good army tactics, a sealed unit. It also means that if we can get to Ferreira before he gets to Holly then the chances are no-one's going to follow us up. Ferreira is very probably dispensable. Is that right, Ted?'

'Yeah, I'd say so.' Welsch flicked his front tooth with his thumbnail. Problem was, it made Holly dispensable as well.

'So why Paris?'

Welsch looked round at Jill. He shrugged, still flicking his tooth. 'Probably because he knows Blandford is in France, or was at the last count.'

Kit nodded.

'It's out of the way of any investigation the Met might be doin', and it might possibly be home ground. He has contacts there. I don't know for sure, but I reckon it's easier to get away with murder, literally, over there than it is over here.'

Jill stepped back. She could see the huge topless Hawaiian girl winking at her from above the bar in the next room and she moved across to the archway, leaning against it, and stared at the bar.

'You wanna a drink?' Welsch asked.

Jill turned. He stood beside her, his hands in his pockets, watching her face. 'No, thank you.'

'Think I will,' he said. He walked through and squeezed behind the bar, reaching for a bottle of Malibu. He poured a measure into a long glass and added some lemonade. 'Kit? You want something?'

'I'll have a whisky, thanks. And then I have to make a call. Can I use your phone?'

'Yeah, no problem.' Welsch came round the bar with Kit's drink and his own. 'So? What next?'

Kit drank. He said nothing until he had finished the whisky, sipping slowly, then he answered. 'I'm going to Paris, tomorrow morning.' He walked across to the bar and placed the empty glass down on it. He turned and faced them. 'And I'm going alone.'

Welsch glanced at Jill but said nothing.

'Can I use your phone, Ted? I need to make a call to the States, then I've got to ring Adrian White to get some information. Jill, you know his number?'

Jill nodded. 'I've got it in my book, I'll just get it for you.'

'Thanks.' Kit looked at Welsch.

'Phone's over there,' Welsch said, pointing to the phone on the wall. 'But I ain't goin' along with this, Kit. I don't think it's a clever idea at all.' He watched Kit as he crossed to the phone. 'You sure you know what you're doin'?' he asked.

Kit shrugged. 'Do any of us?'

'Maybe not, but you don't need to take all the risks, you know.'

Kit turned round. He stared at Welsch for a few seconds and

said, 'I know.' There was a silence, then he said, 'Thanks, Ted.' And he picked up the receiver to dial New York.

Welsch sat in the passenger seat of the Range Rover and watched Kit cross the road, his small holdall in his hand. He had declined Welsch's invitation to stay and had booked into the hotel he had stayed in previously. He had said very little on the journey back into central London – all of them had. It had been a depressing forty minutes and Welsch was glad it was over. He turned away as Kit walked into the lobby of the hotel and looked at Jill. They exchanged a glance, then she put the car into gear and drove off.

'Is that it?' she said, slowing into traffic. 'We let him go on his own and just wait to see what happens?' Her voice was tightly controlled but Welsch could detect a desperate edge to it. He took his cigarettes out and put one in his mouth. Jill wound down her window. 'Light it,' she ordered, 'I can't bear to see you fiddle with it again.'

Welsch did so, wound down his own window and blew the smoke out of the corner of his mouth towards the cold night air. He smoked silently for a while, then lobbed the butt out onto the street. Jill frowned.

'We don't do anything,' he said. 'I don't think you should be involved any more.'

'What?' Jill turned to look at him, incredulous. 'You must be jok . . .'

'Jill! *Look Out!*'

Jill turned back and slammed the brakes on, narrowly missing the car ahead. They stopped with a thud and both jolted forward. Jill immediately looked at him. 'Ted, you can't mean that! How can I not be involved, after everything that's gone on?'

Welsch kept his gaze ahead. He nodded towards the line of traffic and Jill followed his eyes. She shifted into gear and moved off again. 'Answer me!' she demanded. 'How can I not be involved?'

'Because your husband wouldn't have wanted you to be, because Holly doesn't want you to be and because I sure as hell ain't gonna let you be! Awright?'

Jill's nostrils flared. Who the hell did this peculiar, arrogant little man think he was? She pulled sharp right into a side street, drove up onto the kerb with a thump and stopped abruptly. 'No, it's not all right!' she snapped. 'It's my decision, I can do . . .'

'You can do whatever you want, yeah, I know, sure you can.' Welsch took out his cigarettes again and this time lit up without asking her. Jill made no comment. 'You ain't got no responsibilities, no ties, you can go an' get yourself killed, no problem, can't you?' He looked at her. 'Can't you?'

Jill stared down at her hands.

'One minute you're scared shitless and the next you want to hop on a plane and walk right into something you might never come out of. You think Holly made a mistake with that message? Think again, lady, 'cause she didn't make any mistake. She knows what she's doin', she rumbled that bastard and she don't want you involved in any of it.' He drew deeply on the cigarette, blew the smoke out of the open window and flicked the ash into the palm of his hand. 'Nor does Kit and nor, for that matter, do I!'

He chucked the lighted butt out of the window again and Jill glared at him.

'So what?' he snapped. 'It gets swept up!' He wiped his palm on his trousers.

Jill sat in silence, knowing Welsch was right: she couldn't go to Paris and she was scared.

After a long pause, he said, 'I don't intend to let Kit handle this on his own either, if that's what you're thinking.'

She turned to him. 'I don't know what I'm thinking,' she said. 'All this has gone way beyond me, if you want the truth.'

Welsch looked at her face for a few moments, then he did something very unlike him. Reaching over, he took Jill's hand

and his mouth dried up suddenly, causing him to run his tongue over his teeth to try to lubricate it. He coughed and squeezed her fingers. 'Certain things have gone beyond me as well,' he said.

Jill stared at him. She thought she caught the glimmer of something in his eye and instantly looked away. She must have been mistaken – it was impossible; they were poles apart. She gently eased her hand away and back onto the wheel. With her other hand, she started the engine.

'I'll leave for Paris at the same time as Kit tomorrow morning, but on a different flight,' Welsch said. 'I don't want him to know I'm behind him but I want to be there, just in case.' In truth he wasn't at all sure what good he would do. He wasn't a hero; he had never done anything brave in his life before.

'And me? What do I do?' Jill asked

'Sit tight,' Welsch said. 'Think about Harry and Sophie.'

'Is that all?' She felt useless, redundant.

'It's enough,' Welsch answered. He wanted to add something meaningful but couldn't think of anything. It *was* enough for him that she just stayed safe, that they all stayed safe. 'It's quite enough.'

Chapter Twenty-Four

Holly came down the marble staircase of the Queen Elizabeth Hotel on the Rue Pierre Sorbie and her gaze swept the lobby for signs of Guy or Lucie Renaud. There were none, and with relief, she carried on to the reception desk and handed in her key. She wanted half an hour to herself; she was running out of time and needed to think. Digging her hands down into the pockets of her huge cashmere overcoat, she turned towards the door and tucked her velvet hat down over her ears.

'Holly! Darling! Over here!'

She stopped. Looking round, she saw Lucie; a dark, brooding, half-French, half-American woman, forty-something, with a long, lean body in head-to-toe black Jean Muir, a black neck-length bob, a pale face and a slash of red for her mouth. She stood in the entrance to the bar, just off the lobby, smoking a small cigar and waiting.

Suppressing a flash of panic, Holly gave up all idea of solitude and walked across.

Lucie Renaud kissed the air on either side of Holly's cheek and took her arm. 'You can't sneak off. We have things to discuss, darling. I've been on the phone to Lynne Banks this morning and London's been alerted. Imagine! One call and the whole of the art world is buzzing with your name!' She led Holly over to a sofa and a low coffee table where she had obviously decamped and set up her office. She even had flowers and her own personal ashtray. 'The rumour is that Adrian White is about to become the hottest property in the business and you are the gallery representing him. *Voilà! Très facile!*' She clicked her fingers sharply for the waiter.

'*Deux espressos, s'il vous plaît,*' she ordered, without asking Holly. '*Et deux verres d'eau. Merci.*' The waiter hurried off, knowing this client only too well, and Lucie took a large brown card folder, tied with cream silk ribbon, from her briefcase. 'Things are really moving, Holly,' she said, in a peculiar mix of Anglo-American with a touch of the French accent. 'The advert went out this morning in *Le Monde* and *Le Figaro* – I have copies for you in this bag here.' She tapped a glossy carrier bag from Tiffany and Co. 'I'll give them to you before you leave. I've booked the gallery. Durand-Desert is between shows and have just opened a new space on the Boulevard Saint-Germain, *très* expensive, but my dear, so worth it, heaps of prestige, so important!'

She drew breath quickly, and carried on with hardly a pause. 'I've been on the phone to the most important invitees this morning and I've had acceptances from Hervé Cadot at Guy Ludmer, the auction house, and Kate Left, an American from Ader Tajon, the other main house. Galleries coming are Daniel Templon, Alain Blondel, Karsen-Grève and personalities . . . oh God, where did I put that list . . .' She flicked through the file. 'Ah! Here, I've got the Minister of Culture, hardly surprising, he'll go anywhere for a free drink and a bit of good food; three pop stars; two minor film actresses, French, I won't bother you with their names; Kate Moss – she's here doing some work for Gaultier – and her boyfriend, the photographer chap; Gilbert and George; Charlotte Rampling and Jean Michel Jarre, and the racing driver Alain Prost.'

She looked up at Holly, expecting praise. 'There's more to come, but I needed a few firm yeses to set things in motion. Already tongues are wagging. This exhibition is not to be missed! Now, let me see, press already coming are . . .' She read out a list of names, people and magazines Holly had never heard of. Holly tried to look impressed but the whole thing depressed her. She was in it up to her neck and she was scared. What was going to happen when Jill and Adrian didn't show up she had no idea. If Guy realised she hadn't told them, if she wasn't able to stall him, if . . .

She glanced up.

'Holly, darling, are you all right?' Lucie Renaud placed her hand on Holly's arm and Holly stared down at the long, thin fingers, the sharp red nails.

'I'm sorry. I didn't sleep well; it's made marshmallow of my brain.'

Lucie flicked her hand in the air dismissively. 'No matter, dear thing, it's a strain, I know, having so much to think about at such short notice. It would usually take me months to set up a "name" and here I am doing it in just three days!' There was an emphasis on the last few words and she stopped expectantly. Holly said nothing. She knew the brief must have been extraordinary but she wasn't sure what connection Lucie Renaud had to Guy She wasn't about to tell her anything.

'So, does he or doesn't he?' Lucie went on. 'You didn't answer my question. I can only assume that he probably does; most artists do. It's not a problem, only we need to book things up, to get the top stylist, and it'll be expensive. I've told Guy already that there might be extras . . . What is the matter, darling? Is it something I said?'

Holly frowned. 'What question? Does he or doesn't he what?'

'Does he need a makeover?' Lucie smiled, enjoying the moment. 'I, Holly my darling – don't ask me how, but mainly through a great deal of cajoling on the phone last night and a huge amount of good will – have managed to get a feature in the April issue of *Vogue*!' Lucie uttered a small cry of triumph as she said this and Holly jumped. 'Oh, I know, it's way too late for your and Guy's purpose – he did say immediate publications only, weeklies or dailies – but my dear, you don't turn down *Vogue*!' Lucie gave a small, shrill laugh. 'Imagine such a thing! Anyway, I'll have to book it up and we'll have to get it done tomorrow morning, as soon as he arrives. What time is he coming? You'll have to let me . . .' Lucie broke off and looked up at the waiter, hovering by her side.

'*Oui?*' she snapped. The young man bent and whispered into her ear. Holly thought she heard her name and tensed. Lucie took the message, dismissed the waiter with a wave of her long, thin hand and then smiled at Holly. 'The question is irrelevant,' she said. 'My dear, you should have said!' She stood, smoothed the line of her skirt and shook her head to resettle her bob. 'Adrian is here in the lobby.' Her face had set into its customary hauteur. 'He is asking for you.' She waited for Holly to stand. 'Shall we?'

Holly's jaw dropped. She stood up, her legs slightly unsteady. What the hell was going on? She followed Lucie out into the cream marble lobby and stopped dead in her tracks.

'Adrian White?' Lucie said to a lone figure by the reception desk. The man turned and Holly caught her breath.

'Yes?' Suddenly his face broke into a smile, an easy, relaxed smile, one Holly knew only too well. 'Hello, Holly,' he said. He turned to Lucie.

'Lucie Renaud,' she said, extending her hand. 'I'm handling the public relations for your show tomorrow night.' They shook.

'Delighted to meet you,' the man said. 'I'm sure I'm in very capable hands.'

Lucie smiled. 'More than capable, my dear, expert!' She turned to Holly. 'And he doesn't need a makeover, thank God! He's perfect as he is.' And beckoning to them both to follow her, she walked back to her office.

Holly stood where she was for a few moments.

'Are you all right?' the man murmured.

She nodded and looked away, her eyes filling with tears. 'What the hell are you doing here?' she whispered fiercely.

'I should ask you the same thing,' he said. Reaching out, he brushed the beginnings of a tear from under her eye. 'You haven't even said hello yet,' he whispered.

Holly closed her eyes for a moment, so relieved at his closeness that she felt dizzy with it.

'Hello, Kit,' she murmured. Then she opened her eyes again and followed him into the bar.

'Ah, Guy, darling! I thought you'd want to know. Isn't this a surprise? Adrian's here!'

Guy Ferreira walked across to them, leant forward and stubbed out his cigarette in the ashtray on the sofa table. He didn't like surprises; they made him decidedly uneasy. He neither smiled nor spoke and a tense silence ensued, interrupted by Lucie's mobile phone ringing. Holly jumped.

'Oui, Lucie Renaud.' Lucie turned away from the other three to take her call, reaching for her notepad and scribbling as she spoke.

'How nice that you're early,' Guy said finally, shaking hands with Kit. 'Did you travel alone?' There was something odd about this chap: he was older than Guy had expected – mid-thirties – and he was well groomed, a little too Ralph Lauren for a struggling artist.

Holly tensed.

'I had to,' Kit answered. 'I don't like to be parted from my work for too long. When we got the tickets I decided I couldn't wait. Jill and Sophie are on their way tomorrow.' He glanced at Holly as he said this. 'It's a bit of a shame; I couldn't change that economy ticket you got me, I . . .'

'Let me reimburse you,' Guy interrupted. 'I know how you artists struggle.'

Kit smiled. 'Thanks a lot.'

'So!' Lucie turned back to them, having finished her call. 'You all relieved the star of the show is here early?'

Holly nodded. She was holding a smile so tightly on her face that her cheeks were aching.

'Good. It's all shaping up nicely, I must say. An almost impossible brief, Guy darling,' Lucie turned to him and smiled, 'but I say *almost* – nothing is insurmountable, for the right fee!' She laughed again, the same shrill tinkle. 'And I think we're getting there. Now . . .' She picked up the file and dropped it into her briefcase. 'Why don't we take a taxi across to the Boulevard Saint-Germain and have a look at the gallery? Adrian, you can talk us through how you and Holly would like the work hung.'

'Yes, I'd like that,' Guy said. He sounded suspicious and Holly swallowed back the urge to scream. How the hell was Kit going to handle this? She glanced across at him but he seemed perfectly at ease. Digging her nails into the palm of her hand, she looked up to catch Guy's eye; he had been staring at her.

'Have you made a choice yet, Adrian?' she said quickly. 'You were very undecided before we left. Do you still want to leave most of it up to me?'

Kit shrugged. 'Whatever you want. Let's wait and see the space, but I do have a couple of pieces I think should definitely form the bedrock of the exhibition.'

'Really?' Guy said. 'How interesting, which ones?'

'Violet affairs probably,' Holly jumped in, 'or . . .'

'Marine lives,' Kit said; Holly caught her breath. 'Maybe both series together, I'm not sure Let's have a look when we get there. The space might not be big enough to take them.'

Holly let the breath go. She unclenched her hands and reached for her coat and hat. As she put the velvet cloche on and pulled it down near to her eyes, she realised her hands were shaking and quickly tucked them into her coat pockets.

Kit said, 'Can I wash before we go? I hate travelling; I always feel grimy after a journey.'

'You can use my room,' Holly said quickly.

'What a good idea.' Guy stood. 'If you give me your passport, Adrian, I can book you into the hotel while you're doing that. It'll save you the bother.'

'Oh, thanks, but there's no need,' Kit answered. 'I'm staying with a friend who lectures at the Sorbonne.'

'I see.' Guy raised an eyebrow. 'Are you sure? It's no problem to book you in and it would probably be more convenient.'

'Thanks again but it's an old girlfriend, actually, and I think she'd be offended if I stayed elsewhere.'

Guy looked at him for a moment, then smiled and walked out into the lobby. Adrian was very plausible, but Guy felt tense. There was something odd about him, something too easy and almost familiar. He crossed to the reception desk. Behind him, Holly and Adrian headed for the lift to go up to her suite. Guy turned just before the lift doors closed and stared at them for a moment, then they disappeared from view. Crossing to a sofa, he sat and took up a copy of the day's *Figaro*, but he found it impossible to concentrate on reading the paper. He had the oddest feeling that he had seen Adrian White before.

Just inside the door of the suite, Kit turned to Holly and before she could speak, drew her body into his and held her tightly, pulling her hat off and burying his face in her hair. She closed her eyes and they stayed like that for as long as they dared. Then, pulling back, he broke away from her. 'What the hell are you doing here?' he demanded.

Holly stared at him, speechless. The moment was ruined and she turned angrily away.

'Holly? I asked you a question!'

'I heard you!' she snapped, her voice thick with tears. 'I'm not deaf!'

'No, but you're pretty damn stu . . .' Kit bit his tongue as Holly swung round again. He saw her face and felt such intense longing that it took his breath away. He stared at her, then down at the ground. 'I'm sorry,' he said. 'I've been so scared . . .'

She cut him off. 'I know.' She waited for him to look at her. 'In answer to your question,' she said, 'I don't know what I'm doing here.' She bit her fingernail nervously and when she spoke again, her voice had changed. She was obviously terrified. 'I made a snap decision in London,' she stammered, 'a stupid decision, when I found out that Guy Ferreira wasn't who he said he was, and that he was involved in all this. I wasn't thinking straight. I was so frightened, it was in the middle of the night, and I thought, I thought that maybe he would make a mistake, get careless in some way and I'd see a way out of all this!' Suddenly she slumped back against the edge of the table. 'Christ, I was so naïve! I don't know what I could have been thinking! I saw his washbag, the drugs, the books in the safe, pictures of me and you in the phone box, and I just panicked. I thought, I thought . . . Oh God . . .' Holly put her hands up to her face.

'Whoa, wait a minute!' Kit crossed to her and gently removed her hands. He wiped away a tear on her cheek. 'What drugs? Books, photos? I don't understand.' He held both her hands. 'Holly, look at me. Tell me.'

'There isn't time, not now, I . . .'

'Tell me! There's time, tell me quickly.'

'I went to Guy's hotel, after he'd talked to me about this Paris thing. I wanted to ask him a question; it was important. I . . .' She stopped and took a breath. Her chest had begun to constrict as she spoke. 'He assaulted me . . .'

'He did *what*?' Kit sprung forward but Holly held up her hands to restrain him. He swallowed back a rising anger. 'Go on,' he said.

'It was a sort of pass but it was terrifying, violent almost. I don't think he knew what he was doing – he was stoned – but I got away, into the bathroom, and that's when I saw he'd left the hotel safe open. It was careless of him. I saw some photographs on the top of it as I went to the bathroom, black and white. They looked odd, and when I looked closer it was me and you, close-ups of us, I mean, in the phone box . . .' She swallowed, embarrassed at the memory of them.

'And?'

She took a deep breath to calm herself. 'I looked in the safe. The books were there, the gallery's books, and a packet of cocaine – I think it was coke, because he had all the things in the bathroom, spoons and a razor blade and stuff like that.' She wrenched one of her hands free and wiped at another tear on her cheek, then her nose, which had started to run. 'I just thought that if he'd made one mistake, then he'd get careless and make more and . . .' She stared at Kit, suddenly wild-eyed. 'I didn't want Jill and Sophie and you involved, not once I knew he was out to get me. I had to do this on my own – that's the main reason I came. I just had to disappear, then you'd all be safe . . .' Again she wiped her nose on the back of her hand and Kit instinctively searched his pocket for a handkerchief. He handed it over without thinking. Holly took it, and blew her nose, then they looked at each other. Suddenly they both smiled.

'Shall I keep it?'

Kit nodded. He held one of her hands to his mouth and kissed it.

'We should go.' Holly's voice had an edge of panic to it. 'Guy will be waiting, he'll . . .' She didn't finish her sentence.

Kit leant forward and kissed her. Moments later, he pulled back and placed a finger on her mouth. 'Don't think about him any more,' he said gently. 'It'll be OK.'

Holly stood smoothing her clothes and running her hands through her hair, then over her face to wipe away the traces of tears. 'How, Kit? How will it be OK?'

He stared back at her. In truth he had no idea but he couldn't tell her that. 'Just trust me,' he answered and Holly nodded. But it was the second time she had heard those words in the past forty-eight hours and despite the warmth of the hotel, she shivered.

Kit finished talking to Lucie and saw Holly standing across the large gallery space, watching him. They had been working all day on the exhibition. Most of the work had been chosen and placed, ready to hang in the morning, and the last few drawings were being framed there on site. He was relieved Ferreira had left early – he had been thinking on his feet for hours, trying to remember what Adrian had told him on the phone the night before, trying to assume the air of an artist, an air he didn't possess. At least Lucie Renaud wasn't looking for clues. Ferreira was; he was certain of it. Kit was tired but he was pumped full of adrenaline, his mind buzzing with the answers he had learnt by heart overnight. He'd got away with it, for the moment.

'So you're ready for the press tomorrow?' Lucie said. He tore his gaze away from Holly.

'Yes, pretty much.'

She reached up and touched his hair, gently flicking a strand off his forehead. 'Good boy,' she said. She had lit up another small cigar, one in a chain of almost twenty that day, and the air was heavy with stale smoke as she took a long drag. 'We have *Beaux Arts* at nine, *L'Objet d'Art* at eleven and then we do *Vogue*. I've yet to confirm with them and I'm hoping to God they don't let me down!' She stared off into the distance for a few moments and then said, speaking more to herself than to Kit, 'You can never be sure, though. It's not as if it's a big feature. You're not well known, even known at all really but . . .' She broke off and shrugged. 'Ah well.' She waved her hand in the air dismissively. 'We'll see tomorrow.'

Kit smiled grimly. 'Yes, quite. Is there anything else you need me for?' Lucie smiled. 'I could think of one or two things,' she answered, laying a fingertip lightly on his chest. Kit stared down at the glossy red nail for a moment, then he inched away.

'Holly, I'm utterly exhausted,' he called across theatrically. 'I really ought to get back and get some rest. I've got a very heavy day tomorrow.' He glanced at Lucie. 'Flying plays havoc with my energy levels,' he said. 'I'm not half the man I usually am.'

Lucie Renaud laughed, a sharp trickle of noise that seemed to bounce off the white walls. 'Get some sleep and restore the other half then,' she said. She laid her palm against his cheek. 'I want to see the life-size product tomorrow, OK?'

He nodded and her hand fell away as Holly joined them.

'Take this darling man back to his accommodation and put him to bed,' Lucie commanded. 'I shall see you both tomorrow morning for breakfast at the Queen Elizabeth.'

Another time, another place, Holly would have laughed but instead, she nodded bleakly and went across for her coat. Tomorrow, she kept thinking, tomorrow.

'You may have done it in a hell of a rush, my dear,' Lucie said, coming up behind Holly and whispering, sotto voce, 'for reasons I couldn't possibly understand . . ' She left the sentence hanging but Holly didn't fill it in for her. 'But he's worth it! This darling boy has talent.' She gestured towards a large deep purple and red canvas. 'Real talent.'

Holly nodded. She fastened her top button and yanked her hat down over her eyes. She wanted to cry.

'So, onward and upward!' Lucie called across to Kit.

Kit smiled. 'Onward and upward,' he said. 'Holly, you ready?'

'Yes. Lucie, can we give you a lift anywhere in the taxi?'

'No, thank you, darling, but I shall stay on here and finish making a few calls. Guy might call in later to see how his money has been spent.' She fluttered her fingers in the air. 'So much to do and so little time!'

'Quite,' Holly said. Kit opened the door for her and she turned to wave at Lucie. Smilingly, Lucie waved back, then the phone rang and she moved away from the door to answer it. Holly and Kit were instantly forgotten.

'If we walk up to the corner of . . .'

'Let's just walk,' Kit said, glancing behind him at the gallery and taking Holly's arm as they moved out of sight. They were alone, or so he thought.

'But we . . .'

He moved towards her and silenced her briefly with his mouth.

'Later,' he said gently. 'First things first.'

It was a freezing cold night, Paris was lit up and clouds of white fog hung round the street lamps. The cafés were busy, their windows steamed up; loud voices and warm, smoky air spilt out onto the pavements as people came and went. And Holly and Kit walked unnoticed in a city where lovers were commonplace, up along the Boulevard Saint-Germain, into the Rue des Ecoles and along past the Musée de Cluny into a small back street behind the Sorbonne and the narrow, shabby streets of the Left Bank.

Kit stopped in front of a small hotel, with old painted wood doors and a bay tree in a terracotta pot outside. He glanced up at the name, Hôtel d'Arrivée, and pushed open one of the doors. Holly went in first and he followed.

'*Bonsoir*,' he said to the lady on the desk. '*Une chambre double, s'il vous plaît.*' She peered at him over the rim of her metal-framed reading glasses, then at Holly for a few moments and finally she nodded. She had grey hair scraped back into a tight, oiled bun and wore a black dress with a cream lace collar and lace cuffs. She pushed the cuff back as she filled in her forms and then passed them across.

'*Pouvez vous remplir cette fiche, s'il vous plaît, et signez en bas. Ce sera deux cent quatre-vingt francs, s'il vous plaît. Taxe et service compris.*'

Kit signed and dug in his pocket for some cash. He counted

the notes, handed them across and the woman stood up and reached for a key. She held it out for Holly, her eyes steadfast on Holly's face, her features set in a grim expression of disdain. Holly took the key and glanced at Kit, and suddenly the woman smiled. She winked broadly at them both and Holly flushed. The woman nodded, sat back on her stool and returned to her book. She didn't look up again as Kit took Holly's hand and led her silently up the stairs.

'This is what the wink was for,' Kit whispered as he pulled Holly towards him and kicked the door shut with the heel of his foot. He kissed her and tugged at her hat, throwing it onto the floor. Holly broke away. She looked at him for a while, not knowing whether to laugh or cry, then she moved back towards him and stood very close. 'In the words of Lucie Renaud,' she said quietly, 'take this darling man back to his accommodation and put him to bed!'

Kit laughed and she smiled at the wonderful expression of love and laughter in his eyes. 'Quite,' he said, the laughter evaporating. He reached out and slowly unfastened her coat, slipping it off her shoulders, letting it drop heavily to the floor. He pulled her sweater out of the waistband of her skirt and she lifted her arms so he could take it off.

'Same grey silk underwear,' he murmured, tracing the curve of her breast with his fingertip under the line of her bra. She shivered and he pulled her close, just holding her for a moment. Then he slid his hands up under her skirt and pressed her pelvis hard into his, his fingers digging into the flesh of her thighs and buttocks, slipping inside the sheer fabric of her stocking tops, the silk that covered her bottom. She moaned and he moved his mouth over hers, kissing her, sinking down and back, pulling her roughly on top of him.

'God, Holly, I love you, I . . .'

She had straddled him and reached behind her back to unclip

her bra. She leant forward and he frantically kissed the smooth, perfumed skin of her breast, taking her nipple in his mouth as her fingers struggled with his trousers.

'Wait, I . . .' He lifted her hips and unfastened his fly underneath her, letting her fingers do the rest, catching his breath as she touched him and eased him towards her. Then suddenly she stopped. She broke away from him and pulled herself up, looking down at him, her eyes on his.

'Holly, what . . . ?'

With shaking fingers, she unzipped her skirt, dropped it to the floor, peeled off her stockings and slid her knickers down over her hips. She stood over him, naked, then slowly knelt down astride him. He moaned as she sank down and reached up to catch his hands in her hair.

'I love you too,' she whispered. And slowly she began to move the length of him, making him tremble, grinding down onto him until he called out her name over and over again.

Later, they lay together on the muddle of their clothes, covered with their coats, Holly's head on Kit's chest, and he stroked her hair, winding strands of it round his fingers, touching the soft, fine down on her neck. They didn't talk; neither of them wanted to. They stayed like that for as long as they could and then Holly moved. She sat up and reached for her underwear, breaking the intimacy, spoiling the moment and bringing them both back to reality.

Kit watched her.

'You OK?' he said.

She nodded, pulling her coat over her shoulders, trying to ignore the terrible ache she felt in the pit of her stomach.

'We need to talk.'

Holly looked back at him. 'No, Kit, not now. I can't talk now . . .'

He reached forward and caught her wrist. 'When then? I want to tell you how I feel, I . . .'

She broke her hand free and touched his face. 'You just have.'
Then she stood, hugging her coat around her, and walked to the
window. The room was only semi-dark, the curtains were open
and it was lit by the peculiar pink neon of a tabac sign on the wall
opposite. Holly stared at it, wanting to be anywhere but there at
that time and yet so terrified that the moment would disappear that
she was physically shaking. Kit stood and moved across to her. He
stood behind her for a few moments, both of them staring down
at the empty street below, then he eased the coat off her shoulders
and wrapped his arms around her, stroking her, his mouth on the
nape of her neck. She stood motionless for a while, then her back
arched as his hands moved down her body to between her legs and
she moaned gently, throwing her head back, letting him kiss and
bite her shoulders, her neck.

'Oh God, Kit.' He pulled her round to him and lifted her,
wrapping her legs around his hips. 'Kit, I . . .' But the words
tailed off. She cried out as he entered her and closed her eyes,
lost to everything but him.

Across the street, in the shadow of a side alley, Guy Ferreira
watched the window with a sick lust in the pit of his stomach.
It ached so much that he could hardly stand, could hardly bear to
watch, and yet he couldn't turn away. He was fascinated; he loved
it and he hated it. His brain was on fire.

Leaning back against the cold stone wall, Guy took several deep
breaths. He was feeling sick, dizzy; he'd done too much coke and
his whole body was on overload. He put his hands up to his face
as they moved away from the window and covered his eyes. He
was sweating despite the chill wind, and the perspiration clung,
cold and damp, to the back of his neck. He started to shiver.

He had to have her, he knew that, he had always known it.
After Blandford he would take her, in front of that bastard she
was with now. He'd use her, fuck her, make her cry out. Guy

snapped his eyes open as a surge of adrenaline pumped through his veins. He moved away from the wall and stood straight, wiping the back of his neck with his handkerchief. Again he took several deep breaths, holding the air down in his lungs and letting it out, slowly. He felt better, strong again, more in control. He dug his hands deep into the pockets of his overcoat, and without looking back at the window, he walked off. This time he knew exactly what he was doing.

But Guy Ferreira was wrong. He had just made the one mistake Holly had been convinced he would make. He was out of control, and he had decided on a course of action that was about to give Holly what she had been praying for. A chance.

A last way out.

Chapter Twenty-Five

It was four thirty pm, almost forty-eight hours since passport control had confirmed Holly Grigson's arrival in Paris, and the incident room was virtually deserted. DS Eames sat by the phone, a pile of airline computer printouts in front of him, a full ashtray by his side, along with a half-empty pack of cigarettes, the second that day, and his lighter. He drank a cup of coffee but he couldn't really taste it; he was too wired up. In the awful silence, he drummed his fingers on the desk, heedless of the stares from DC Dobson across the room 'I wish they'd bloody get on with it,' he said, 'How long does it take to get a frigging warrant?'

Dobson shrugged. 'Can't hurry a judge,' he remarked. 'You should know that, Eamsie.'

The phone rang. Eames picked it up instantly. DS Eames. Oh good, right, sir.' He put his hand over the mouthpiece: 'They got the warrant and they're there now.' He went back on the line. 'Yes, as soon as we come up with anything. Right, sir. Bye.' He hung up.

'Welsch is definitely away by the look of it; the house is empty. They're just starting the search now.'

DC Dobson stretched his arms behind his back, then flicked his own pile of computer paper with his fist. 'Well I hope they find more than I have,' he said. 'God knows where he's buggered off to. You come up with anything yet, Sarge?'

Eames reached for another cigarette. 'Nothing. It's like looking for a needle in a haystack.'

'You're telling me.' DC Dobson stood. 'Want another coffee?'

Eames shook his head, then went back to the list of passengers on yet another Air France flight to Paris and the search for the name T. Welsch.

Ted Welsch sat in a small bar in a back street off the Avenue Marceau, a short distance from the Queen Elizabeth Hotel, and drank his last coffee of the day. It was five pm; there were two hours to go before the Adrian White exhibition at the Durand-Desert Gallery. He lit a cigarette and counted his change on the table in front of him. He had done it several times already and was stalling for time. He had to ring Jill, to let her know what was happening, and he wanted to say something to her, something that summed up the way he felt about her. The trouble was he just didn't have the nerve.

'*Désirez vous la même chose?*' the waiter asked.

Welsch held up his hands to indicate that he didn't speak French.

'You want anozer *café*?' the waiter tried.

'NO, THANKS. WHERE IS THE PHONE?'

'*Le téléphone?*'

'*OUI.*' Welsch spoke loudly, as if talking to an idiot, not simply a foreigner.

'Out in ze back. 'Ere, follow me, monsieur.'

'OH RIGHT. THANKS.' He stood and swept the change off the table into his hand. Oh well, he thought, can't put it off any longer. The waiter showed him to the telephone and he thanked him again, even louder this time, to show his appreciation. He waited until the young man had gone, then dialled, slotted his money in and waited for Jill to answer.

'Hello?'

'Jill? It's me, Ted. Awright?'

'Yes, fine.'

Welsch was amazed at how clear the line was – it sounded as if she were just down the road, and that filled him with trepidation.

'What's happening?' she asked. She sounded tense. He wished he could have seen her face.

'Not very much so far. It was a quiet night last night an' it's been a quiet day.' He didn't mention Kit and Holly's visit to the hotel on the Left Bank; there was no need. 'Things seem to be moving awright; the gallery looks ready; I guess I just gotta get meself prepared for tonight.' He slotted some more coins into the box. 'What about you?'

'Well, I've been at the gallery and we've had umpteen calls about Adrian, so I've directed all enquiries to the Art 'ninety-four show. We've just finished choosing what's left of the work to exhibit there. I don't know what's happened in Paris but it's had one hell of an effect over here. There's some kind of rumour that Adrian White is the next Francis Bacon!'

Welsch heard the smile in her voice. 'Keep it up, Jill,' he said. 'Well done.' He stubbed out his cigarette. 'Look, Jill?'

'Yes?'

'Jill, you will be careful, won't you? I mean, there's no guarantee that Blandford's gonna turn up here, you know. I mean, you just don't know . . .' He stopped. He didn't want to frighten her. 'Just be careful, awright?'

Jill frowned on the other end. 'I will be,' she said. 'You too.'

'Yeah, thanks. Look, Jill?' Welsch hesitated, searching for words to express how he felt. There was a pause, then a silence opened up. He couldn't do it. The divide was just too great. With a simple goodbye, he hung up.

In Sussex, Jill sat and stared at the phone for a long time, feeling infinitely depressed. She was sure she had missed something, something important, and was powerless to do anything about it. She liked Ted; they might one day end up as good friends, but that was all. She hoped he understood. Glancing up as Sophie came downstairs, she said, 'That was Ted Welsch.'

Sophie put her hand on Jill's arm. 'He's a nice bloke, Jill.' Jill nodded. 'I'm pleased you're friends with him. It's important to him; he told me.'

'Perhaps I shouldn't have been so open with him – there can be misunderstandings. We're so different.'

Sophie shook her head. 'That's the old Jill talking.'

Jill patted her hand. 'Yes, perhaps you're right. I suppose it's all about learning, no matter how hard the lesson.'

'I suppose it is,' Sophie said. And because of Alex and Holly and Kit and Ted Welsch, the two women smiled at each other. It was a smile of understanding.

Lucie Renaud glanced down at her small gold Rolex and sighed heavily. Providing the caterers arrived in the next five minutes, she had just under an hour to get back to her apartment, shower, change and return to the gallery, and she hated to rush. She hated it with a vengeance. Most days it took her an hour simply to apply her make-up. She crossed to her bag to take out her compact and inspect her face. She might not have to strip it right back, she thought, touching the pale matt skin of her cheek. She might just get away with redoing her eyes and mouth. She shut the silver case, engraved with her initials from Tiffany & Co., New York, and turned as the floral display artist, fresh from London, stood back from the last huge vase of arum lilies to admire his work.

'It's beautiful!' Lucie announced as she walked across to the young man and embraced him. 'Absolutely divine!' The young man sighed and wiped a tear from underneath his eyes. He was feeling emotional. He had worked all afternoon on the three vases and they were perfection. 'Now, off you go, dear boy, and pamper yourself ready for tonight,' she said, tapping him lightly on the behind. 'You will be overwhelmed with compliments and I want you to look your best to receive them!'

He smiled and sighed again, then crossed the gallery to pick up his leather jacket and rucksack from a chair. 'Go on, see you later!' she called, seeing him glance back at her. She followed him to the door, closed it after him and stood there until he had disappeared from view. Then she slumped down on a chair and dropped her head into her hands.

God, what a job this had been! She was absolutely exhausted. If she hadn't desperately needed the money and if that money hadn't been quite such an obscene amount, she would never have touched it. It worried her and if she was really honest with herself, it was beginning to scare her. Guy Ferreira might be terribly pukka, but he was weird; in fact the whole brief was weird. She couldn't wait for it to be over. Ever since he'd paid half her fee up front in cash, alarm bells had been ringing. Who nowadays had a hundred and sixty thousand francs in used notes?

Lucie stood up and turned to her favourite painting. She had a good eye – she had been collecting for years – and had already reserved two pieces. She took a sheet of small red stickers out of the pocket of her tunic and placed one by the title underneath the painting. This one was hers and she sure as hell wasn't going to pay full price for it. She didn't know what this lot were up to but if that Adrian guy was the real artist she was a flying pink pig. Thank God *Vogue* had cancelled – whoever he was, there was no photographic record of it, she'd made sure of that. She left the stickers by the catalogue on the pale ash desk and collected up her coat and bag. She turned to leave then jumped as the door opened.

'Guy!' She couldn't keep the edge of fear out of her voice. He was stoned, had been all day, only now he looked a little out of control. She plastered a smile onto her face. 'How charming!'

'I don't pay you to be charmed!' he snapped. 'Is the upstairs unlocked?'

'Yes, I think so. I have the key here . . .' She turned and fumbled on the desk, searching for it. 'It is definitely here somewhere. I had it earlier; the wine merchants delivered the champagne up there, I . . .' She found it. 'Here!' She turned to give it to him. 'I'm sure I left it unlocked, I . . .' But she didn't finish her sentence. He had slammed out of the gallery, leaving the door wide open. She stood motionless for several moments, staring after him, then she heard the scrape of tyres against the kerb and the catering van pulled up outside. 'Thank God for that,' she murmured under her breath. She threw her coat over her arm, grabbed her bag and hurried out of the gallery.

'I'll leave you to it,' she called to the woman in the front seat. They were a firm she used frequently; they knew exactly how she liked things. 'See you later!' And without a backward glance, she dashed across the road and disappeared down a side street, not at all sure why she had this terrible instinct to run.

Holly took the top off her lipstick and held it to her lips. She stared at her face in the mirror, perfectly made up, her hair swept back into a chignon at the nape of her neck, jet drops at her ears and a Victorian jet necklace at her throat. She had packed her best clothes for tonight, laying them in her case with macabre care before she left London. She had thought that if she died, these would be the clothes she would like to be found in, and now, as she looked at the ankle-length sheath of deep green crushed velvet, the high-heeled black velvet shoes with straps that laced over her feet and the jets her grandmother had owned, she was pleased. Her fingers shook as she traced the line of her mouth and filled it in with dark crimson, the finishing touch. She was hanging on to her nerve with every sinew of her body and as she turned away from the mirror she knew it might be the last time she would ever look at her own face.

She picked up her evening bag from the bed, wrapped her cloak around her shoulders and with her head up, she left the suite.

Down in the lobby, Holly waited. There was no sign of Guy or Kit, and that made her nervous. She stood uneasily by the entrance, clutching her bag, and watching the scene in front of her: the woman waiting by the floral display, the crowd of Japanese tourists by the lifts, the couple booking in, all the comings and goings of a busy hotel. She took in none of it. As she stood alone she could think of nothing but her husband, Sandy Turner. Her ex-husband, not even her husband, simply a silent partner. A thief. She realised she was gripping her bag so tightly that her fingers ached. She took a breath and relaxed her hand, transferring the bag to the other one. Hugo Blandford, she thought, and a hard knot of anger expanded then contracted in the pit of her stomach. If I ever had the chance, I'd kill him.

Guy reached for his jacket off the bed, eased it on and fastened the centre button. He looked at himself in the full-length mirror to check that the gun didn't show, then patted his pocket and moved across the room to the door. It wasn't ideal, a .38 Smith & Wesson, but it was all he could get at short notice. It would do the job. He walked through to the sitting room of the suite, past his bags, packed and ready by the door, and called reception. In answer to his question, the clerk told him Holly was waiting for him. He took his coat off the sofa and left the suite. He had done his last line – after tonight there would be no more coke. No more shit from the top either. No more mistakes. Stepping into the lift, he glanced briefly at his reflection in the mirrored panel. It didn't enter his head that Blandford might not show up; it simply wasn't an option. Money and sex were the ultimate bait: Holly Grigson was the sex, the paintings were the money. Guy mindlessly watched the lights flash up on the panel as the floors slipped past. Money, sex and power, he thought, and smiled tensely. Tonight he would have the power.

Kit hung around outside the hotel for as long as he could, watching the building, the entrance, the street. He stood in a shop doorway, the collar of his overcoat turned up, his eyes scanning the scene. He didn't really know what he was looking for and he was bloody scared if he was honest with himself. He had called Ted Welsch three times that evening but all he got was the answerphone. Time was running out.

Glancing down at his watch, he realised the waiting was over. He had to go. He stepped out into the glare of a street lamp and hoped to God that he knew what he was doing. At this stage, he didn't have any choice.

'Hey!'

Kit stumbled for a moment, then righted the small chap he had just banged into. '*Pardonnez* moi . . .' He looked at the man. 'Jesus! Ted! What the hell . . .'

Welsch shoved him back into the doorway, out of sight, watching the road. They stayed there while a black saloon car drove past and parked opposite the hotel entrance. Welsch released Kit and patted him on the arm.

'Sorry, mate, awright?'

'Yes, fine, but what . . .'

'Don't ask, 'cause I don't know. I came out the café three roads down and I saw that car over there. I started walking towards the hotel and I saw it again, twice. It's doin' a circuit, waiting for someone.' Welsch ran his tongue over his teeth. 'You, probably.'

'You sure?'

'Nope.'

'Shit.'

Welsch dug in his pocket for his cigarettes. 'Nicely put, couldn't have said it better meself.' He lit up and dropped the match on the ground between them. 'You'd better go. You're late, Monsewer le artiste!' He smiled grimly.

'Yes, you're right. But before I do, tell me – what the hell are you doing here, Ted?'

'Sightseeing,' Welsch said. He flicked the ash. 'Go on, bugger off!' He swivelled round and walked off in the opposite direction.

Several minutes later, Welsch watched Holly, Guy Ferreira and Kit climb into a chauffeur-driven car. It pulled off and was followed by the saloon car. He stepped out of the side street and hurried into the hotel. Crossing to the reception desk, he asked for the phone. One was brought up from under the desk and Welsch looked at it, hesitating for a moment. Then he dialled a number he knew off by heart: Bromley CID.

'DCI Reg Carter.' He was straight through to the office. 'Is he there? Yeah, you can, tell him it's Ted Welsch.' Welsch waited. He was sweating and the phone felt oily in his hand. Carter was on the line in a matter of seconds. 'Reg? Yeah, I have gotta problem. I'm in Paris and I need help.' Welsch swallowed, his mouth suddenly bone-dry. 'I need all the fucking help I can get!'

DS Eames picked up the phone on the first ring. 'DS Eames. No, I'm sorry, DCI Heeley isn't here at the moment. Can I take a message?' He instantly sat forward. 'Where? Yes, I've got that.' He scribbled frantically on the back of a printout. 'Can you spell that for me? Right, got it. Yes, I will, I'll call him right now and get on to Interpol. Thanks, yes we will.' He hung up and immediately dialled again. 'Dobbo, we're on!' he called across the room. 'Shit!' He slammed the phone down. 'Bloody Heeley's engaged. You got any other mobile numbers, Dobbo?'

'None. What the hell's happened?'

'Welsch is in Paris; he's just rung Bromley CID.' Eames dialled again. 'Jesus! Get off the phone, sir, please!' He dialled a third time. 'There's something going down there, something big. He wants armed assistance and he bloody wants it now!'

Dobson whistled through his teeth.

'Can you get up to the CAD room and ask them to radio one of the cars to go over to Bromley? I've got to get hold of Heeley.' Eames glanced at his watch. 'We're running out of time. Shit! I'd better get onto the Chief Super.'

'He's not in,' Dobson said. 'On leave, remember?'

'Oh Christ, that's all we frigging need!'

Dobson scribbled down Welsch's address on the corner of a piece of paper and tore it off. 'I'll be back in a few minutes.' He darted out of the room.

Eames rang Heeley's mobile again – this time he got through. 'Is the boss there?' He bit his fingernail. 'He's what? Oh Jesus! Can't anyone get hold of him?' He listened to the reply. 'Great!' he snapped. 'Just fucking great!' And he slammed down the phone.

'Heeley's gone walkabout,' he said as DC Dobson appeared in the doorway. 'Out of radio control. Gone for a frigging sandwich, would you believe?'

Dobson stared at him. 'I'll have to ring Special Branch myself,' Eames said. Dobson continued to stare and suddenly Eames dropped his head in his hands. 'Shit, shit, shit!' he exploded. 'What the hell do I do now?'

'You ring Special Branch, get them to contact Interpol on an emergency code.'

'What if it's a false alarm? How the fuck am I going to explain that?'

'You'll just have to.'

'You know how much this is going to cost, Dobbo?' Eames stood up and took a deep breath. 'Sorry, I don't know why I'm shouting at you. On my head be it.' He picked up the phone and smiled tensely. 'And who said graduate intake were wimps?'

The gallery was packed. The noise level rose as the champagne flowed, red sold stickers sat on almost every title, and as Kit circulated, trying to say as little as possible and to avoid the cameras, he found that Adrian White's reputation was escalating without any help from him. The paintings spoke for themselves, and when they didn't, he feigned a total incomprehension of the French language. It worked, and he was able to stay out of the limelight and watch the room. He didn't intend to let Holly out of his sight for even one moment, although where the hell Guy had got to was really beginning to bother him. He sipped a glass of champagne and kept one eye on the door. He reckoned that if Blandford was going to turn up, he'd do it in the midst of a crowd – if he was as smart as Kit thought he was.

Holly talked to the valuer from Ader Tajon, explaining how Adrian White had been discovered by her husband several years ago and how they had been building his reputation. She attempted to give the impression that he had been slowly developed towards this solo exhibition in Paris, but it was hard work. She didn't want to lie outright but she was finding it almost impossible to concentrate. Her hands shook and she had to grip her glass tightly to stop it from showing.

She stared at the work in front of them as the young American asked how the gallery could justify the prices for a virtual unknown and for a moment lost her train of thought.

'I'd say the paintings answer that for themselves, wouldn't you?' a low voice said quietly behind her. Holly jumped.

'Are you OK, Miss Grigson?' the American asked.

Holly turned to her. Now her whole body had started to shake, and she stammered over the words. 'Oh, yes . . . er, yes, I'm fine.'

'Keep your eyes front, then excuse yourself,' the man whispered in her ear. She could feel his breath hot against her neck and shuddered. 'Upstairs, now,' he hissed.

'Will you excuse me?' Holly managed to say.

The American nodded and smiled. 'You sure you're OK? You look awfully pale.'

'I'm fine, thanks, I . . .' She looked behind her but couldn't see anyone. Her eyes scanned the crowd. 'Just a bit faint, the excitement . . .' Her voice trailed off. She shrugged and moved towards the door, squeezing through the packed bodies, searching frantically for Kit. The door was open and several people were spilling out onto the pavement with their drinks. They carried Holly with them. In the cold air she suddenly shook herself and took a deep breath. There was an old wood door to the side of the gallery frontage and Holly pushed it open. It led to the upstairs space, a huge glass-ceilinged room, split into two and used for private showings of art films, musical recitals and experimental theatre. Holly climbed, holding onto the wrought-iron rail for support, her legs weak, her breathing rapid and short. At the top, she walked through the glass doors into the gallery space, her footsteps echoing on the polished wood floor.

Suddenly she spun round.

'Hello, Holly.'

She caught her breath.

'You look lovely, very much the gallery owner.'

Hugo Blandford stood at the far side of the room by the fire exit. He was thinner than she remembered, and tanned. He wore a coat she recognised but apart from that he could have been anyone, a total stranger.

She dug her fingernails into the palms of her hands by her side, so frightened and angry that she wanted to cry.

'Is this an unexpected pleasure or did it cross your mind that I might show up?' He moved into the centre, closer to her. 'You were always a clever little thing.' He smiled. 'But not quite clever enough. You know about the money, presumably?'

She nodded, unable to speak.

'And that's what this little charade is in aid of, I suppose? To try and salvage your precious little gallery?' He raised an eyebrow. 'The prices are very steep, but you've managed it well, I'll give you that. and he's good; he probably will be the next Francis Bacon. Very neat. I'm glad I made it. I had to come and see what you were up to, Holly, and, of course, to collect what's owed me.' He lifted his arm and Holly let out a cry.

'You were never frightened of me before, Holly, why now?' He moved even closer to her, watching her face. 'You even used to like me a little, I think.' He was very close now and Holly started to shake. 'We were a good team; I'm surprised you didn't suss me.' He reached out and touched her cheek. She forced herself to stand absolutely still. 'I liked you, Holly. We had some good times, didn't we? You know, I even used the date of our wedding anniversary to number my account in Geneva.' He smiled, then, as he watched the shock on Holly's face, the smile turned to a quiet snigger. 'You don't like that?' He shook his head. 'Oh dear, poor Holly.' He touched her again and she flinched. 'Poor, poor Holly.'

'Poor Hugo too, I think!'

Hugo jerked round.

'Guy!' He stood perfectly still and the smile died on his lips, his face drained of all colour. 'Guy, how nice, I . . .'

'Shut up!' Guy snarled. He held a gun at both of them and motioned with it. 'Get up against the wall, both of you!'

Holly was shaking so much, she stumbled back, knocking hard into the wall. She stood there, holding onto it for support, her eyes locked on Guy's face, wild and terrified.

'What's the date?' he suddenly shouted. 'When was it?'

Holly's body slumped down, and she hugged her arms around herself, biting her hand to stop herself from sobbing. She was so frightened she couldn't think, let alone speak. Guy crossed to her. There was something about her pathetic fear, her vulnerability, that excited him. He hadn't meant to touch her, not yet, not until this was over, but he couldn't control himself,

'When was it, Holly?' he asked quietly. He squatted down in front of her, the gun trained on Hugo, and stroked her face, her hair. He cupped her breast in his hand and felt the nipple harden. She stared blankly at him, too terrified to move. 'You like that, do you?' He seemed to have forgotten Hugo. His breathing quickened. 'Do you?' He pinched her nipple hard and she cried out. 'Tell me!' he suddenly shouted, grabbing her hair and yanking her to her feet. 'Tell me, you bitch!'

Holly started to sob.

Kit pushed through the crowd towards the door. He'd lost sight of Holly. Lucie said she was at the back of the gallery, but by the time he had squeezed and shoved his way across she had moved. He began to panic. He shunted people to the side as he struggled to get out, knocking glasses and ignoring the shouts. He could see the door. It was blocked by a crowd on the pavement, but he had to get out. He called to someone to let him through but as he battled past the bodies he felt himself almost lifted and thrust to one side. The noise level suddenly dropped.

'*Restez calmes, s'il vous plaît! Restez calmes, s'il vous plaît!*' A man in the doorway was talking to the immediate crowd in the entrance, speaking calmly and carefully in order to be heard. '*Veuillez évacuer la galerie, s'il vous plaît, en petits groupes, en continuant de parler. Merci!*'

'What's he saying?' Kit called to an English woman in front of him. 'What's happening?'

She looked back over her shoulder at him. 'They want us to leave the building in small groups but keep talking.'

Kit started to sweat. He attached himself to the person in front of him and shuffled forward, inch by inch, until he was finally out of the door. Glancing behind him he saw the same man move on into the gallery repeating the instructions. Out on the pavement the street had been sealed off. Armed police and ambulances lined the road some distance from the gallery and police walked among the crowd, escorting people away from the building. '*Dégagez, dégagez! Le plus loin possible.*'

Kit scanned the crowd fearfully for any sight of Holly, calling out her name. He ran the length of the pavement and back, dodging the small group just leaving the gallery. There was no sign of her. He panicked. Without thinking, he slammed through the door next to the gallery and ran up the stairs.

Seconds later, he burst into the room.

'*Kit!*' Holly screamed.

Guy spun round. His instant reaction was to shoot. He pumped two bullets in the direction of the door and Kit dived to the floor. He lay there and held his breath. There was silence. When he opened his eyes he saw Guy's foot in his face.

'Get up!' Guy snapped. Kit knelt, then staggered to his feet. Guy held the gun to his head and motioned for him to stand over by Blandford. 'You're just in time,' he said. Kit could see a stream of perspiration running down the side of his face. 'Come here!' Guy shouted at Holly. 'Or I shoot his face off!'

Holly stumbled forward, still sobbing.

'Now!' Guy shouted.

She made it across to him, biting on her hand again to try and stop the uncontrollable sobbing.

'Good.' He was still breathing hard but his voice was controlled. 'Kneel down.' Holly moved towards him and he glanced at her every few seconds as he kept the gun trained on the two men. 'Here . . .' He gesticulated with the gun. 'Down here.' Holly inched forward, then suddenly he reached out and ripped the neck of her dress. She screamed and fell off balance with the impact of it as Kit sprung forward. Guy jerked round with the gun. 'Stay!' he shouted. Kit stopped.

Guy smiled slightly, then looked at Holly. The sight of her overpowered him; he seemed almost crazed by it. 'Take it off.' He pointed the gun at her dress. 'The top of it, so I can see your breasts.' She had stopped crying; the fear seemed to have paralysed her. She fumbled with the dress, her hands shaking, and managed to half unzip it, half pull it down over her chest.

'Now get down on the floor.' Holly dropped to her knees and Guy lunged forward, grabbing her hair and pulling her head down into his crotch. He couldn't think of anything else; the image of her last night in the window burnt in his head as he fumbled with his trousers. He stared at Kit, watching him try to swallow down the bile that rose in the back of his throat. Finally managing to free himself with the one hand, he held the gun above Holly's head and the excitement took him over. 'Suck,' he snarled, not even looking at her. 'Do what you did to him . . .'

That was his mistake.

Ted Welsch pressed his face against the fire exit and held his breath. He could hear voices and the thud of his own heart, but nothing else. He didn't know what the hell was going on in there. He glanced up at the roof from where he stood. It was a three-storey building and he was on the fire escape at the top. He spotted the guttering and took a deep breath. Climbing onto the metal railing, he reached up, dug his fingers into the lead piping and jumped. He held himself against the wall, clawing at it with his shoes to get some sort of footing, then, with an almighty effort, he managed to heave himself up, just catching the edge of the brick with the tip of his shoes. He got his leg up onto the roof, and then dragged the rest of his body up.

'Jesus fuck!' he muttered, staring down at the ground below. It was a hell of a way down. He closed his eyes for a moment and turned his face away, then looked up the roof. Slowly he knelt, then stood, crouching low and holding the tiles with his fingertips. He could see where the glass ceiling started, and edging up and round, he lay against the tiled roof and peered down through the glass into the room. He could see Kit and another guy. He craned his neck. He saw Guy and Holly.

'Oh shit!' Ducking down, he covered his head with his hands, an automatic reaction. 'Fuck!' he muttered. Then seconds later he dropped his hands and stood, keeping low. He moved round the glass ceiling, watching Guy all the time, feeling each step with his feet and hands. He was shaking and his legs felt funny, but he kept his breathing even, his eyes locked on the scene. Just above Guy he stopped. He could hear talking, a monologue. He calculated the drop. Ten feet, maybe fifteen. He would have to be accurate. Untying his scarf, he tied it up over his head and zipped his jacket to the top, turning up his collar over his face. He pulled the elastic cuffs on his sleeves well down over his hands and tucked his trousers into his socks. He hadn't any idea of the danger of what he was about to do; there wasn't time for it to register. He wasn't a hero. All he could think of was Jill. If that bastard got away she would never be safe. Never.

Taking a pace back, he held his breath, clenched his fists and then, closing his eyes for an instant, hurled himself at the glass. Guy heard the resounding smash. He jerked his head round towards the door as Welsch fell through the roof and cracked down onto his body. Glass flew everywhere and Holly covered her head with her hands, screaming as it shattered over her. Welsch, amazed he was still alive, rolled off Guy and dived for the gun, scrabbling on the floor for it. But Holly got there first. As she snatched it, Welsch looked up and saw Hugo run for the door.

'Hold it!' Holly screamed.

Hugo stopped. He was only halfway across the room and Holly had the gun pointing right at his head. 'Back!' she shouted. 'And you!' She pointed the gun at Guy. 'Get up! Over to the wall!' Guy struggled to his feet. He was in pain and sweat glistened on his face. Holly was shaking so much she could hardly hold the gun steady.

'Holly! What the hell . . . ?' Kit ran forward.

'Stay where you are!' she screamed. He stopped as she trained the gun on him. 'I'm going to fucking shoot them, so you'd better stay there. Stay out of the way, Kit!' She was trembling and the gun shook so violently she had to hold her wrist with her other hand to steady it.

'Holly, stop it! Don't be stupid, don't . . .'

She jerked round and the gun was pointing at Kit's head. 'Get out, Kit, go on, get the fuck out of here!' But Kit couldn't move. He stood frozen to the spot as Holly started to cry, the tears streaming down her face. Welsch moved forward. Out of the corner of his eye Kit saw him do it, slowly, carefully, one step at a time, behind her, inching closer.

'Give me the gun,' he said gently. 'I'm behind you, Holly, just give me the gun . . .'

'And what?' she cried. 'Let them get away with it! Ruin my life! No way . . .' She glanced over her shoulder, then instantly back at Guy and Blandford. 'I hate them both, the bastards. They've both raped me, both of them, they . . .' She choked back a sob and the gun jerked dangerously. Kit flinched.

'Give me the gun, Holly, and I'll shoot them,' Welsch said quietly, 'I promise. But not you, you've got a life ahead of you. You don't want this on your conscience; you don't want to have to pay for it . . .' He was right behind her now and he spoke so quietly Kit could hardly hear him. 'Give it to me, Holly, let it go, awright?' He gently put his arms around her body. Kit held his breath. He saw Blandford put his hands up to cover his head but Ferreira just stood and stared.

'Holly, please . . .' Welsch had his hands over hers on the gun. 'Holly . . .'

Suddenly a shot rang out and Ferreira slumped to the floor. 'Shit . . . !' Welsch grabbed the gun and threw Holly to the ground. He glanced up at the roof, saw two figures and started pumping bullets up into the air. He couldn't aim, he didn't have time; he just fired as Holly lay underneath him, her hands over her head, screaming as the shots ricocheted off the walls. As Welsch fell on top of her, a spasm of fear shot up through her body and she bit through her tongue. The last thing she knew was blood: the smell of it, the taste of it, the feel of it, warm and thick on her face.

When she came to, Holly was lying on her back, with a blanket draped over her. She opened her eyes but it took her a while to focus. Then she felt the pain in her mouth and struggled to sit up. A paramedic appeared by her side.

'Don't try to speak.' The young man reached out and placed a reassuring hand on her arm. 'We will take you to the hospital very soon.' She struggled again, turning her head from side to side to try to see what had happened.

'It's OK, please, try and stay still.' Again the man's arm came across her, reassuring but restrictive. He held her gently down and Holly lay with her face to one side, helpless and in pain. It was then that she recognised Kit's shoe. Silently she began to cry.

Chapter Twenty-Six

It took six hours for Holly to come round from surgery. As she gained consciousness, she turned her head to face the blank, white hospital wall and the tears streamed down her face.

'Holly?'

She jerked round, wincing at the pain, but unable to say anything. Her mouth was wired up and she wore a head brace.

'Just how I've always wanted you,' he said. 'Silent and in bed.' He attempted a smile, then came across to her, took her hand and pressed it to his mouth. She began to sob.

'Hey, sssh, it's OK . . .' He kissed her wrist and stroked her fingers, locking them in his own. 'Thank God you're all right. I thought . . .' He broke off and put her hand up to his face, covering his own tears.

Even when Holly stopped crying, a short while later, she still wouldn't let go of his hand, gripping it so tightly that his fingers were white. With her other hand she made writing motions, and Kit opened her bedside drawer to look for a pen and paper. 'Here.' He found a pad that a former patient had obviously left and searched in his jacket pocket for a pen. Holly reached forward and touched the blood stain on his chest. Without responding to the question in her eyes, he handed over the paper and pen and watched her write. She held it up and he read it. There was a silence. 'Are you sure? Wouldn't you rather leave it until you're feeling better?'

She shook her head and wrote in capital letters, 'NO, I WANT TO KNOW NOW.'

Kit sat staring at his hands, at her fingers wrapped in his. It was he who'd rather leave it. He didn't want to talk about it; he wanted to forget it had ever happened.

'Ted Welsch died,' he said. Again he had to swallow back his tears and look away, embarrassed by his show of emotion. 'Look, I'm sorry but I really don't think you're ready for this.' He heard her scribble something and pass the paper to him. He read it. 'All right,' he said, against his better judgement. 'I'll write it down, if that's what you really want, but I'm going to give it to the nurse. You can look at it tomorrow, when you're feeling stronger.' Kit took the pen. He didn't know how to begin and sat there for several minutes just staring at the blank paper.

Then he wrote. 'Two men came for Ferreira. They shot him from the roof and opened fire on all of us. Welsch started firing back; he was shot, fell on top of you and took two more bullets. Blandford ran for the door and was killed.' He broke off. Holly waited. A few moments later he continued. 'I crawled the few yards to Ferreira and pulled him on top of me. I was heading for you, then the next thing the room was swarming. The door burst open and armed police were everywhere.' He put his hands up to his face.

When he eventually let his hands drop down, he saw that Holly had read what he'd written and was looking at him with horrified comprehension. 'I don't really know exactly how it all happened,' he said. 'God knows how we got out of there alive . . .'

Holly leant forward again and touched his face. Kit looked up at her. 'I honestly believe that,' he said. 'That only God knows why we didn't get hit . . .' She left her hand there, against his cheek, and he closed his eyes. It was a fucking blood bath, he wanted to shout. I was so scared, you nearly died, I nearly died. Ted Welsch, what a fucking brave thing to do, he saved our lives, he . . .

Kit opened his eyes again. 'The police will want to interview us,' he said. 'There'll be lots of questions, raking it all up. I'm sorry, it's not over yet.' He looked away from her. 'At least you've got the gallery to go back to. Adrian White's going to be a big success; you've still got that.'

She nodded, and he felt that answer with every part of his body. She still had the gallery; that was all that mattered to her. 'I'd better go,' he said. 'Let you get some rest.' He stood up.

Holly scribbled something on the pad and Kit glanced down at it. 'How much do I think you'll get for it?' He frowned. 'The gallery, you mean?'

Again she nodded. 'God knows,' he mumbled, turning towards the door. 'You can get someone to value it, they'll tell you.' He pulled open the door and Holly uttered a cry behind him.

'For God's sake,' he said sadly. 'What do you want now? You want me to find an agent for you, is that it . . . ?' He turned, looked across at her and his voice trailed off.

Holly held up her piece of paper, her hands shaking as she waited for Kit to read it.

'Yes, I do think it'll raise enough money for a one-way ticket to New York,' he said. He stared down at the ground for what seemed like forever and Holly held her breath.

'Is that what you really want?' he asked finally. He didn't look up at her; he couldn't bear to.

She scribbled again and he heard the scratch of the pen on the paper. He glanced over. 'YES, YES, YES, YES, YES, YES, YES!' he read and at last he smiled.

'Typical bloody Holly,' he said. 'You would have to pay your own way, wouldn't you?'